OTHER NOVELS BY GENE COYLE

EVERYBODY LIES IN WARTIME

A Tale of WW II Espionage in Moscow

Gene Coyle

authorHOUSE®

AuthorHouse™
1663 Liberty Drive
Bloomington, IN 47403
www.authorhouse.com
Phone: 1 (800) 839-8640

Published by AuthorHouse 08/13/2018

ISBN: 978-1-5462-5525-3 (sc)
ISBN: 978-1-5462-5524-6 (e)

Library of Congress Control Number: 2018909587

Print information available on the last page.

AUTHOR'S NOTE

Several of the characters briefly mentioned in the story, such as General William Donovan, Vincent Astor, Ambassador Harriman, General Deane and NKVD Director Beria are true historical individuals. The other main characters, specific events and methods of tradecraft attributed to the wartime OSS within this novel are fictional and any resemblance to real people and facts is purely coincidental and unintended.

My thanks to Kelsey Biers Haberly for her fine editing assistance.

Dedicated to the several Russian intelligence officers who I knew, who wanted to help bring change to Russia, and who inspired this novel.

CHAPTER 1

PRELUDE – HISTORICAL SETTING

W W II has been raging since Nazi Germany invaded Poland on September 1, 1939 from the west, while the Soviet Union invaded from the east. Upon Hitler's action, England and France declared war on Germany, but by summer 1940 France had surrendered and the alliance of Germany and Italy basically controlled the European continent up to the border of the USSR. Hitler and Stalin had signed their Pact of Steel in 1939, but that alliance came to a dramatic end when the Germans invaded Russia on June 22, 1941. Despite secret warnings to Stalin from England that such an invasion was coming, and from his own Intelligence service, Stalin ignored such warnings and was caught totally by surprise. The German Army drove deep into Soviet territory in those opening months and eventually was only brought to a halt by the brutal Russian winter. But by late 1943 the tide of war had dramatically changed. The Germans had been defeated in North Africa, pushed back to the north of Italy and were retreating all across the Russian Front. No one thought that the war was about over, but certainly the tide had turned in favor of the Allies. The Russians were waiting for the long-promised invasion by the Americans and British of Western Europe, which would help relieve pressure on the Russian Front.

The United States and the Soviet Union politically had not been friends prior to 1941, but the war had created strange alliances of necessity. America needed Russia in the war with its millions of soldiers to keep "bleeding" the German Army on the Eastern Front. Russia needed food, military supplies and even railway cars from the Americans as part of the Lend-Lease Act to keep from collapsing, so both sides pretended that they liked one another.

MOSCOW

Large, fluffy snowflakes fell outside on the colonnaded, pre-First World War Russian mansion, giving it a fairy-like appearance in December 1943. Inside, a balalaika quartet played in one corner of the large ballroom while Russian Army privates served as waiters. Some carried gold-trimmed dinner plates from the Czarist-era with food, while others circled the table with a bottle of Russian vodka in one hand and a bottle of champagne in the other, to make sure that the glasses of the American guests were constantly full. The Soviet-American dinner meeting was being held in the ornate, grand dining room of a mansion which had been built by a prosperous aristocrat around 1890, and which had been "expropriated in the name of the people" after the Bolshevik Revolution of 1917. The bloody revolution that had swept away the old Romanov dynasty and brought in the Communists of Vladimir Lenin. Despite wartime shortages of most everything in the Soviet Union, the long, mahogany dining table was amply covered with food and drink, and lighted by dozens of candles. Heat was the only thing in short supply in the room; there was frost even on the inside of the large windows. Despite all of the armed soldiers guarding the house, the famous Russian winter with its extreme cold was not to be denied entrance to the house.

The sixty-year-old American in military uniform with one gold star on each shoulder and a full-head of lovely white hair sat quietly while listening to the music and smiling at his Russian hosts. He gazed around the opulent chamber at the elaborate cornices near the top of the twenty-foot high ceiling and at the trim around the windows. He guessed correctly that they were covered in genuine gold-leaf and not just gold-colored paint. He sipped gently at his full glass of Russian vodka, knowing the potent effect of the clear liquid. Being of Irish heritage, he was accustomed to the tradition of drinking alcohol among friends and making toasts to cement partnerships, but the Russians took the practice to a new level of indulgence. Several of his aides had repeatedly downed their entire glass of the chilled vodka in one shot, as their Soviet counterparts were doing across the dining table. Actions which they would regret the following morning. The leader of the American delegation was General William Donovan, Director of the Office of Strategic Services, America's first true intelligence service. He only sipped from his glass as he wanted to maintain some degree of sobriety for the upcoming official meeting with his Soviet counterpart in the NKVD. Donovan was a recipient of the Congressional Medal of Honor from the First World War. He enjoyed the befitting sobriquet for the head of an intelligence service of "Wild Bill", but that was not for the audacity of some of the operations he'd ordered into Occupied France over the last eighteen months as director. He'd gotten the nickname from his football playing days in college. Donovan had come to Moscow with a proposal to open a direct channel of communication between the two intelligence services, so as to exchange mutually useful information between America and the Soviet Union, to aid in fighting Nazi Germany.

By December 1943, the tide of the war against the Nazis had started to turn on the Eastern front, but there was still much fighting ahead throughout Europe for the Allied forces in order to bring about the total defeat of the German Army. But before there could be any negotiations that evening, the Soviets had insisted upon a formal dinner to welcome their honored guest. Traditional military officers within the U.S. Army considered Donovan and his secret warriors of the OSS as interlopers who were not really needed at all. However, within the Soviet system of government, the head of any intelligence service was considered a very powerful man and therefore, Donovan's visit merited an elaborate dinner. Such official Russian dinners were always well lubricated with abundant amounts of vodka and champagne. The country might have shortages of food, ammunition and housing, but even during wartime there seemed to be no shortage of vodka!

After the mandatory numerous toasts to friendship, cooperation and victory, Donovan and Lavrentiy Beria, the Director of the NKVD, along with their senior aides and interpreters, retired to a separate room. Comrade Beria saw no real purpose in an exchange of information on sabotage and subversive field techniques being used by the two services against the Germans. However, as America was the primary supplier of badly needed aid to the Red Army, he was perfectly willing to make General Donovan happy by agreeing in principle to such a program.

Once they were all comfortably seated, the youthful-looking Beria in wire-rimmed glasses began the meeting, speaking though his interpreter. "General Donovan, I have read your proposal that General Deane of the

US Military Mission here in Moscow sent us last week in preparation for this meeting. I think I can save us all a lot of time by simply stating here at the start that I think your proposal is an excellent one. I'm sure that both our organizations have developed some techniques and procedures that have been very effective and the NKVD looks forward to benefiting from the experience of the OSS."

General Donovan was somewhat surprised by how easily Beria had agreed to the proposal without any modifications or reservations, but he kept his face from showing his surprise. "And what do you think of the proposal of placing one of your officers in Washington and one of mine here in Moscow, in order to further this collaboration and exchange of information?"

"It may not be possible to place one of my officers in Washington anytime soon, because of the shortage of qualified officers to fight against the Germans, but I would welcome the arrival of an OSS officer here in Moscow at any time."

"Excellent. I will get back to you shortly with a precise arrival date, but I think I can have a man here by next month."

The forty-four-year-old head of the NKVD, who looked more like a school teacher than the head of a brutal intelligence service and who'd personally executed his predecessor, smiled and said, "Agreed. Well, unless you have something else to discuss with me this evening, I think we've finished our business and we can now return to the party going on in the next room." Beria thought to himself, how easy it was to make a naive American happy.

Donovan smiled back and stated, "I agree with you. Let's go back to the party!" He thought to himself, how easy it had been to achieve what he wanted.

The following morning in Beria's opulent office on the third floor of the NKVD Headquarters in the Lubyanka Building, the two sides met for the formal signing of the memorandum for the exchange of tactical information and for the posting of an American OSS officer to Moscow. While waiting his turn to sign the document, the Russian black humor joke came to his mind, about how the Lubyanka was the tallest building in Moscow – because from its basement prison cells one could see all the way to Siberia. The destination point for thousands of people who'd passed through its basement on their way to prison camps in isolated Siberia.

After the signing, Beria proposed a toast, "To our gallant American ally. May this agreement be but the first leading to ever greater cooperation and friendship between our two services and our countries."

They all drank.

Then it was Donovan's turn. "To the brave men and women of the Soviet Union, who are helping bring lasting peace and democracy to all of Europe."

They all drank.

Everybody lies.

An hour later, General Donovan boarded his specially outfitted C-47 cargo plane to begin the long journey back to Washington. Beria went back to fighting a war against the German Army, as well as spying on Soviet citizens to guarantee their total loyalty to Comrade Stalin. A number of Donovan's staff were nursing terrible hangovers from the previous evening. During the flight, one of his aides began a discussion over the loud drone of the engines with Donovan on how to proceed with implementing this new agreement.

"Who do you want to handle the selection of information back at Headquarters for passage to the NKVD?"

"To see that things get started correctly, let's initially run this out of my office, with you in charge of selecting material."

The major was not thrilled with that idea, but smiled and immediately concurred with his boss' proposal. "An excellent idea, sir. And who do you have in mind to send to Moscow as our representative in Moscow?"

"I have a couple of people in mind, but let me give that some further thought on the flight home before I reach a decision."

"Between your accomplishments in London last week with MI6 and the SOE, and now this agreement with the Russians, I'd say you've had a very successful trip."

"Yes, I'll have a few good things to report to President Roosevelt in a few days about my journey. I know this agreement with the Russians is mostly just BS, but it looks good on paper and who knows, something useful might come out of the exchanges. If nothing else, it will give the

OSS our own eyes and ears in Moscow to try to learn what's really going on within the Soviet Union. I never believe a word that those cookie-pushing State Department diplomats of ours send back in their reports about what a great guy Uncle Joe is. Half of them are themselves Communists and the other half are sleeping with little Russian ballerinas or male dancers!"

Both laughed, then Donovan reclined his seat to try to get a little sleep during that leg of the journey. With good tailwinds, he could expect to be back in Washington on Wednesday and get in to see President Roosevelt by Friday. Before he fell asleep, his thoughts did turn to the question of who to send to fill this new position in Moscow. One person immediately came to mind. Not that he was an obvious choice to send to Russia, but it would help Donovan to fulfill an outstanding promise to the man to get him another overseas assignment.

OSS HEADQUARTERS, WASHINGTON DC

The regular Monday morning meeting within the Morale Operations Branch of the OSS had just finished and the twenty or so members who'd attended that day were slowly filing out of the room. Army Captain Charles Worthington, in his late twenties with sandy-colored hair and hazel eyes, had made no comments during the meeting. In fact, he'd barely managed to stay awake. The MOB was tasked with coming up with imaginative ideas by which to spread Allied propaganda within Germany, with the official goal of demoralizing the will of the German soldier and populace at large to continue fighting. Some of its product was obviously put out by America, but they also printed fake German newspapers and even ran a clandestine German radio station supposedly staffed by German soldiers who wanted the German people to know the truth of how badly the war was going. Most of its staff consisted of former Ivy League professors who allegedly knew something about the "German mentality" or who'd at least studied or traveled within Germany sometime before the war. Captain Worthington, who was a Harvard-educated lawyer, and had served abroad in Portugal before being assigned to this Headquarters position in August 1943, knew little about Germany or German society. He privately thought that many of the proposals were rather far-fetched. However, he admitted, at least to himself, that as he neither knew the German language, nor had he ever been in Germany, what did he know?

Worthington, originally from Chicago, did think that the particular propaganda idea that had been discussed that morning had set a new record for insanity. Timothy, who used to teach 19th century German poetry at Yale, had suggested that the OSS go buy thousands of the largest condoms made in America and have them placed in specially manufactured packages stamped SMALL. These were to then be thrown out of American bombers while flying over German cities. The concept was that when German citizens would find them and see that they were marked SMALL, this would create great panic as the Germans wondered just how big and tall were American soldiers! The proposal had been tabled until the next meeting on the following Monday, so as to give members of the branch further time to consider the proposal.

Captain Worthington shared his small office with no windows with another OSS officer, Lt. Dallas, a younger man from a small, rural town of southern Virginia. Charles himself was six feet tall and of medium build, but his six foot five, 280 pounds office mate made him look small. In contrast to all the academics of the branch, Dallas had actually seen combat in North Africa and had several pieces of shrapnel in his shoulder to prove it. His innocent, baby-like face seemed to contrast sharply with the bronze star on his chest for action in the Libyan Desert. Behind a closed door, they often joked about their academic colleagues and about some of their strange ideas for propaganda efforts to help win the war.

Worthington at least knew why he'd been banished to the MOB. He'd screwed up while serving as the OSS Chief of Station in Lisbon. General Donovan had sympathized with most of the actions Charles had taken in Portugal, but he'd had to publicly rebuke him, as an example to others within the OSS not be too "imaginative" in their actions, and to mollify certain powerful Congressman. He'd privately promised Worthington "that he would take care of him" once the political storm had passed, but five months had passed and Charles was beginning to wonder if Donovan had forgotten him. His tall officemate with a soft Southern drawl, however, had no idea as to what sin he'd committed that had landed him in the Morale Operations Branch. That made his situation even worse than Worthington's, as he didn't know to whom he should apologize or for what. He'd been working out of the OSS office in Cairo, Egypt in the summer of 1943 and suddenly he was ordered with no explanation back to Washington and dumped at OSS Headquarters in the MOB. His official transfer orders had only included the infamous phrase, "for the needs of the Service."

"So, what do you think of the condom caper?"

Dallas, a former college All-American football player replied with a smile in his soft, Southern drawl, "I hope I can steal some of those special packages. It's hard for a man my size to acquire XXXL condoms."

Charles laughed and replied, "Perhaps they should put a picture of your 'anatomy' on the box – that should scare the Germans!"

The two bachelors decided that they'd contributed enough to the war effort that morning by attending the lengthy staff meeting and decided to leave for an early lunch. The cafeteria food in the Headquarters building in downtown Washington DC actually wasn't too bad, but Dallas knew of a nearby restaurant which sold alcoholic drinks served by very attractive waitresses – and the food was also pretty good.

Once they'd ordered their meals, gotten their drinks and admired their waitress, both coming towards them and walking away, their conversation drifted back to office issues. In violation of discussing classified information in public places, Worthington raised with Dallas the rumor that Donovan's just completed overseas trip had included a stop in Russia. Charles leaned forward with his elbows on the checkered red and white table cloth, so as to come closer to Dallas.

"Do you think that 'Wild Bill' actually met with Uncle Joe while he was in Moscow?"

"I heard that the trip did include a visit to Moscow, but I doubt if he actually met with Stalin. Rumor has it that Stalin is quite paranoid about with whom he meets, as he's afraid of being assassinated."

"Assassinated by the Nazis?" asked Worthington.

"Not by the Germans. By his own people." Dallas offered a broad smile.

Charles shook his head in mock disgust. "The way you talk about our glorious ally. No wonder you were brought home and assigned to the MOB!"

The rest of the conversation drifted over who was about to go overseas, had recently returned from overseas and who would never be returning. Nobody really knew the official statistics, but office rumor had it that service in the OSS brought the fastest promotions of any branch of service and the shortest life expectancy.

When they returned to their office some two hours later, Charles found a note on his desk telling him to report immediately to General Donovan's office. He started thinking about who he might have offended in recent days. No one in particular came to mind, so he straightened his tie and headed for the General's office.

He half suspected that someone was simply playing a prank on him by leaving such a note on his desk, so he announced himself to the outer office secretary by simply saying, "I found a note on my desk stating that General Donovan wished to see me immediately." He then showed her the note as proof of his claim. She did seem to have actually heard of him and sent him to the secretary in the inner office, which had a much nicer quality of wood paneling on its walls and a thick carpet on the floor. He repeated his claim of having been summoned.

"Yes, General Donovan wishes to speak with you, but he's with someone at the moment. Please have a seat over there and I'll let you know as soon as he's available." She then turned her face back down to papers on her desk. She wasn't unpleasant, but she didn't waste words or time at being pleasant either. Charles happened to know that she'd been Donovan's private secretary at his New York law practice before the war, but the rumors that she'd personally killed several German officers behind enemy lines with a garrote were also popular in the building. In either case, people moved when she gave instructions in her very authoritative voice. Charles went and sat down as told. He noticed that there was a coffee pot and cups just beyond the secretary's desk, but as a mere captain, apparently he didn't merit an offer of coffee. Probably just for majors and above, he thought silently to himself.

While seated in a comfortable leather chair, Worthington continued to try to think of why Donovan might want to meet with him personally and apparently with some urgency. He passed on reading any of the magazines on the coffee table in front of him and simply stared at several of the oil paintings of Confederate Major John Mosby's raiders, wreaking havoc behind Yankee lines. Supposedly Mosby's hit and run raiders were one of General Donovan's inspirations for how OSS military operations were to proceed in Occupied Europe and Japanese-held Pacific islands. Worthington still hadn't come up with any particularly good idea for his summons when ten minutes later the secretary informed him that General Donovan would now see him. She opened the impressive mahogany wood door, while stating loudly his name so that Donovan would for sure know with whom he was about to meet.

"Captain Worthington is here at your request," the fifty-year-old, no-nonsense secretary announced.

Captain Worthington proceeded to the front of the General's massive desk, came to attention and saluted. He'd met Donovan on two previous occasions, but had never noticed before what broad, square shoulders the man had. He could imagine why he'd been a force on the college football field when a student at Columbia University several decades earlier. Donovan returned a proper military salute and then pointed at a chair. "Take a seat Captain. How are things going down in the Morale Operations Branch?"

"Just fine, sir. Everyone is putting in long hours."

"Good, glad to hear that."

Donovan was well known for getting directly to the point and therefore cut out any further typical social chitchat and proceeded to the purpose of the meeting. "Are you happy down there Charles?"

"Well, sir. I'm not sure that I bring much to the table, as my knowledge of the German people is rather limited."

"I see. So you wouldn't be opposed to the idea of my sending you back overseas?"

A smile instantly came to his face. "No, sir. I was hoping to get overseas again where I might perform a little better than I had in Portugal. What do you have in mind for me?"

"Ever been to Russia?"

"No, sir, but I understand you were recently there." Both men smiled at how quickly that allegedly secret part of his recent overseas trip had spread around the building. Donovan proceeded to brief Charles on the agreement he'd signed with the NKVD while in Moscow, including the provision of assigning an OSS officer to Moscow to help facilitate the exchange of information between the two intelligence services.

"Would you like to be that officer sent to Russia?"

Charles really didn't know much about the Soviet Union. And he only knew about ten words of the language, which he'd learned from a previous Russian girlfriend named Olga. She'd been part of his disaster in Lisbon, but that was another story. Three of the limited words he knew were, "I love you", which he doubted would be of much value in discussions with NKVD officers. However, he recognized that this was the long-awaited offer for a chance to redeem himself, which Donovan had promised him upon his recall from Portugal five months earlier. There was clearly only one answer to give.

"Yes, sir. I think that would provide an excellent opportunity for me to again contribute to the war effort. How soon will I be leaving for Moscow?"

"We're still working out the fine points with the State Department and the Army's attaché command, but I suspect you'll be away shortly after the New Year. You'll be assigned to the US Military Mission, which is part of the American Embassy in Moscow. Go see Major Powell about your paperwork. He was there with me at the meetings in Moscow with the NKVD and can give you some further points on your upcoming duties, but get on my schedule to meet with me a day or two before you depart."

"Yes, sir. Thank you for the second chance." Charles rose from his chair, but then hesitated. "Is there by any chance a second officer will be assigned to Moscow with me?" He presumed that if there was to be, Donovan would have mentioned it, but he thought he'd at least try to get Lt. Dallas a job as well. "I'd heard that we often send men out in pairs," he added optimistically.

"If going into a jungle or Occupied France, yes, but I think you'll be able to sleep safely at night alone in the American Embassy in Moscow!" General Donovan came from behind his desk with a broad Irish grin upon his face and firmly shook Charles' hand.

"I told you that I'd get you back in the game once things had calmed down over the Lisbon fiasco. It's an assignment off at the far end of the earth, but that's actually a good thing, as then I won't have to explain to many people why you're going back overseas. Hardly anyone will even know that you're there! In fact, try to just quietly depart Headquarters without any great fanfare. Here is your second chance." Donovan then added, "please don't fuck up again" and gave Charles a fatherly wink. Charles could see why men in Donovan's command during the First World War had fought so well and willingly for him.

Worthington knew he should just leave the office with the good news in hand, but he couldn't resist asking. "One other thing while I'm here. I just noticed your special assistant, Duncan Lee, pass through your outer office. I take it you didn't really believe me when I passed to you the information back in Lisbon that Lee is working for the Soviets."

The smile quickly faded from Donovan's face. "It's not so much that I don't believe you, but you offered me no checkable proof other than that Russian girl's word and even she then disappeared. I've moved him to a different job, mostly doing with arranging my appointments, but without actual evidence that I could take into a court room, I can't just fire the man." Donovan shrugged his shoulders. "He has lots of friends in the Roosevelt Administration. And if it's true he is working as a spy for the Soviets, at least keeping him here in a relatively harmless position where I can keep an eye on him is better than sending him onto some other component of the Government."

"Understandable. Thanks for explaining the situation to me." Charles saluted once more and went on his way. He'd consoled himself over the past five months of internal banishment that at least one good thing had come out of his assignment to Lisbon, the uncovering of Lee as a foreign spy, but apparently nothing had really been done with the information. One more confirmation in his mind that from then on he should just take care of himself and not worry about anything else!

Captain Worthington practically floated back down to his office, where Dallas naturally wanted to know what General Donovan had wanted of him.

"I'll tell you, but you won't believe me until I disappear from here in a few weeks! I'm headed for Moscow to open up direct liaison with the Soviet's NKVD."

Lt. Dallas was genuinely happy for his officemate, but did inquire, "Don't suppose that's a two-man post?"

"Sorry, no. I even hinted at that myself with Donovan, but got told no."

Dallas quickly recovered. "Well, hardly any point in my going all that distance. Once we start dropping all those extra-large condoms on the Germans, they'll be surrendering within just a few weeks anyway!"

When Worthington got back to his small apartment that evening, he finally had time to sit and really reflect about his upcoming assignment. Donovan had indeed finally come through with his promise to get him back overseas. It would remain to be seen how good of an assignment the Moscow job would turn out to be, but at least he was back in the game. It was a new position, so it would be up to him to define the parameters of the job. He was getting a second chance to salvage his career. From now on, he would solely be looking out for the welfare of number one – himself. There would be no more foolish considerations of what was good or fair for others, as he'd mistakenly done in Lisbon.

Aside from reading the occasional newspaper article, all he really knew about the Soviet Union were things that Olga had told him in the past and much of that was not very flattering. Stalin certainly seemed to be quite a brutal dictator, but he was not going to Moscow to help bring about democracy and happiness among the Russians. He was going there to help defeat the Nazis. Charles remembered a great statement made by Winston Churchill in 1941. Churchill had been well known for his harsh criticism of Stalin and the Soviet Union throughout the 1930s, and he was questioned one time about the change in the tone of his comments about Stalin after the German invasion of Russia in June 1941. Churchill had replied that if Hitler invaded Hell, he would find a few appropriately positive comments to make about the devil! He decided that the first thing to do the following morning would be to pay a visit to the OSS library and browse through what books might be available on the Soviet Union. He could hardly become fluent in the Russian language in two or three weeks, but he would immediately try to find someone who could at least quickly teach him a few basic greetings and useful phrases. With a game plan in hand, a tired but happy Charles Worthington crawled into bed.

The next couple of weeks passed quickly. Some of it spent trying to find the warmest clothing available, given what he'd been reading about Russian winters! With the influence of the OSS, getting a priority space on a flight to England was not a problem for him. The major hurdle was how to get from England to Russia. There were numerous cargo ships headed to Murmansk and Archangel, after a stop in England or Scotland, but the particulars of sailing dates for supply convoys were considered Top Secret and the U.S. Navy didn't care who he worked for or why he needed to get to Russia, it wasn't talking. The best that could finally be arranged was that he should fly to London and then contact the US Naval attaché at the American Embassy there. His office could then assign him to a particular ship that would be sailing from the United Kingdom to Russia. Cramming as many tinned cans of meat and bars of chocolate into his duffel bag as he could fit with his clothes was also recommended. Apparently, food supplies were very limited in Moscow, even for American Embassy personnel. Where he would be billeted in Moscow would be worked out once, and if, he physically arrived there. The State Department explained to him that a number of personnel enroute to Moscow had been killed when their ship sank or their plane had crashed. Therefore, no housing assignment would be made until Worthington actually arrived. That tidbit of information about men not even making it to Moscow was not the most encouraging news that he'd obtained about his upcoming assignment!

His departure to Moscow was supposed to be kept low key, but Dallas and a few close friends did throw him a nice farewell dinner at a restaurant across the river in Alexandria, Virginia two nights prior to his departure. The precise mortality rate of OSS personnel serving overseas was closely held only within General Donovan's office, but enough men and women had gone overseas in the previous eighteen months and never returned for all OSS personnel to know that they were involved in a dangerous business. Farewell parties, therefore, had a very special meaning for OSS officers. As a matter of superstition, the practice at such affairs was to never use the phrase "good-bye"; everyone ended such events by simply saying "till next time."

The day before his scheduled departure, Worthington had his final meeting with General Donovan. He looked tired and only had about ten minutes before he was scheduled to meet with a visiting delegation from Shang Kai-shek's Chinese Government, so he again skipped quickly over the social chitchat.

"Charles, you know why officially you're going to Moscow in this new position. You're to promote and facilitate the exchange of information between us and the NKVD that will be helpful in fighting the German

Army. Maybe this will prove beneficial, maybe it won't, but it's at least worth a try. Secondly, I think it will also be useful having someone there in Moscow who can occasionally send me unbiased reporting about the nature of the Soviet government. I'm not asking you to spy on the Soviets in the traditional sense of that activity, but I'd appreciate hearing your opinions about Stalin, the Communist Party, and anything else about the political life within the Soviet Union that you think might be useful for me to hear. We're going to have to work with that SOB and his brutal government after the war with Germany ends and it's best if we start now getting a better understanding of that country and its postwar intentions."

"I understand, sir. I'll keep my eyes and ears open."

"You know that official Allied policy is that we don't spy on each other. Of course, it's pretty clear that the Soviets are spying here within the United States every day of the week, but we're not supposed to do anything in return. What I'm telling you is, don't do anything that looks like spying on the Soviets. Or to put it another way, don't get caught spying on the Soviets! Because if you did, naturally I would have to disavow any such activity by you and once again call you back to Washington, and probably fire you." Donovan gave Charles a big smile. "Don't make me have to fire you."

Worthington smiled back and said, "I would never think of violating Allied policy regarding our good friends in the Soviet Union."

Donovan came over and gave his young officer a firm handshake and a pat on the back as he started for the door. "Good luck and good hunting."

The following day, Worthington headed for the nearby military airfield with his luggage. As he was going PCS to a diplomatic posting, he was allocated to take with him two Army regulation-sized duffel bags instead of just one. The ground staff looked at him as if he was slightly crazy, as it was a relatively mild day in Washington around 30°F, yet Charles was wearing a coat suitable for the North Pole.

Seated in the waiting lounge was another Army officer.

"That's a hell of a coat you have there. You headed to the top of Canada?"

Charles returned the grin from his fellow passenger and responded, "No, but close to it." Discussing with strangers where any soldier was

headed was a violation of security regulations. I'm Charles Worthington"
He extended his hand.

"I'm Tom Parkington, glad to meet you." The two captains shook
hands.

"That's a pretty serious coat you have there as well," observed Charles.

Tom laughed. "Aw, this is just my summer coat. My winter one is
back home."

At that moment, the sergeant at the assignment desk called both of
their names. "You the two guys headed for some place called Archangel,
Russia?" After he received confirming nods, he handed both of them a
packet of tickets. "These will get you as far as London. Once there, check
with the military dispatcher at the airfield about how to get to Archangel.
Once you land in England, you become his problem. Your plane leaves in
about twenty minutes." He then turned to walk away, shaking his head as
to why on earth anyone wanted to go to Russia in wintertime!

"I guess that's why you have such a serious winter coat," commented
Tom as he laughed and pulled out a small pack of Lucky Strike cigarettes,
one of the free packs that the USO ladies passed out to GIs. "Want one?"

"No thanks, I'm a cigar man," he replied, as he took out a small silver
cigar case. "You just going out, or returning to Russia?"

"I'm just going back after three weeks of medical leave. I got some
sort of lung infection and medical care in Moscow is practically medieval,
so the medic we have assigned there at the Mission finally just decided to
send me home to see somebody who'd actually gone to medical school."

"And the closest real doctor was here in Virginia? Don't they have
doctors in England?"

Tom smiled. "Well, for three bottles of Scotch the medic decided that
the best lung specialists were only in America!"

"I'll keep that mind, should I stub my toe or sustain some other kind
of serious injury while in Moscow."

"You coming out to replace somebody or are you a new guy?"

"I'm one of General Donovan's boys, coming out there to do something
so secret that I don't even know what it is I'll be doing," he replied in a
joking manner.

"Ah, I have a few old school friends who wound up with you 'Oh So
Social' guys, but two of them bought the farm out in Burma. The third,

Duncan Lee, he has some cushy job in the General's office. You ever run into him?"

Charles tried to maintain a bland face about Lee. "Yeah, I've met him a couple of times just in passing. You know him well?" Given what Charles knew about Lee being a recruited agent for the Soviet NKVD, he was automatically a little suspicious about anybody claiming to be his friend.

"We overlapped at Yale for a couple of years and we get together for a drink now and then here in Washington. A very likeable guy."

"And what is it you do out in Moscow?" asked Charles, wishing to change the subject off of Duncan Lee. He knew he shouldn't judge a guy just based on who his friends were, but Charles figured he'd watch what he said around Tom, at least until he knew him better.

"I worked in the shipping business before the war in New York City. It was my uncle's company and all I ever did was take major clients to dinners, but the Army figured that qualified me to help arrange shipments of war materiel to the Red Army. They tell me what they want, which is everything, and I send the lists to Washington. Any trained monkey could handle my job."

"Well, you're a trained monkey with a degree from Yale," kidded Charles. "I attended Harvard, so I suppose I shouldn't be seen talking to a Yale man!"

The sergeant called their names once more and informed them that their plane up to New York was ready for boarding and to head out to the field. Worthington gathered up his possessions and thus began his journey by airplane and ship of almost two weeks before his feet landed on territory marked Moscow on the map.

CHAPTER 2

MOSCOW

After ten days at sea, the convoy of mostly American freighters, protected by five British destroyers, bringing war and food supplies to the Soviet Union arrived at Archangel. The Baltic Sea area had generally been cleared of German U-boats and surface ships, but the freighters still traveled under black-out conditions just in case. The merchant seamen seemed to calmly take the threat as simply part of the job, but Worthington and Parkington found it a very stressful journey, especially as they were not allowed up on deck at any time. It did give the two of them a lot of time to talk and get better acquainted. Tom tried to give Charles as much insight as he could on his future colleagues and how life operated for men at the US Military Mission and within the American Embassy Moscow. Charles was glad he'd crammed as many paperback books and chocolate bars into his two duffel bags as possible, as it certainly didn't sound as there was much in the way of recreation or even food for American personnel in Moscow – especially in wintertime. The two parted company in Archangel as Captain Parkington was staying on for a few days to check on operations at the port. Technically speaking, Archangel was well below the Arctic Circle, but Charles had never been so cold in his life as when he stepped off the ship and was outside for the first time in Mother Russia. Thank god Tom had advised him to layer on a heavy flannel shirt and two sweaters beneath his winter coat, but his legs, even with the wool long johns, were freezing. He wondered how anyone could fight in such weather. Close to a million German soldiers had been wondering that same thing for the past three winters. Worthington caught a flight headed down to Moscow the day after his arrival at the port. He hoped it would be slightly warmer six hundred miles further south. It wasn't.

As the United States was a massive supplier of war materiel to the Soviet Union, the Americans were allowed to conduct two US Army Air Corps flights per week between Archangel and Moscow, shuttling personnel and bringing down supplies for the Americans assigned in Moscow, not that the Soviet Government liked it much. Given their paranoia, the Soviets did insist that a Russian pilot be on board each flight, supposedly to offer any needed navigational advice to the American pilots. Everyone understood that the Russian was really on board to guarantee that the American flight did not deviate from the approved route and thus conceivably see or photograph anything on the ground that the Red Army considered secret. And the Red Army considered almost everything a secret! Fortunately, after several months of such flights the dozen or so Russian pilots who performed such escort duty became totally bored and usually just sat up with the American pilots where it was warmer than the cargo area and stayed out of the way. They enjoyed the free American cigarettes and chocolate bars and looking at pornographic magazines. The Russians could only speak a few limited phrases in English, and could read even less, but they could understand the photos of semi-naked women just fine.

US Army Master Sergeant Kowalski from the US Military Mission Moscow was waiting to meet Captain Worthington within the small American air terminal, at the Soviet airfield several miles outside of Moscow. It had been fenced off from the rest of the airfield to keep the Americans in and any Russians out, though the mounds of snow were almost as high as the fence and someone probably could have just stepped over the barbed wire if they really wanted to enter or exit the compound. Every morning started at the airfield with snowplows attached on the front of trucks doing their removal duty. There never seemed to be a massive snowfall, but it snowed three-four inches almost every day, which required daily plowing to keep the runways open during the six-month-long winter.

Initially, Red Army troops insisted on stopping every American vehicle entering or leaving the American sector of the field and demanded to examine the documents of every person in each vehicle. The same rules applied up in Archangel. The American ambassador prior to Ambassador Harriman thought that excessive and finally made a trip over to the

Soviet Ministry of Foreign Affairs to protest such treatment of an ally. A Deputy Foreign Minister shrugged his shoulders and turned up his palms in the universal gesture of "there was nothing he could do." He told the ambassador that it was Soviet territory and they would run the airfield how they wished to do so.

Having heard of the failure of his ambassador to achieve anything on the matter, the following day, General Deane, who was in charge of the US Military Mission in Moscow, called on his counterpart at the Soviet Red Army Headquarters to discuss the situation. After getting an initial, similar "shoulder shrug" response, he announced that any further shipments of American supplies out of Archangel and Murmansk would be indefinitely delayed from that day forward. He explained that the Americans were going to have to make a detailed inventory of all equipment and supplies down to every single can of spam before any unloading of the ships could begin. When the Russian protested at such delays, the general shrugged his shoulders and turned up his palms, and said, "American ships, American rules." The following day, the Soviets announced that henceforth, only the driver of vehicles entering or leaving the two American airfield sectors would have to show identification. Amazingly, the American inventory of supplies on the cargo ships was completed that same afternoon, and the unloading of war materiel from the ships began again. Such was the nature of American-Soviet relations.

Sergeant Kowalski, a native of Chicago, was nearing forty years of age and had been in Moscow for over a year. He had nearly twenty years of Army service and two ex-wives, which his craggy face showed. Prior to the war, he'd been at nearly every US Army post around America and throughout the Pacific. He'd been sent to Moscow by some Army Personnel captain who'd read somewhere about how the Polish and Russian languages were practically the same. The theory was that Kowalski would be able to serve double duty and act at times as an unofficial interpreter for the American Military Mission. Unfortunately, that captain hadn't also read somewhere that Poles and Russians had hated each other for several centuries. At least with his childhood in Chicago, he was accustomed to harsh winters.

He found Captain Worthington in the terminal standing in front of a small wooden desk, being questioned in halting English by a Red Army Sergeant about the purpose of his arrival and starting to demand that

Worthington open his two duffel bags for inspection of all contents. Per the Memorandum of Understanding between the two countries, the Soviet official had no authority to inspect American luggage. The enterprising Soviet Sergeant was simply hoping to have found an American officer who had not been properly briefed about the procedures allowed at the terminal and get him to turn over a desirable item or two within his luggage – claiming for example that a bottle of whiskey or a carton of cigarettes was forbidden and had to be confiscated.

"Are you Captain Worthington?" asked Sergeant Kowalski.

"Yes, I am."

Kowalski began speaking in Polish to the Soviet sitting behind the desk. Without knowing a single word of Polish, Worthington could tell from the tone of the voice that he was giving the Red Army Sergeant hell and probably suggesting that he go attempt a sexual act upon himself that was physically impossible.

The Russian never said a word. He just waved a hand at Worthington to move on. Kowalski then picked up the two duffel bags, as if they were filled with feathers and stated, "Follow me Captain, if you would please." Worthington's arrival interview was over.

As they neared the exit door of the shoddily-constructed wood building, Kowalski explained to Worthington how the Russian had been trying to shake the Captain down. "Those little Russian shits have no right to inspect any of your possessions. They can ask to see your identification documents, but actually aren't allowed to even question them. I was speaking Polish to him, not Russian, but I think he got my point."

Worthington smiled. "Yes, Sergeant, I think he understood what you meant."

Once they were in their official vehicle, a standard US Army staff car, Kowalski continued to give Worthington a few pointers on how things worked at the airfield, and around Moscow in general.

"This is your assigned vehicle Captain. Everyone in Moscow who merits the use of a vehicle is given one of these. If you tried to drive a Jeep in this kind of winter weather, you'd freeze your ass off in the first five minutes. We've added heavy duty batteries and a special oil to these cars, so they will usually start in such cold weather. You'll also notice that there are no official US Army markings on the outside of the vehicle. This was done at the request of the Soviets, as Stalin doesn't want the Russian people to know that a foreign country is actually here helping to fight the Germans. It does have a diplomatic license plate on it, so you shouldn't be stopped too often by local or even Soviet military police."

As they were entering into the city proper, Worthington noticed that there was a great deal of damage to many buildings in Moscow. Obviously, it had sustained heavy German bombing early in the war. Even the undamaged buildings, however, had a drab and shabby look about them. The city was filled with three-four story tall apartment buildings with gray, concrete walls that all looked alike. The buildings and the streets actually looked better, covered with the nice, white snow.

"Do you know if I've been assigned permanent housing yet?"

"Yes, sir. You're one of the lucky ones. You've been assigned a room in the Ambassador's residence, a place called Spasso House. It had been built by some rich Russian aristocrat prior to the Russian Revolution, and the US Government has had it ever since 1933, when we opened an embassy here."

"And why does living there make me lucky?"

"Because the heat always works in the Ambassador's residence and the small mess hall in there generally has the best food available in town as well. It may still suck, but it's the best available. We fly in every week most of what we eat here, especially during the winter. And the Soviet secret police, the NKVD, can't always blatantly search through your possessions, like they do to those of us assigned to other housing blocks in the city. That being said, don't go leaving anything in your room that you don't want the NKVD to know about because there are a number of local staff, repairmen and servants around the house who snoop in your room when you aren't there. Door locks don't mean a thing since it was the Soviets who put in the locks and kept a set of keys for themselves. All of the Soviet staff in the house are either informants or actual NKVD officers."

Worthington smiled. Life in Moscow was going to be just as it had been described to him back at Headquarters. "Yes, I can see that I'm clearly one of the lucky ones! How long have you been serving here in Moscow?"

"A little over a year, sir. I keep being told that I can leave just as soon as they find a volunteer replacement for me who can speak some Russian.

But it's a volunteer position and there ain't nobody in the US Army fucking stupid enough to come here. So I guess I'll be here until the war is over."

"So how did they get you to volunteer to come here?"

Kowalski kept a perfectly straight face. "I'm Polish, sir. All of us are fucking stupid, especially those of us born in Chicago. Plus, the Personnel Officer told me it would be career enhancing!"

"And where do you live Sergeant?" inquired Charles. "Are you living at Spasso House as well?"

"No enlisted men in Spasso House, sir. I'm over at Mokhovaya House that is another old aristocratic mansion, which has some office space as well as the sleeping quarters. Not a bad place. I've slept in worse during my career in the Army, sir. All of us, however, are allowed to come get chow at Spasso House."

Just then they pulled up to an outer gate of Spasso House, which was manned by Red Army soldiers who requested to see Kowalski's and Worthington's identification cards. Thirty yards later, there was another gate; this one manned by US Army soldiers, who also checked their IDs.

"I guess we don't have to worry about pesky Fuller Brush salesmen just dropping by to annoy us," sarcastically remarked Worthington.

"The Soviets claim that there are still German sympathizers and saboteurs around the city and they want to make sure that we're all safe," replied Kowalski. "Actually, they just try to limit as much as possible any contact between us and locals. I don't know what they think would happen, but they don't like any unauthorized contacts."

Within an hour, he'd been officially checked in, given his embassy identification card and assigned his room up on the second floor. He unpacked his worldly possessions from his two duffel bags and easily managed to place them within his allocated space, which was about twenty by twenty feet in size. He merited a single room. The walls were covered in the most hideous-looking wallpaper he'd ever seen. He had a bed, a fairly comfortable chair in which he could sit and read and a small desk with a wooden chair. He had two clothes dressers and a couple of book shelves on one wall. Such would be his home for the next year or so – presuming he didn't screw up and get suddenly recalled home – or freeze to death! He put his hand on the old-fashioned steam radiator and learned that Kowalski had been right. There was heat!

He was quite exhausted by his journey and slept like a rock in his small, but comfortable bed. The following morning Worthington found the small dining room near the kitchen, which served as the mess hall for officers billeted at Spasso House and any US soldiers in the city. Prior to being turned into an Army meal facility, it had been the "informal" dining room of the mansion. The formal dining room could accommodate a hundred guests or more. There were already some twenty men at the tables, which could accommodate forty if every chair was taken. Charles thought the massive crystal chandelier hanging from the ceiling added a nice touch while he ate his powdered eggs, mystery meat and bread and drank his coffee. The small stick of bread served in the mess was actually quite tasty and he soon learned it was baked out in the kitchen each morning, giving the entire room a lovely smell. The coffee was even better. After his first sip, he commented to the captain seated across from him, "This is amazing coffee. Is it always this good?"

"It is usually," he responded. "About the best thing served in here. Turned out that Ambassador Harriman is a fan of good coffee and he pulled some strings so that a really nice coffee brewing machine was shipped here, along with a grinder and around the first of the month, 200 pounds of Brazilian coffee beans are flown down here from Archangel."

"Well, I may enjoy this assignment more than I'd expected." He took another sip and offered a wide smile. He then ate a bite of the powdered eggs, which brought him back down to reality. "Does Ambassador Harriman ever come in here?"

"No, he told General Deane that he considered this the Army's room and he didn't want to go making us feel uncomfortable by his coming in here for any reason. He and his family eat in another room, served by an entirely different kitchen."

Charles just nodded and drank more of his coffee.

"I don't recall seeing you here before. Are you a new arrival?"

"Yes, just got down from Archangel last evening. I'm Captain Charles Worthington."

"Welcome to Moscow. I'm Ted Collins. I deal with Soviet requests for artillery and mortar shells."

Worthington had noticed a slight Irish accent, which matched well with the flaming red hair on the head of the thirty-something year old fellow officer talking to him. "I'm the new OSS guy in town, originally out of Chicago. My last overseas assignment was Lisbon, Portugal. You wouldn't be from up around 'Bawston' by any chance?"

Collins laughed. "Don't tell me my accent gave me away!"

"Just a wild guess," replied Charles as he continued to eat. Not having gotten any dinner the day before, he was indeed hungry. "Are seconds allowed at this small facility?"

"Man, you must be hungry!" replied Collins. "They probably are, though no one has ever wanted or asked for seconds until today. The cook out in the kitchen will faint from shock when you go ask." A thin smile crossed his lips. "Well, you'll have to excuse me. I have a daily meeting to attend at 0800 over at the Mission building. If that is where you'll be headed shortly, any of the guys here can show you the way."

Charles looked around the room at the men eating their breakfasts. The décor was much nicer than a regular Army dining facility, but the behavior of the officers and NCOs was about the same as at any base he'd had occasion to visit. Some were chatting with the guy across the table; a few simply staring down at their food. Nobody looked that thrilled at being there. As most of them had already endured three months of Russian winter, he could see how that would wear on a person. He'd only been in the country just over two days and already he was longing for home and sunshine. He finished his breakfast, went back to his room to gather up his civilian winter coat and headed for the front door. He'd noticed already that the regulation about wearing Army-issued coats was either officially waived in Moscow or simply ignored by all, for he had yet to see anyone wearing one. He was glad to see that common sense outweighed a silly rule. Just as he exited Spasso House, he encountered an elderly Russian shoveling the snow that had fallen during the night from the driveway. He now had a chance in the pre-dawn light to get a good look at the residence. It really was quite a mansion. He stood and stared at the architecture of the grand house.

"Quite a house, isn't it, sir!" commented someone from behind him, in excellent, British-accented English.

Charles turned around expecting to see a British military colleague, but instead found himself facing the elderly Russian worker. "Yes, it is," he managed to mumble.

The Russian tactfully ignored Worthington's befuddled expression and simply continued talking about the mansion. "It was built just before the First World War, in 1913 by a rich Russian businessman named Nikolay Vtorov. He'd made lots of money in the textile industry and wanted to create a mansion befitting his stature in the city. Moscow wasn't the capital in those days, but still, there were lots of wealthy individuals in the city with whom to compete for having the most ostentatious home."

Charles had recovered from his surprise that a Russian common laborer spoke such excellent English. "It was already dark last evening when I arrived, so this is my first chance to get a really good look at it."

"Wait till you see it in the sunshine, sir. Then the place really impresses. By the way, I'm Viktor. I take it you just arrived in Moscow." He removed a glove and extended his hand.

Worthington did as well and they shook. "Captain Charles Worthington. Yes, I just flew down from Archangel yesterday. Nice to meet you. I'm to be an aide to General Deane." That was the polite way that Charles was to introduce himself to the locals, rather than saying he was with the OSS.

"Very good. Well, as you can see, one of my duties is shoveling snow during the winter and a variety of other tasks all year round. I believe your American word for me is that I'm a handyman."

"A pleasure to meet you Viktor. I don't suppose you could point me in the right direction once I go out the gate to arrive at the US Military Mission. All of my colleagues seem to have already departed for work. Wouldn't do for me to arrive late on my first day," he added with a friendly smile.

Viktor started leading Charles to the front gate." Do you want to go to the main Mission offices at Mokhovaya House, or the nearby annex?"

"I believe I'm to report first to the nearby annex."

"Ah, well, then you're in luck. You simply go out the front gate, turn right and you'll come directly to it in about ten minutes. It's an ugly, three-story concrete building. You can't miss it. I take it you'll be living here at Spasso House?"

"Yes, I will."

"Ah well, then you are one of the lucky ones. Plenty of heat and the food in the small cafeteria is good as well I'm told. I'm sure we'll be seeing a lot of each other."

At the American gate, Viktor repeated his instructions and bid him farewell. "Have a good day, Captain"

Worthington gave him a small wave of the hand and headed off to help win the war against fascism.

His first hour at the Military Mission was spent getting introduced around to a variety of colleagues and he was eventually escorted up to the top floor, where he was shown his own relatively small, but private office. On the lower floors, he'd noticed that most everyone shared offices. Officially listed as "Aide to Mission Commander", apparently someone had decided that he merited a private office. The walls of the room were bare concrete, with not a single picture, photograph or even a calendar hanging anywhere. There was one official US Army-isued metal desk and wooden chair, two metal filing cabinets, one with padlock and one without, two uncomfortable-looking, wooden guest chairs in front of the desk and a couple of small side tables. The concrete floor was covered with an industrial-grade, black and white, small check linoleum. He went over and touched the radiator; it was lukewarm. He was beginning to see why he was considered lucky to be living in Spasso House with plenty of heat! He found in the middle of his desk a note stating that he had an appointment with General Deane at 1100 hours.

There was a knock on his door, and then it opened without waiting to hear any response. In entered a tall, thin man with just the first few hints of gray hair around his temples. "I'm Major Barry Singell. I presume you are Captain Worthington."

"I am." Charles came around from behind his desk to shake hands with the Major. "Nice to meet you, sir."

"Welcome to Moscow. I trust you're getting settled in OK."

"Yes, thank you. I got into my room in Spasso House last evening and a Sergeant Kowalski has been taking through my paces this morning to get me officially checked-in and assigned an office. I'm to meet the Commander, over at the main building, in about a half hour."

"Excellent. You'll like General Deane. He's a competent and easy going fellow. He only arrived a few months back, but has already improved things around here. I've been here eight months. Deane understands that this is Moscow, not Washington and appreciates that dealing with the ever demanding Soviet officials on top of the tough weather, bad food, etc. requires a certain patience and practicality."

"Glad to hear it."

"Well, I'll let you get on with settling in. By the way, a few of us are going to go to a local restaurant tonight. If you'd like to come along and experience some genuine Russian food, please join us. It will give you a chance to get acquainted with a few of your new colleagues."

"Thank you for the offer. "I'd like that."

"We'll head out at 1800 hours, from the front door of this building. In the meantime, you have any immediate questions I might help you with?"

"No, I think I'm... well, actually there is one thing. I met an interesting Russian worker this morning on the grounds at Spasso House. Viktor was his name. Spoke beautiful, British-accented English and sounded quite educated. What's his story?"

Singell laughed, "Ah, Viktor the snow shoveler. Yes, his English is amazing. Nobody knows for certain, but given his excellent English and his friendliness, most people assume he works for the NKVD as an informant. Either way, quite a pleasant fellow."

"Ah, I sort of suspected that might be the situation. Thanks. I'll see you at 1800 to head off to dinner."

Worthington arrived at Major General John Deane's outer office five minutes in advance of his appointed time. Charles didn't know much about him, other than that he was a career Army man, originally from California and had a son who was a West Point graduate. He was in his late forties. Promptly at the minute of his appointment, the adjutant nodded at Worthington, then proceeded to the General's door, knocked loudly twice and opened it without waiting for a response. He didn't wait for Charles, but went straight in, so Worthington figured he should just do the same. The adjutant was laying some folders in General Deane's in-box and announced, "Newly arrived Captain Charles Worthington, reporting for duty, sir."

General Deane stood. Worthington walked smartly to the front of the desk, came to attention and saluted. "Captain Charles Worthington, sir."

Deane looked to be in his early fifties, had thinning brown hair, but appeared to still be in good physical shape. He smiled, pointed at a chair and replied, "Welcome to Moscow, Charles. So, you're to be Donovan's man in Moscow with the NKVD."

"Yes, sir, that's what I was told my assignment is. To facilitate the exchange of useful information between the OSS and the NKVD, to help fight the German Army."

"Yes, I know. I was at the signing of the Protocol with the NKVD by General Donovan. I told him at the time and I'm honestly telling you now, I think it's a complete waste of time, but as long as you stay out of the way and create no problems, I'm glad to provide you an office."

"Yes, sir, I shall endeavor to follow both of your requests. As to whether it will be a complete waste of time, I guess we'll find out over the next few months. General Donovan didn't ask me my opinion of his plan, he simply told me to travel here and open the liaison relationship. I presume someone here at the Mission knows how I can get in touch with a Colonel Suvarov of the NKVD."

"Yes, a plan on how to get started was worked out while Donovan was still here last month. I shan't accompany you to your first meeting, as officially, you are not really part of the Military Mission, though obviously you are under my command as all US military personnel in the area of Moscow are."

"Understood."

"I naturally wish you luck in your assignment, but unfortunately my staff can provide you very little assistance once you're settled in and put in contact with the NKVD. My people are all working twelve-hour days as it is just trying to get the Red Army requests back to Washington, and seeing as best as we can that the supplies get here in a timely fashion and are put to good use in fighting the Germans. We're in the middle of the third annual protocol with the Soviet Union and it's almost impossible to meet the promises made by people back in Washington for how much tonnage can be supplied every month. 'Supplies' means everything from trucks and tanks to railroad engines to sacks of flour. We supply the goods over three routes. They come across the Pacific Ocean to Vladivostok and then by rail across Siberia; up from Tehran and thirdly, across the northern route to Archangel and Murmansk. The Soviets are frequently a pain in the ass to deal with, but they are essential to defeating the Germans, so we humor them in every way we can. We need them more than they need us."

"Yes, sir, I understand."

"Good, if you can help the NKVD be more efficient at killing Germans, great, but don't cause any problems. I've never quite understood why the Army needs an OSS, or even exactly what you do, but do remember the Allied Agreement that we don't go around spying on our fellow allies."

"Yes, sir. General Donovan expressed similar thoughts in my farewell meeting with him a few weeks ago."

"Are you by chance a Russian speaker, Captain?"

"Just a few words, sir. I was told back in Washington that whomever I would be interacting with at the NKVD would be an English speaker."

"Yes, I'm sure they'll have someone who can speak English with you. Too bad you don't know Russian though. We could have made some use of you in your spare time." Worthington felt that there had been a clear emphasis by the General on the word "use", insinuating that what Charles had officially been sent to Moscow to do wouldn't be particularly useful.

General Deane then seemed to visibly relax as he reached for a cigarette from a box on his desk. Apparently, having made his speech, he was returning to being the more congenial person that Major Singell had told him he was. While Deane was lighting his cigarette, Charles glanced around the room, beginning with several very nice oil paintings on the walls, a handmade Persian carpet on the floor and the beautiful 19th or even 18th century wooden desk at which the General sat. While Charles had worked before the war for multi-millionaire Vincent Astor in New York City, he'd been in his home and office many times and knew quality furniture when he saw it.

"That's quite a lovely desk that you have General," observed Charles.

General Deane laughed. "I see that you know something about antique furniture. The Soviets apparently have the interesting philosophy that any visiting general should be taken care of in a first-class fashion. Two days after my arrival this past fall, several trucks arrived with all of this stuff for my office, courtesy of Marshal Zhukov."

Charles offered a small smile. "Very considerate of him."

"Don't suppose you're a bridge player?"

"No, sir, I'm afraid I've never acquired a taste for the game. I'm more of a poker player, if I play cards at all."

"Ah, I thought being a Harvard man, you'd be a bridge player. Oh well, welcome to Moscow. Would you please tell my adjutant to come in, while you're on your way out."

Charles took that as a signal that his "welcome call" was over. He stood, saluted, and exited. He told the adjutant on his way through the outer office that the General wanted him, and departed. Once back to his own building, he sought out Major Singell in his office.

"I just had my meeting with General Deane. He claims that it was all worked out last month on how I should go about getting in touch with the NKVD once I arrived, but he didn't bother sharing any of the details. Don't suppose you'd know who would know that minor detail?"

"As a matter of fact, I do – it's me. I just wanted to wait until you'd had your meeting with General Deane, before I brought it up with you. How'd your meeting go with him?"

"Fine. As long as I stay out of the way and don't cause any problems, I'm completely welcome to an office in his building. And I'm not to ask for any assistance, as everyone else is busy doing something useful, in supporting the Red Army," Charles offered a grin.

Singell laughed. "Yes, that sounds like General Deane. Handling the requests and deliveries for the Russians does take a lot of time. They aren't the easiest fellows to deal with either, but then they've been through quite a lot and need all the supplies we can send them – so from General Deane's view point, nothing should interfere with that work."

Charles looked around Singell's office and noted the large photo in a nice wooden frame on his desk of a woman and two teenaged children. "You're wife and children I presume?"

"Yes - my wife Shelley, my son, Tom, who will graduate from high school this spring and my daughter, Annie, who's two years younger. All of them safe and sound back in Oregon."

"A lovely family." Charles pointed at the desk. "You don't seem to merit the same grade of furniture as the General," he kidded the Major.

"We're all waiting to see if they allow the General to ship any of that stuff out of Moscow at the end of the war, or if they will expect its return."

"Well, the Soviets presumably stole all of those things from some rich capitalist back in 1917, so it would only be fair turnaround, if Deane managed to steal at least the desk from them!"

Singell laughed and looked at his watch. "It's almost lunch time. "Let's head over to Spasso House for some food and we'll worry about making a phone call to the NKVD once we get back. I heard that you're not a Russian speaker yourself, so we'll get one of our enlisted men interpreters to make the call and to accompany you on your initial call – wouldn't want you to get lost and get shot in the first week of your assignment."

"Sounds like a good plan, for both lunch and a Russian speaker going with me on my first visit to the NKVD."

During lunch, Major Singell introduced Worthington to several other officers. Newspapers and letters took weeks to reach Moscow, so everyone always welcomed a new guy, if only for the "current" stateside news and gossip that he brought with him. As planned, a phone call was made after lunch to the NKVD and an appointment made for Charles to go to the main NKVD Headquarters at 1000 hours the following morning. Master Sergeant Gau, who was an interpreter, happily reported the good news that the Soviet Colonel he was finally connected to had actually heard of Captain Worthington and was expecting him. "The bad news, sir, is that I don't think Colonel Suvarov speaks any English at all."

"Well, I guess we'll find out tomorrow morning. At least they did know I was coming."

Charles spent the next hour or so, putting together a package of material that he would pass to the NKVD at his first meeting. OSS Headquarters had done a good job of sending him ten reports, in both English and Russian translations. There had also been the promise that he would receive a similar packet via HF radio transmission on a weekly basis. Charles was skeptical that such a promise would actually occur, for a number of possible reasons, and decided to only take on his first visit what he considered to be the three most interesting reports. He would thus have a small reserve for subsequent meetings in case the promised weekly reports didn't arrive as scheduled. He also didn't consider all of the reports in his possession particularly exciting and decided he'd be better making a good, first impression with quality rather than quantity.

It was only 1600 hours, but there was really nothing else for him to do that day at his office, and as General Deane had stated, Charles wasn't really part of the US Military Mission, and therefore, Charles decided he could come and go as he felt. Fifteen minutes later as Charles was entering Spasso House via a side door – rather than using the formal, grand entrance at the front – he once again encountered Viktor. The well-educated snow shoveler had just come inside himself, to warm up a little and take a break from his manual labors.

"Greetings, Viktor"

"Ah, Captain Worthington. How was your first day?"

"Well, I didn't get lost going to work or coming home, so I think we can mark it down as a good day!"

Viktor laughed. "Ah, the famous American sense of humor. You joke much more than the British do."

"Given your British-accented English, I presume you first knew and spoke English with British citizens, or Russians who'd studied in England?"

"Correct. My governess and first tutor was from York. And back in the early years of this century, most of the foreigners around St. Petersburg were from England or France."

"Do you also speak French?"

"Oh, once as a young man I did, but I've forgotten most of it. You look a bit cold Captain. Come down here to the worker's warming room and let me show you something valuable to know." Viktor had lowered his voice, as if about to share a great secret. He indicated with his hand for Charles to follow him. They went down a flight of stairs to the basement of the house and there was a twenty by twenty foot room, with several wooden tables and benches, a sink and a simple stove. On the walls were lovely pictures cut out of magazines from cities around the world.

"This is where we local workers can have our meals and take breaks. Most importantly for you to know is that we keep a samovar running down here all day and night with nice hot tea. If you're ever in the mood for some tea, please come down here and help yourself." He pointed at a large, electric, plain-metal samovar over on a side table. It was made in the style of the famous czarist-period tea urns made of brass, but this was a cheap, modern-day device.

Charles saw a number of the traditional Russian tea "glasses" sitting beside the samovar. They were made of glass, but set in metal holders with small finger hooks, so one could lift the glass without burning your fingers. The holders were contemporary, mass-produced items made of some cheap alloy, but the glasses were cut-crystal and looked quite out of place in a workers' warming room, even if in the basement of the American Ambassador's official residence. Near them was a glass container containing one kopeck pieces and another with sugar in it.

Charles pointed at the beautiful glasses and noted, "These seem a little out of place."

"Very good," responded Viktor. "I see that you have an eye for quality and beauty. They had belonged to an elderly aunt of mine who had lived near Moscow. She gave them to me a year or so ago, shortly before her death and I brought them here. I have no use for such things in my home."

Viktor poured himself a cup of hot steaming tea from the samovar and sat down on one of the benches, with a bit of a moan. "I'm afraid I'm not as young as I once was." He laughed.

Charles decided to have some tea as well. He poured himself a glass and added a one-ruble coin to the "treasury."

"You have donated way too much Captain Worthington. My colleagues will think that the Little Father himself has visited!"

Charles remembered that Olga had once told him how the last Czar of Russia was sometimes referred to by that phrase, but he'd also read in one of his library books that since the war with Germany had begun, Soviet propaganda sometimes also referred to Joseph Stalin with that phrase. He silently wondered to which "Little Father" Viktor was referring.

Viktor had taken from an inner coat pocket a bit of bread and a small piece of cheese, to have with his tea. From another pocket he pulled out a very worn and smallish hard-covered book and laid it on the table. Apparently, he was going to read while having his late afternoon break.

Charles was about to leave with his glass of tea, but first pointed at the book with the title in Cyrillic and asked, "What are you reading?" He presumed it would be some political tract, or one of the horrible Soviet-era novels about how a boy fell in love with his tractor, that Olga had joked with him about once in Portugal.

"Ah, I just started yesterday reading War and Peace by Lev Nikolayevich Tolstoy."

Charles wasn't sure what to make of that choice of literature as Viktor's leisure reading. He'd heard of the famous book of the previous century, of course, and had even read a few chapters in English in school, but he was a bit surprised that such material was even allowed in the Soviet Union. He couldn't think of anything appropriate to say, so just said, "Good evening, Viktor." He took his hot tea up to his room and decided to start reading one of the books he'd brought with him – a nice detective story by Dashiell Hammett.

Just a little before 1800 hours he headed back over to the Military Mission so as to meet up with Major Singell and whoever else was going out to dinner with them. Large, fluffy snowflakes were gently falling. He saw that Viktor was back at it, removing snow from the front steps of Spasso House. If he was an NKVD officer, or informant, he certainly took his cover duties seriously. If he wasn't, Charles felt sorry for the nice old man, who'd obviously started out life better than he was finishing it.

CHAPTER 3

Major Singell, Captain Worthington and Captain Collins pulled up to the Hotel Metropole for dinner about 1830 hours. It was the premier hotel of the city, which had been built in 1907 in the *Art Nouveau* style. There was no formal parking lot, as so few people had vehicles, so they just parked out on the street near the grand entrance. The Military Mission had phoned to the restaurant that afternoon to make a reservation. Not that one was really needed to insure a table, but at least this way the kitchen of the hotel would know that they had to find enough food to feed at least three people that evening. For the more cynical members of the Mission, phoning was also considered a "courtesy" to let the NKVD surveillance squad know that some of them might have to have to work late that day. No one at the Mission seemed to merit being watched every day, but most all of them had noticed at least occasionally that they were being followed, and none too subtly. The educated guess was that the surveillance was meant more as a message that they shouldn't be out doing anything the Soviet Government hadn't authorized, as they'd be observed if they did. It wasn't that the NKVD necessarily thought any of them were out committing espionage; the Soviet Government was simply paranoid about any foreigner having "unauthorized" contact with any of its citizens. All information or even casual impressions gained by the Americans was to be tightly controlled. However, a few of the Americans thought that NKVD coverage was more devious – surveillance at times was intentionally conducted in an obvious manner, so that when they conducted very discreet coverage on other days, the American would think he didn't have anyone following him. Most of the American military personnel in Moscow didn't really care if they had surveillance or not.

Collins, who had driven, remarked to his colleagues as they exited their vehicle, "We seem to have 'friends' with us this evening, and not being subtle at all." He nodded his head in the direction of two cars with two men each, stopped about 50 yards up the street from them. "They must want to know what the new guy likes to eat for dinner!" He and Singell laughed"

"You mean we were followed here from the Mission?" inquired Charles.

"The NKVD keeps an eye on us and the Brits in town," replied Collins. "Can't blame them much I suppose, given all the effort the U.K. and America put into trying to overthrow the Bolshevik Government in its first few years, and perhaps still do. Is that why you're here Charles – to overthrow the Bolsheviks?" he asked with a joking smile on his face.

Worthington joined in with the humor and replied, "No one told me to overthrow nobody. You were the one driving Ted. Maybe they think you're trying to overthrow Stalin!"

"Me, a former member of the Communist Party of the USA! That would be a laugh. The FBI used to think I was trying to overthrow the American Government. An awful lot of suspicious people in the security services of the world. Doesn't anybody trust me?" He gave his best injured look as they headed for the front door.

"Well, I've long suspected that you cheat at cards," chimed in Barry, "but I've never suspected you of being a subversive. It would require way too much hard work. And we all know where you stand on hard work!"

Once inside, they were immediately seated at a nice table near the center of the dining room. The reservation had indeed been unneeded, as there only about eight other people seated in a restaurant that could accommodate at least a hundred fifty patrons. Over dinner, Charles passed along what popular news and gossip he could remember from back in America, such as what female movie star was dating what politician or baseball player. Neither man had any questions about how the war was going, as both had been around long enough to know that a lowly Army captain, even if fresh out from Washington, knew nothing more than they could read in a month-old copy of Stars and Stripes.

When they'd first received their English-language menus, Charles started carefully studying the extensive menu of multiple pages. Barry interrupted the newcomer, "Charles, there are never more than just one or two items actually available. The polite method is to simply ask the waiter 'what he recommends.' He will then inform you as to anything they actually have today. In that manner, you don't embarrass him."

"Ah, good to know. Thanks for the tip." He laid down his menu, which was the signal to the waiter that they were ready to order and he came over to their table.

After they'd ordered, the musical "ensemble" for the restaurant, consisting of one elderly accordion player and an even older violinist, started playing some lovely, traditional Russian music. There were only a few men at three other tables off in far corners of the restaurant. Charles finally took a good look around the restaurant and guessed it had been built back around the turn of the century. The tall columns were beautiful, as was the art work painted directly on the walls and the wooden floors were still gorgeous, though rather scuffed and scratched. The well-worn table clothes and mismatched crockery did, however, reveal that the grand old hotel had fallen on hard times since the Bolsheviks had taken over ownership.

"Were you really in the Communist Party?" Charles asked of Ted.

"Absolutely, joined when I was a student at CCNY in Manhattan during the latter part of the Great Depression. I was an early supporter of FDR's New Deal programs. It's a shame he hasn't gone further. If it hadn't been for this stupid war, he could have really gotten America started down a proper road to government ownership of all means of mass production."

Singell chimed in. "Pay no attention to him Charles. He gets Karl Marx mixed up all the time with Groucho Marx! His old man has owned an enormous auto sales dealership out on Long Island for years. Probably plays golf with Vanderbilt and Astor on the weekends. Ted here is the richest Marxist I've ever met, and fortunately for the rest of us, he's willing to keep raising in poker games when he's only got a pair of sixes."

Even Ted laughed at the gentle ribbing from his colleague and then asked of Charles, "Are you a poker player?"

"I've played a few hands," he responded with a perfectly straight face.

"Ah, I don't like a response like that," remarked Singell. "We'll have to keep an eye on this guy in the first game with him!"

At that moment, their first course of borscht soup was brought to the table by their elderly and rather frail looking waiter. Rumors around

Moscow had it that the Russian Army had scraped up every man in the country between the ages of fourteen and seventy during the darkest months of the German invasion, when the Germans had been killing tens of thousands of Soviet soldiers every day. Apparently, their waiter, who looked in his early seventies, must have just barely missed being drafted.

About ten minutes after the Americans arrived, a Russian male in his mid-thirties and two attractive young women entered the restaurant and were seated by their waiter at a table right next to the three officers – despite the fact there were dozens of other tables available that would have afforded both parties more privacy. Given the outdoor temperature of below zero, the ladies seemed quite underdressed. He was wearing a typical, locally-made suit, at the cheaper end of the price scale. They were speaking Russian as they sat down at their table. They only ordered a large bottle of vodka and some bread. Within a matter of minutes the Russian gentleman turned and spoke to them, in quite competent English.

"Excuse me, if my ears do not deceive me, you gentlemen are Americans, yes?"

As the ranking officer of the three, Singell courteously answered for the Americans, who were in civilian clothing for the evening outing, so as not to draw attention to themselves. "Yes, we are," and left it at that.

"I am sorry to disturb you, but it is so rare that I have a chance to speak English. I am Boris and these are my younger sisters, Maria and Natasha." There appeared to be at least fifteen years age difference between Boris and his "sisters", who both appeared to be eighteen or nineteen. The two ladies smiled broadly and both said in heavily-accented English, "It is pleasure to meet you."

Charles was already thinking to himself, what a coincidence. Hardly anyone spoke English in this country and now three of them just happen to sit down next to the American trio. The Americans nodded politely and tried to go back to their food, but Boris was not so easily deterred.

"Today is Natasha's birthday. Will you do us the honor of joining us in a toast to her?"

There was no tactful way to say no to such an innocent sounding request, so again Singell replied for the trio. "We would be honored."

Boris snapped his fingers and like magic their previously disinterested and rarely seen waiter was at their table with three vodka toasting glasses. Boris himself was immediately at their table pouring generous amounts of vodka into the glasses. He then raised his own to Natasha and said, "Happy Birthday, Natasha!" The three Russians downed theirs in the traditional one gulp manner. The three Americans all only took a sip until Boris informed them that it was considered bad luck to the birthday person, if all the toasts were not fully consumed. Charles thought that this guy was really good.

The Americans' glasses were barely back on the slightly grayed-from-age, white table cloth before he proposed a toast to the great alliance of the Soviet Union and America, and for a great victory against the nasty Nazis. Hard to say no to such a proposed toast. The three Russians again emptied their glasses, while the Americans demurely sipped from theirs. The two-man band started into a nice, slow waltz and Natasha in her very form-fitting red dress immediately stood and requested a birthday dance with Charles. He rose and gallantly accepted her request. Natasha was several inches shorter than Charles, a natural blonde with Slavic cheek bones and full lips. She was, as they used to say back in polite Manhattan society, "full bosomed." She unbuttoned her sweater and left it on her chair as they headed off to the dance floor. The sweater removal showed that she was wearing a very plunging neckline dress and no bra. He humorously thought to himself that along with a variety of other wartime shortages, apparently brassieres were in very short supply in the USSR.

Apparently, to keep her breasts from jiggling so much and possibly even from falling out of her dress, she decided that leaning firmly up against Charles' chest was the best way to dance with him. Whatever her motive, he certainly found it a pleasant experience. Her English was not as polished as Boris', but still good. Her first comment to him was, "I hope your wife won't mind you dancing with a poor, lonely Russian student on her birthday?"

"I'm not married, engaged or have any particular girl waiting for me back home." He figured he would save her time by covering all possible situations of "commitment" in one answer. He suspected that this was not news to the girl, if the NKVD had done their proper homework on him, but she almost squealed with delight at hearing that he was not taken.

"Perhaps then you can help poor Natasha improve her English. I am a student at the Moscow Polytechnic Institute and must do well on my English exams in two months. You will help me pass and in return I will show you some of the beautiful architecture and museums of my city. Yes?"

Charles had wondered just how far and how fast her approach would go. A second dance and Natasha would have their wedding date selected! He decided it was time to extract himself from this plan to occupy all of his free time while in Moscow. "Unfortunately, I have much work to do every day fighting the Nazis, which keeps me in my office until late in the evenings, but naturally whenever I'm free I would love to help you with your English."

"I have no classes at night," she announced with a beautiful smile. "We could very well get acquainted."

Just to be a bit devilish, he then revealed to her his sad personal tale of having been in love with a blonde in the recent past, who'd broken his heart, and so blondes at the moment just brought back bad memories. That seemed to stymie her plans for a few minutes, until she announced that she shouldn't monopolize all of Charles' attention, as her sister, a brunette, was jealously waiting to have a chance to dance as well with such a handsome American.

Maria was suddenly in his arms, dancing closely and telling him of her need to also pass an important, upcoming English language exam and asking if Charles could help her.

"I would be so grateful to you in so many ways," she added with a mischievous smile. She didn't even bother mention taking him to see historical sights of the city. He observed that for a Russian family so poor that neither sister could afford a brassiere, they could manage to come to one of the most expensive restaurants in town to celebrate Natasha's birthday. Fortunately, the band came to the end of a song and he managed to excuse himself and get back to his own table.

"Let's get out of here, now, before Boris has any more toasts to propose, or any more of his sisters arrive!" His two colleagues laughed and immediately stood. Rather than wait for a check to arrive, Singell simply threw on the table a number of rubles, which he was sure would be at least double what the bill actually would be and they all stood to leave.

41

Boris, Natasha and Maria all protested that the evening was still young, but the Americans were insistent. While hugging Charles goodnight, both women managed to slip into Charles' front pant pocket a slip of paper with their home phone numbers. As the three were getting their overcoats from the check room, Charles commented, "Such shy, reserved women they have here in Moscow!"

The other two laughed. "Don't feel so special, Charles. Almost everyone upon arrival bumps into a beautiful woman or two, who finds him irresistible."

"Oh, and I was thinking it was my charm!" Charles sat in the back on the return drive to Spasso House. The threesome had fallen into silence. The view of Natasha's large breasts, half uncovered brought back to his mind another Russian beauty in a low cut dress – his Olga of New York City before the war, who also favored red. He forced himself to think of something else. Thinking of Olga and their brief, but happy days together made him sentimental and sad.

The following morning, Worthington and Sergeant Gau were on their way to the NKVD Headquarters building by 0930, with Gau behind the wheel of Charles' assigned vehicle.

"I know it seems like we've left rather early to get to a 1000 hours appointment in a building that is only ten minutes away, but you have to allow for a certain amount of extra time to get through all the security checks and just bureaucratic nonsense that the Soviets love."

"Understood. By the way Sergeant, what is the background of the name Gau? I'm not familiar with it."

"It's French, sir. I was actually born in a Parisian suburb, but the family moved to America while I was still a baby. If you're wondering why a Frenchman speaks Russian, it's because my mother was Russian. Several hundred thousands of White Russians and Monarchists fled Russia when the Bolsheviks came to power. She and her mother wound up in Paris. And no, we weren't of some noble family and related to the czar. My mother worked in the kitchen of a wealthy French businessman. My father was the family's French chauffeur. One thing lead to another, marriage, then me, and then they moved to America to find their opportunity and riches. We hardly ever spoke French at home, as my father wanted us to become 'Americans' as quickly as possible, but my mother taught me Russian. The

US Army appreciated my mother's efforts – and here I am in the ancestral homeland. Lucky me!"

"Wonderful story. Hollywood should make a movie about your life," replied Charles.

Sergeant Gau had been correct; it took almost twenty minutes to get through the various gates to get onto the grounds of the NKVD Headquarters in their vehicle and then several more checkpoints at doors within the building, manned by uniformed guards with machine guns, before the two were placed in an office to await Colonel Suvarov.

"Not much of an office for a colonel," Worthington said softly to Gau. "No photos, no plaques upon the walls."

"It's just an office the NKVD uses with visitors. I've been here a couple of times before, and regardless of with whom the meeting was scheduled, we always met in here. Apparently, they don't want any foreigners up on the actual working floors of the NKVD," explained Gau in an equally soft voice.

There was indeed only the one plain wooden desk and chair in the center and two similar chairs in front of it. All of which looked as though they had been in use for many years. There were two small tables in the corners closest to the window, which had a metal grill over it. None of the desks had so much as a single piece of paper on them. The walls were unpainted concrete. If the NKVD architect had been going for the Spartan prison-look, he'd achieved it, thought Worthington. He certainly agreed with Gau's assessment that this was simply a "visitors" office.

Charles' thoughts were interrupted by Colonel Suvarov, who emerged from the same door though which the Americans had entered. He was a broad-chested, thick-necked man of perhaps fifty. He had short-cropped hair and a clean shaven face. He strode directly to the chair behind the desk and sat down, without stopping to shake hands with his guests. Charles thought the man had a cruel-looking face and a thought passed quickly through his mind that there was little the OSS could teach this man about killing Germans – or any other nationality.

Suvarov started speaking in Russian and paused after every few sentences to give Sergeant Gau a chance to translate. He clearly knew that Worthington spoke no Russian and why the sergeant was there. The gist of his opening comments was that he was aware of the contents of the Memorandum of Agreement that had been signed between the two services back in December and looked forward to working with Captain Worthington. He then paused.

Worthington took that as a sign that it was his turn to speak, also with breaks to give Gau time to translate into Russian. "I am Captain Worthington and General Donovan chose me to come here to begin our exchange of information and ideas on how best to conduct guerrilla operations against the German military and government officials. Unfortunately, I do not speak Russian, but the reports I will be bringing to pass to you will have already been translated back in Washington into the Russian language. We will gladly receive reports from you in Russian or English. I'm sure that with your excellent success at killing German soldiers behind enemy lines, you have many techniques and knowledge of such warfare equipment which would greatly benefit OSS efforts in Occupied France and elsewhere around Europe."

Charles then pulled from his leather satchel the three reports he'd chosen to pass at this first meeting and rose to lay them on the Colonel's desk. "This is a first example of information that Washington believes might be useful to the NKVD."

Suvarov didn't even glance at them, but simply and politely replied that he would read them with interest later that day. "I have nothing for you today, but shall in the near future have three reports for you in return. I was waiting to make sure that you arrived in Moscow before I ordered the preparation of any reports."

The Colonel then sat there in silence. Charles concluded that there was to be no offer of tea or anything else and that Suvarov considered the meeting at an end. So Worthington inquired if Colonel Suvarov would care to set another specific date to meet again, perhaps in a week or so?

"I think it would be better to wait until I have our reports ready for you before setting a specific date to meet again."

Charles could take a hint. He stood, saluted and headed for the door. Sergeant Gau hurriedly expressed a few words of farewell in Russian and followed his Captain out the door.

Once they were back outside, he stated to no one in particular, "So glad I traveled 8,000 miles to have that meeting. What a fucking asshole!" He said nothing else the entire drive back to the US Mission. He thanked the Sergeant for his assistance and went straight to his office. He fumed and paced around his small office for almost ten minutes, before he sat down and began to write a report to be sent via classified telegram back to General Donovan. He had worked out in his mind on the return drive how he would explain to Donovan what an asshole Colonel Suvarov was and that he saw no point in even being in Moscow. The Soviets clearly had no interest in the relationship they had agreed to the previous month. He even toyed with the idea that Donovan had simply sent him out there to fail.

He then sat down, too a deep breath and typed:

Had first meeting with NKVD Colonel Suvarov on the morning of the 12th. The Colonel was very gracious and expressed his appreciation for the three reports that I passed him today. He said that he would have their initial batch of reports for the OSS in a few days. He stated that he was looking forward to working with me in the future in building our new relationship. Will advise further once we have received their first reports. (Col. Suvarov only speaks Russian, so meeting was conducted in Russian, using US Military Mission Master Sergeant Gau as translator.)

He then took his draft to the Communications Section and requested that it be sent Priority precedence to Washington/OSS Headquarters. He had a brief squabble with the lieutenant in charge of the section over the fact that no one had signed off on the release of the message. Charles explained that no one was in charge of him, so no one cleared his telegrams for sending. If the lieutenant had a problem with this procedure he and Charles should immediately go see General Deane and the General could explain it to him. The lieutenant decided that there was no reason to bother the Commander of the Mission on such a trivial matter. After Charles walked away, the lieutenant put it on the bottom of the pile of messages to be sent and figured he might get to it by quitting time.

Worthington went back to his office, gathered his coat and left for an early lunch back at Spasso House. As he walked through the snow, he thought about what a "misleading" message he'd just sent off to Washington, but came to the conclusion that he'd simply reported what General Donovan clearly wanted to hear. Donovan had obviously "misstated" the situation Charles had been sent to in Moscow, so now he felt no reluctance in lying a little in return. He remembered what happened in Lisbon, when he'd reported the truth and what he'd gotten in return for his trouble – recalled to Headquarters and stuck on a lousy desk for five months. He'd learned his lesson and would now report what Headquarters wanted to hear – and get his career back on track. Fuck'em. Everybody lied. Worthington was simply looking out for Worthington.

There were only a few others in the Spasso House mess hall and he ate by himself; he wasn't in the mood for company. After lunch, he went up to his room and took a nap. He hadn't slept well the night before – anticipation jitters over his upcoming first meeting with the NKVD. He concluded that he'd certainly lost sleep over nothing! He gave thought as to how he might still make a mark for himself in this assignment – absolutely nothing came to mind.

Around 1700 hours, he felt the urge for some tea and took one of his own coffee mugs down to the worker's warming room that Viktor had introduced him to the previous day. He found the white-haired Viktor there, reading. He seemed to be nearing the finish of War and Peace.

"Isn't it about time for you to be going home, Viktor?"

He looked up from his book. "It's going to start snowing again very soon and the Ambassador has guests coming for dinner tonight. Shoveling will be needed soon. It's easier to just wait here till I'm needed."

Worthington had just looked outside a few minutes earlier and hadn't seen a cloud in the evening sky, but figured the locals knew better than he what were the signs of snow coming. "Have you always lived in Moscow, Viktor?"

Viktor laughed. "No, I was born and raised in St. Petersburg, but when it became Petrograd, I moved out to Siberia for many years. I only came to Moscow about two years ago, to work – after the Nazi invasion. My knowledge of English was found useful."

"What were you doing out in Siberia?"

Viktor smiled. "Whatever I was told to do."

Charles smiled himself, out of embarrassment. "Ah, so it was the Government that had suggested that you move to Siberia?"

"Yes, unfortunately my parents were minor aristocrats and I was a young teacher of Literature at the university at the time of the Revolution. I wasn't considered enough of a counterrevolutionary threat to bother shooting, but clearly I had to be sent away so that I couldn't "infect" the students' minds with my ideas. There seemed to be plenty of empty space out in Siberia where I could do no harm."

They both smiled again. "But the war made you useful again?" asked Charles.

"Yes, tens of thousands of us in Siberia were suddenly needed in the Army. Past sins of almost any kind were forgiven, as long as we could carry a rifle. The German Army was creating many job vacancies in the Red Army in late 1941. I wasn't actually any good with a rifle, but someone noticed my knowledge of foreign languages, so I was sent to the Department of Services within the Foreign Ministry. My father had always wanted me to go into the Diplomatic Service and here I am, a snow removal specialist of the Ministry of Foreign Affairs!"

Viktor kept a perfectly solemn face while saying that, but Charles couldn't suppress a grin. He silently thought to himself that if Viktor really was an informant for the NKVD, sent there to spy on the Americans, he was certainly the most irreverent Soviet spy.

As if he had read Charles' mind, Viktor commented. "What are they going to do? Send me back to Siberia!" A smile formed on his face.

Wishing to change the subject, Charles pointed at the book. "Surely, you've read War and Peace in the past?"

"This reading makes the 37th time. There wasn't much else to do out in Siberia but read and I only owned a few books. I make a little tick here on the last page each time I finish it." He showed Charles the last page which was indeed dotted with little pencil check marks, to prove his claim of multiple previous readings. "I try to focus on a different character each reading, or imagine how the plot might have proceeded down another path if a character had acted differently or had died, or not died."

"Well, having read it so many times, what do you think Tolstoy was really trying to tell us about life with this story?"

"That will make for an interesting discussion, but on another day, for as you see it has just started to snow and I am now needed out on the white battlefield!" He laughed as he stood and began to put on his tattered winter coat. He wore two sweaters under the coat.

"I look forward to that discussion," replied Charles. He then topped off his mug of tea and headed to his own room upstairs, thinking to himself, what an interesting and charming fellow Viktor was – even if he was an informant.

CHAPTER 4

It was two days before Worthington received a reply from OSS Headquarters in Washington to the report on his initial meeting with NKVD Colonel Suvarov. It was brief, but complimentary. Charles hadn't figured out yet just how he would sustain this "creative" image of the new relationship with the Russians, but at least nice things were being thought of him for the moment by General Donovan. Perhaps, Suvarov would warm up in the coming weeks. Perhaps something else would come his way; he needed to keep his eyes open for opportunities.

The rest of the week went by without his hearing anything from Suvarov. Aside from the problem that created for maintaining the illusion with Washington that the liaison relationship had started well, it left Charles with damn little to do. He'd barely been in Moscow for a week and already he was bored. It was winter time and there certainly wasn't much to do in war damaged Moscow. He suspected there hadn't been much to do in peacetime Moscow prior to June 1941, either. He jokingly thought to himself that perhaps he should phone up Natasha and give her "English lessons" just for something to do! He did get invited to a poker game with some of his fellow officers on Sunday afternoon, where he managed to at least come out ahead by a few bucks at the finish. Sunday evening, he reorganized his room, for the third time since his arrival. At the rate he was reading the books he'd brought with him, he'd be finished with all eight by the end of the following week. He did write a short letter to Lt. Dallas back in Washington asking him to immediately mail him some more books. The weight restriction meant he would only get two or three books per shipment. He'd also been told by Collins that given the travel time of outgoing mail and for the return of packages from America, it was usually four to five weeks before anyone received anything requested from back home.

He was sitting in his drab office on Monday morning, reading an old magazine he'd borrowed from Singell, when he received a call from down at the front reception desk, informing him that a Red Army official courier had just dropped off a package for him. He hurried down and retrieved the one inch thick envelope. He waited until he was back in his office before he opened it, only to discover that everything in it was in the Russian language. It looked like three reports on something and a short, handwritten covering letter. He immediately went searching for Sergeant Gau to translate for him.

Once Gau had had a few minutes to look through the materials, he gave him the news. "Colonel Suvarov has sent you three NKVD reports. It is he who wrote this short explanatory letter and signed it. He says he'll be in touch when he has anything else to communicate."

"I was hoping that he'd at least have me come back to his office for a little chat, when he gave me these promised reports."

Sergeant Gau shrugged his shoulders and said, "Doesn't look like he's all that anxious for direct contact with you."

"No he doesn't, but I'll make that SOB like me, whether he wants to become acquainted or not. Sergeant, does the Mission or the Embassy ever have any social events? Cocktail parties, movie nights or anything like that? When I was in Lisbon, the various embassies were always holding dinners or parties for one reason or the other."

"This new ambassador, Averell Harriman, does seem keener on such things than his predecessor. He brought some playwright named Sam Spewack of the Office of War Information with him to spark up more cultural exchanges with the Russians. Harriman also brought his daughter, Kathleen, with him to serve as hostess for his social events."

"Oh yes, I've seen her in Spasso House, but not had a chance to actually speak with her."

"Since he arrived in late November, he's been having one or two events per week. I can check with Spewack for you, sir. It's just that there isn't much of a diplomatic community here in Moscow to invite."

"Understood, but do find out when the next couple of events are planned by anybody, and find out from whomever if I might be allowed to invite a few Russian officials to whatever they're holding."

"I will do so, sir. Anything else?"

"Yes, two things. Will you take these three reports and just scan through them. Don't bother with a word-for-word translation; they'll do that back in Washington, but just give me a quick, oral or written gist by tomorrow morning. Second, if you can, come back here about 1000 hours tomorrow and we'll make a phone call to Colonel Suvarov."

"I should be able to get that done by tomorrow, sir. See you in the morning."

An hour later, Charles' phone rang.

"Captain Worthington here."

"Good morning, Captain. I'm Sam Spewack. Your sergeant was just here, inquiring about upcoming social events. Since you're apparently interested in my cultural calendar, I thought it might be good if we met and got acquainted."

"Yes, that would be useful. By the way, just for the record, Gau is not my sergeant. As I don't speak Russian, he's just been kindly helping me get settled and get started. I wouldn't want General Deane to think I've claimed him as my own."

Spewack laughed and replied, "Understood. I'm free today from about three o'clock onward, if you'd like to come by my office yet today, or about the same time tomorrow."

Charles checked his watch. "Three-thirty today will work fine. I'll see you this afternoon."

"Good, I look forward to meeting. Just ask at the reception desk when you arrive here at the embassy and someone will show you the way to my office."

Charles leaned back in his chair and pondered what the protocol between a civilian of the State Department and a US Army captain was? He concluded that whatever the diplomatic protocol manual said, Spewack figured that as he was Ambassador Harriman's personal man, he outranked Worthington and thus it was he who should go to Sam's office. Charles then wandered into a few colleagues' offices to try to get any information on Spewack. Captain Collins was the only one who knew anything at all, and even that wasn't much.

"Ambassador Harriman personally requested that he be assigned here to the Embassy to help improve relations with the Soviet Union. Specifically, he is to arrange a number of cultural exchanges and bring about better knowledge and understanding of the Russians by Americans and vice a versa. I believe he was with the Office of War Information since early 1942. Prior to the war, he and his wife were a team, writing plays in New York City. He speaks Russian reasonably well, because the two of them spent four years here in the early 1920s as journalists for some socialist newspaper in America. I had heard of him in the 1930s because of his efforts on behalf of workers and socialists, though I believe he has toned down his public statements about political issues since he joined the government. I don't recall whether he's a true Marxist or only a socialist, although I suspect such didactical differences don't mean much to you." He smiled. "What's your interest in Spewack?"

"I'm meeting with him in about an hour. I was just curious as to what sort of fellow he is."

"The couple of times I've spoken with him, he came across as a fairly pleasant fellow, though he does seem to enjoy dropping the names of various Broadway and Hollywood stars that he claims to personally know. I'd guess that he's about forty-five years old."

"Thanks for your help. I suspect that I'll see you at dinner."

Worthington arrived at the Embassy promptly on time for his appointment with Spewack. The fellow might consider himself quite important since Ambassador Harriman had personally requested his assignment to Moscow, but he apparently didn't merit a secretary or assistant. Charles simply knocked on the door that bore his name and upon hearing a "Yes" coming from inside, entered the room. He found Spewack to be a handsome man with dark brown hair, who cheerfully greeted his guest.

"I presume you're Captain Worthington. Do come in." He rose from his desk and came around to shake hands with Charles and pointed to one of the chairs in front of his desk. He took a nearby chair, rather than going back behind his own desk. "I understand that you've only recently arrived in Moscow, correct?"

"Yes I've only been here about ten days and I'm still getting accustomed to everything, including the weather."

"I have some bad news for you Charles. I lived here from 1920 until 1924 as a journalist for an American newspaper and I can tell you that it has actually been quite mild these past two weeks. You have yet to experience real Russian winter!" He laughed and pulled a pack of cigarettes from his pocket. "Those were exciting days, seeing the Communist experiment just getting started. My wife and I loved every day here, despite the weather."

"I'm sure they were," politely replied Charles.

"What is it that you do here at the Military Mission, Charles? When I asked a couple of my State Department colleagues, they were rather vague about your duties, or had never even heard of you."

Charles saw no point in being evasive or mysterious about his assignment, particularly as he was gearing up to ask for some favors from Spewack. "I'm here as the representative of the OSS to the Soviet security service, the NKVD. I presume that you're aware that General Donovan was here back in December for talks with the NKVD and signed an agreement to open up a direct liaison channel between our two services. The idea is to exchange information pertaining to our peculiar type of warfare, you might say, that will be helpful to both sides in fighting the German Army."

"I knew about the signing of the agreement, but was not aware of any of the particulars, such as the assignment of an OSS officer here to Moscow. How is the new relationship going?"

"Well, we're just getting started, but I've already exchanged several reports with them and I'm optimistic about the future."

"Excellent. As you may know, I put out a weekly newsletter here in Moscow for the benefit of journalists and other embassies, but I suspect that you would prefer that I not mention this special relationship," he said with a smile.

"No, I suspect that everyone would be happier if this allegedly secret relationship remained a secret, at least for a few weeks!" They both laughed.

"So what can I do for you Charles?"

"I'm finding the few NKVD officers that I deal with to be rather hesitant and withdrawn in our meetings and I would like to have them invited to a few of your cultural or social events that I understand that you arrange. I'm hoping that they and I could get to know one another better in a more relaxed atmosphere."

"An excellent idea and I'm sure I can be of assistance to you. That type of socializing is one of the reasons I'm here and Ambassador Harriman is all in favor of such interactions." He reached over to his desk and picked up a piece of paper with the schedule of events to be held at Spasso House by the Ambassador in the coming two weeks. "See if you think if any of these events might interest your Soviet contacts. If so, just give me their names and official addresses and I will see that formal invitations are sent to them. Or, if it would be easier, I can simply give you the printed invitations and you can personally deliver them to the NKVD."

Charles took a quick look at the upcoming events and stated that, "Several of these should work quite nicely. I'll get the names to you in just a day or two, although it might initially be better if I personally delivered the invitations."

"That will be fine. In fact, why don't I just send to you two or three of the official invitations for each upcoming event and then you can fill in the cards and deliver them in person as needed. The cards do ask that the invitee respond to let us know if they're coming, but I've been finding that the Soviet officials don't seem to like to commit themselves in advance if they're coming or not. So, don't be surprised if you don't get a firm yes or no yourself, even when you present an invitation in person."

The official purpose of his visit achieved, Charles turned to more personal issues. "I understand that in your civilian past you were a playwright. Is that correct?"

Spewack lighted another cigarette. "Yes I was, but not one anyone most people have ever heard of, even in Manhattan."

"I think you're being overly modest," responded Charles. "I used to live around New York City and I recall seeing a Broadway show at the Imperial Theatre around 1938, called *Leave It To Me*. And as I recall, you and your wife were listed as the playwrights, correct? The music by Cole Porter."

"You have a very good memory, Captain."

"Sometimes my memory works. I remember there was a very catchy tune, titled *My Heart Belongs to Daddy*, sung by a charming young lady named Mary Martin. She had a sparkling personality and a wonderful voice. Do you happen to know, what has become of her?"

"Oh yes, Mary was such a charming young girl. Most recently, I believe she has been singing regularly on the radio, but I'm sure you will be seeing more of her on the stage in the future. There was also an exciting young man with a real future, named Gene Kelly in that show. And of course, hanging out with Cole Porter was a real joy."

"Well, I should let you get back to work. Thank you Mr. Spewack for your kind assistance. I'm sure I'll be seeing you around the embassy and at Spasso House events in the future."

"It's been a pleasure meeting you, Charles. By the way, what were you doing when you were living around New York City?"

Charles decided that he would do a little name dropping of his own and responded, "I was working as the personal secretary for Vincent Astor in those prewar times."

Spewack nodded appreciatively, certainly recognizing the name of one of the richest men in America. He stood and shook Charles' hand. "Until next time."

As Charles was walking out of the embassy, he concluded that their meeting had gone exceptionally well. He was beginning to wonder, however, just how many American communists and socialists worked in Moscow!

When he returned to his office at the US Military Mission, he found that there was a letter waiting for him on his desk that had arrived via the Soviet postal service. This was truly surprising, as he was under the impression that the Postal Service of the country was barely working. He immediately opened it and found a brief, hand written note in English, signed by his former Russian girlfriend, Olga.

"Dearest Charles,

I imagine this letter comes as a surprise because I've not seen you since we met in New York City several years ago, before the war. I'm working in the war effort out here in Novosibirsk, in Siberia. All is with me good. A friend of mine from the Soviet Foreign Ministry was out here visiting recently and mentioned that there was this new American military officer working at the American Embassy, who was quite handsome! And when she mentioned your name, I almost fainted with surprise. Don't know when I might have a chance to visit Moscow, but would love to hear from you and how you doing.

You can write me through my friend there in Moscow, Tatyana, and she can arrange for your letter to travel to me here in Siberia.

Your good friend,
Olga"

A wide smile came to Charles' face. The author of the letter didn't seem to be aware that he'd last seen Olga in Lisbon, not New York City and most likely she was now somewhere in the Mediterranean Sea area not Siberia. She was waiting for the opportunity to create a Jewish homeland, with all of the gold she had stolen from him in Portugal! Other than those minor factual errors, it was a great letter. He could think of no one but Olga's old employer, the NKVD, who would have written the forgery. When she'd met him in NYC, she must have filed some reports on their early contacts. Nice to know that the NKVD was efficient in their record keeping and that he had a dossier in their files dating back to 1941. As to why they sent such a letter, he was less certain. Perhaps since he hadn't taken up the offers of Natasha or Maria from the night of the dinner at the Hotel Metropole, the NKVD decided to approach him in a more roundabout manner. He presumed that this imaginary Olga would never quite be able to arrange a visit to Moscow, but her supposed friend, Tatyana, would be happy to be his companion in the evenings, or even over a long winter night.

He started to lock the letter in one of his filing cabinets, but then decided to take it back to Spasso House. He would leave the letter laying in plain view on the small desk in his room. He wanted one of the NKVD informants who worked at Spasso House to be able to report that he had indeed received the letter and had opened it. When he never responded, he was curious as to what would be the next ploy to offer him a "friend." He hoped they didn't conclude that he didn't like women and would start arranging for him to meet handsome men or young boys who wanted to improve their English! Another smile came to his face, but which quickly faded. He wondered whether Colonel Suvarov was part of the "targeting plan" of him and thus the NKVD intentionally planned on keeping him bored, with little work to do in the liaison relationship, so as to help encourage him to seek out Russian women, if only for something to do.

The following morning he had Sergeant Gau place a phone call to Colonel Suvarov, to thank him for the three reports that he'd sent over the day before. If it was hard working through an interpreter with all three persons in the same room, it was even more of a nightmare on the telephone! Charles stated that he had several new reports to pass that week and asked when would be a good time for him to call on the Colonel at his office. Suvarov noted that a face-to-face meeting was not necessary, but Worthington falsely claimed that General Donovan had instructed him to personally deliver all OSS reports to the NKVD. Charles did make the offer that Suvarov could come to the US Military Mission, if he preferred, rather than Charles going to the Colonel's office. Suvarov quickly caved and agreed that Worthington should come to his office on Thursday at 1000 hours. Score one for Charles! That only left him with forty-seven and one-half hours to kill before their next meeting.

Worthington sat staring out his office window for almost an hour while smoking a cigar and watching the gentle snowflakes drift slowly to the ground. There was little wind, so it was a fairytale view of the surrounding old mansions, almost obliterated from view by the snow. They reminded him of the heavy snowfalls he'd experienced as a teenager in Chicago in wintertime. He suddenly thought of Viktor. It wasn't a great job, being a snow shoveler, but it was guaranteed work for six or seven months of the year in Moscow! And he seemed to work to his own schedule; Charles had yet to see anyone to whom Viktor reported or answered. He certainly had a better life now than his two decades out in Siberia in Internal Exile – that was presuming that the story of his past he'd told Charles was actually true and not just a cover story to make his work as an NKVD informant easier. A thin smile came to Charles' face as he slightly shook his head. "God, I am getting suspicious. I no longer believe anything that anyone tells me," he thought silently to himself, but then again, everybody lies. He wondered if he could get something like that engraved on the Worthington family crest: "Never believe anything that anyone tells you." Since the family name of Worthington was an invention, he presumed he could also make up a family crest and motto to go with it.

He checked his watch. It was almost 1130 hours. He noted that he seemed to be getting better at letting time pass by while doing nothing. He decided that he'd go on over to Spasso House for a long and leisurely lunch, perhaps to be followed by a nap. He recalled the famous John Milton line, "They also serve, who only stand and wait", and wondered if that also applied to those who lay down while waiting? He enjoyed his walk to lunch in the large, fluffy snowflakes. He needed to find out if in the Russian language they had different words for different types of snow, the way the American Eskimos supposedly did?

There was only one other person in the cafeteria when Worthington arrived, so he went over and joined his fellow officer, a first lieutenant who appeared to be in his mid-twenties He'd seen him in there a couple of times previously, but they'd never been introduced.

He placed his metal tray on the table and extended his hand. "Hi, I'm Charles Worthington. I just arrived about a week ago."

The young man looked up from his food and offered a friendly smile. "Have a seat Captain. I'm Bobby Penkovsky." He shook Charles' hand and stated with a distinctly southern drawl, "So you're the new fellow in the house. My room is on the second floor on the backside."

"Your family name and your accent don't seem to go together Lieutenant."

"Well, you see Captain, I was born down in the Caucuses, but then my parents left for America in 1919 and wound up down in Georgia. Apparently, they mistakenly thought that Georgia, Russia and some place in America named Georgia would be similar!"

Charles smiled. "And I suspect nobody down in Soviet Georgia speaks with a drawl."

"You are correct, Captain! Anyway, I grew up down around Atlanta which explains my beautiful accent and clearly distinguishes me from you Yankees."

"Do your folks still live around Atlanta?"

"My father died several years ago, but my mama still lives down there and now speaks the most god-awful Russian you've ever heard, which she was kind enough to teach me!" He offered up a big, good ol' boy smile. Bobby started speaking Russian, but with his southern drawl to demonstrate. "Now you can see why the Russians here in Moscow absolutely cringe when I speak Russian to them!"

"Do you still have any relatives down there in the Caucuses?"

"I suppose there must be some cousins wandering around somewhere, but it's been about fifteen years since mama got a letter from anybody back home. Maybe they've all been shot by now."

Wishing to change the subject to a more pleasant topic, Charles moved on to the typical questions as to how long Bobby had been in Moscow, whether he was married, what were his duties at the Military Mission and what had he found to do for entertainment, especially during winter?

He'd been there almost eight months, was divorced, filled out request forms to get the Red Army more of everything and played a balalaika for self-amusement. Not only did Penkovsky speak slowly as many Southerners did, but it took him a long time to get to the main point of what he was trying to say. It had taken him nearly two minutes to provide Charles those four simple facts.

"Well, it's been a pleasure meeting you. I'm sure we'll see each other around here often. It's time for me to get back to work and fill out more forms."

"It's been a pleasure, Lieutenant. I'll see you soon." When he'd finished eating, Charles poured himself one more cup of the good coffee and took it with him up to his room.

He read for a bit, but when he started feeling a bit sleepy, he put down the novel, pulled a blanket up over his chest and drifted off to sleep in his chair. He awoke at 1645 and feeling the desire for some nice hot and sweet tea, took his mug and went down to the workers' warming room to get some of the beverage. He found Viktor in there alone, just staring off at a blank wall. It was the first time that Viktor looked old and tired to Charles. He could only guess at his age, but he suspected that twenty years out in Siberia had not been an easy period in his life.

"What, no book? I usually find you reading. Did you finish War and Peace?"

"Oh yes, several days ago I finished that." A pleasant smile returned to his face.

Charles sat down across from the elderly Russian. "So what was Tolstoy trying to tell us about life in that book?"

Viktor laughed lightly. "I don't presume to understand the mind of a genius like Lev Nikolayevich, or to speak for him, but I suppose there are a few obvious points."

Charles simply sat in anticipatory silence.

"You read the book I suppose at university and tried remembering who was killing whom, marrying whom, sleeping with whom. One needs a chart to keep track of all the characters from the Czar and Napoleon down to various sergeants and peasants." He shrugged his shoulders and shook his head in dismay.

Charles laughed. "I don't really remember many of the characters, but it did seem like half of the population of St. Petersburg was in the story!"

Viktor smiled. "Exactly, but maybe what was truly significant in the story was when various characters realized that what was important was not what trivial things happened on earth, but what happens afterward. Is there an afterwards? Is there a soul? He certainly talked a lot about the irrationality of man's actions."

"And is there a soul and an afterlife?" asked Charles.

Viktor again shrugged his shoulders. "Tolstoy only makes you think about such questions. He doesn't know anything more than you or me, but if he can at least get people asking the right questions about life – that's a good thing, that's a good first step."

Charles looked a little skeptical. "Lots of people have questions. It's answers that I'm looking for. I think Tolstoy is also overly optimistic about the goodness of man. My personal experience so far in life is rather the opposite and given what I know about your personal history, I would think that you'd share my low opinion of your fellow man."

"Well, I certainly used to own more possessions, ate better and wore better clothing – and that was pleasant – but is that what is truly important in life?"

Charles saw he was not going to win that argument with Viktor and simply responded with his own shoulder shrug of "who knows."

"Well, I must get back to my task with the snow. It has been a pleasure chatting with you. We will have to discuss life again another day." He bundled up, preparing to go back outside where the temperature was a few degrees below zero Fahrenheit. The Russian approach to warmth was layering. His coat seemed rather thin, and frayed, but he had on two sweaters and wore two pairs of gloves.

The American filled his mug and headed back up to his room. He was amazed that Viktor could hold such an optimistic view of his fellow man, given the way he'd been screwed by the Soviet system. Charles figured he'd stay with his own current philosophy of looking out for number one – himself – thank you very much.

CHAPTER 5

Prior to going over to the NKVD Headquarters on Thursday as planned, Charles had received from Spewack invitations to the next two cultural events at Spasso House. Sergeant Gau had managed to come up with the name of Colonel Suvarov's deputy, a Major Petrushkin, so Charles filled in two of the invitations with their names for a string quartet recital the following Sunday afternoon at Spasso House. The musicians were Russians, but according to Spewack they were to play several pieces by American composers. The invitation cards also noted that there would be a buffet dinner after the performance, so even if Suvarov wasn't into classical music, hopefully he would be into good food!

Once seated in Colonel Suvarov's sterile "show" office, Worthington began with the presentation of three more OSS reports for the NKVD. One was mostly a dry medical report about the most fragile parts of the human anatomy, beginning with the neck and laryngeal prominence of the throat, and of the kidneys. Charles had found it boring, but he noted that of the three reports he handed over, after seeing the title, Suvarov actually opened the cover and read the first paragraph or two of the report and nodded approvingly. He figured that told him something about Suvarov's personality!

Again, no offer of tea or coffee, so Charles quickly moved on to presenting to the sour-faced Russian behind the cheap wooden desk the two invitations from Ambassador Harriman for a string quartet concert on Sunday. Worthington managed to suppress a smile as it flashed through his mind that the burly and probably not terribly educated Russian might think a "string quartet" was the garroting of four people at once.

Sergeant Gau offered an explanation in Russian as to what the invitations were for, while Charles handed them to the Colonel. From his facial expression, he didn't seem impressed, but Charles had saved his "big gun" for the finish. "General Vorontsov will be there on Sunday for the performance. My Ambassador understands that the General is quite fond of classical music. Are you acquainted with General Vorontsov?"

General Vorontsov was quite famous in Russia for his part in stopping the German Army at the gates of Leningrad, and Charles was reasonably certain that Suvarov had never met him, but probably would like to make his acquaintance. Russians and Americans were different people, but had certain traits in common. Charles was fairly certain that Suvarov would like to become a general – and in any army or intelligence service, who you knew became ever more important the higher you rose.

Suvarov didn't immediately say "yes" to the invitation, but after hearing who else would be there from the Soviet side, he did respond, "I will check my calendar to see if I am free."

Charles rose. "Excellent, Colonel. I hope that you and Major Petrushkin will be available on Sunday to join us for music and food."

Once back in their official vehicle, Gau commented to Charles, "Did you see the way Suvarov's eyes opened wide when you told him that General Vorontsov would be there at the concert!"

Charles laughed and replied, "I sure hope that Vorontsov actually shows up and that Spewack wasn't just being optimistic that he's coming."

On Sunday, just a few minutes after the official invitation hour of 1600 hours, Colonel Suvarov, Major Petrushkin and two captains that Charles had never seen before came through the front door of Spasso House. General Vorontsov had arrived a few minutes earlier. Charles suspected that Suvarov had been sitting outside the compound in his car waiting to see Vorontsov actually arrive, before he committed to coming into the house. Worthington thought he could have been mistaken, but he believed that he saw for the first time ever, just a trace of a smile of happiness on Suvarov's lips. Charles had Sergeant Gau standing by to translate, but it turned out that the two captains were interpreters and served as such for Suvarov and Petrushkin.

It was a little awkward having casual "chit-chat" through an interpreter, but it worked. Worthington had forewarned Spewack that his Russian "guest" that day was anxious to get to meet Vorontsov, so when there appeared to be an interlude of anyone else talking with him, Charles led Colonel Suvarov over to meet the General. Spewack acted as interpreter and while the conversation only lasted a minute or so, Suvarov was clearly a happy man to have shaken hands with the famous hero of Leningrad.

The musical performance started fifteen minutes later. There were one hundred wooden chairs arranged in the grand hall of the house and everyone took a chair. Worthington thought the players were quite good, but it was probably a good idea that Ambassador Harriman kept it short. Apparently, he was smart enough to know that not all of his guests were great music lovers, and generally kept all performances to one half hour in length. Other doors were then opened and the audience of a hundred or so moved into another room to retrieve food from a long buffet table, which featured caviar, smoked herring and various cheeses shipped in from Wisconsin.

Charles found his four Russian guests back in the grand hall, with plates filled to capacity. He suspected that the NKVD cafeteria did not normally serve such splendid fare! He again engaged Colonel Suvarov, through his interpreter, on trivial topics such as where Suvarov had been born and whether he was a keen fisherman, like so many of his fellow Russians. Suvarov had already downed at least five shots of vodka and had become almost sociable.

"When you have any free time, perhaps on Sundays, what do you do in winter time for relaxation?" Charles inquired of the Colonel.

"We have a type of relaxation here in Russia where one jumps into freezing water and swims about." He slapped his chest and added that, "It is very good for the circulation. The people who do this are called 'polar bears' or 'walruses' and afterwards one drinks vodka."

"I think Russians drink vodka after almost everything!" commented Charles with a small smile.

Once Suvarov heard the translation, he laughed and slapped his big hand onto Charles' back. "Very true."

Thirty minutes into the dining portion of the afternoon, General Vorontsov announced his departure and within a few minutes, most all of the other Russian guests also headed for the cloak room to retrieve their coats. Apparently, no Soviet official wanted to be left alone with the Americans. Charles found Spewack near the door, after the man had shaken hands with every single Russian on the way out.

"How did your guests enjoy themselves today, Charles?"

"Well, my Colonel Suvarov almost smiled at one point, so I'd say it was a success."

Spewack laughed. "Well, in that case I'll keep sending you several invitations for all of our events."

On Monday afternoon, a Soviet courier from the NKVD dropped off an envelope for Captain Worthington, containing three reports for the OSS about German defense procedures at installations near front line fighting areas. He might have had a good time on Sunday, but he still wasn't interested in having face-to-face meetings, at least not at his initiative. When Sergeant Gau phoned on Tuesday to propose a meeting, at least Colonel Suvarov agreed to 1000 hours on Thursday.

Upon entering Suvarov's office on the appointed day, he did find Major Petrushkin sitting with the Colonel, and a silver serving set, with coffee, on the desk. The set was better than the coffee! Charles figured that per Russian etiquette, having been to Spasso House for entertainment and food, Suvarov felt he should offer a refreshment in return. He noted that the engravings on the set gave it a Romanov dynasty look; Charles presumed it had been "confiscated in the name of the people" from some Russian aristocrat somewhere along the line. Using Gau to interpret for everyone, they managed to carry on a friendly conversation for about ten minutes. Suvarov had had a wife and eight year old son when the war started, but they had been killed by the German advance on Leningrad in the fall of 1941. Major Petrushkin on the other hand, had always been a bachelor. Using an old Russian peasant proverb, Suvarov even made some sort of joke about how there would be so many disappointed girls if the Major ever married.

Gau simply gave Charles the rough idea and said, "It's a proverb; I'll try to explain it to you later."

Worthington didn't want to press his luck on all this friendly camaraderie and after ten minutes of polite conversation, he opened his folder and took out his three OSS reports for the week. "I suppose we should get down to some work. Suvarov took a quick glance at the titles of the reports, but seemed disappointed not to find another one on the weak points of the human anatomy. Charles had in fact sent a telegram back to Washington telling them how much Colonel Suvarov had enjoyed the one on the neck and Adams' Apple from the week before and asked for more reports along those lines. Maybe in the future Headquarters would come through.

Petrushkin poured another round of coffee and Suvarov inquired via Gau if he might ask a personal question of Captain Worthington?

When Charles responded in the affirmative, Suvarov asked, "Have you ever personally killed a man?"

Gau was slightly shocked by the question, but translated it directly, without comment. Suvarov stared directly into Charles' eyes after he asked the question. Charles didn't even turn his head towards Gau while answering. He stared straight back at the Colonel and without hesitation, said, "Yes, I have, with my bare hands. It took place out in the South Pacific." He thought about asking the same of Suvarov, but was sure he knew already what the answer would be.

Upon hearing Worthington's translated answer, Suvarov gave a small, approving nod of his head. "I will see you next week, Captain Worthington."

Everyone shook hands and the Americans departed.

Once back in their car, Sergeant Gau commented, "That was a great answer, Captain. I'm sure the Colonel never suspected that you were joking."

Without even turning his head towards his sergeant, he replied, "What makes you think I was joking." The two rode in silence the rest of the way back to the Mission. Gau was wondering if Worthington was bullshitting him. Charles was silently remembering all the vivid details that led that day in late 1940 to his killing of a Japanese spy. He'd accompanied Mr. Vincent Astor, as his personal secretary, on a vacation tour of South Pacific islands. He stumbled across a hidden HF radio of a Japanese spy on Guadalcanal. They got in to a fight and Charles killed him in self-defense. And it was with his bare hands.

Charles spent the rest of the drive staring out the window at civilian Russians going about their everyday lives on the streets of Moscow. Everyone was bundled up in multiple layers of clothing to fight the bitter cold. When he could see their faces, everyone looked depressed and rather sad. He'd never been in a Russian's home, but at least out in public, everyone looked perpetually sad. Their lives under Stalin had been hard, the winters were harsh, the German invasion had killed millions and while the war was now going better, the end was hardly in sight. He admired the Russians for their resilience and ability to suffer and carry on.

Once back in his office, he typed up another enthusiastic report to send back to his Headquarters about that day's meeting with the NKVD. He'd yet to receive a response from Washington to his message reporting on Sunday's social event, but presumed that today's report about establishing a real rapport with Colonel Suvarov would surely prompt a nice "atta boy" telegram from Headquarters. If he could just keep up this positive image of the relationship, this should surely help get his career back on track. He doubted, however, he could con Headquarters along for another ten months, so he knew he still needed to keep his eyes open for an opportunity to actually accomplish something, so as to impress General Donovan. He remembered an OSS training briefing about Nazi Propaganda Minister, Joseph Goebbels, who'd once said something about how a lie repeated often enough became the truth. A senior Nazi official was not exactly an ideal role model, but this one statement did merit some recognition – report to Headquarters long enough that there was a great liaison relationship underway with the NKVD because of Charles' efforts, and Headquarters would eventually come to believe there was a great relationship. A bit of an exaggeration, but then everybody exaggerated – stock brokers did to their clients, politicians to the voters, all gave the most optimistic views of situations.

Having taken his report to the Communications Office, to be enciphered and sent off to Washington, Charles decided to head home for lunch and maybe to read some. No one else at the Military Mission knew exactly what Worthington did, but he calculated that if he was often out of his office, colleagues would assume that he was out and about doing something useful! He did in fact start in his third week to take his official car, and guided by an out-of-date street map of Moscow, start exploring the city. His Russian language lessons, which he took every afternoon on Mondays, Wednesdays and Fridays had him up to a level of where he could be polite and ask a few simple questions, such as "how much" and "where is____?" He practiced his few phrases on Viktor, who graciously lied to him and told him how well he was pronouncing the words, but he wanted to try out his language on a few real Russians. He also wanted to get to know the city. Charles had no specific purpose in mind; he simply figured that an intelligence officer ought to be reasonably acquainted with his city, just in case something came along requiring area knowledge.

Sergeant Kowalski had told him of a couple of interesting places in town, known as "commission stores." These were places where local citizens came in and left a few personal items for sale, and the store kept a small percentage of the sale price for its service when the item sold. Often these were very practical items such as fur gloves and coats, but occasionally there were also lovely old family heirlooms for sale, such as samovars, beautiful tea sets from the Czarist era and jewelry – items that people had managed to hide from Communist Party confiscation over the past twenty years. In one store, Charles found a used light-weight winter jacket that appealed to him and he bought it. He thought it might be useful to have something like that, in case he didn't wish to wear his "Nanook of the North" heavy, winter coat. Perhaps if he ever needed to change a flat tire or something and didn't wish dirtying his good coat. He just stored it in the trunk of his vehicle.

Visiting such stores and a few antiquarian book shops, which had a few old books in English, would give Worthington an explanation as to why he was driving around, just in case the NKVD did follow him and wondered what he was up to that day. He hadn't truly made up his mind about Viktor yet, but just in case he was working for the NKVD, Charles mentioned to him one afternoon about his plan for going out and exploring such stores. He figured it wouldn't hurt if Viktor passed this "story" along to the NKVD – might spare them the effort of bothering to tail him about the city. Only on a few occasions so far had Charles concluded that he was being followed on a trip somewhere and on those days it had been so blatant, it seemed that they wanted him to know he had surveillance.

Several days after Charles had told him of his plan to visit commission stores, Viktor stopped him in the courtyard after lunch one day. "Captain Worthington, I have the names and addresses of two good commission stores you might want to visit someday. They are not very well known to foreigners and while small, both have some very nice 19th century items for sale." He handed him a small sheet with the information written down for him.

"Thank you, Viktor, I shall try to find them tomorrow when I'm out." Charles had determined that "19ᵗʰ century" was Viktor's politically correct way of referring to the Czarist period. "Don't suppose you have hidden away any nice old pieces of pottery or jewelry that you'd like to sell?"

Viktor laughed. "No, I'm afraid that other than those tea glasses that my aunt had kept that are now downstairs in the worker's room, the Rostov family 'donated' all of its possessions to the Bolshevik cause long ago."

Charles appreciated Viktor's sense of humor and responded, "And a good cause it was."

"Indeed it was, Captain. Do let me know if you find anything worthy of purchase at either of those stores. I'd like to see them – to remind me of the old days."

"I shall do so." It was vaguely worded, sarcastic comments like that, poking a little fun at the Communists that made Charles doubt that Viktor really was an informant, as many of his colleagues suspected. If, however, Viktor was an NKVD officer, or informant, he was at least a friendly and helpful one.

On the following Sunday, Colonel Suvarov came again to Spasso House to see several short films featuring Laurel and Hardy. He even brought a few more of his colleagues with him, as well as the two interpreters. There was no attempt to translate the dialogue of the movies as they played. Mr. Spewack simply give a brief synopsis of the plots at the start of each film. The slapstick comedy of Laurel and Hardy didn't require one to understand the spoken lines of the film and its very thin plot line. Once again, Charles actually saw Suvarov smile. There was no famous Red Army general present this time, so apparently the Colonel simply came to enjoy himself, or to perhaps show that the Americans and Russians were actually allies against the Nazis.

After the films, during the buffet, Charles went up to Suvarov and his NKVD colleagues to show him one of his small purchases from a commission store the previous day. He held out his right hand to show a ring made with a stone of Russian amber. "I've been visiting a few of the commission stores in the city recently and found this lovely treasure yesterday." Charles figured it wouldn't hurt if he told Suvarov why he was driving around town. He obviously wasn't in charge of surveillance teams, but Charles was certain he would pass along to whomever was, his explanation.

"It's very nice. Glad to see that you rich American capitalists are helping out broke Russians by buying their personal possessions." Suvarov kept a very stern look on his face for about three seconds, then let out a big laugh at his own joke.

NKVD Captain Nosenko, who was acting as their interpreter was trying to explain why Suvarov thought his comment was so funny, but wasn't making much progress. Charles figured he'd help the poor man out and let out a loud laugh of his own, which made Suvarov happy. Suvarov saw a Soviet Foreign Ministry officer he knew and excused himself to go say hello, leaving Worthington and Nosenko alone.

"So, Captain Nosenko, what part of Russia is home for you?" inquired Charles.

"I was born near Vladimir, which is a small town 200 kilometers east of Moscow. It is an ancient place that was founded 900 years ago."

"It must be very beautiful," replied Charles.

At first, Nosenko looked and acted a little nervous that he'd been left alone with the American spy, but lots of Russians were talking to other Americans, so he eventually relaxed.

"And where is your home in America, Captain Worthington?"

"I was born and grew up in Chicago, before going to college near Boston and had been working in New York City before the war."

"Ah, yes, Chicago. It was home of Al Capone. My English teacher told me all about that famous gangster. Is there still much danger of being killed on streets by machine gun fights between rival gangs in Chicago?"

Charles smiled just a little at Nosenko's knowledge of the Windy City, based on Soviet propaganda lectures and insights from an instructor who'd probably never been there. "Well, it's much safer there now than it was in the 1920s. Probably more danger of being hit by a car while crossing the street than of being hit by machine gun bullets." He'd definitely have to tell Salvatore and Lou, his two Italian gangster friends back in Manhattan, next time he was there about the Soviet view of continued gang warfare in Chicago. Nosenko's question did trigger a brief flashback to how his own father had died in Chicago back in the Capone era, but then his mind returned to the present.

"Do you have any hobbies?" Charles asked. This required further explanation of what a hobby was, but then Nosenko grasped the meaning of the word.

"Yes, I play balalaika for entertainment when I have free time. My father had played this instrument and he taught me. Did your father teach you how to play any musical instruments?"

"No, unfortunately, he died while I was very young." The thought of machine gun fire again shot quickly through Charles' mind. "But I have no musical talent in any case. I can 'play' records on a phonograph machine, but nothing else."

Nosenko laughed. He understood Worthington's sense of humor.

Nosenko saw Suvarov waving for him, in need of his interpreting skills. "Excuse me, Colonel Suvarov needs me. It was very nice talking with you and thank you for the invitation. The movies were very funny."

"My pleasure. I hope to see you again in the future."

Charles then drifted over to a small circle of British officers. As he got closer, he saw that at the center of them was a woman. She was also in a uniform, like all around her, but definitely a woman, with short, chestnut-colored hair and porcelain-white skin, as English women often had. Charles started a conversation with a British lieutenant from the Gordon Highlanders, assigned to the British Embassy in Moscow, but he quickly maneuvered himself closer to the female soldier. When there was a brief lull in the conversation between her and a fellow Brit, he quickly stepped towards her and simply said, "I'm Captain Charles Worthington. I don't believe we've met before."

She offered him a smile that would have melted any man's heart and made any Hollywood agent immediately take out a contract and pen. She responded, softly, "I'm WREN Jane Summerfield. No, I don't think we've met before."

Charles tried to think of something terribly clever or witty to say, but out of his mouth came only, "So, you're a WREN. I've heard of such women, but never met one before."

Jane tossed off a quick, comical salute and responded, "Women's Royal Naval Service at your command, Captain."

Charles decided that she had more than a passing resemblance to Vivien Leigh of *Gone With The Wind* fame, but managed to suppress a thought of offering up his best Clark Cable impersonation. Instead, he returned his own fairly nice smile and simply asked, "Have you been in Moscow long?"

"Do you mean actual months, or just how long does it seem that I've been here at the edge of nowhere?" she answered, while maintaining a straight face.

He noticed that her wine glass was almost empty and so he replied, "Why don't we find you some more wine. I'm sure it will make it seem as if time is passing more quickly."

"Yes, why don't we do that," she responded with another thousand watt smile. Charles then smoothly stole her away from her British colleagues and monopolized the next twenty minutes of her life. Once they had fresh glasses of wine, they found a small couch off in a side room and began the usual round of get-acquainted questions and answers.

She admitted to being twenty-three years old, an only child and having been raised in a rural area of Norfolk County, in East Anglia.

He stated that he was from Chicago and having done his undergraduate studies and law degree at Harvard, then working for a couple of years prior to the war as a private secretary for a wealthy businessman in New York City.

Charles had noticed the plain gold wedding band on her left hand and finally addressed that topic. He pointed at her ring and inquired, "And is your husband in the British military?"

"He's in the Army, serving in North Africa, but..." There was a slight pause, before she added, "But he's been Missing in Action for the past year."

Charles quickly searched for something optimistic to say and responded, "Probably off in some Italian or German prison camp and official notification simply got lost somewhere while passing through the Swiss."

"Funny, that's my opinion as well. One hears all the time of clerical errors in getting notifications from those awful Germans. I think sometimes they intentionally screw up the records just to cause unnecessary concern in English families."

Charles wanted to move on to a more pleasant topic. "How about your mom and dad? They still in Norfolk?"

"Dad's been a school teacher for many years and now he's quite proud of being an Air Raid Warden in our village near the coast. Mom's been helping out in a pub and a shop, now that all the men are off to war, and she has big victory garden going behind our house. It's a beautiful area of England, with gardens everywhere, just like you see in all the movies set in England."

She finally inquired about his love life. "How about you? Surely there must be a girl or two back home waiting anxiously for letters from you?" she teased.

"Oh, dozens, actually. I get my sergeant to run off mimeograph copies of my letters, so I don't tire out my hand too much."

She laughed, but wouldn't let him off the hook that easily. "Come on, fess up. A good looking fellow like you must have someone special waiting somewhere for you."

Charles stared down at his wine glass for a second. "Well, there had been someone very special, but it got very complicated and I haven't seen her for some time now – not sure if I ever will again."

This time it was she who realized she'd unintentionally touched on a clearly sensitive point and moved on to a different topic. "So, what is it that you do here in Moscow to help win the war? Or is it terribly secret and a mere WREN shouldn't know of such things?"

Charles quickly thought about how close to the truth she'd come. "Oh, I just push paper in the US Military Mission, from my in-box to my out-box. General Deane tells me I'm very good at it and if the war goes on long enough, I might even make Major some year down the road!"

"Well, if that ever occurs, I'll buy you a bottle of good champagne out on the black market, to celebrate."

He took her hand to shake it. "That's a deal and I'll hold you to your offer."

She saw that one of her British colleagues was discreetly waving at her. "I see that my friends are getting ready to leave. It's been wonderful meeting you and I hope I'll run into you again in the near future."

"It's been great chatting with you. I hear that Moscow is a pretty small town, so I'm sure we'll meet again. And if not, I'll just phone over to the British Embassy and track you down."

They shook hands and exchanged smiles. And then she was off. His Russian guests had already departed, presumably while he'd been off chatting with Jane, so he too decided to call it a night. One additional benefit of living at Spasso House was that it only took him thirty seconds to get to his room after an evening's social event. As he lay in bed before falling asleep, he found himself thinking about what a wonderful young lady Jane was. He also rather strangely found himself thinking that it was good that she was married, as that removed from the equation any issue of romance or intimacy. They could just be friends and in a tough place like Moscow in winter, he thought that having a good friend was more desirable than a girlfriend.

CHAPTER 6

Over the coming weeks, Worthington's life settled down to a rather dull routine. He'd meet once a week with Colonel Suvarov to exchange materials, the substance of which became ever-more irrelevant. Neither side intended to share anything too sensitive, or perhaps didn't even have anything sensitive to give regarding guerrilla warfare. The battle on the Eastern Front was simply one of hundreds of thousands of men and thousands of tanks slugging it out, as the Germans slowly, but steadily withdrew from Russian territory. Suvarov seemed to almost begin to take pity on Charles' predicament. He'd been sent to do a job in Moscow; a job which simply didn't really exist. The Russian had taken to offering coffee at each session just so they'd last a little longer. Charles had explained at one meeting that Sergeant Gau wasn't really his to command and asked if Captain Nosenko might serve as interpreter at their future meetings, to which Suvarov assented. This did give him a chance to spend a little time around Nosensko, who would meet Charles at the main entrance at his appointed arrival time, and also walk him back out to his vehicle at the end of a meeting. At one meeting, Charles inquired of Colonel Suvarov if he had any objection to his inviting Captain Nosenko out for lunch one day. Nosenko looked terribly embarrassed at this surprise invitation, but fortunately, Suvarov gave his concurrence in principle. Charles said he would be in touch shortly to propose a particular date, perhaps in the coming week.

That same evening, there was a large party at the British Embassy on the occasion of the birthday of their ambassador. Charles looked forward to the event, figuring that he would again have a chance to bump into Jane. He passed on several offers of rides to the party. He wasn't sure just how long he might want to stay, if indeed he encountered the WREN again and they were having as pleasant a time together as at their first meeting. A light snow was falling as he drove to the British Embassy and he had to park several blocks from the building, just to find a parking space. There weren't that many social occasions among the foreign diplomats in Moscow and apparently a large percentage of such bored individuals who'd been invited, had accepted. Charles was enjoying a small cigar on his drive to the social event, as he often did. Word had filtered down to him at Spasso house that Ambassador Harriman didn't really enjoy the smell of cigars, so he rarely smoked them there, except occasionally in his room with the door closed and the window open. Despite the cold, he put the front passenger window down several inches to let the cigar smoke out of the car. If he didn't, after only ten minutes or so his clothes and hair would reek of smoke.

By the time he reached the party, a good crowd had arrived to celebrate Ambassador Sir Archibald Clark Kerr's birthday. Rumor had it he was turning 62, but Sir Archibald would only admit he'd been born sometime in the last century. He'd been serving in Moscow since early 1942. Charles found Jane loitering near the front entrance to the chancery, which made it easy to find her among the large crowd of more than a hundred. He flattered himself with the thought that she'd been standing in that convenient spot, waiting for him.

"Ah, you've finally arrived," she said to him as he kissed her on the cheek. "I was beginning to think that you weren't coming this evening," she added, thus confirming his thought and flattering his ego.

"And miss seeing you again? Never." Her took her by the arm and headed in to the main room. "Do they have a bar somewhere in here?" he inquired.

"What a question! Our Ambassador was born in Australia. Do Russian bears sleep in the woods?"

After getting their hands on a couple of gin and tonics, they moved off to a quiet corner to have a little privacy. After the usual chit-chat of what was new, done anything interesting this week, etc., she moved the conversation on to more interesting subjects. "I understand from a colleague that you're the spooky OSS man here in town for the Americans. Is that true?"

Since she obviously already knew it was, he simply replied, "Yes, I am, though I tend not to advertise it, unless it serves some purpose."

"OK. I understand. By the way, I do know how to keep a secret."

"Excellent. So we both know how to keep secrets." He leaned in closer and whispered in her ear, "Now if one of us only knew a secret, we'd be all set."

She grinned and slapped her hand on his chest, but then left it there for several long seconds. She then started asking questions about his childhood and the other sorts of questions that people ask when they're genuinely interested in knowing more about another person.

"Do your parents still live in Chicago?"

No, unfortunately, they were both killed in an automobile accident when I was young teenager, so I lived mostly at this boarding school for young boys before I went off to college."

"Oh, so sorry to hear that. And you were an only child?"

"Yes."

"Do you ever get back to Chicago? I mean, do you still have any relatives around that area?"

"No. There was a fellow who sort of looked out for me that I called 'uncle', but he had just been a friend of the family and once I moved east I lost contact with him as well."

"Well, perhaps you're just as well off. I have several aunts who are absolutely horrible people that I have to go visit whenever I'm back in my hometown." She laughed.

Their private conversation was interrupted a half hour later when the birthday cake was brought out and all the guests assembled to sing Happy Birthday to Sir Archibald. Charles sang very softly, being totally tone deaf and not being able to distinguish one note from another. Jane on the other hand, sang beautifully. She said she'd had several years of singing lessons when a young girl. After the cake cutting, Jane was drug off in to other circles of British diplomats and officers, and thus ended their conversation for the night. Charles was among the first guests to depart. He was of low enough status that he was not called upon to bid Sir Archibald goodnight; he could just gather his coat and make for the door. He did catch a glance of Jane, chatting in a circle of other guests. She gave him a warm smile and waved at him. He returned a gesture indicating that he would phone her, and then he was gone.

He departed in a very good mood. He greatly enjoyed her company, not for any particular reason that he could articulate, but just in general. It was still softly snowing and he walked in silence the few blocks to his car parked on a narrow side street. He did like the sound of the snow crunching under his boots. He'd rarely heard such a sound when walking in the snow around Boston. He guessed that maybe it had something to do with how much colder the snow was around Moscow than in Massachusetts, which give it that special sound.

He got into his staff car and was pleased that it did turn over and start. It was then that he noticed the Russian match box on the front passenger seat, which he swore had not been there when he'd parked the car. He took a quick glance all around his car to see if anyone was watching him. Seeing no one obvious, he pushed the box open and saw that the matches had been removed and there was a small piece of paper folded up neatly within the box. He shoved the box closed and put it in his side coat pocket. Though he was dying of curiosity, he'd wait to read it until he was back to the privacy of his own room at Spasso House.

He drove the legal speed limit and kept a sharp eye out for surveillance on the route back home, but saw nothing that struck him as cars following him. Of course, if this little note was some sort of NKVD entrapment ploy, why would they bother putting surveillance on him that evening as well?

Once back in his room, he carefully pulled open the match box again, took out the note and was pleased to see that it was in English, not great English, but at least English. It read:

> "I Russian officer with important information for your government about Stalin's plans for after defeat Nazis. If you interested, park your car on side street by restaurant Odessa this Friday between 12 and 1 PM. Leave back window little bit open and you will receive another note with specific instructions when you from lunch return about how we meet one day soon.
>
> Your friend"

Worthington wasn't quite sure what to do with such an offer, presuming it wasn't simply a ploy of some kind by the NKVD. He knew that if he reported the note in official channels, taking any action would be rejected because of Allied policy about not working against their ally, the Soviet Union. But he thought that one of the ways to get out of the OSS doghouse would be to have a big success of some kind, while in Moscow. His official liaison job was a joke and certainly not going to achieve anything.

He contemplated this offer from all sides for the next half hour. If he went forward, this would present several dangers. First, he was occasionally under surveillance by the NKVD, despite being an ally and he could be caught meeting with this Russian. And of course, this could simply be a provocation by the NKVD so as to have an incidence of an American assigned to Moscow attempting to spy on Russia. He couldn't fathom why they'd want to create such a public incident, but maybe they would keep it private and have "one" in the bank, so to speak. Thus, if a Soviet spy got caught one day in America by the FBI, the Russians could cite the "Worthington episode."

He also faced the challenge of what exactly he would do with any intelligence obtained? There were several more senior officers than he at the Military Mission and Embassy who were very pro-Soviet, with clear communistic political leanings. There'd be trouble in even being allowed to send reports to Washington which put the Soviet Union in a bad light. And given the "no spying on an ally policy", just how would he source any such intelligence?

If the whole thing did blow up in his face, he'd be sent home and General Donovan would have to outright fire him from the OSS. That would be embarrassing, but at least it would get him out of this meaningless job in miserable Moscow. Besides, the war was not going to last forever and he could simply go back to the law profession.

Worthington pondered such problems while he smoked a cigar, but finally decided to go ahead and at least learn more of what was being offered and by whom. He would park his car at the designated spot and time as requested, in order to signal his further interest. He did have one clever idea on how to protect himself, in case this "volunteer" was indeed an NKVD entrapment operation against him.

The following morning, he phoned Captain Nosenko at his NKVD office and invited him to lunch for that Friday at 1200 hours. As he already had Suvarov's approval, he readily agreed. He also accepted Worthington's gracious offer to pick Nosenko up and drive him to the restaurant. Worthington's thinking was, if it did turn out to be a "provocation", how could he be accused of meeting an "agent", or any such improper activity, since he had invited an NKVD officer to go with him to the alleged meeting!

The following three days passed incredibly slowly. Charles kept envisioning all the various possible outcomes of his taking this risk. He liked best the ones in which this volunteer would have incredibly valuable intelligence and regardless of the minor technicality about spying on an ally, his initiative would be highly regarded back at OSS Headquarters. He didn't dwell on the scenarios where he was arrested and then sent home in disgrace!

Nosenko was waiting outside the front gate of the NKVD compound at 1145 hours as agreed upon. He had mixed feelings about going to lunch with Charles. On the one hand, it was rather prestigious to be lunching with an American and he did like him. To the negative, he remembered how many NKVD officers back during the Great Purge of the mid-1930s simply disappeared off to Siberia for nothing more than being acquainted with someone who had previously been arrested. A number of NKVD officers in those years who had been serving abroad had been brought home and shot on the grounds that their thinking might have been contaminated by contact with Westerners – even though their assignment had been to meet Westerners with the goal of recruiting some as Soviet spies!

Upon arrival, Charles left it to Nosenko to get them a table and to select a few items from the menu. He saw that Nosenko was being hesitant about what to choose.

"By the way, lunch is on the US Army today – I insist." Nosenko did not argue with him over who would pay and seemed to relax. Either his portion of the bill was to come out of his own pocket, or Suvarov had only allocated him a very small amount to spend. Once they'd ordered, Charles launched into a few personal questions about Nosenko's past. "How did you come to work in the NKVD?"

"I had been active in the Komsomol, the organization for young Communists, and had been noted by my group's leader for my loyalty and dependability. That was back in the early 1930s. In those days, one's loyalty was considered the most important quality." As soon as he said that, he worried that if anyone else had heard that, it might be considered a questionable comment, but noted that there was no one within many meters of their table.

"And when did you start studying English?"

"When I first entered the Soviet Army, I was given various tests. I don't remember this English word – something about having a natural ability for something."

"The word is 'aptitude.' The test showed you had an aptitude for learning a foreign language?"

"Yes, that is the word. So, I was sent off to study English." Nosenko didn't feel comfortable going into the details of his career and just jumped ahead. "And then the war started, and here I am."

"Well, your English is very good. I've been having Russian lessons for many weeks now, and I fear that I will never have much command of the language."

The Russian laughed. "Don't get discouraged, we have many sounds in our language that the mouths of Americans don't normally make, and our grammar is rather complicated compared to English. You will one day be fluent!"

"I hope the war doesn't go on long enough for that to happen!"

Nosenko picked up his vodka glass to offer a toast. "Za pobedy!"

Charles had been in town long enough to have learned that popular Russian phrase – "To victory." He picked up his glass and repeated the phrase, then they both downed their glasses.

After they'd finished their soup course, Worthington excused himself, allegedly to go to the Men's Room, but instead went quickly out to his car to check for a "message." He'd left a window cracked as directed and indeed found another matchbox inside on the back floor of his car. He simply put that in his pants pocket and would read it later. In case someone had been watching him, he also opened the front passenger door and got into the glove box, as if searching for something. As he walked away from his car, he kept his right hand in his pocket, holding the match box. If he suddenly saw men running towards him, to grab him, he intended to toss the match box into the snow and rush for the hotel. No one approached him, though an elderly "babushka", Russian grandmother, severely chastised him in Russian for being outside without a hat. These legendary ladies of Russian society were well known by all for offering unsolicited advice on everything to one and all! He hurried back to the table and his guest.

The rest of the meal was general chit chat, mostly about what Charles intended to do after the war.

"Will you stay in the OSS?"

"No, this is strictly a wartime job for me. I'll probably go back to being a lawyer – find a wife, have two or three kids, get fat and watch my hair turn gray."

They both laughed and Nosenko offered another toast, as he once again raised his glass. "To watching our hair grow gray!"

After dropping the Russian off back at the NKVD compound, Worthington drove straight to the US Military Mission. He wanted the safety of his office with the door closed, before he began examining the contents of this second missive.

Once he'd grabbed a cup of coffee and was seated at his desk, he slowly opened the match box and excitedly unfolded the sheet of paper inside, upon which his military future might depend.

> "I will meet you in nine days on Sunday at 2 pm in Patriarch's Pond. A polar bear group swims in pond in park on Sunday afternoons in winter. Be in water but away from others. I know you and will come to you. I will say that water in Siberia is better. You will answer me that it is best in Finland. Then you will know it is me. We can then discuss future plans when I will pass to you important information and make agreement on what I want from you. That will include move to America before war ends."

Worthington had hoped that the note would contain some spectacular intelligence and thus clearly justify continuing with the case, but it did not. He could understand why the cautious Russian hadn't wished to leave any more than necessary on the piece of paper tossed into his car, which someone else might have got their hands on, but it didn't help him much to decide whether to continue or not. After sitting and staring at the far wall for a good ten minutes, he made his decision. He decided that if he was in for a penny, he was in for a pound and would make the meeting to see just what this volunteer offered. In the meantime, he would report nothing to OSS Headquarters.

On the following Sunday, the last one in March, he drove to this famous park and pond. He went over to the bank where twenty-five or thirty men were already naked and in the frigid water. They'd broken up the ice in a large area of the pond. He couldn't decide if they were incredibly "manly" or were just insane. Many others were watching, drinking vodka and cheering them on. Fortunately for him, it was a relatively mild winter's day, by Russian standards. It was only 2° below zero Fahrenheit, with little wind and the sun shining. He disrobed quickly and got into the water. Entering slowly would not help and he wished to minimize the chance of others on the shore talking to him and realizing he was an American. If he was going to have a heart attack, he would just as soon have it immediately. He went over to one side, away from most of the men in the pond, hoping that the volunteer would approach him sooner rather than later. He kept rapidly moving his arms and legs, trying to generate some body heat.

In approximately two minutes, another bather came towards him. He was a man in his early 40s with a short, military haircut. He stated the anticipated oral parole in heavily accented English about Siberia and Worthington replied appropriately about preferring Finland.

"I am Captain Sasha Turgenev, of the NKVD. I was going to wait longer to make sure no one seemed to be watching you, but from look on your face, I was not sure how much longer you would survive in our cold water! Charles would have returned the Russian's broad grin, but he was too damn cold to smile – if that comment had been an attempt at humor. Maybe it was just an obvious statement of fact.

"Thank you for coming to me sooner rather than later. I'm not accustomed to bathing in such cold water, so perhaps we should proceed quickly with our business."

"Agreed. I work in counterintelligence section of NKVD responsible for keeping watch on foreigners in Moscow. I have some information in that field, but most importantly, I have intelligence about plans of Stalin to permanently occupy any territories in Eastern Europe that Red Army will have conquered from Nazis by end of war. I know Stalin has made agreement with your President Roosevelt about holding elections and other such nonsense after the war in those countries, but Comrade Stalin has no intention of giving up any captured territory. I know this because NKVD has been ordered to start drawing up plans necessary to control those countries."

"Do you have any official documents to show what you're saying about such preparations by the NKVD? I don't doubt what you are telling me, but it will be easier to convince Washington of what you say if you have documents."

"Yes, I have and can give you copies next time. I also have other important information about work of NKVD, if we come to agreement. In return, I want you to move me to America before end of war, provide new identity documents and whatever amount of money you think my information has been worth to America. Then I will simply disappear."

"I don't personally have the authority to promise you such things, but once I've gotten some verifying documents from you to send to Washington, I'm sure you will get what you want. I do suggest that next time we meet, it be on dry land so that it will be easier for you to pass me documents!"

"Yes, good idea. Plus, I am not sure you can survive another 'walrus' dip in Russian waters in winter."

Charles felt no sense of national pride or masculinity on the line and readily agreed. "Do you know where the winter market is in the food hall on Gogol Street?"

Sasha nodded positively.

"Good, I'll be there at 1000 hours on next Sunday and carrying a typical wicker shopping basket. It's always crowded at that time and you will be able to come very near to me without anyone noticing and place something in my food basket. Also, you propose to me in a note you place in my basket the day, time and place for the following meeting, maybe two weeks later."

"That market on Sunday mornings will be good place to pass messages. I will be there at 1000 hours, but if for some reason one of us is not there, the alternate meeting will be the following Sunday at 0930 hours."

"Agreed," was all that Charles could say between his chattering teeth and the onset of hypothermia.

"Good. You should go now, before you have heart attack," replied the Russian. He wasn't trying to be funny.

Charles needed no further encouragement and immediately headed for the shore and a towel.

Once back in his room at Spasso House, in fresh dry clothes and sitting on his desk chair a few inches from his radiator, Charles was finally starting to feel warm and comfortable. *The things I do for my country,* he silently thought to himself as he started to make some notes on a single sheet of paper laid on the hard cover of a thick dictionary. They'd taught him at OSS School not to just write on paper within a notebook or tablet, as it would leave impressions on the sheets below the one he actually wrote on. He didn't try to write a word-for-word exchange of the two men, but just to get down the important highlights before he forgot anything said at the meeting with the Russian volunteer. He started with the man's name and place of work, followed by the story of Stalin's plans for any countries that would come to be occupied by the Red Army. There was the vague claim that Sasha could provide information from his work in a counterintelligence unit of the NKVD. Charles regretted not having pressed Sasha for more details on that claim, but admitted freely that he'd not been at his intellectual best while freezing in the cold water.

Having gotten the facts down on paper, he turned to considering the next step. He concluded that he should continue to act unilaterally, until at least the follow-up meeting, when hopefully Sasha would provide documentary proof of his claims about the future of Eastern Europe. What he had at the moment was tantalizing, but there would be hell to pay when he advised Washington he'd violated the rules about not targeting an ally and he knew he would have to have great intelligence in hand to counteract that "minor detail" – not just the promise of great things to come. He rationalized to himself that he hadn't "targeted" Sasha; the man had volunteered himself to Worthington. He thought that what Sasha was offering to provide was valuable intelligence, but then just maybe, Sasha was lying to him, as many agents do to their handlers. He might actually work at the NKVD, but was simply trying to scam his way to America.

Charles had an early and quick dinner. He wasn't in the mood to socialize in the mess room with his colleagues. He went to bed early. He was exhausted. Aside from the toll of being in the cold water, the emotional stress of the day had had a wearying effect on him as well. A goodnight's sleep would do him good, both physically and mentally. He'd already decided that he would make the next meeting with Sasha, so that wasn't an issue to focus on in the coming days. However, he could use some clever ideas on how to handle the case safely in the future, right under the noses of the NKVD in downtown Moscow!

Not having anything to really do on Monday at the Mission, Worthington came back to Spasso House for lunch, then simply went up to his room to read and when he started feeling sleepy, he walked the eight feet to his bed and began a genuine, horizontal nap. He knew that some people claimed that rainy afternoons made them sleepy, but since arriving in Moscow, Charles swore that afternoons of steady snow fall had the same effect on him.

He awoke about an hour later and feeling the urge for some hot tea, he made his way down to the worker's break room. He'd just finished filling his mug when in came Viktor, looking very cold and very tired.

"Greetings Captain Worthington," he uttered as he started removing his outer coat and a few layers underneath.

"Greetings Viktor. You look very tired. Is the snow winning today?"

Viktor laughed. "Maybe so. Maybe my mind still thinks I'm a strong young man, but my body is telling me I'm not."

"It's been snowing non-stop today. I think any man of any age would look tired after fighting the snow for so many hours, and by the way, please call me Charles. You're not in the American Army, so I'm not your captain."

"Very well, Charles, if you are comfortable with that. You know, Tolstoy once observed that men who truly deserved to lead others didn't care much about titles or rank, while the men who so gloried in their rank and title, often didn't deserve to be in charge of anyone."

"I don't know about the Russian Army, but I've seen a few in the American Army who perhaps fit Tolstoy's comment very well."

"Oh, we have such people in the Russian Army as well." They both laughed.

"How are you settling in, here in Moscow among us Russians?"

"Well enough, I think. The truth of the matter is that there is nothing very exciting or glamorous about moving paper in an office, arranging for supplies to be ordered and delivered. One day has quickly become like any other. I know it's necessary work, but rather tedious, and winter is not the most exciting time of year either."

"Some ancient Greek, I forget who, once said that victory goes to the slow and steady, and that victory comes from the preparations made before the first spear is thrown. So, helping get all the supplies here that the Red Army needs to kill Germans is perhaps not exciting, but still necessary."

Charles nodded in agreement. "I think that idea might well apply to many endeavors in life. A number of philosophers have commented about how life is the process, not any specific end goal."

"Perhaps, but one still needs at least a few goals in life, at least to serve as a compass, to help you choose the path of that process. I don't think I'm smarter than you, but I have lived many more years than you have yet, so perhaps I have some keener insights about life. And one of those insights is about how you treat your fellow travelers on the road of life. As Jesus said at his Sermon on the Mount. 'Do unto others as you would have others do unto you.'"

"Yes, well, my experience is an old Chicago proverb: 'Do unto others, before they stab you in the back.' I once was quite the optimist about my fellow man, but now, I look after only me, and everybody else can look after themselves."

"You have become a very cynical man, Charles, and at a very young age. I take it something very damaging to you happened in your life, for you to have adopted such a cynical outlook of your fellow man."

Charles just shrugged his shoulders in response "What about you Viktor? If all you have told me is true, you were screwed pretty badly in life – sent to a prison camp in Siberia for many years, and from what I've heard about life out there, you've seen plenty of the darker side of mankind. Are you not yourself a cynic?"

"I was for some years out in Siberia, but I came to my peace with my fellow man and yes, I have seen the worst in mankind. My own wife testified against me as secretly being a counter revolutionary at my brief trial in St. Petersburg before the Cheka shipped me off to a Siberian prison camp. But I couldn't go through the rest of my life hating her and everyone else who had done me wrong. She simply did what she had to do to survive herself. So, I am a foolish optimist about my fellow man, but I sleep better now at night than I did when I thought only of myself."

There was a long silence in the room, before Charles stood up and said, "I sleep just fine at night, knowing that no one will ever betray or hurt me again. Good evening, Viktor."

"Good evening, Charles."

CHAPTER 7

With his decision to continue to keep the operation strictly to himself for the present, Charles was again forced into the unpleasant situation of just waiting. Finally, the designated day for the next encounter arrived. On that Sunday morning, he parked close to the market and immediately swapped his heavy-duty American-made coat for the Russian-made one he'd bought that day in the commission store. The American entered the market as planned, along with hundreds of locals looking for food products, which were always very scarce in winter and especially in wartime. At six feet tall, he was a little taller than most Russians, but then many of them wore thick, fur hats which added four or five inches to their height. Charles had chosen a flatter, cloth hat. After about twenty minutes, Sasha slowly approached him in a crowd, and without stopping or speaking, dropped a large loaf of bread into Worthington's shopping basket. He then just drifted away in the crowd. Worthington himself purchased some sad looking apples and some pathetic turnips and then returned to his car and drove back to Spasso House. Once he'd parked, he took the items from the basket and placed them into a cloth chopping bag to carry past the Soviet guards and in to the house, leaving the basket in the trunk of his car.

Once in the privacy of his own small room, he took out the gift loaf of bread and discovered that it had been hollowed out and the center replaced with a number of paper documents. Six of them dealt with plans of how to take control of any new territories captured during the fighting. They were in Russian, but Sasha had attached to each of them a short summary in English. There was also a hand-printed note, three pages in length, fortunately in English, giving more information about Sasha's background. After eliminating comments by Sasha blatantly sucking up to

America and his grammatical mistakes, what Worthington learned about his volunteer was:

Sasha had started learning English back in his university days, but had also received training by the NKVD when he went into the counterintelligence section, where he was charged with watching the activities of foreign diplomats posted to Moscow – especially the British. After the signing of the Nazi-Soviet Pact of Steel in August 1939, there were many more Germans assigned to their Embassy in Moscow and Sasha began to have official contact and attend diplomatic events at which he met Russian-speaking German officials. Among them was German Army Captain Holger Schmidt, who was ostensibly in Moscow for meetings concerning cooperation between the two armies. In reality, Schmidt was an officer of the Abwehr, German Army Intelligence. By mid-1940, their relationship had turned into a social one in which they would go fishing or out drinking. In September, after many months of socializing, Schmidt recruited Sasha. He claimed that he had come to realize what a horrible leader Stalin was; a man who had ordered the killing of millions of his own people in the Purges. He'd admitted to Schmidt that he thought eventually there would be war between Germany and Russia and he wanted Germany to win so as to get rid of Stalin. However, he had also accepted money from Schmidt.

His relationship with the Abwehr progressed nicely in early 1941 and Sasha was even able to inform the Germans that the NKVD had recruited a mid-level German diplomat in their Embassy in Moscow, for which he received a nice bonus. Sasha had been given a shortwave radio to hide and to use to maintain communication with the Abwehr should there be war. After the Nazi invasion of the USSR on June 22, 1941 and their rapid advances everywhere, Sasha was convinced he had made a wise decision. However, once the invasion had bogged down that winter and the Soviet Army started pushing the Germans backward by early 1943, Sasha began to have doubts. He knew that the NKVD was very active in monitoring of HF radio activity to find spies like himself. He therefore destroyed the radio and thus lost contact with Schmidt. As the war turned in favor of the Red Army, he also came to fear that once the Soviets had defeated the Germans and took control of Berlin, the GRU or the NKVD would find records of his recruitment by Schmidt. The Germans were well-known for their meticulous record keeping. It was at that moment that Sasha concluded that making a deal with the Americans, in which he received a secret move to America, was his only real chance for survival. He'd heard second hand from colleagues that an OSS officer had arrived in Moscow in January and that was when he began his plans on how to discreetly make initial contact with Worthingon.

Having finished writing out this succinct summary of what he then knew about Sasha's background and his motivations, Charles just stared silently at the far wall of his room for several minutes, almost in a trance. He finally muttered softly, "holy shit", while shaking his head slowly in disapproval. While he appreciated, sort of, Sasha's honesty in telling him about his previous association with Abwehr officer Schmidt and his motivation for helping the Germans, it certainly complicated Worthington's situation. His hole just kept getting deeper. Not only had he violated Allied policy on not recruiting a citizen of a fellow ally, but his agent had now freely admitted to having previously been a spy for the enemy! He sympathized with Sasha's anti-Stalin's sentiments, if Charles could truly believe that was his motivation – and not just a simple case of greed to make easy money. However, he could think of no way to sugar coat that horrible detail to his Headquarters, should he ever find a way to report the case at all to Washington. He finally concluded that that detail of Sasha's past would just have to be forgotten about. What was one more little lie? Assuming Sasha did eventually get to America, Charles doubted if the Russian would be inclined to bring up his past work for the Abwehr, especially if forewarned by Charles not to do so!

He skimmed the brief summaries in English of the six documents provided, which provided details on how the NKVD would work in any future occupied lands, as part of Stalin's plan to incorporate them into his empire. Ostensibly, they would remain independent countries and not technically become part of the USSR, but that independence would only be on paper. Soviet officials would be posted throughout those governments, especially in the ministries of Interior, which ran the police and security organs. Only citizens of those countries who were considered loyal Communists would be allowed to hold upper-level positions. The documents looked genuine. Worthington determined that these documents should certainly show to Washington that Stalin had no intention of living up to promises made to President Roosevelt for a post-war Europe. But would they be enough to buy Sasha a free trip to America, and salvage Charles' career?

The final part of Sasha's handwritten note proposed that they next meet at the same market, again on a Sunday morning, in two weeks' time, with an "alternate" of every following Sunday until contact was reestablished. He would again place a loaf of "special" bread in Charles' basket, and if Charles had anything for him, he should have a small note ready, and discretely put it in to Sasha's hand when they were very close together in a crowd of people.

Charles' brain was exhausted from thinking about his problems, so he decided to head downstairs for dinner as soon as the mess opened at 1700 hours. He also had to find a short-term solution for where to hide the Soviet documents. He stared at his dresser. When moving it to a different spot in the room a few weeks earlier, he'd noticed that a layer of the thin, decorative wood constituting the back of it had slightly separated from the underlying piece of cheaper wood. He'd found a couple of tiny nails on the floor, which had probably been used in holding the two pieces of wood together. He pushed the dresser out a bit from the wall and examined the separation of wood on the backside. It was a perfect cavity into which he was able to slide the documents from Sasha. He then used one of his boots to hammer one of the small nails he'd found back in to the outer piece of wood, to secure it to the underlying piece. A small separation still showed, but at least one couldn't see that there was paper hidden in the cavity. Better than nothing for the moment. Sasha's handwritten note he simply shoved down into his side pants pocket.

When he reached the small mess, he found Ted Collins was the only person there and so sat down across from him. "Good evening, Ted."

He looked up from a book he was reading while poking occasionally at his dinner. "Oh, hi Charles. How are you?"

"Fine. Mind if I join you, or are you deep in to your book?"

Collins laughed and closed it. "No, do join me. I was just reading for something to do."

As he sat down, he looked over at Ted's book. "You're reading *Das Kapital* by Karl Marx. God, you sure know how to have fun on a Sunday evening!"

Ted laughed. "I've been having trouble sleeping the last few nights – figured this would help."

"I vaguely remember having to read a chapter of it in an economics course at Harvard, and I could barely manage that! Don't know how anyone could read the whole thing."

"Actually, there are some very sound principles in here, but you're right, it's not exactly a page turner." He pushed the book off to the side. "So, how are you settling in here in Moscow?"

"Living in Moscow isn't exactly a page turner either," replied Charles. "And this weather! It snows every miserable day and it gets dark by 1500 hours. I can see why Russians drink so much vodka. I'd be depressed and become an alcoholic if I permanently lived here as well!"

"I think you're exaggerating, Charles. I saw you at the British Embassy the other night, completely occupying the time of that lovely young WREN, and you didn't look the least bit depressed!"

Charles felt his face flush. "Oh, we were just having a nice chat. Pretty tough on that gal, having her husband M.I.A. all these months."

"Yeah, that would be rough on anybody. I've chatted in the past with a few of her British colleagues about her and her missing husband. They've all said there isn't a chance of his being alive in some German POW camp after more than a year of his being missing. His bones are likely bleaching somewhere out in the Libyan desert, but nobody wants to be the bad guy and take away what little hope she has that he's still alive."

"Yeah, war sucks on a lot levels for a lot of people," mused Charles as much to himself as to Ted. He wanted to move to a different topic and pointed at Das Kapital. "So, when did you get interested in all this socialism, communism BS?" Charles had encountered several similar fellows like Ted back at Harvard. Those men would start dating some cute female Marxist and start going to meetings with the gal, mostly in hopes of getting her in to bed, but then get seriously interested in "scientific socialism."

"I had a freshman world economics class at Yale and my old professor was quite the true believer and he made us read several books on socialism, especially as developed by Lenin here in the Soviet Union. The more I read, the more sense it made. Capitalism certainly proved it was a failure during the 1930s, with the Great Depression and all." He could see he was starting to bore Charles, so he swiftly wrapped it up by saying, "We'll see what develops with socialism around the world once we all stop trying to kill each other."

"Yeah, a lot of things are on hold for a whole lot of people until we get rid of the Nazis." That somber thought brought both of them to silence as they continued eating their dinners.

The next two weeks plodded along in the same boring fashion, with one meeting taking place each week with the NKVD. It continued to snow almost daily. The most efficient, and perhaps the only efficient thing the Moscow City Government did was remove snow from the streets of the city. If it didn't everything would have just come to halt until about late May! He and Viktor had more interesting chats about a few more famous works of Russian literature, beginning with *The Brothers Karamazov*, by Fyodor Dostoevsky.

He still hadn't made up his mind as to whether the nice old man was an informant for the NKVD or not. He certainly made irreverent comments at times about the Soviet government, but perhaps that was just a ploy on his part. On the other hand, maybe he really was just a nice old guy who'd been dealt a pretty tough hand in life after the Russian Revolution, being sent to Siberia for two decades. Shoveling snow for a living at Spasso House had actually been a step up in life for him and was about as good as it would ever get for Viktor. Charles admitted to himself that he genuinely did like the old gentleman, even though he thought Viktor was naively optimistic about his fellow man. It was this very optimism that Charles found surprising, given what the Russian had suffered at the hands of his fellow man, but to each his own. Charles had learned his lesson in Portugal about being too concerned about the welfare of others. He had no intention of making that mistake again. His attention needed to stay focused on how to make himself look good to his superiors back at OSS Headquarters!

The next Sunday, a little sunshine peeked through the afternoon sky, so Charles went out for a long walk to enjoy it. It was also good to just get out of Spasso House and his own room; he was feeling a bit claustrophobic.

He walked down along the river and had turned towards the Kremlin when he saw Major Singell just about to enter a typical, four story tall Russian apartment building. Odd in itself, but even more surprising was the attractive young blond on his left arm, presumably a Russian woman. He only had sight of the two of them for four or five seconds, so he probably was mistaken, though the black-colored winter coat on the man certainly looked like the one Singell often wore. He finally dismissed the whole sighting, as family-man Singell had never struck Worthington as the philandering kind. He continued the walk for almost another hour, then realized that he was freezing cold. Sunshine or no sunshine, it was still well below zero degree Fahrenheit and he turned himself towards Spasso House. His thoughts now focused on the welcoming samovar down in the local workers' room, with its nice hot contents. Before even reaching home, he was already mentally enjoying the thought of the warm glass container in his hands and the pleasant feeling he would have as he poured some of the hot tea in to his mouth. He was mildly astounded at how simply the thought of some hot tea could bring such pleasant anticipation to his mind! He wondered what he would be like after a full year in Moscow.

The following morning at the Military Mission, Charles was wandering into different offices to see who might have a fairly recent magazine he could borrow to peruse. Many officers were sent various American magazines and newspapers from friends and family, and the standard practice was that once a person had finished reading something himself, he would leave it in plain view in his office, to let others know it was theirs for the taking. He wandered into Major Singell's empty office and discovered a Time magazine, only a month old, on a side table. He was leaving with his lucky find when he noticed the Major's coat on a hook by the office door. There was no way to be sure, but it certainly looked like the one that Charles had seen going into that local apartment building the day before. It still seemed unlikely, given what he knew about Singell, but one just never knew, particularly when a guy was far away from his wife for many months. None of his business, was his final thought on the matter as he started thumbing through the newly acquired Time magazine on the way back to his own office.

A few minutes after returning to his office, Sergeant Kowalski came in with a package for him.

"How you doing, Captain?," asked Kowalski as he laid the package down on the desk.

"Good, Sergeant. How about yourself? I haven't seen you for a week or two."

"I was sent up to Archangel for ten days to help them with all their paperwork. God, it's even colder up there than here in Moscow."

Charles laughed. "After all the months you've been here, I would have thought you'd be accustomed to cold weather by now. What kind of an old Chicago guy are you?"

"Being accustomed to and liking something are two different issues, sir. You said you'd grown up in Chicago. You've experienced real winter back in Illinois, when that wind would come in off of Lake Michigan, but it doesn't make you enjoy winter here in Moscow does it, sir."

"Fair point, Kowalski. Maybe it just seems worse here because it's practically dark outside by three o'clock in the afternoon here."

"Yeah, it being dark eighteen hours a day does get a little depressing. Well, I'll leave you with your package."

"Thanks for bringing it up. See you later."

He turned his attention to the package and saw that it had come through official mail channels from his old office mate, Lt. Dallas, back at OSS Headquarters. He hadn't been expecting anything in particular from Headquarters, but receiving a mystery package was always fun in boring Moscow. He quickly tore open the brown wrapping paper and discovered eleven books – nine fictional novels and two non-fictional history books. The accompanying manifest sheet simply noted that per Worthington's official request, here were the books he'd wanted to use as presents with his local liaison contacts. Lt. Dallas had obviously received the personal letter he'd sent back to America a month earlier, saying that he was fast running out of reading material and had asked that Dallas send him some more books. Knowing that an official package would arrive quicker than a personal one, his old friend had cleverly manipulated the system and declared them "official" books, needed for liaison work. Those Virginia boys were pretty crafty! Charles started scanning through his newly arrived trove. There was a history book on President James K. Polk, which looked a little dull, but then beggars couldn't be choosers in Moscow. The second was about the life of frontiersman Kit Carson, which held a little more promise. The next eight out of the box were an assortment of crime novels by Raymond Chandler and Dashiell Hamett and two Earl Derr Biggers' *Charlie Chan* detective stories. And at the bottom of the stack was a copy of Margaret Mitchel's *Gone With the Wind*. Now, these looked more like what he could really enjoy on a cold Russian night!

The following day, he had a mid-morning meeting with Colonel Suvarov at the NKVD, which was quite uneventful. The range and quality of reports from OSS Headquarters was drifting downwards, as had what the NKVD cared to share in return. The fact of the matter was that given the restrictions by both sides on what sort of information could be shared, there was only so much to say about effective techniques to quietly, or not so quietly, kill Germans! Even more reason for Charles to find some other way to have a success while in Moscow, which revitalized the need to find some way to report on Sasha and to forward his intelligence to Washington. He kept racking his brain, but so far nothing very promising was rising to his conscious level. He was wishing Lt. Dallas had sent him a book on creative thinking!

He was scheduled to take Jane Summerfield out to lunch one Friday and arrived promptly at 1300 hours at the British Embassy to pick her up. He'd tried a few different restaurants around town, but had found that the food at the Metropole Hotel was about the best in the city – and that was a sad comment, given its questionable quality on some days.

She was waiting just outside the front gate of her Chancery and climbed right in. "Good afternoon, Charles. You're looking well. Had a good morning?"

Her cheerful demeanor immediately put him in a better mood. There was nothing exceptional in what she'd said, but she always wore that winning-smile and she had such a pleasant, soft voice! She was dressed as usual in her WREN uniform, but she'd clearly put on make-up. Amazing how just a little red on a woman's lips could perk a guy up in a drab, gray place like Moscow.

"Oh, about typical for a day in Moscow in the dead of winter. How about you? What have you done today to bring victory on the Eastern Front, or to improve mankind?"

"Well, as it's almost the end of the month, so I've started moving information from weekly reports to the monthly report, which Mr.

Churchill is no doubt anxiously awaiting to arrive so that he can read it some night soon – in case he's having trouble getting to sleep!" They both laughed.

"Oh well," remarked Charles, "We can't all be generals and heroes on the front line. Some of us have to generate and send useless reports, so that people back in our two capitals have something to read."

Charles recognized the same elderly Russian waiter who'd been there the night he'd met the two young Russian girls who'd wanted English lessons. He presumed that as he was lunching with a woman, no other local beauty would just happen to be having a birthday or looking for an English tutor that day!

Charles had learned the skill of not even bothering to look at the menu, with its long mythical list of dishes, and simply asked in Russian, "What do you recommend today?"

"Grandpa Ivan", as the Americans who frequented there had named him, simply responded, "beef." Charles nodded his agreement and used two fingers to indicate that both of them wanted the same dish. To impress Jane, he also showed his growing command of the Russian language by saying, "champanskoe" and used his multi-lingual fingers to indicate that they would both be drinking champagne. Grandpa Ivan nodded and shuffled away.

Charles told her of his literary windfall and promised to give her first choice of which book she would like to borrow.

Unrelated to anything they'd been discussing to that point, she then asked, "How much longer do you think this war is going to last?" Lots of people asked the same thing, but he noted such a depressing sigh in her voice as she asked it, that he wondered if something had happened to prompt her question. It was atypical for her to deviate from her usual upbeat demeanor.

"God only knows," was his honest answer. "The Russians tell us that they're pushing forward almost everywhere on the Eastern Front, and if they're casualty and captured figures of Germans are at all realistic, you have to wonder just long the German people will put up with this slaughter. It is becoming ever-more clear that Germany cannot win."

She nodded in agreement. "We hear the same optimistic reports from the Russians, though nobody really believes most of the things that the Russians tell us on any subject."

"Anything happened in your life to bring that particular question to mind today? You sounded rather depressed when you asked it."

"Nothing special. Perhaps I'm just tired of hearing about people suffering and dying. Tired of not knowing for sure about my husband. Tired of being in Moscow with all the snow, cold and the sun setting at two o'clock in the afternoon. I wish they hadn't sent me here in the first place. I knew that taking that evening course of Russian for three months had been a mistake. Once they saw that in my personnel file, I was doomed!" She forced a small laugh.

Charles wished he had some highly insightful, cheerful comment to offer her, but he didn't. He was fairly miserable himself in Moscow. His opinion on the fairness of life had been pretty low even before he'd arrived and had grown ever more cynical while there. "I'm afraid that there are millions of people around the world who are also weary of this war and all that has come with it." He started to also say to her that for many of those millions, it was going to be miserable for years to come after the war as well, as devastated countries tried to rebuild, but figured there was no need for him to make her feel even worse than she already did. All of which reconfirmed his post-Lisbon philosophy to look after yourself first, as no one else was going do that for you. For most of the rest of lunch, he managed to shift the conversation to the more pleasant topic of her describing the part of England, East Anglia, from where she came.

"It all sounds so lovely and tranquil. I've never had the opportunity to visit England. I'm definitely putting that on my 'to do' list after the war.

Once back out to his car after lunch, he opened his trunk and let her peruse his windfall of newly arrived books. She opted for Raymond Chandler's *Farewell, My Lovely*, with a lurid cover of a young lady in a low-cut blouse, smoking a cigarette. "Is this what all women out in Los Angeles look like?" she teasingly asked.

"I don't know, I've never been to L.A. Perhaps I should plan a visit there just as soon as the war is over!"

"You should stop and see English girls on your way back home, just so you'll have something to compare with those California girls." They both laughed. She felt comfortable enough with Charles to make such joking remarks, as they both knew she was only joking and not flirting with him, or was she? After dropping her off at her Embassy, he thought fondly of their times together. She was one of the few positive aspects of life in the depressing capital of the worker's paradise. One good thing of the almost daily snowfall was that it covered over the dirty streets and gave a little shine to the gritty city of gray, pre-fabricated concrete.

After work and his return to Spasso House, he went down to the workers' warming room to see if Viktor was there. He was, sitting there, but looking older and more tired than usual as he sipped his hot tea. Charles was almost tempted to ask if he could take Viktor's photograph one day sitting at that table, for he thought that the pose of his wrinkled face slowly sipping tea encompassed perfectly in just one photograph the Russia of early 1944 – tired, cold and barely hanging on. He wouldn't ask to take such a photo because he knew it would embarrass the proud, old man. He did catch himself sadly thinking that he'd come down there one day and be told that Viktor had died of a heart attack or just of old age while shoveling snow. It would be one more example of how hard life could be.

"Viktor, how goes the battle against the snow?"

Viktor looked up and a sparkle came to his eyes. He saluted and said, "We are winning the battle. I know because Comrade Stalin has told us we are winning." Viktor didn't smile, but Charles did. "Ah, well, then it must be true." Viktor was poking fun at the frequent radio broadcasts and articles in the state-owned newspapers in which Stalin spoke of one glorious victory after the other. Hard to believe there were any Germans left alive after reading the claimed casualty statistics along the Eastern Front.

Charles laid on the rough-hewn wooden table in front of Viktor the newly arrived copy of *Gone With the Wind*. "I have a book to lend you to read. I'm not sure how well Margaret Mitchell compares to Tolstoy, but it's an interesting story of one family's struggle through the adversity of wartime and post-war life in the Old South. I've never actually read the book, but it made a heck of a movie back in 1939."

Viktor eagerly picked up the book and opened the cover. "I've heard other Americans talk about that movie. It's about the American Civil War, yes?"

"Before the war, when all was good for the family, and then its downfall and recovery after the war. I hope you'll enjoy reading it. I received today a box of books from a friend back in Washington."

"Excellent, I shall start on it this very evening. I'll keep it here in the warming room… so I can read it while on my breaks." What Viktor really meant Charles suspected, was that way there wouldn't be any questions from NKVD personnel or neighbors at his apartment building as to whether he was reading subversive, foreign propaganda.

"After you've read some of it, you can tell me what you think of the story," commented Charles as he was leaving the room. He was anxious to get up to his room and get started on one of the Charlie Chan mysteries. As he was going up the stairs, he thought again to himself on the question of whether Viktor was an NKVD man, put there to spy on the Americans. He'd pretty well concluded that such was not the case. If he was, why would he worry about what any of his apartment neighbors thought about what he was reading?

He passed through the mess room and got himself a nice cup of the Brazilian coffee and took it to his room. He shed his heavy winter coat and extra sweater, then settled into his reading chair. The opening paragraph about warm, soft breezes blowing across the beaches of Honolulu and of swaying palm trees immediately made him forget about the snow and bitter cold of Moscow!

CHAPTER 8

The day of the next contact with Sasha finally arrived, which was good as Charles was just about stir crazy from waiting. At 0915 hours on the appointed Sunday, Charles walked out of the front gate of Spasso House, nodding in a friendly manner to both the American guards inside the grounds and to the Russian ones on the outside. He tried to convey the look of simply a bored guy on a Sunday morning, out to take a stroll and enjoy the unexpected sunshine. He'd left his car parked about a block from the Military Mission on Friday, figuring he might draw less attention driving away from there, than if parked out in front of Spasso House. He'd also left in the trunk of his car his small wicker shopping basket. During his fifteen minute stroll to reach his car, no one seemed to be showing any particular interest in him. He presumed that like most bureaucracies, employees at the NKVD, even its surveillance squads, liked to have Sundays off from work and thus the chance of having surveillance on that day was less than say on a work day. Once in his car, he drove away slowly. If anyone was watching him near the Mission, he still wanted to give the impression that he was just out and about, going nowhere in particular. After about ten minutes, he stopped at a small bread store that he knew was open on Sundays, and bought a stick of fresh bread. He actually nibbled on it as he drove around Moscow for the next half hour.

He neared the target farmer's market a little before 1000 hours and parked a block away. Not so far away as to raise in a surveillant's mind a question as to why he wasn't parked nearer to one of the doors, but not right on the actual street of the market. He didn't want people in the market to associate him with an official vehicle. Not that he had a typical "Russian" face, but he wore the coat he'd bought locally and a Muscovite cap pulled well down on his head, which he'd put on just before leaving

101

his car. He'd seen no other car following him up until then, so he exited his vehicle in a positive mood and fetched his basket from the trunk. The market was very full; apparently the sunshine had brought out many people on that morning.

There was no point in even trying to look for surveillance in such a crowded place, so he just went about his shopping as everyone else was doing. There was a great deal of noise as the stand owner's shouted out appeals and prices and many people were talking to one another. Most items available were "pickled", which kept them preserved since they'd been jarred the previous summer and that smell permeated the air – a smell Charles found quite revolting. That smell was mixed with human body order. Russians didn't wash often in wintertime, neither themselves nor their outer clothing. Added to this potent mixture, on the coats of most of the men was the smell of cigarette smoke. Having noticed this peculiar aromatic phenomenon at the market the first time, this time Charles picked out his dirtiest clothes to wear and hadn't showered since Friday morning. He could only do so much to try to not dress like an American, but he could at least try not to smell like a freshly bathed American! His was not a typical Slavic face in structure, but what most all the shoppers shared was a tired, worn-out look on their faces, so he tried to maintain as sad and exhausted an expression as he could, so as to blend in with the locals.

He again bought a few apples and was slowly working his way up and down the outer aisles of the large hall, keeping an eye out for Sasha. Finally, he saw him approaching about twenty feet ahead, so he stopped at a table to eye some jars of pickled carrots. Dozens of people were milling all around him. Suddenly, he felt someone bump into the side of him and saw that a long, thin loaf of bread had been placed in his basket with his apples. Charles had taken his small, folded note for Sasha out of his right hand pocket once he'd come to a standing stop in front of the table. After placing the bread in Charles' basket, Sasha remained standing there for a few more seconds, staring as well at the jars of pickled carrots, but with his left hand slightly open in a cupped position. Charles pushed the note into the hand and it immediately closed around the paper. The body belonging to the hand then pushed its way to the right, between two other shoppers – and then he was gone, in to the sea of humanity looking for food.

Charles spent another ten minutes pretending to carefully shop and then fought his way to an exit door and returned to his car. He put the bread into a cloth bag along with his apples and took it to the front seat, returning the basket to the trunk. He also put back on his American winter coat and returned the Russian jacket to the trunk. He then slowly made his way back to his parking spot near the Mission; his original spot was still available. There were so few private cars in wartime Moscow, and hardly anyone out on a Sunday, that finding parking was rarely a challenge. He arrived back in his room at Spasso House by 1100 hours, locked his door and removed the "secret ingredients" in his loaf of bread. There were no documents this time, just a two-page, hand-printed note from Sasha. At first, he was disappointed that there were no official documents enclosed, but as he started the second paragraph, he stopped munching on the loaf of bread which had contained the missive. He read completely through the note once and then again a second time. Had there been secret microphones in his room – which he sometimes did suspect there were – they would have heard Charles again softly exclaim, "Holy shit."

He then took out a piece of notebook paper, and again using the hard back cover of one of his books to write on, he copied the important phrases from Sasha's note, with improved grammar and spelling, on to a clean sheet of paper. As he did that, he resumed munching on the bread. The nice thing about a bread "concealment" device, he could easily destroy the evidence. His copying duties done, he leaned back in his desk chair and silently read through his own note:

"Last weekend, I spent an afternoon drinking vodka with an old NKVD colleague of mine. We've known each other since 1934 and occasionally celebrate the fact we survived the Purge years together in our service. He works in the section that tries to recruit Americans and he was bragging that about four months back they had managed to recruit one. He was not specific as to where this American worked, but it sounded as if it was someone at the Military Mission, not in the Embassy. And naturally, he didn't say the name, but it is a man. I doubt if I will be able to learn anything more about this person, because while I work in the CI Section, I am concerned with activities of British and American spying, not our efforts to recruit officials of those two countries. I might get some information now and then from that Section, if it might help my work, but I can't just go asking for details and certainly not ask anything about sources they've recruited. But there is definitely a penetration within your ranks, so be very careful who you tell about me.

On the 15th of this month, there is a reception by your Ambassador at Spasso House and I have arranged an invitation for myself, in return for four bottles of good vodka. Major Petrov will also likely be there. Maybe you have already met him. He is the NKVD officer in charge of targeting you for recruitment. While you are talking with him, I will come and join the conversation. I want you to pretend in front of Petrov that you enjoy my company. You will bring up topic of chess and I'll mention that I play and then you will suggest idea that perhaps we should play a few games some evening – then I'll move on. Petrov has had no luck so far in getting you interested in spending time with any Russian he has sent to try to meet you. I'm hoping that he will come to me after this reception and suggest that I give it a try, since he'll have seen that we got along well together – perhaps invite you to play chess. Then we will be able to openly have meetings, while I pretend to target you. Later in the evening at the reception, we can find each other and have a quick private conversation."

At first, Charles thought that the news about there being a traitor amongst the Americans, and probably within the US Military Mission, greatly complicated his problem of how to eventually report about Sasha to OSS Headquarters, but then he realized that it actually simplified the challenge. Once he did finally advise General Donovan somehow of what was going on, he could explain that he had waited many weeks to do so because he couldn't risk sending any message through regular Army communications at the Mission about the case.

That would explain why he hadn't reported sooner about Sasha, but he still had to find a way to get a report directly to Donovan? He would either have to get someone to confidentially courier a hand-written, secret report directly back to General Donovan, or Charles would have to arrange a personal or official trip home for himself. The latter seemed more feasible. Perhaps a medical problem, which had gotten Tom Parkington a trip back to Washington. Charles would have to give this further thought, but in the meantime, perhaps he should start frequently coughing.

Charles felt his stomach growling from hunger and looked at his watch; it was 1800 hours and all he'd eaten since breakfast was bread. He took Sasha's original note over near his window, which he opened wide. He folded and stood the paper in an ashtray, then lighted it from the top, so that it would burn slowly downward through the note, as he'd been taught at OSS school – that would insure that it burned thoroughly, rather than lighting it at the bottom. Once burned, he then broke up the ash in to a fine powder in the ash tray. He'd take that to the lavatory at the end of the hall and flush it down the toilet. His newly printed version of Sasha's information, he folded up and placed in his trouser pocket. He would renew his contemplation about the case once he'd gotten some dinner downstairs.

He sat with Captain Parkington and two others and engaged in mindless, idle chatter while they were eating. When it was down to just Charles and Tom, Charles broached the topic of Tom's "medical leave" back to Washington.

"Say, I've been meaning to ask you, just how did you arrange that medical trip of yours back to America that you told me about when we first met?"

Tom laughed. "Getting tired of Russian winter are you? Feeling some illness coming on, which defies local diagnosis?"

Charles feigned a couple of coughs. "As a matter of fact, I have been feeling rather poorly the past few days. Who was the medical technician that saw you and sent you all the way to America for a cure?"

"Got some bad news for you. He shipped out three weeks back and his replacement apparently believes that two aspirins will cure anything. When Lieutenant Lafleur even very subtly hinted last week at a little quid pro quo for the 'correct' medical opinion of his condition, the new medic threatened to go to General Deane himself, if he heard anything further along those lines. Lafleur told the technician that he'd totally misunderstood what Lafleur had been saying, and that he was sure a few aspirins would pick him right up! So, I'm afraid you're going to be right here in lovely downtown Moscow until spring arrives, which I understand is about the end of June."

Charles went back to eating, concluding he'd have to find another excuse for a trip back to Washington in the near future. After Tom finished his dinner and left, Charles remained to drink more coffee and started staring around the room at his colleagues, wondering if one of them might be the NKVD mole? While waiting for an inspirational thought to come to him about finagling himself a TDY home, he could at least start paying more attention to his colleagues as he tried to figure out who might have gotten himself recruited by the Russians a few months back. One of his first thoughts turned to Captain Collins, who was quite the socialist. Perhaps he'd decided that it was his internationalist workers' duty to help the Soviet Union? Then there was Bobby Penkovsky, with possible relatives still living down in the Caucuses, through whom maybe the NKVD was working to put pressure on Bobby to cooperate with them? And then there was Major Singell and the funny incident of Charles possibly seeing him going into a local apartment building with a blonde. By that point, Charles did need two aspirins for the headache he'd given himself thinking about who might be the traitor. He decided he'd done enough to protect America for one day and was going to spend the rest of the evening with one of his new books and see how private eye Phillip Marlowe was progressing in finding out what had really happened to Sean Regan in *The Big Sleep*.

Charles left the Mission about 1600 hours Monday afternoon and returned to Spasso House. After several month's presence there, the Russian uniformed guards at the outer gate knew him well on sight and didn't bother anymore with the regulation mandating that everyone was to be stopped before entering to show their identification. They did for the first month or so, but as the weeks had passed, even the guards had grown weary of the needless requirement. If there was no officer present, the guards would just nod and pass him through. The same phenomenon occurred on the American side. They had their differences of course, but in some ways, the life of an American and a Soviet enlisted man was quite similar. They just followed orders and tried not to create problems, either for others or themselves. Charles always smiled and said "hello" to both Russian and American guards. One difference he had noticed between the American and Soviet guards at the gate were that the Russians were all well over six feet tall and very solid looking. While the Americans were just your typical nineteen or twenty year olds. Charles had commented on this one day to Viktor, who laughed and leaned across the table and whispered to him that this was no coincidence. He said, "Everything has a political purpose in our country. Our guards at your gate must appear bigger and stronger than yours. It's all about image. Personally, I'd rather see all those great big peasant boys of ours out fighting the Nazis!" They both laughed.

Charles observed that afternoon that the driveway and the sidewalks on the grounds of Spasso House were well cleaned, so he suspected that he'd find Viktor down in the warming room, taking a break. Indeed, he was, sitting there at the table with a glass of hot tea, reading *Gone With the Wind*. He looked up as soon as he saw Charles enter and said, "This is quite good," pointing at the book. "Very good character development and a fascinating story of a family trying to survive in wartime. Margaret Mitchell is quite good. How many other books had she written before producing this epic tale?"

"That is the only book she ever wrote," Charles answered. "I read somewhere that she spent eight or nine years working on it."

"That is amazing that on one's first try, any author could produce such an intricate story with such well-developed characters. Do you think it's very accurate of the times in America which it describes?"

Charles had never really focused on history in his schooling, but wanted to believe that it was somewhere near the truth. "I don't really know. I guess there are good and bad people, brave and cowardly ones in every century, in every country. I have an older friend, who has traveled and seen much of the world." It was Mr. Astor whom Charles was thinking of, but didn't bother naming him to Viktor. This fellow commented once to me that if there aren't at least a few real Rhett Butlers in the world, we'd have to invent them, so as to feel better about ourselves as a people."

"You have a very wise friend. Tolstoy once said something very similar when asked about the accuracy of characters in *War and Peace*. We shall have to have a long chat about this book once I finish it."

"Gladly, but I have a different question for you today. Do you play chess?"

Charles saw a distinct twinkle come to Viktor's eyes as he smiled. "Yes, I have been playing for many decades. Asking a Russian if he plays chess is like asking a Frenchmen if he drinks wine! Are you a player?"

"I've played a little in years past and thought I should try to improve my game while here in Russia. Perhaps we could have a game some afternoon and you could give me a few pointers."

"Gladly, gladly. There is a set up there on the shelf. Any afternoon you come back to the house a little early, we could play. But I am out of practice and may not be able to give you a very good game."

Charles knew immediately that the sweet old man was setting him up and he was no doubt going to kick Charles' butt in their first few games. His ego could handle that. What was important was that he would be establishing a nice backstop for his upcoming request to Sasha to play chess one evening. He presumed that Viktor would report to the NKVD on their games of chess.

Three nights later was the Ambassador's reception at Spasso House. About a half hour in to the event, Charles saw Sasha talking with a Soviet Army major. He appeared to be about forty, slightly graying hair and just a hint of Oriental ancestry in the shape of his eyes and high cheek bones. Over the next few minutes, Charles slowly moved himself closer and closer to his target. He finished exchanging a few words with a British diplomat and then turned, which just "happened" to place him directly in front of Sasha and Petrov. He said, "Good evening" to them in Russian and then in English, "I am Captain Charles Worthington."

Sasha responded in English. "I am Captain Sasha Turgenev and this is my colleague, Major Nikolai Petrov. The three shook hands.

"Have you been in Moscow long, Captain?" asked Major Petrov in excellent English.

"Just a few months. I'm still getting accustomed to the Russian winter."

All three forced a little laugh to that typical comment by a foreigner.

"And in what section of the Embassy do you work?"

"I'm not at the Embassy. I'm in our Military Mission, working for General Deane." Charles found this line of questioning by Petrov rather amusing, given that Sasha's last note had said that Petrov was the NKVD officer in charge of targeting him and obviously knew everything there was to know about Charles.

"Ah, one of the American soldiers arranging for a few supplies to be shipped to the Soviet Army."

Charles found that an insulting way of putting it – a "few supplies" – given that America was shipping everything from cans of Spam up to train engines and box cars, not to mention all the ammunition, rifles and trucks to Russia! He was taking an instant dislike to Petrov.

"And what are your duties Major Petrov" asked Charles.

Petrov smiled. "Oh, nothing of any consequence. I work in a policy development department of the Red Army."

Charles then turned to Turgenev. "Where is home for you Captain?"

"I was born down in the south, in Georgia, spent some years in Leningrad, but I have lived here in Moscow for a number of years. And what about you?"

"I was born and raised in Chicago, but was in college near Boston and before the war, I was working in New York City."

"Ah, so you are a Chicago gangster, like Al Capone," joked Turgenev.

Worthington forced a grin, as he knew it was meant to be a good-natured joke, even though it had accidently hit very close to the truth – at least in regards to his father.

"So, are all you Russians great chess players, like I keep hearing?"

Turgenev smiled and replied, "Well, I am, but Petrov here is terrible, so we can't say that 'all' Russians are great players." He laughed and slapped his colleague on the back.

Charles noticed that Petrov didn't seem to think that remark was all that funny, but Charles kept with the planned script." "I've been wanting to improve my game while here in Russia. Perhaps we can arrange a game some evening."

"That would be a pleasure," was his response. He passed one of his official calling cards to Worthington, who reciprocated with one of his own. Turgenev said goodnight and moved on to another circle of guests. Charles didn't offer one of his cards to Major Petrov. The last thing he wanted was that prick calling him up with any sort of invitation.

A minute later, Worthington and Petrov also said goodnight and parted. Charles spent another fifteen minutes or so with other guests, then drifted off to a small room, sat down and lighted a cigar. He figured Ambassador Harriman would never know if the smoke was from him or one of the guests, seeing as how at least two out of every three Russians there were smoking the foulest-smelling, unfiltered cigarettes on the planet. Charles thought to himself that Sasha's ploy had gone exactly as planned. It had gone so well in fact, that Charles found himself wondering again if this whole game with Sasha wasn't some elaborate entrapment ploy by the NKVD. If it was, he personally thought it was overly complicated, but he'd been briefed by one old OSS staffer of Russian background that Russian security people loved such intricate espionage games, going back even to the Czar's secret police. Before he could ponder that idea any further, Sasha ambled in to the room and lighted a cigarette.

"May I join you Captain Worthington?"

"Yes, of course. Please sit down."

They stuck with their charade for a few minutes more of having just met, then Sasha passed over a nearly empty packet of Russian cigarettes to Charles. "Here, you should try a real cigarette sometime."

Charles looked down in to the pack and saw that there was a piece of paper folded inside. "Thank you. I'm smoking my cigar now, but I'll try one of these later." As no one in particular seemed to be looking their way, he casually slipped the packet in to his coat pocket.

"Our conversation earlier seemed to go well," Charles commented, while staring out at the crowd in the other room.

"Yes, very well. Petrov came up to me a few minutes ago and told me to stop by his office tomorrow morning."

"Can't say that I enjoyed meeting the Major."

Sasha laughed. "A number of people he has personally shot over the years would probably agree with you. He is not a pleasant man, but he is very clever and a man not to be taken lightly, as I think you Americans say. If I am correct how his mind works, he will come to me and tell me to invite you to play chess. If that doesn't happen, then we'll meet again at the market in two Sundays, at 1100 hours."

"Understood," replied Charles as he blew a large cloud of cigar smoke up into the air. He'd always wanted to be able to blow smoke rings, but had never mastered the skill. He wondered how all those actors managed to do it so easily in the movies.

Turgenev stood to leave. "I think you'll enjoy my cigarettes," he said with a mischievous smile. They shook hands once again and Sasha slowly headed back into the main ballroom area. As he departed, he blew a perfect ring of smoke in to the air above him.

Damn him, thought Charles, as he unsuccessfully tried once again himself to blow a smoke ring. He stubbed out his cigar and left the reception, heading up to his own room.

Once he'd locked the door of his room and drawn his curtains, he took the cigarette pack from his pocket and carefully removed the hand-written note from it.

"Dear Friend,

Last week, General Beria personally called me to his office. You can imagine what I first thought it was about and I expected perhaps a bullet was waiting for me, but it turned out he is transferring me to very special section. He told me that he'd seen that I knew English and that I had worked for several years in the NKVD records section. Told me that he needed such man to be in charge of how to handle and distribute very secret intelligence coming in now from America. I am to file such information in correct manner and decide which of four different groups of scientists should receive what information – and to keep exact records of who is shown what reports. Approximately every two weeks, I am to personally fly out to a secret research base in Central Asia to hand-deliver certain of these reports. Don't know yet where this base is and what it is working on.

This very secret information is coming out of America and concerns development of new type of super weapon, called atomic. I could not find this word in any English dictionary??? Your American research work has code name of 'Manhattan Project.' That is all I know to date. Once I start there on Monday and see some of reporting I should be able to know more. Beria told me that our Soviet project has no name and section I am being assigned to doesn't even have name. He joked that this way, no one can talk about this section since it has no name. If someone asks me, I am to just say that I work directly for General Beria. On bureaucratic chart within NKVD, I will still be listed in my old section, but my boss will be told to just forget about me! There was no mention about our agent or agents in America on this project, but there must be at least one, or there wouldn't be any information for me to be filing. I will have to be very careful, but will try to find out more about who our agents are or at least where they working in America.

Other reason I think the General chose me is because my son, who was killed at the end of 1943 had been fanatical Communist. He had been very active in Komosomol (youth wing of CP) and was raving lunatic in support of Stalin. Was very embarrassing to me, but I kept my mouth shut, or he would have denounced me. Very funny, now that he dead, Beria thinks I must be very loyal Stalin man, like my son. I tell you one day how I came to work in records section of NKVD in 1936.

Hopefully, we will be able to play chess soon and can talk. If not, see you in two weeks on Sunday at market at 1100 hours.

Your friend."

Charles once again found himself quietly muttering "Holy shit!" This made his traveling as soon as possible to Washington essential, but how could he arrange such a trip, and in a non-alerting manner? If Sasha wasn't greatly exaggerating about this new job, it seemed to him that intelligence about Soviet agents working in a super-secret American weapons program ought to make Charles look really good in the eyes of Donovan. It might even get Sasha his free trip to America and a new life. Charles went over to the shelf and looked in his own dictionary; the word "atomic" was nowhere to be found. He vaguely recalled from a college science class that there was a tiny particle called the atom, but didn't see how that could have anything to do with a super weapon. As he fell asleep that night, he was having a very nice dream in which General Donovan was pinning a medal on his chest.

CHAPTER 9

SANTA FE, NEW MEXICO

A clean-shaven young man, who looked to be at most twenty, sat at a bus stop on a neighborhood street in the small city of Santa Fe, in the American southwest. It was only about noon on a Saturday, but the sun was bright and the wind was already very hot and dry. The area was neither particularly affluent nor poor, just an average street with modest, standalone houses and a few small, two-story apartment buildings. He'd been sitting there almost twenty minutes, beads of sweat dripping down the sides of his face. He was wearing an inexpensive white dress shirt, slightly wrinkled black slacks with a snake-skin leather belt he'd bought himself for Christmas in a Santa Fe department store. He sported men's lace dress shoes of a moderate quality. They were a bit scuffed at the toes. He obviously didn't have a job where having one's shoes polished was particularly important. He had brown hair, slightly unkempt. His overall appearance was of a man who didn't really focus on such things as his personal appearance. He was wearing wire-rimmed glasses and had an academic look about him. Lying next to him on the wooden bench was a small package in plain brown paper and tied up with twine. It looked as if it might contain a couple of books. He was rather anxiously looking up and down the street, as if he was expecting someone.

A mildly attractive woman, about thirty, with shoulder-length brown hair wearing a nice blue dress and practical walking shoes was coming down the street. The dress didn't appear very expensive, nor did the white handbag she was carrying. She seemed to be staring directly at him as she approached the bus stop. Damn, he thought to himself. He really didn't want another passenger sitting there waiting for a bus, as he was to meet his contact at that bus stop any minute now. They would need privacy to speak freely, so he could explain what he'd brought with him. He wondered whether he should get up and wait down the block a ways, until his "friend", whom he'd met several times before in this manner, finally appeared.

She sat down next to him on the bench, then turned to him, smiled and casually said to him, "I don't think you get the kind of rain here in Santa Fe like we do in Seattle."

The young man was taken aback. That was indeed the parole sentence, but he'd been expecting Harry, the man with whom he normally met. He finally regained his composure and gave the appropriate countersign. "No, but I think it rains even more in San Francisco."

"Hello, I'm Elizabeth," she said in a pleasant voice.

"Where is Harry?" he replied.

"Harry couldn't make this trip, so I was asked to come in his place this month. She looked down at the wrapped package. "Is that for me?" Elizabeth had been performing this sort of secret courier service for the Soviets for several years and was much calmer than the young man. She wished to quickly receive the "package" and be on her way.

"Yes, it is," he somewhat stammered, still clearly surprised by having a woman meet him. "My name is Ted," he blurted out, just in case more evidence was needed that he was the correct person to be meeting with at the bus stop. "Are you from the Special Service?" He used the term that Harry had used on a few occasions to refer to the people who were receiving his information and who were so grateful for his contribution to the workers' cause.

"Yes, I am," she replied. She actually had no idea what he was referring to, but clearly he wanted to pass his "package" to the Special Service, so she was happy to confirm to this young man that that was indeed who'd sent her.

He handed the package to her. "My notes and a schematic diagram are inside the two books."

"Very good. And you already have the meeting instructions for next month?"

"Yes, I do. Will it be you again, or will Harry be back?"

"I don't know. It could even be a third person. As long as they have the oral parole, you will know that he is from Moscow."

"Very well."

A bus was nearing the stop. She stood and approached the curb, without any further words to the young man. She didn't care which route number it was. She simply wished to separate herself from him as quickly as possible, as good espionage tradecraft dictated. The bus pulled away as Ted continued to sit there. He was much relieved that the passage had gone without incident. In fact, he felt even better than usual. He jumped to the conclusion that Moscow was very impressed with his work and had elevated him to being handled directly by a member of the NKVD, rather than just an American cut-out, as Harry clearly was. She'd spoken quite good English, but the young man had convinced himself that he'd heard a slight Slavic accent in her voice.

In truth, she was just an American courier like Harry, and even further down the bureaucratic ladder than he was. She'd simply been chosen to make the long trip from New York City out to Santa Fe, because she was available and Harry wasn't that week. Plus, the NKVD Rezident in New York City had thought that a woman traveling by train across the country would attract less attention than any male courier.

Elizabeth took a seat in the back of the sparsely populated bus. There she undid the wrapping paper and from each book she removed the sheets of hand written notes and the one very detailed schematic drawing. She took a quick look at it, which to her almost resembled a washing machine, but with many more parts. She didn't know exactly what they did at the secret military facility at nearby Los Alamos, but Harry had told her one night in bed that it was a very secret research facility, and he was quite privileged to be involved in handling one of the NKVD's agents working there. She placed the sheets of paper down inside a small box of Kleenex, with several tissues on top and put the box in her purse. She then rewrapped the two books in the brown paper. At the next stop, she exited the bus, walked away from the path of the bus, until she came to a trash can next to the wall of a pharmacy, where she nonchalantly tossed the package. Eventually, she flagged down a taxi which took her to the train station. She retrieved her one medium-sized suitcase from a pay locker, consulted the time schedule, then sat down and waited for the next train headed east.

She had a momentary scare as she and some twenty other passengers were lined up on the platform, waiting to board the express flyer headed for Kansas City, and which in a few days would have her back in New York. There was a US Army soldier at each passenger car entrance, checking the suitcases and hand baggage of all the passengers. Harry had never mentioned such a check to her, so she didn't know if this was some routine procedure or they were on special alert. She decided she would look suspicious, if she suddenly walked off the platform, instead of boarding her train, so she inched forward in the line like everyone else, trying to keep a relaxed look upon her face.

Finally, flashing a nice smile, she placed her suitcase up on a small, wooden table for one young Army private to open and quickly look within it as he had everyone before her. The other private asked to see her ticket. She wasn't sure if they were going to search her purse or not. She played the flustered woman and pulled out first her Kleenex box which contained the documents and handed it to the private to hold for her, so she could dig deeper in her purse to find her ticket. He gave her an exasperated look, until she did find and showed him her ticket all the way east to New York City. He thanked her and handed her back her Kleenex box. She boarded the train, where a nice elderly porter helped her place her suitcase in the overhead rack. She sat down and let out a long and deep sigh of relief! She didn't know exactly what sort of papers she was carrying, but presumed it was nothing that could have easily been explained as to why they were in the purse of a civilian woman. She doubted that prison was a very pleasant place.

Three days later, she was sitting in an unpretentious family-run Italian restaurant in the Little Italy section of Manhattan. She had now placed Ted's documents inside an inexpensive child's doll, which was wrapped in brown paper and tied with string. She saw the man she was expecting come in and seat himself at a small table covered with a red and white-checked linen table cloth near the front of the restaurant. After ordering something, he stood to go use a phone booth near the back, in a corridor, which led to the restrooms. It was almost three o'clock in the afternoon, well past the peak rush hour of the restaurant, and there were only a few other customers in the establishment. She already had the check and had the needed cash at the ready. She placed two one-dollar bills on the table to cover her check and for a modest tip. Not small enough to appear miserly, nor overly generous. In other words, not an amount that would stick in a waiter's mind and help him remember her if asked later about who had been in the restaurant that afternoon. As this latest customer passed her table, he gave her a very subtle nod. She waited ten seconds and then took her large purse, which contained the wrapped doll, and headed back to the ladies room. No one else was in the back corridor. As she passed the phone booth, she slowed just enough to hand the package to the man wearing a blue suit and sitting in the phone booth. The door was partially open. When she came back out a few minutes later. The man was back at his table, enjoying a glass of red wine. She headed straight for the front door without looking at him and exited out onto Mott Street. She mixed in with the crowd of people out on the street and disappeared. Her task was completed.

By four o'clock, the man was back at the Soviet Trade Mission in mid-town Manhattan. He took the "package" up to the restricted NKVD section of the Mission. By the following afternoon, the original English-version of Ted's note, and a quickly translated version into Russian had both been encoded and sent as diplomatic messages via HF radio back to Moscow. There was no way to send the schematic via radio; it had to be photographed and would go out in the next diplomatic pouch. All such intelligence as this on the American project to build an atomic bomb was considered extremely important and time-sensitive, but the decision had been made that to send off special couriers with a diplomatic pouch, rather than the standard once-a-week pouch, might be alerting to the FBI that something special was happening. The scientists working on the Soviet bomb out in Central Asia would just have to wait a few more days. Fortunately, the regularly scheduled diplomatic pouch was to depart in just two days.

While there had been some theoretical discussion within the physics world in the 1930s as to whether one could in fact "split" the atom and start a chain reaction, which might release amazing power, no one had yet figured out how to build such a device. Whoever did so, would be the undisputed military super power in the world. Stalin had no intention of letting America be the sole atomic power and had told the NKVD that targeting the American scientific efforts in this field should be a priority.

The NKVD had been very lucky and had had several American and British scientists working within the secretive Manhattan Project volunteer their assistance to the Worker's Paradise. They hadn't even had to search out and find these well-placed scientists. The NKVD's biggest problem was how to stay in touch with several of these American agents who were working on unlocking the power of the atom, while living and working at a top secret military base far away in Los Alamos, New Mexico – out in the middle of nowhere. It would have seemed strange to the FBI had any Soviet official in New York or Washington traveled to New Mexico more than once and thus began the use of well-trusted American Communists to serve as couriers to the American Southwest.

CHAPTER 10

MOSCOW

Four mornings after the diplomatic reception during which he met Nikolai Petrov and Sasha Turgenev, Worthington's office phone rang and the Corporal on duty at the switch board transferred an outside call to him.

"Captain Worthington here."

"Captain, it is Captain Turgenev," said a male voice in English, with a Russian accent. We met last week at reception at your Ambassador's home."

"Oh, yes, Captain. How are you?"

"I am doing fine, thank you. We spoke that night about chess. I am calling to invite you for game of chess one evening soon – if you still interested?"

"Yes, I think that can be arranged. I'm fairly busy the next couple of days, but I'm sure we can find a weeknight when both of us are free in the next week or two. Or perhaps it would be easier to meet on a Saturday or Sunday?"

"Yes, Saturdays are better. Does this Saturday work for you?"

"I have plans in the evening, but if you would like to meet around one or two, we could play a few games. Where did you have in mind?"

"There is small restaurant called "Pushkin House." It is located near center of city, on Kropotkin Street. It is very easy to find. I wait you there at one, on Saturday."

"Agreed. See you Saturday."

Charles smiled to himself as he thought that Major Petrov must have really liked the idea of using Turgenev to target him and told Sasha to waste no time in contacting him. Charles was glad that the NKVD had

120

moved quickly as he would like to see Sasha once more before he made his trip to Washington – which would happen just as soon as he thought of a ploy to get himself such a trip!

On Thursday, Charles arranged to have a game with Viktor down in the warming room of Spasso House, so he could get in a little practice before facing Sasha. It didn't really matter if he won or lost on Saturday, as it was after all just a cover for their meeting, but he still felt a little pride was on the line. He figured he would lose, but wanted it to at least be a competitive game.

Charles won the toss and had the whites and thus the honor of moving first. The first ten moves or so went OK, and he felt he was holding his own, but then he realized he'd been sucked into a lovely little trap in which he lost both his knights and a bishop. There was no longer a question as to who would win, it was just a question of time to finish the game. Still, Charles was getting what he wanted, some practice.

There was little talk during the game, as both men were concentrating on their moves and the progress of the game, but once Charles had capitulated, Viktor suggested some tea.

"You didn't play too badly, but I don't think you calculate very far into the future your potential moves when you play. That is the sign of a good player, to look ahead. Also, maybe it is part of the Russian mentality, not just of our style of chess play, but we are willing to make sacrifices to lead to later gains. I led you into that trap by sacrificing my bishop. You could not resist that short term gain, even though it was leading you into a terrible situation."

Charles laughed. "It wasn't that I took the short term gain, no matter what was coming later – I didn't see what was coming!"

Viktor laughed as well. "Keep in mind, any time that a Russian player offers you an opportunity that looks too good to be true, probably it is a deception leading you into a trap."

"I'll keep that in mind in the future." Charles silently thought to himself that that might be a good rule of thumb to remember in dealing with a Russian in any field!

They said goodbye and Charles went up to his room to relax a bit before dinner. He returned to thinking about whether Sasha was perhaps just leading him into a trap, with his claim of suddenly being given a new job through which he had learned about supposed Russian agents within some super-secret American weapons program. But, there was really no backing out now. He would show up Saturday, regardless of what might be coming.

On the scheduled day for chess, Charles drove directly to the Pushkin House restaurant. He saw no reason to take maneuvers to check for surveillance in route, since the NKVD already know where he was headed. There would be no reason to follow him from Spasso House. When he entered the small, rather drab restaurant, he saw that Sasha was already seated at a wooden table over by a window and had a chess board set up on the table. He saw two other games in progress around the room.

"Good afternoon, Captain Turgenev." He reached out to shake the Russian's hand.

"Captain Worthington, good to see you again."

He had already ordered a plate of "snacks", *zakuski* in Russian, some black bread and a bottle of vodka for them to share.

Charles took off his coat and hung it on a peg in the wall and took a seat, while looking around the restaurant. There were some fifteen men sprinkled around the room, mostly in twos and threes and doing more drinking than eating. However, there was one man seated alone, up on a raised area of the restaurant. He had a bottle of vodka and a newspaper on his table. He was still wearing his coat and his fur hat. He was, Charles guessed, a surveillant sent by the NKVD to keep an eye on the chess game.

After their first toast of vodka, they began their game. Charles said softly, without looking up from the board, "I see you brought a friend with you."

"Yes, the fellow with the hat on, pretending to read a newspaper. I guess Petrov thought I might need protection."

"He might as well be wearing a sign that says, 'NKVD surveillant' on him."

They both laughed lightly. Sasha added, "Please don't defeat me, Petrov will have me sent to Siberia if I disgrace the service. Let's just concentrate on the chess for a while."

The first game took about twenty-five minutes for Sasha to win, which made Charles feel good, thinking that perhaps he was better at the game than he thought. His second loss came in less than fifteen. Charles finally realized that his erratic play in the first game had deceived Sasha in to thinking that perhaps he was playing some clever strategy. By the second game, Sasha had figured out that the American just really didn't know what he was doing!

By this point, "Mr. Hat" appeared to have grown quite bored and seemed to actually be reading his newspaper and had ordered some soup to eat as well.

By the start of the third game, Sasha said softly without looking up from the board, "I think we can now discuss something besides chess, while we play. Our friend seems satisfied that is all we are doing."

"You invited me very quickly for a game of chess. I take it Petrov liked the idea?"

Sasha grinned. "Yes, he loved it, especially since he believed it was his own brilliant idea! He called me to his office the morning after the reception and raised the topic. He thinks he is brilliant for having noticed your interest in chess. When I suggested that we wait a week or two, he insisted that we move much faster. He already authorized me to agree to any thing you suggest for further contact."

"Excellent, as that solves the danger of anyone seeing us together in the future at the market or any place else."

"Just be sure to tell me a few personal things about your background, so that I have something interesting to report to Petrov."

"I'll do that right now, so we don't forget. I was born in Chicago, an only child. My mother stayed at home with me. My father was an accountant, but he and my mom both died in an automobile accident when I was only fifteen. I attended Harvard University on an academic scholarship. I then immediately started law school, at the same university. I haven't had much actual court room experience as a lawyer, but I did pass the New York bar exam. Before America entered the war, I dated several different woman, but nothing serious. I like readying mystery novels and I really enjoy the music of Glenn Miller. There, that should be enough to make Major Petrov happy!"

"Yes, I think so, though next time, he will want me to find out more about your political views – are you secretly a socialist, just waiting to help the International Proletariat rise up against the exploiting capitalists of the world? But that can wait till next time." He smiled.

"Good, now tell me more about this Manhattan Project that the NKVD has penetrated in America."

Sasha took out of the side pocket of his officer's tunic a folded propaganda brochure about the life of Stalin, with a large picture of him on its front and gave it to Charles. He demonstratively held it up before handing it over, so that anyone watching could see what it was. "I think you will find reading this quite interesting, and it will be good practice for your Russian."

Charles looked at the cover for a few seconds and then simply laid it beside the chess board. "Sasha, tell me about your background and your career until now. Such information will help me convince Washington that you're worth moving one day to America."

"I was born in Tbilisi, Georgia; the same area as Stalin, though I am Russian, not Georgian. My father was a fairly successful merchant in Tbilisi and sent me to the university in St. Petersburg in 1912 to study science. Despite my bourgeoisie background, I became a political radical. When I went into the Imperial Army in 1916, my father arranged for a nice, safe job in the Engineering Corps – you know, to build things, not actually fight. When the Revolution got underway in 1917, I immediately became a supporter of Lenin's Bolsheviks and by pure coincidence I became a part of the CHEKA, the security organ of the Communist Party. I started as a private."

"So, you have been with the Soviet security apparatus for many years. Why are you only a captain?"

Sasha smiled. "I may only be a captain, but I am still alive. Let me explain. I had no problem shooting rich capitalists and czarists in the early years, or of Western spies later on. But then came the rise to power of Stalin. Many colleagues saw me as a fellow Georgian, like Stalin. I was given preferential treatment, though never by Stalin himself, who didn't even know who I was, but by sycophants around Stalin. They thought it would do them good to treat me well, so maybe when I rose to higher ranks, as a fellow "Georgian", I would remember their kindness to me – or maybe even mention their name to Stalin. Such was the sick state of the Soviet Government that I came to see in later years. And by the way, I was a captain by 1930.

"So, you were on your way up, despite your family's background," observed Charles.

Sasha moved his knight on the board. "Yes, but then the Purges began in the mid-1930s under Stalin's paranoiac leadership. I was smart enough to keep a low profile. I shunned assignments in operational units, where I might receive promotions. In fact, I asked to go in to the administrative/records department and took a demotion back to lieutenant to do so. Many thought me stupid for doing so. However, by 1938, when many in the NKVD had themselves been sent off to Siberia or shot, I knew I had chosen correctly. Still, my wife's father and sister had been anonymously denounced by somebody and just disappeared one night. Such was life in the Soviet Union in the mid-and late 1930s and right up until Hitler attacked Russia in June 1941."

Charles made his move on the board and commented, "Pretty tough times. I see that you've always been a 'survivor' and wish to continue to be one."

"Yes, and speaking of that, by our next meeting, I expect a firm answer on whether we have a deal for me to be taken to America before the end of the war. If you don't have an answer by then, I will look elsewhere to solve my problem."

Charles realized he'd strung Sasha along for as long as possible and agreed that by their next meeting, he would have a firm answer for him. Since he hadn't even told Washington yet about Sasha, Charles figured it would be easy enough to make up his own decision and he could just tell the Russian anything he wanted. How would Sasha know? Besides, what's a little lie between friends?

"Yes. By next meeting, I will have a firm answer for you, which I'm quite sure will be a positive one."

"Very good. Just to finish my story, at the end of 1940, I was promoted back to the rank of captain and moved out of the administrative/records section and in to the counterintelligence department. I had been very careful and had kept my opinions of Stalin to himself. One reason I was allowed to transfer to the CI Department was because so many officers of the NKVD had been shot or shipped off to Siberia, so there were plenty of openings! And though my son's politics appalled me, in an ironic twist, the fact that he was seen as such a fanatical supporter of Stalin helped make me look like a loyal person as well. My son was a political commissar in the Army. You know what that is?'

"I think so. He's a person who teaches the soldiers about communism and checks on their loyalty to the Communist Party."

"Yes, that is correct. He was killed in combat in spring 1943, and in another bit of irony, I was given my son's awarded medal after his death, which also made my superiors regard me even more as above suspicion. I had a reputation of being competent, though I suppose a bit of a simple man with no real ambitions, and thus a perfect candidate to work in counterintelligence. And so, here I am today, a lowly regarded captain within the NKVD, but a highly regarded spy by the OSS." He gave Charles a wide grin, moved his queen on the chess board and said, "Checkmate!"

"Mr. Hat" had finished his soup and had returned his attention to the two of them.

"My ego has suffered enough for one day. I think I shall head for home while I still have any pride left at all, but thank you for a pleasant afternoon," He reached across the table and shook hands with Sasha, then stood to get his coat. He stuffed the propaganda brochure in an outer pocket of his winter coat and started to reach for his wallet to pay his share of the bill.

"No, no, Major Petrov would insist on me paying the whole bill," stated Sasha with a perfectly solemn face.

"OK, but next time General Donovan will pay for lunch." He exited without even stealing a peek over at their surveillant.

Worthington drove straight back to Spasso House and went directly up to his room. He locked the door and again drew the curtain over the window. He realized that unless the NKVD had a trained pigeon, there really was no way for anyone to see into his room, but closing the curtain was just a habit. He was dying of curiosity to see what Sasha had given him further about this super-secret American weapons project. He took out the propaganda brochure and saw that in the margins and any blank spaces, Sasha had printed out his information in small letters, which made it even more difficult than usual to read his writing. After about thirty minutes of effort, he had managed to write out on a clean sheet of paper the important parts.

"Dear Friend,

I've only worked in my new job for a few days, but have determined a few valuable facts. This secret American project is called Manhattan Project. Some research done at a university in Chicago, but real work at building this special bomb is done at a military base near Los Alamos in state of New Mexico. This makes it very difficult for the NKVD handlers in New York City to meet with our agents working in this project. It appears that we use a few trusted Americans to go out to Southwest America to meet these agents, because it would be too suspicious if Soviet official traveled to New Mexico. It appears to me from the reporting that we have at least three penetrations of this project, but one is very important because he works on actual design of this 'bomb.' I still don't understand what kind of special bomb they are trying to build, but from one description it appears that it is indeed just one bomb, which would be dropped from an airplane. No one knows for sure just how powerful an explosion it will be because no one has ever built one before. In one report, there is an estimate that this one 'atomic' bomb would be the equivalent to the bomb effect of the total load of bombs carried by a thousand of your large American bombers!

All I know so far about our agent penetrations is that we use the word to describe them that we use when a person has volunteered to assist for ideological motivations. They're not helping just for money or being blackmailed. This primary agent who works on actually designing the bomb has a code name in Russian of 'Starik', which means an 'old person.' Normally, these code words are supposed to hide the identity of an agent, but there have been a few comments about him in two reports, which make it sound as if he is in fact an 'old man' who suffers from arthritis and who had long ago taught at the Carnegie Institute of Technology of Pittsburgh. Another agent seems to be a lowly 'mechanic' who simply makes parts for the bomb, but who can occasionally steal copies of design schematics. As for the third agent, I have so far seen no clue as to his current job in Los Alamos or his past. I will try to learn more about these three, or others, but must be very 'delicate' in my searching or asking questions. This operation has the highest priority by Stalin himself. There are unlimited funds available for this operational work.

As for our research facility in Central Asia, where we are trying to duplicate this 'atomic' work, I know nothing. Perhaps after I make my first courier trip to there, I will know more.

Your friend."

Charles then sat in his room, eating the last Hershey's chocolate bar he had, and thinking about what to do next. It certainly seemed as though he had stumbled onto an amazing Soviet espionage effort with incredible potential consequences. A case that should earn him an immediate recall to Washington, a promotion and possibly a medal. However, Viktor's recent comment came to mind about the Russian mentality in chess of being very deceptive and even willing to take short term losses in order to lead the opponent down the wrong path and eventually to disaster. For the moment, he wondered what that "greater gain" later could be that would justify giving up one or two of these incredibly sensitive agents in a super-secret American weapons development program – a weapon that sounded as if it could change the course of the war. This was certainly a possibility that deserved more of Charles' analysis, but for the moment he had to proceed on the assumption that there really were penetrations within the Manhattan Project.

Whatever the final truth, his getting back to America to personally brief General Donovan on these allegations by Sasha was essential. He fell asleep still trying to think of a method to get him a trip home. When he awoke at 0600 hours, he lay in his bed having a bizarre thought. He remembered an undergraduate psychology lecture at Harvard in which the professor said that the human brain was often its most imaginative and creative during the short period of time after first waking up – when the brain was still drifting between wake and sleep. His professor had no explanation as to why that was, but he definitely claimed that it was true. Charles hoped his old professor was wrong, because the "imaginative" idea that had entered his brain at 0600 hours that morning was that Sasha's story about penetrations of the Manhattan Project might be a total deception scam. What if the Soviets had simply only learned of the existence of this secret "atomic" program called the Manhattan Project, but had no real details and in fact had no penetrations of it? What if the NKVD goal was to simply slow down the American effort, while Soviet scientists conducted their own research in this field? What better way than to make the American Government *think* the program was riddled with Soviet spies? This might start investigations and witch hunts of all kinds and Sasha's allegations could cast doubts about the whole program. But why would the Americans believe Sasha? Well, if he had correctly identified an NKVD agent within the Military Mission there in Moscow – that would certainly enhance his bona fides. It would be like sacrificing a few pawns, or even a knight, in chess, in order to capture the opponent's queen!

As soon as the dining hall opened, Charles was down there and having breakfast all alone, reading through a month old New York Times newspaper that someone had kindly left on the table. On the third page was a large photo of his old boss and mentor, Vincent Astor. He looked elegant in his black tuxedo, presiding over a ball to sell war bonds to the upper class folks of Manhattan. The article claimed that the evening had set a record amount in sales and quoted the mayor as giving much credit to Mr. Astor. It stated that the beautiful Hollywood film star, Hedy Lamarr, had also been at the podium, and gave a kiss to each purchaser of bonds. Charles presumed that might have helped sales just a bit as well! The solution to his problem of how to get back to Washington came to him as he finished reading the article – Vincent Astor, richest man in America and former Coordinator of Intelligence in the New York area was the answer. Worthington had worked as his private secretary on an interesting cruise on Astor's yacht to the South Pacific before the war, and had also assisted him in an intelligence operation in 1941. It was he who suggested Charles apply to the OSS and no doubt had personally phoned Donovan to recommend him. All Charles had to figure out now was how to get word to Astor that he would like to get an official invitation from somebody to him to come back immediately to Washington for some reason. The solution to that challenge walked into the mess hall for breakfast just thirty seconds later.

Army First Lieutenant Parr had just finished his twelve months of duty in Russia and was leaving the very next morning to start his journey back to America to begin a well-deserved R&R. Once he had his tray of food, Charles waved for him to come over and join him.

"Reilly, you're getting so short, I could hardly see you come in the door." It was an old line, but Parr didn't care, he was about to go home.

"Charles, how you doing?" They hadn't been real close friends, but the Military Mission was a small enough place that everybody knew everybody else to some degree.

"Pretty good. It was nice to see some sunshine yesterday, but of course you're down to being such a short timer, you don't even care about the lovely Moscow weather you'll be leaving behind!"

"Not in the least. As long as the weather is good enough tomorrow morning for my plane to take off, I'm happy with weather of any kind." A wide grin confirmed his spoken words.

After a minute of discussion of how Reilly planned on spending his leave back in America, Charles got to the point.

"Hey, could you do me a small favor – take a personal letter with you and mail it once you hit stateside? I'll have it stamped and everything; you just need to find a mailbox at whatever airport you land at back in America. I need to get word quickly to an old friend who's waiting to hear if I might be interested in a job with his firm after the war, so I need to get it there sooner rather than later."

"Sure, just get it to me by this evening and I'll put it in with my socks." A number of guys asked for personal mail to be hand-carried in such fashion, and thus circumvent the official censors. Soldiers often wanted to avoid censors reading pretty personal stuff to wives and girlfriends back home. For some reason, the practice had acquired the phrase that such mail traveled "with a guy's clean socks" in his duffle bag.

"I'll give it to you at dinner tonight. Thanks a lot for doing this."

Before even going over to the Mission, Charles went back up to his room and began to write.

"Dear Mr. Astor,

Everything is going well over here in the land of cold and snow. A friend was traveling back to America, so I asked him to bring this and mail it once back home in order to save time. I do need a small favor. I'd like to discuss a few things in person with Uncle Bill down in Washington. Perhaps you might talk with one of your friends down that way who could arrange a brief, official TDY back to DC for me so that I could do that.

I've been keeping my eye out for an appropriate souvenir from here for you, though nothing has appeared yet. I trust all is well with you. Saw a picture in an old newspaper of you and Hedy Lamar selling war bonds at a ball – tough duty working with Miss Lamarr!

If I get invited soon back to DC, I'll probably come through New York City and we can have lunch.

Regards,
Charles"

He sealed up the letter, addressed it to Mr. Astor at his New York City mansion on 5th avenue and applied the stamp. He put it inside a pocket and headed off for the Military Mission. He'd find Lt. Parr right now, so that he couldn't possibly miss him before his departure. He realized that his letter was quite vague, but he was sure that Astor would read between the lines and realize that it was something very important for Charles to resort to this circuitous manner to arrange a trip back to Washington. That was one small hurdle taken care of. Parr would fly to Archangel, then he'd catch an empty freighter to England and probably merit a ride on a plane the rest of the way home. The Germans generally didn't bother trying to sink empty freighters, so odds were good that Parr and Charles' personal letter would safely reach America within two weeks. As is often the case in the world of espionage, waiting was one of the most annoying features of the game.

Now all he had left yet to do was figure out who was the Soviet mole in their midst in Moscow and the several traitors in the super-secret weapons program back in America, prepare a good explanation for General Donovan as to why he'd broken US Government policy and recruited a Soviet national – one who used to work for the Nazis no less – and then be able to smuggle him out of the Soviet Union. Other than that, he pretty much had the case wrapped up! He probably also should brush up on his chess game, if he was going to continue to use that pretense for future "public" encounters with Sasha. Lt. Paar departed the following morning as scheduled. Worthington had no doubt that he would safely mail the envelope once back to America. The real question was whether Astor would be at home in Manhattan at the current time. Multi-millionaires did have a tendency to go off to warm and sunny places during winter, or he could be off on government war business – making American industry more productive. He'd just have to wait patiently to see if "official travel orders" arrived one day at the Military Mission.

The following day around 1700 hours, Charles returned to Spasso House in the middle of a snow blizzard. He'd given up wondering how much snow fell in Moscow during one winter, as it had to be a number of feet beyond his mental capacity to even comprehend. He presumed that Viktor had been out shoveling at some point in the afternoon, but there was absolutely no sign of his efforts, if indeed he had been. After shedding his coat, he went down to the warming room to see if Viktor might be available for some chess.

He found Viktor sitting at the table. He looked very tired.

"How goes the battle with the snow today?"

Viktor shrugged his shoulders, in a dejected manner. "I shovel and an hour later there is no sign that I had even been there! It is somewhat like life. In one hundred years, who will know that I had been here – or in even ten years? Political leaders are no better and never seem to learn from history. Over the millennium, they all thought they were so special and that history would remember them. They put up monuments to themselves and leave heirs to carry on their dynasties in the delusion that if they are remembered, it will make them immortal. Hitler's thousand year Reich will be over in just a few years more. The great pyramids are still there, but who remembers who built them? Comrade Lenin thought he could create a new socialist man, who didn't think of his own individual welfare." He shrugged his shoulders in a gesture of who knows.

"You're certainly in a rather pessimistic mood today, my friend," commented Charles. "Anything in particular that has brought on this change from your usual optimistic view of life?"

"No, nothing in particular. Having lived through years in labor camps out in Siberia, there is little left I haven't seen in life. I saw men kill one another just for a crust of bread. I've seen men and women just give up and sit down in the snow, and wait to die. But then I also saw a hungry person willing give up a crust of bread to another who was starving. I shovel snow and every day there is always more snow. I think life is simply a process versus reaching any particular goal. And, of course, I sometimes do think about the fact that I've had many more years behind me than I have yet ahead of me."

"Oh, you have many years yet ahead. You're still quite a young man." Neither of them believed that lie.

Charles was surprised by Viktor's negative comment about Lenin. It seemed odd, if he was indeed an NKVD officer or informant. He decided to take an aggressive move. "Viktor, many of the Americans think you're an informant for the NKVD. Are you?"

Viktor laughed. "Every Soviet citizen is an informant to some degree. Wives report on husbands, friends on friends. I meet once a week with someone from the NKVD who wants to know what is happening within the American community? I always have some tidbit for him, or I might lose my job. One has to report something, but from me, it's usually something harmless and meaningless, and that everyone else has probably observed as well. I tell them, 'Charles seems rather sad in recent days. John got several letters from his wife this week, apparently with some good news about something. I will try to find out what.'

Charles smiled and nodded. "So, everybody plays the game. What's the most interesting thing you've ever reported about me?"

"Well, I hate to say this, but you lead such a dull life that I rarely have much to say about you. When pressured to try harder, I have in fact just invented a few statements that you supposedly had made. For example, I once reported how you had commented about how impressed you were with the bravery of Russian soldiers. And then there was the time you supposedly had gotten a few letters from a young lady back in America, in New York to be precise, and they had greatly improved your spirits. I was to find out more about her."

Charles laughed. "I wish!"

Viktor gave one of his frequent deep shoulder shrugs. "I lie to my handler. He pretends that he believes me and repeats my lies to his superior, and so on. This entire country is a pyramid of lies."

Charles rose to leave. "You may report next time that the young lady's name is Jane and that she has just moved from New York up to Boston. You can also tell them that I said that she has very beautiful… no, I probably wouldn't have shared that fact with you!"

They both laughed.

He stopped at the doorway. "Say, what have you reported about my chess game?"

"I simply said that you are a very enthusiastic player, but lack experience."

Charles waved goodbye and headed on out the door without replying. He thought to himself that that was a generous assessment by Viktor of his skill level. It did at least help support his rationale for meeting with Sasha to play chess.

CHAPTER 11

On the following Sunday afternoon, Charles took Jane out for lunch. It was still quite cold, but at least the sun was shining and there was almost no wind. The buildings, trees and bushes were still totally covered in snow, which made the city look like a winter scene on one of the famous lacquered, miniature hand-painted boxes from the village of Palekh. She lived on the second floor of a shabby three-story tall apartment building just a few blocks from the British Embassy. It was actually only eight years old, but looked as if it had already been deteriorating there for fifty or sixty years. The foreigners in Moscow joked how new buildings were built to fit right in with old and dilapidated ones! She was waiting in the sunshine out on the sidewalk. He picked her up in his official car and as she entered, she let her green wool, military coat come open. Charles immediately noticed that she was wearing a plaid skirt, a light pink blouse and a blue sweater with small flowers around the collar. First time he'd seen her in "civvies."

He wanted to say something appropriately flattering, but just sat there in silence for several long seconds as he admired her attire.

"Thank you," she said with her Hollywood-quality smile. "I take it from your mouth hanging open, you approve of my kit today?"

Charles grinned. "Well, it has been several months since I've seen a woman in such lovely and colorful clothing and yes I heartily approve."

"I decided today that perhaps some cheerful clothing would put us both in a better mood. I'm so tired of wearing my WREN uniform every day. Whoever designed that outfit should be shot!"

"Cheerful clothing is an excellent idea and your timing is perfect, as we're going someplace special today – a restaurant other than the Metropole Hotel or any of the other four places in the city that the Westerners use. Viktor, the old Russian worker at Spasso House I've mentioned, has given me directions to an 'unofficial' restaurant he knows of through a friend that only Muscovites frequent."

"Sounds like a great adventure. Is the fact that we don't speak much Russian going to be a problem?"

Charles pulled from his coat pocket a folded sheet of paper. "Not a problem. Viktor has written out an explanation to the owner who we are and a first and second choice for our meal. And not that it won't be obvious, but the note even explains that we don't speak Russian!"

She laughed. "No, I don't think we need a note explaining that we can't speak Russian!"

"I thought you'd taken some Russian earlier in your life?"

"I did, but I didn't learn any vocabulary particularly helpful in ordering food." She laughed.

He had another sheet upon which Viktor had written instructions on how to find this restaurant with no name, and no sign outside identifying it as a restaurant. It took about twenty minutes to find. Many street signs had disappeared when the buildings they were attached to had been destroyed by German bombings. Others had intentionally been taken down so as to confuse the German Army, had it reached Moscow – and no one in authority had ever thought about putting them back up, even though the German Army was no longer within five hundred miles of the city.

Fortunately, there was a number above a cellar door, which allegedly led to this semi-private restaurant. Charles knocked loudly and almost immediately a young boy opened the door and greeted them in Russian. He pointed them down a hallway to an inner door. Charles opened that one on his own and once inside, the first thing they noticed was the wonderful smells permeating the room. There were a dozen or more couples eating at simple, mismatched wooden tables, all lighted with candles, thus confirming that it was a restaurant. It appeared that the building lacked electricity. A middle-aged woman came to them, smiling and greeted them in Russian. Charles immediately handed her his note from Viktor. He hadn't counted on the fact that the woman couldn't read, but she called over her husband after he'd delivered two plates of food. He quickly read the note, gave them a broad smile and said, "ah, Viktor." He led them to an empty table.

They'd received some attention from the other customers upon entering, as they didn't look like locals, but when Jane removed her coat and showed off her colorful attire, everyone unashamedly stared. Charles had noticed on previous occasions that Russians had no shyness about staring at anybody or anything that caught their attention. All of the Russians were dressed in their bland, gray clothing, like every other person in the country. Several had left their coats on, as it was definitely on the cool side in the restaurant. A number of women started whispering to their male table companions. Charles presumed it was about Jane's colorful clothes, not about his unknown uniform. Charles smiled at a number of the people, which he knew from experience they wouldn't return, but he enjoyed doing it anyway.

The host, who'd patted his chest and informed them that his name was Boris returned a minute later with a bottle of red wine, two cheap glasses and a basket of clearly homemade dark bread. Charles decided not to even try speaking his few sentences of the Russian language, for fear that it might make Boris think he understood the language. The other guests finally went back to eating their own food. He noticed that as Boris walked away, he had a serious limp with one leg – that probably explained as to why the late-forties male was no longer in the Red Army.

"Well, we certainly created a stir with our entrance," remarked Jane. "You said this wasn't a place visited by foreigners and you were correct. I'd say we're the first!"

"Yes, we'll certainly be the first to send the Baedecker Travel Book Company a review of this establishment," he quipped, which got a good laugh from his British dining companion. He poured them both a glass of the red wine, from the bottle with no label of any kind on it.

"To our health!" he toasted.

"To our health!"

The wine was not to be mistaken for a vintage French red from the Bordeaux region, but both of them had drank worse in Russia.

Boris returned a moment later with two bowls of borscht soup, which smelled wonderful. Small wisps of steam rose from the soup.

"How do you think this place acquires the needed ingredients to serve meals?" asked Jane.

"I presume it's totally 'on the left', as the Russians say – underground and illegal, buying the needed meat and produce on the black market. Viktor told me to expect to pay two or three times more than I would at the Metropole Hotel."

She dipped her spoon in to the soup, and her eyes lit up. "Oh my God, this is wonderful. It's worth any price."

After he gave it a try, he agreed with her. "So, this is what borscht is supposed to taste like!"

"You explained where they get the ingredients, but how do you think they get away with running this place in downtown Moscow, under the nose of the Soviet Government?"

Charles rubbed his thumb and two fingers of his left hand together. The universal symbol of a bribe. "I'm sure for a small monetary consideration, and a bowl of this soup, the local police and NKVD officers all turn a blind eye to the existence of this establishment."

"Ah, I see. I've heard stories of places around London that are probably operating on the same basis – a few quid passed into the right hands and ration cards are no longer a problem."

"Wartime or peacetime, some folks always know how to make the system work, for them. They take care of 'Number One' and let the other poor suckers play by the rules."

"You have a pretty grim view of mankind, Charles. Have you always been this cynical?"

"A grim view of mankind? My God, the whole world is at war and millions of people have already died in the last few years. What is there to be optimistic about?"

"A lot of people would agree with you about the madness of this war, but has something particularly happened to you personally?"

"Some day I may tell you the whole story, but I'll simply say for the moment that when I served in Lisbon, I foolishly thought of others and tried giving a few of my fellow men a break. It didn't turn out well for yours truly, and here I am in downtown Moscow, carrying out a shit job. I won't make that mistake ever again."

There wasn't much she could say to counter what Charles had stated and she realized her view of the world wasn't much different, but she still felt had a small spark of optimism about her fellow man. In any case, she was having such a wonderful time, she didn't want to spoil it with some pointless philosophical argument about the goodness of man.

Boris arrived with the main course, which he called "goulash." Charles saw that there were a few carrots and potatoes in addition to small chunks of beef in the bowl. He lowered his nose towards the dish and inhaled deeply. The smell brought back some childhood memories from Chicago. His Irish neighborhood was right next to a small Hungarian one. One of his school friends was Hungarian and he'd eaten several times in the one-bedroom apartment of his friend. His mother was a wonderful cook.

After inhaling deeply several times, he said to Jane, "It's paprika. That's what gives it that glorious smell." He took his first bite and his face told her it must be wonderful. In the end, they both used the brown bread to wipe up every last trace of the goulash from their bowls.

Both of them were in a post-luncheon nirvana, as they finished off the red wine. She turned the conversation to the topic of his parents. "What did your father do? Was he also a lawyer?"

"No, he was an independent accountant out in Chicago. He kept the books for small-time companies like mom-and-pop groceries or gas stations – nothing special. Unfortunately, my parents died when I was a young teenager, so an uncle raised me." Charles had told this lie so many times, he'd almost come to believe it himself, and it came out of his mouth smoothly. He'd discovered over the years of telling it that it generally created a certain amount of sympathy for him. Probably more so than had he told the truth – that his father had been a bookkeeper for the Capone Gang in Chicago and that his mother had stopped by the "office" to see him one day, at just the wrong time. The time that a rival gang was making a "hit" on that office. The claim he'd become an orphan at age fifteen was true. The "uncle" however had been Murray Humphreys, one of Capone's lieutenants who'd felt sorry for him and took him under his wing, including changing his name.

"I'm so sorry." Like most people, she wanted to change the subject as quickly as possible to something more pleasant. "What do you want to do after the war?" she asked.

"Oh, I'll probably go back to being a lawyer, but doing exactly what I don't know. I'd worked before the war for a rich financier in New York City, dealing a lot with property investments." He rarely mentioned to people that his employer had been Vincent Astor, one of the richest men in America, as he thought it sounded a bit pompous and that he was trying to show how important he was because of for whom he'd worked. "I'll just see what comes along, when this war ever ends." He had the attitude of a lot of OSS operatives, who never took it for granted that they would live to the end of the war, given the mortality rates of OSS officers who'd gone overseas. So, there was little point in doing much post-war planning in the present.

"What about you? If…, well if you husband doesn't return…" Charles just let his voice trail off, having regretted he'd started the sentence as soon as the first words left his lips.

"I've given that some thought, more so in recent weeks. At first you tell yourself that he'll show up someday, somehow. Second stage, you tell yourself that you could never love anybody else, but then reality starts creeping in to your thoughts after so many months. You realize that you probably will find someone else, as you don't want to live alone the rest of your life. It finally just becomes a question of what is a respectable waiting period, before you start moving on. Start accepting invitations to parties or to dinners." She stopped talking as she looked at Charles, hoping he didn't think that she was implying that she was at that stage now and was accepting his invitations to do things together because she did want to move on… or was that exactly what she was doing?

Fortunately, Boris came to the table at that moment with the check, sparing either of them from having to say anything further along that line of discussion. The check actually consisted of a small corner of some newspaper that Boris had torn off and written a number on, presuming correctly that the American couldn't understand spoken Russian numbers. The proprietor spoke some words that Charles presumed correctly was telling him what an honor it had been to have him there and he hoped they'd liked the food.

Charles called upon his brain for one of his few Russian phrases and responded, "ochen vkustno", very tasty, which brought a big smile to Boris' face. They gathered their coats and departed, with the eyes of all of the remaining customers again upon them. They didn't speak much on the drive back to her apartment. They were both in such a good mood, that talking just didn't seem necessary. As he pulled up in front of her building, he said, "I may be taking a short trip back to Washington within a week or two, so not sure when I'll see you again. I might not get much advance notice of when I'll be leaving."

"But you will be back?"

"Oh, yes. We may be able to see each other again before I leave, but if not, definitely as soon as I return."

That statement once again brought a smile to her lovely face. Sometimes, people said a lot, without saying hardly a word. He leaned over and kissed her on the cheek as she squeezed his gloved hand. Hardly the passion often described in one of Raymond Chandler's novels, but it was the first time he'd kissed her in any fashion. He drove off smiling like a teenage boy at the end of his first date.

Captain Worthington was in an excellent mood the rest of the day, as he loafed about Spasso House, reading more of his Charlie Chan mystery and indulging in one of his cigars up in his room, with the window cracked. He finished his cigar and his book just as it was time to go downstairs for dinner. He hadn't had a clue until the very last chapter as to who'd murdered the wealthy businessman that night on the beach of Waikiki! Clearly Charles was no Charlie Chan.

Even Major Singell noticed Charles' cheerful demeanor at dinner. About ten minutes in to the meal, Barry commented, "You must have had a good day. You seem to be in a very good mood this evening."

"The sun was shining today and I finished one of my mystery books." He then just shrugged his shoulders, indicating that that was all he could think of to explain his pleasant mood.

"Reading doesn't seem to usually put you in such a good demeanor. What else did you do this weekend?"

Charles gave out a school boy grin. "Oh, British WREN Summerfield and I went to lunch today. What a charming young lady."

"So I hear and most importantly, she's right here in Moscow."

Charles was a bit befuddled for a moment, not understanding what charm and geography had to do with each other, but then he understood. For a married man, like Singell, separated by several thousand miles from his "charming lady", he thought about how geographical location affected a man's opinion of a woman, who happened to be present. It was the old joke about how absence makes the heart grow fonder – for the one close at hand! He then remembered his possible sighting that day of Barry with a local blonde, headed in to an apartment block.

Their further discussion of Miss Summerfield was interrupted by the arrival of Captain Collins with a tray who sat down next to Charles. He had an old copy of the Daily Worker newspaper under his arm, which he laid on the table, next to his tray. "How you fellas doing today?" he inquired of Barry and Charles.

"Charles was out on a date today with that good-looking British WREN, Summerfield," replied Singell. "He seems to be in a very good mood this evening."

"Ah, I see," replied Ted. "I guess she's OK, if you like women with pretty faces and nice bodies who laugh at your jokes!" He winked at Singell.

Wishing to change the topic, Charles pointed at Ted's commie newspaper and inquired, "Gus Hall got any advice on how to win the war faster?"

"Mr. Hall has a lot of good ideas. This issue is six weeks old, but I'll be happy to lend it to you to read."

Charles shook his head, "I'll pass. Barry here has a copy of the Oregon Fish and Wildlife Guide for 1939, which he's offered to loan me in return for one of my Charlie Chan novels."

Ted smiled as he started his dinner. "You guys just laugh, but one of these days you capitalists are going to wake up and discover that we've just elected the first Socialist president of the United States."

Singell didn't want Ted to get started on one of his political lectures, so he turned the conversation to the semi-neutral topic of sports. "You guys heard about this women's professional softball league some guy started out in the Midwest? Craziest thing I've heard of."

Charles likewise wished to avoid getting Collins started on politics and joined the softball topic. "Yeah, the chewing gum millionaire, Wrigley, out in Chicago started it last summer, since there aren't enough men around to play in the professional baseball league." The ploy worked and for the next fifteen minutes the three were arguing over whether women could play even softball well enough to make for an interesting game for the fans. Several other guys joined them at their table and got into the discussion as well. As he finished his dinner of mystery meat in sauce, instant potatoes and green peas out of a can, he fondly remembered his delicious lunch. The treat for the night was dessert, which was chilled, canned pineapple chunks. Most of the guys always complained about the food, but Charles was still rather impressed at what the three enlisted men out in the kitchen managed to put together for meals in the middle of Moscow in wintertime. Most everything came out of boxes or cans. He promised himself that if he did get this trip arranged to get back to the states, he was only going to eat real eggs while there, as he had had his fill of powdered eggs!

He made his weekly meeting with Suvarov at the NKVD Headquarters, but his mind was totally on the question as to whether Astor would be able to arrange official travel orders to bring him back to Washington in the very near future. And exactly how he would explain to General Donovan about Sasha, the alleged mole within the American Military Mission in Moscow, and then the big one – was there really some super-secret weapons development program in America called the Manhattan Project, which the NKVD had supposedly penetrated?

During the day, while sitting in his office with little else to do, he thought about his military colleagues within the Mission. Did any one of them strike him as acting "unusual" in trying to find out what sections other than their own were doing? He still didn't understand what good a penetration within the Mission would do for the Soviets, as most everything that went on there simply dealt with getting requested supplies to the Red Army. Perhaps their hyper-paranoia was at play. They simply wanted confirmation from a secret source that what the Mission told them about availability of supplies and delivery dates was the truth.

He also speculated on what would have been the motivation for one of his colleagues to be spying for the NKVD. He didn't know most of the men well enough to make an informed decision and found himself just again going over old ground. Captain Ted Collins was a socialist or a communist, or whatever he wanted to call himself, so perhaps he felt he should help the only communist country there was. Captain Tom Parkington was a longtime friend of Duncan Lee, who Charles knew was an NKVD source, but exactly what did that prove? Bobby Penkovsky still had relatives down in the southern parts of the USSR, so perhaps he was vulnerable to blackmail. And speaking of blackmail, there was still the possibility that Major Singell, a married man, had taken up with a local cutie. There were a couple of other officers who occasionally seemed overly nosey about what Charles was really up to for the OSS while in Moscow, but who knew what that indicated. Life was generally so boring in Moscow, a colleague being nosey about Charles' activities, was as likely caused by boredom, as it was from the possibility the fellow was working for the NKVD.

His final conclusion was that as long as he kept his "Sasha operation" a secret from anyone else within the Military Mission, a Soviet mole there wasn't really a threat to him, or a pressing concern. Getting more information about the NKVD sources within the Manhattan Project, before he left for Washington, now that was an urgent matter. He wanted to wait as long as feasible before having another chess evening with Sasha, but he definitely wanted to see him before he left on his trip. As a matter of safety for Sasha, he knew he shouldn't press his luck and see Sasha too often, whether they had a good cover story or not. Also, he wanted to give his asset as much time as possible to learn more about these moles, before they met again. As usual, he was having to do what he hated the most – calmly wait!

Eight days had passed since Reilly Parr had started his journey for America with Charles' letter packed "in his socks" and Charles decided he could wait no longer before triggering a "chess meeting" with Sasha. He called him at his work number on a Wednesday morning, but received no answer despite several tries. He didn't want to look too anxious to get in touch – supposedly just to arrange a chess game – so he waited until the following afternoon to try again. He remembered that Sasha had told him he was to make periodic trips to Central Asia. He was to hand carry secret reports to their scientists out there, who were working on a Soviet "atomic" bomb. The other explanation for his not answering was that he was sitting in an NKVD cell, being tortured.

Again, no answer on the first try, but a half-hour later, Sasha answered. In passing conversation, Sasha did mention that "he'd been traveling" and they agreed to another session of chess on the coming Sunday afternoon at 1400 hours, at the same little place as last time. Friday came and went at the Mission with still no telegram for him from Washington.

He drove directly from Spasso House to the little restaurant on Sunday. He saw no sign of anyone following him that afternoon. Charles found

Sasha already seated at a table off in a corner, which provided a good view of the entire room. The same man who'd "just happened" to be there reading a newspaper the last time was in the same spot today. He was either a surveillant, or this was his favorite restaurant in all of Moscow!

Sasha stood and warmly greeted Charles. "My dear friend. How are you today?"

"Very good, thank you. And you?"

"Good. Here let me take your coat." Charles shed his heavy coat and handed it to his Russian friend, who took it and hung it on a hook next to his on the nearby wall. Both Sasha and Charles were in civilian clothes, so as to draw as little attention to themselves as possible. Charles noticed that Sasha had subtly slipped something into the right-hand pocket of his coat while hanging it up.

"You're in for trouble today Sasha. I've been practicing since our last match and I'm feeling lucky today," said Charles with a friendly smile.

"It's going to take more than luck to defeat me, my capitalist friend."

There was already a small loaf of brown bread, a bottle of vodka and two glasses on the table, next to the chess board. For the benefit of their "friend" watching from nearby, they got straight to the chess game with little conversation. Sasha again won, but indeed, Charles did put up a better challenge this time. Before starting a second game, they engaged in a little conversation while exchanging a couple of toasts.

"I left a little present for you in your coat pocket."

"Yes, I saw. Further news about the Manhattan Project I hope."

"Yes, there is, but I have to be very careful as I try to find out more about the sources that are providing the intelligence, which I am to file and distribute. I was out in Kazakhstan last week, making my first courier trip there, so I have some information about our research facility out there. You were to have an answer for me. Do you?"

Charles gave him a broad smile. "Indeed I do and one I think you will like. Before the end of the war, you will be smuggled to America and given US$10,000 to start a new life. You will be given a new name and identity documents."

Sasha didn't really understand how much ten thousand dollars was, but it sounded like a lot of money. Her poured both of them generous shots of vodka and raised his glass in a toast. "To America!"

Of course, Charles had yet to even tell the OSS about Sasha, but even if that never worked out, he figured Mr. Astor would be good for the $10,000 and his two Italian friends in Manhattan, Salvatore and Lou, could no doubt come up with some quality, fake identity documents. That just left the "minor detail" of getting him out of Russia and in to America – surely a clever OSS officer like himself could figure out how to do that! Charles sincerely hoped that Donovan would buy in to this operation once he knew the details, and he wouldn't have to personally be that clever. But for the moment, he had made Sasha a happy man. There was no reason to worry him with little details about how all this would work.

"One more thing. I'm making a trip back to Washington in the next week or so. I'm to personally brief General Donovan about our operation. I'll be gone maybe two weeks. I'll call about a chess game when I get back."

Sasha clearly didn't like the idea of Charles leaving Russia, even supposedly on a short trip, before their deal was concluded. "Who will work with me, if you don't return?"

"I'll definitely be back, in just a couple of weeks," Charles lied smoothly. He could think of numerous reasons as to why he might not be back, beginning with General Donovan firing him on the spot, once he'd briefed him on what he'd been doing in Moscow without even checking with OSS Headquarters. But there was no reason to share those concerns with Sasha. He knew that a happy agent produced more and what he needed right now, was as much great intelligence out of him as possible. If in the end, he couldn't get Sasha out of the Soviet Union and to America – well, that would be Sasha's problem, not Charles' – tough breaks happened in this business.

They returned to their chess game. Charles played very well and actually had a chance at winning, before Sasha closed with a strong finish and beat him. Charles played so well, he actually suspected that having gotten the answer Sasha had wanted to hear about moving to America, Sasha had almost let him win!

After their second game ended, Charles quickly gave Sasha a few more personal details about his life and his hopes for the future, so he'd have something to report to Major Petrov. They then bid farewell and Charles was on his way back to Spasso House, resisting the urge to even take a quick peek at what Sasha had placed in his coat pocket.

As upon previous occasions, Charles locked his door and closed the curtain of his window. He took the package of Russian cigarettes from his coat pocket, which Sasha had placed in there, then made himself comfortable in his reading chair. He pulled the folded note from the package and read carefully through it.

"Dear Friend,

We have at least three sources within the Manhattan Project:

1. He is very young, a child genius of mathematics or something. He works on designing how this new type of bomb will be made to explode. Came directly from a major American university where had been student.

2. This man not a scientist, but type of metal grinder. He actually makes metal parts to fit in this bomb. Doesn't know why anything works, but has stolen copies of various "schematics" (if that is correct English word). He is soldier in US Army, came from New York City area. He may have family/relatives who also sources for NKVD. Has a wife.

3. More senior man (scientist), with code name of "STARIK" (old one). Had been university professor for many years. Maybe has wife in Chicago area of America. He has car in New Mexico. His information is about progress this secret program is making. Maybe he more "manager" and overall designer than worker on project.

All three sources are met once every 4-6 weeks in Santa Fe, New Mexico, but not by NKVD officer. This would look very strange if Soviet official wanted to travel from Washington or New York to New Mexico, so NKVD uses very trusted American sources as couriers to travel West, then bring back reports. All three sources are considered to be motivated by their correct political views, not money or blackmail.

Two of the main Soviet physicists involved in our project are Yakov Frenkel and Igor Kurchatov. Program really given push by Stalin in late 1942.

Your friend."

Charles did not bother to make a clean copy of Sasha's report, but sat and read it over and over until he could almost recite the facts in it from memory. He took out the other sheets of paper he'd previously placed in his semi-secret hiding place on the back of his dresser, and read them over many times as well. He dare not take any written notes with him on his trip, nor leave anything behind while he was away. He would burn all these sheets of paper the day before leaving for America, then sit down and make out a new complete report with the pertinent details for General Donovan, once he was on American soil. Presuming he ever got the anticipated orders for him to travel to Washington. He skipped dinner and went to bed by 2000 hours. Between the stress of the operation and the vodka he'd drank in the afternoon, he was mentally exhausted and sleepy.

In hopes there might be a message waiting for him on Monday morning, he arrived at the Military Mission promptly at 0800. The communications and code room worked seven days a week, so something could have come in over the weekend for him, but there were no messages waiting for him. Depending on the atmospherics, somedays they received no messages at all from America, and then there would be a back log of as much as two or three days' worth of traffic to receive and send. He spent two hours that morning in his office, reciting from memory the facts he was taking to Washington in his head. He'd just returned from an early lunch back at Spasso House when he received a phone call in his office from General Deane's adjutant.

"General Deane would like to see you immediately," said the deep male voice on the other end of the phone.

"Yes, I can be there in about fifteen minutes." He grabbed his coat and headed for the door. He didn't know what other qualities the officer had as Deane's adjutant, but he had the perfect "telephone" voice to be making requests and giving orders for a general! Charles hoped the request for his presence had something to do with the arrival of travel orders, but another horrible thought also crossed his mind – what if Sasha had gotten arrested yesterday and had confessed all. The NKVD would have had all night to beat the truth out of him and a formal complaint about Captain Worthington's activity being "incompatible with his assignment to Moscow" could have been made to General Deane by late morning. Thus, the request for his immediate presence could be connected with being informed by Deane that he was being expelled from the country.

When he arrived at Deane's office, Charles got no hint from the adjutant as to why he was urgently needed by the General. After about a ten minute wait, he was ushered in and shown a chair. Deane was holding a telegram.

"I just received this IMMEDIATE message from Army Headquarters, Washington DC. It says that you are urgently needed in Washington and that you are to travel there on a priority basis and report immediately to General Donovan for further instructions. Any idea why you are so urgently needed in Washington?"

Being a practiced liar, Charles kept a perfectly straight face and responded, "Not a clue, sir."

"You sure you haven't been going out and doing something for the OSS that you shouldn't? You've just been conducting regular liaison meetings with the NKVD as ordered?"

"Yes, sir, only my official liaison duties."

"I hear second hand, you don't seem to do much of anything even when you're in your office, and you leave the building frequently. Damn peculiar this special order for you to suddenly travel on a priority basis."

He thought about reminding Deane how upon his arrival he'd told Charles how he wasn't really part of the Military Mission, so what was it to the General what he did in or out of the building and for how much time. Fortunately, he'd been in the Army long enough to know that generals didn't like to be reminded of anything that contradicted them, so he just remained silent. Charles then remembered hearing the rumor a month back that General Deane had been annoyed, as he had put in to travel on a priority basis back to Washington on consultations and had had his request denied. No wonder he was clearly annoyed that Worthington, a mere captain, was to now travel on a priority status!

"If I might speculate, sir, it may have something to do with some topic from my previous duties at OSS Headquarters. I was involved in planning for some sensitive projects to be happening about now. Or it might even be that something has come up concerning my previous time in Portugal." Charles wanted to hint at anything except a subject connected with Moscow, as he was sure the rumor mill would get started quickly about his sudden departure TDY for Washington."

Apparently, Deane liked that possible explanation. He finally grunted, "Uh, perhaps that's it." There was a brief pause as he stared again at the telegram. "It's already been arranged, you're to fly out of here first thing tomorrow morning, so that you can catch a special Army Air Corps flight out of Archangel tomorrow evening that is carrying several Soviet Army officials to America for a conference. You'll change planes in Scotland and then fly directly on to America. With luck, you'll be in Washington by Friday."

"That's outstanding, sir. Thank you for making this happen so quickly."

Having satisfied himself that Worthington's trip was not linked to any bad news for him or his command in Moscow, he then relaxed and even smiled. "I imagine you'll enjoy a little break from the lovely Russian winter!"

Charles didn't even bother to hide his pleasure at the thought of getting out of Russia for a week or two. He smiled broadly, and replied, "Yes, sir, seeing ground without snow on it will be a pleasant change – and have a few meals that contain nothing made from a dehydrated mix!"

Deane reached into his desk drawer and took out a personal-sized white envelope. "Mind taking a letter to my wife and mailing it once you reach Washington? Her birthday is next Monday and it will be a nice surprise for her if she hears from me in a letter actually written just a few days earlier than she reads it. I scribbled out a letter to her just before you arrived."

"I'd be happy to take it with me, sir" Charles took the envelope, saluted and departed. He barely got through the office door his smile was so wide!

Back at his office, he made a call to Captain Nosenko over at the NKVD office and told him in English that he was making a trip back to Washington, apparently to report on how things had been going in the liaison relationship and would get back in touch soon as he returned, probably in two weeks.

He then placed a call over to the British Embassy to WREN Summerfield, who was finally located and came on the line.

"Jane Summerfield here."

"Jane, it's Charles. How are you today?"

"Good, for a Monday. To what do I owe the pleasure of your call?" she asked in that smooth as honey, lovely English accent. He bet the NKVD phone tap translators fought over who got to listen to tapes with her on the line.

"I'm taking off on that little trip I'd mentioned that might come up. Any chance of us having dinner tonight?"

"Oh, I'm sorry, but I have duty tonight at the embassy and they really frown on people trying to switch around at the last minute."

Charles had often wondered why their embassy needed "evening duty clerks", but every chancery did things their own way. He tried sounding upbeat. "Oh, well, I'll only be gone two weeks at the most and I'll see you then. We can have dinner when I return."

"You are… You are definitely returning?" Even over the lousy quality Moscow telephone line, he could hear the sudden sadness in her voice. He knew then that they had become more than just friends.

"Absolutely. Uncle Joe has told General Deane that we can't win the war on the Eastern Front without me here. Say, is there anything I can bring you from America?"

There were a few seconds of silence. "Oh, just surprise me. You know what a woman likes. Listen, when you get back, how about I cook you dinner at my flat? Give me a chance to keep up my cooking skills that my mother worked so hard to teach me."

"That sounds wonderful. What will you fix?"

"A girl has to keep some mystery about herself. Your present to me will be a surprise and my main course will be a surprise for you." He could almost see her smiling at the other end of the line.

"Fair enough. Well, I better get home and start packing and I suppose you better get back to work on those daily, weekly and monthly reports for London."

She laughed. "Alright, Charles. Goodbye."

"In my branch of service, we don't say 'goodbye' – we just say 'until next time.' He thought about saying something more, but didn't know exactly what he wanted to say and simply hung-up the phone. Maybe by the time of his return, he might have a clearer idea in his mind about their relationship.

He headed back to Spasso House to sort through his closet to find a few clean clothes. He hit the mess hall the moment it opened, so he could get in, eat, and get out before having to answer a bunch of questions from his colleagues. He'd carry personal letters if anybody came to his room with such a request, but preferred to avoid conversations as to why was he was suddenly making a TDY to Washington.

He did slip down to the workers' warming room to see if Viktor might be there, which he was. He seemed to be a happier, younger-looking Viktor than the last few times he'd seen him.

"I'm off first thing tomorrow morning for a quick trip back to Washington. Just wanted to say a quick "dosvydonye."

"Give my regards to President Roosevelt while you're in Washington," jokingly replied the elderly Russian with a smile on his face. "By the way, I've nearly finished reading *Gone With the Wind*. We will have to have a chat about it when you return."

"Absolutely. I'll probably be gone about two weeks. Carry on the battle with the snow, while I'm away." He reached over and shook Viktor's hand.

"Go with God, Charles."

As he was finishing packing that evening, there was a knock on his room door.

"Yes?"

"It's Barry Singell."

"It's open, come on in," he shouted at the door. He rarely bothered to lock it during the day.

"Hey, Charles, I hear you're taking off tomorrow morning for Washington." He held up a stamped envelope and smiled. "Don't suppose you'd have room in your suitcase for a letter to my wife?"

"Sure, just toss it in the bag. I'll put it somewhere."

"Thought I'd surprise my wife with a letter she'll receive in the same month I write it," he joked.

Charles thought Barry would then leave, but he went over and sat down in the one chair.

"Must be nice getting an order, directly from General Donovan to travel on a priority basis back to America. Have you and Stalin come up with a clever plan to win the war by the 4th of July?"

Charles smiled. "Nah, you know that only majors and above are allowed to have clever ideas." He paused slightly and then added, "Actually, I don't have a clue as to what Donovan wants. There's nothing I've been doing here that would merit me traveling to the north side of Moscow, much less to Washington."

"Rumors started flying around the building early this morning about you suddenly being called home. They range from several American combat divisions about to arrive in Russia to you sleeping with the British Ambassador's daughter when she visited last month. I personally like the story of you and the daughter."

Charles laughed. "You know, she wasn't really that good in bed." He put on a big grin. "Actually, I suspect that this has something to do with my time back in Lisbon. There were several open-ended operations going on there when I'd left…" He shrugged his shoulders, as if it was all a total mystery to him as well. He definitely didn't want people thinking and talking that his trip had anything to do with his time in Moscow. Talk that could easily get to the NKVD informants.

"Well, I gotta get down to dinner before they close up. Have a safe journey back home you lucky guy."

"I'll be back in about two weeks. Unless, I can figure out a way to stretch it to three!"

After Singell left the room, Charles stared at the letter to Mrs. Singell. He'd never previously seen any evidence that Barry greatly missed his wife or was a conscientious letter writer to her. And his questions as to the purpose of Charles' trip… Of course, most everyone was curious about his trip, but he did wonder if the letter had just been a ploy by Singell to come in and talk to him about his sudden trip to Washington.

CHAPTER 12

Charles landed in New York late Thursday night. He planned to just sleep on a cot in the waiting room out at the airfield, rather than even try to find a hotel after midnight in downtown Manhattan, from where he'd catch the train at 1300 hours the following day for Washington. Despite the late hour, he placed a phone call from a phone booth to a number he had for Salvatore. He hoped it was still valid. After the third ring, a male voice that Charles didn't recognize answered with a simple "yeah?"

"I'd like to talk with Salvatore please."

"It's too late to be placing any bets for today, even for the California tracks. Call tomorrow."

"I'm not wanting to place a bet. I just want to speak with Salvatore or Lou. Tell them it's Charles. I just got in from England."

There was dead silence for twenty seconds or more, then a thick Brooklyn accent came on the line, saying, "Dis is Sally. Who wants to talk wit' me?"

Charles put on his best, upper class, Harvard accent and teasingly stated, "A little more respect young man when you're speaking to an officer and a gentleman of the United States Army."

He heard a booming laugh come out of the phone. "Charlie, my boy, how's are ya?"

"I just landed a bit ago from England, but I'm leaving tomorrow at 1:00 pm on the train for Washington. I need to see you guys before I go. Could you get up so early as to meet me around 11:00 a.m., somewhere down near the Pennsylvania Station?

"Sure, youse comes out of the southside entrance and we'll be there in the same black Packard that we's always had. It'll be great to sees ya!"

Captain Worthington's next phone call was to the Fifth Avenue home of Vincent Astor. Astor was out of the city, but the sleepy-sounding butler remembered Charles' name and previous association with Mr. Astor and revealed that he was staying at the Cosmos Club down in Washington DC. Charles next phoned there and managed to convince the front desk that despite the late hour, it was a wartime emergency and Mr. Astor should be made aware of the call, despite his being in the sacrosanct billiards room where members were never to be disturbed.

After a several-minutes wait, a hearty voice came on the line. "Charles, my boy. I take it you made it to America!"

"Yes, sir, and thank you for your assistance in making this trip happen. I will be on the 1:00 p.m. train tomorrow, arriving Union Station about six. Any chance we might have dinner Friday evening? I hope to see the General on Saturday and I'd like to get your advice on a few things before I do that."

"Well, I'm supposed to be having dinner tomorrow night with some bankers in from the West Coast, but they're a terribly boring lot, so thank you for saving me from them! Shall we say 7:00 p.m. here at the Cosmos Club? And, do you have a hotel room for your stay in Washington? If not, I suspect I can pull a string or two and get you a room here at the Club – might be down in the boiler room or something like that, but at least it will be indoors."

"That would be great, as I was just going to start calling around to different Washington hotels to see if anybody had a room available for a week or two. A room at the Club will save me a lot of effort. I'll see you for dinner tomorrow."

"Goodnight Charles."

"Goodnight, sir."

He left word out at the Duty Desk that he should be awakened at 0800 hours, then headed for his cot. He was quite tired from the journey and within two minutes of his head and feet being at the same level, he was sound asleep.

The following morning at 0900 he placed a call to General Donovan's office, to confirm that he'd arrived in America and would be in Washington that night. Donovan's longtime secretary, put him on hold for a minute, then came back on the line. "The General will expect you at his office at

0900 hours on Saturday morning, and he said to tell you that you're not officially on his calendar."

"Thank you, I'll be there Saturday morning."

Apparently, Astor had managed to convey to Donovan Charles' unwritten desire for a very low key visit and Donovan was doing his part – having the visit occur early on Saturday morning when few people would be around and leaving his name off the official appointment calendar, few were likely to know he'd even been there.

On Friday morning at 10:00 a.m., he was standing by the curb of the appointed meeting spot outside the south entrance of Pennsylvania Station. Promptly on the dot, a black Packard pulled up with Lou behind the wheel and Salvatore jumped out of the backseat to greet Charles.

They gave each other a quick handshake. "Sally" mockingly bowed at the waist as he held the door open for Charles to enter first. He then tossed Charles' bag in on the floor of the back seat and climbed in right behind him. After the usual questions and answers about how was the trip, where'd he flown in from and when did he have to go back, they came to the important question of where to get some food before his train departure.

"You know me, I like anything, but as I vaguely recall they have a few decent Italian restaurants in this town. You happen to know of one?"

The two Italian-Americans laughed loudly, realizing they were being ribbed. "Yeah, we's might knows of one or two," replied Salvatore. "Lou, head da car in the direction of Mama's." He turned to Charles. "I already's phoned her dis morning to let dem knows we'd be in kinda early today and to have somethings special ready for our VIP guest from across the ocean."

"That would be great. Ah, I've dreamed of Mama's cooking all the time I've been there in Russia."

As they headed to the Little Italy section of the city, Charles thought to himself that neither man had changed a bit since he'd first met them almost three years earlier, courtesy of Mr. Astor. They were both perhaps forty years old. They both dressed, acted and talked as if they were straight out of a Warner Brothers gangster picture of the 1930s, except they'd been dressing that way since the 1920s. He always half expected to see Edward G. Robinson or Humphrey Bogart come in and sit down with them. Astor had introduced them to Charles in 1941, when he might have needed some "muscle" to get things done in an investigation there in Manhattan. At the time, he and Astor were searching for a Japanese mole within U.S. Intelligence circles.

"What kinda food dey gots der in Russia? Youse been eating polar bear or anything tasty like dat?"

"I wish. I'm sure a polar bear would be delicious compared to the terrible food those people eat over there." Charles thought about telling them honestly that the food served up in the mess hall at Spasso House was actually decent, but he knew they'd prefer to hear that he'd been suffering.

Mama herself greeted them at the door and escorted the three of them to the VIP table in a corner where Lucky Luciano used to like to sit when he'd dine there in the mid-1930s. Salvatore and Lou were nowhere in stature "within the family" as had been Luciano, but they were well-respected, came from the old neighborhood and when anything needed doing, one of them knew a guy, who knew a guy. They were also known as being tough enough, with or without a gun, that nobody messed with them. Having a vague connection to Mr. Astor also gave them a certain prestige and mystique around Little Italy – not that either of them had any idea of what that latter word meant.

Charles had had only coffee for breakfast out at the airfield and didn't resist at all as Mama started bringing plate after plate of delicious Italian food to the table.

As he ate, he told them several stories of life in wintertime in Moscow, and of his offer from the two Russian ladies to study English with him at night, which got a howl from both of his older male Italian-American buddies.

"Maybes I could go over der and gets some English lessons," kidded Salvatore.

They began bringing him up to date on what had been happening in Manhattan since the last time he'd seen them almost a year earlier. They looked no different. Both of them dressed impeccably in special-tailored pin-striped suits. Salvatore had a bent nose from when it had been broken as a young teenager on the streets of Brooklyn, which was probably the last time anyone had been stupid enough to start a fight with him. Both men had chests and shoulders that made them look like professional boxers.

Sally always liked to wear a red carnation. Both men had slight bulges near their left armpits, caused by the .45s they each carried. Lou had told him once that only pimps in New Orleans whore houses carried a .22 or .38 caliber gun. Astor had never really explained just why he and "the boys" knew each other and Charles doubted he would ever learn the reason. He knew Astor trusted them totally, even on one occasion with his life; another story which had only ever been vaguely explained.

After his third cannoli, he finally got around to a serious matter he wanted to discuss with them. "Fellows, I may need a little assistance in a month or two – off the books."

Both men immediately nodded their assent to anything Charles might need, even before hearing what it might be. "What's youse need?" asked Sally in a lowered voice, while looking around to confirm that no one else was within hearing range.

"I'm arranging for a Russian guy to quietly move to America. He's been helping me out, in return for a new life here. Don't suppose you could arrange for him to get some documents showing that he's a good taxpaying, American citizen?

Lou grinned. "Is da Pope Catholic?"

"I'll take that as a yes," replied Charles. "He speaks fairly good English, but with a heavy foreign accent."

"Everybodys in Manhattan, except youse and Mr. Astor, speaks with an accent. Dats not a problem," stated Sally and both Italians laughed.

"He should have plenty of money, but it might be a week or two before his 'retirement' check arrives, so if necessary, please advance him a few bucks for him to get by on till his dough arrives."

They nodded in agreement.

"He'll have with him that phone number that I used last night to phone you. He'll say that his name is 'Sasha' and simply that he's a friend of mine visiting New York and I'd told him you could show him a good time."

"We's got it," answered Sally. "Maybe's we's should arrange for him to gets a couple of English-language lessons, from one of my lady acquaintances." Sally started laughing at his own joke.

"He's a grown man," replied Charles with a straight face. "He can choose to practice his English however he wants and with whomever he wants!" All three men laughed.

Two hours later, a very satiated Charles was on his train and headed towards Washington. He was glad he'd have five or six hours to digest his "Italian lunch" before it would be time for dinner with Mr. Astor at the Cosmos Club. He slept the first couple of hours, as the train headed south. This was in part due to his full stomach, but also Charles had always been one of those people who found the rhythmic clacking of the big steel wheels on the tracks quite sleep inducing. In between dozing, he did review in his mind the important facts that Sasha had provided to him about the NKVD penetrations of the Manhattan Project and of the US Military Mission Moscow. He'd wait till he was in the relative safety of the Cosmos Club before he put any of it to paper, so he'd have ready to give to General Donovan on Saturday morning.

Promptly at 6:25 as scheduled, his train pulled slowly into Union Station. One thing that he noticed had changed just since last December was how easily he could find a cab. He presumed there was still gas rationing, but there must be more gas available. On the train, he'd sensed something else different as well; people seemed to be more optimistic, happier in general, than just five months ago. Had the war situation so changed?

When he arrived at the Cosmos Club up on Massachusetts Avenue, the Front Desk informed him that they did indeed have a reservation for him, up on the third floor. He wasn't quite sure how many years the elegant club had been there. Everywhere he looked, there was highly polished mahogany wood and marble flooring. It was one of those private clubs for the wealthy and powerful that just seemed to have been there forever. The waiters of the Club, even before the war had taken all the young men away from restaurants, had always been gentlemen of a "certain age." They all spoke in the softest tones. In that regard, so did the clientele whether in the dining room, the bar or the billiard room. There was a note waiting for him at the Desk from Mr. Astor, saying that he would return in time for their 7:00 p.m. dinner. The Desk clerk seemed to know about the dinner appointment.

"If you'll be dining with us tonight, sir, I should inform you that military service uniforms are acceptable in the dining room. The Standing House Rule on formal attire only on Friday and Saturday nights in the public areas has been suspended for the duration of the war."

"Thank you." Charles was glad to hear that everyone was making sacrifices for the war effort!

The clerk leaned forward and added in an even lower tone, "The vote on this 'slackening' of the rules had been a close one and if you do by chance have your tuxedo with you, it would be appreciated if you wore it. If it has been stuffed in your small suitcase, housekeeping could arrange to have it pressed for you on very short notice."

Charles simply replied, "Good to know, thank you." He then took his key and headed for Room 305. It was a rather small room, but elegantly outfitted with solid Cherry-wood furnishings. He did change to a fresh shirt and polished up his shoes, so as not to embarrass Mr. Astor too much at dinner. He still had twenty minutes to kill, so he got started on writing out a concise report to give to General Donovan tomorrow morning.

Promptly at 7:00 p.m., both men appeared at the entrance to the dining room; one in a custom-made tuxedo and the other in an Army captain's uniform.

"Charles, you're looking well. Apparently, snow and cold agrees with you," joked Astor. He knew full well from several of Charles' personal letters over the past months that he was not enjoying life in the least in Moscow.

"It's wonderful there, sir. Perhaps with your influence with President Roosevelt, you could convince him to let you go there for some special negotiations, or even as the ambassador." They both laughed, as the maître d' escorted them to a quiet table in a back corner. Everyone dining there that night knew who Vincent Astor was, but in a classy, thick-carpeted establishment like the Cosmos Club, it would have been considered very bad manners to have blatantly stared. Discrete staring was permissible, and everyone was trying to figure out who was the young Army captain dining with the richest man in America.

Astor was well-known as a martini-man and though their waiter did go through the motion of asking him what he wanted to drink that evening, upon hearing that it was a martini, two of them magically appeared on a silver tray about ten seconds later. He didn't even ask Charles; apparently he assumed that Worthington would drink whatever Mr. Astor drank.

Their initial conversation discussed life in general, the war and a few mutual friends. Only after they'd been served their soup course, did Astor raise the topic of the "unusual" letter he'd recently gotten through the U.S. Postal System from Charles.

"Interesting letter you sent me a week back," began Astor. "By the way, I simply went straight to Bill with this; I didn't fool around being clever with lower-ranking people. He agreed with me that you must have something terribly important to discuss with him – something you couldn't put in regular channels – so he issued the orders for you to come home. I only hope you do have something worth the price of your airline ticket to Washington." They both smiled. Charles did so in part because there were very few people around who called General Donovan, "Bill."

"I think I do and I hope Donovan agrees with me in the morning. This all started about two months ago." Astor put up his hand, indicating that Charles should stop.

"I am naturally curious about what is afoot, but you folks have this concept of 'need to know.' Do you think that I have any direct role to play in this matter? Have any knowledge that will help you and the General decide about what to do next?"

"Not that I know of, sir, no."

"Then I suggest that we leave this matter between you and Bill. I will simply say that I have always found your judgment sound and your thinking clear; whether when we were out in the South Pacific, or later, with that little problem in New York in 1941. If you believe this is an important matter, then that is enough for me." The two sat for several long moments, simply looking at each other.

"Someday, perhaps I'll read about it in a history book," commented Astor.

Astor's position made Charles' life easier. He'd been wondering about just how much he should tell his former boss about the "Sasha operation." Now, he wouldn't be telling him anything.

He simply changed topics. "I saw Salvatore and Lou this morning up in Manhattan; they both seemed to be doing well."

"Glad to hear that. I've not had any reason to be in touch with them for some time. They're quite a pair aren't they?"

"That they are, but if I was to ever be in a tight jam, I'd certainly want both of them on my team," responded Charles.

"Indeed, as long as no one from outside of Brooklyn had to understand what the blazes they were saying, supposedly in English!" Again, they both laughed.

By the time they'd finished their coffee, they had covered all mutual topics. Astor had found the description and story of Viktor quite intriguing.

"Amazing what some men can endure. I suspect he's telling you the truth about simply being the reluctant informant, as everyone must be in that country. If he's the admirer of good literature that you say he is, I'll send you a box next week of some American literary classics that perhaps he'll enjoy reading. Maybe some Hawthorne or Twain."

"I'm sure he would greatly appreciate that."

"And how about you? Anything I can send you in the way of reading material?"

Charles laughed. "My tastes run a little lower than Hawthorne, but if you have some good detective stories laying around your library, do send them along to give me something to do with all my down time."

"I'll have Timothy, my chauffeur, pick you out some books. I've noticed his tastes run similar to yours, if the covers of the novels I see laying on the front seat of my limo are an indication of what he reads!"

"That would be great, thank you."

"When do you think you'll be heading back to Moscow, presuming that you will be returning?"

"I'm not sure. I'm guessing that it might take the General a few days to check out certain facts before he sends me back. So, maybe next Thursday or Friday I'll be on my way across the Atlantic again. Or, he might just have me demoted and reassigned to the motor pool right here in Washington!"

Astor joined in on the dark humor and responded, "Probably not here in Washington, but we do have an Army base up in Alaska you know. Given your experience with the cold and snow of Russia, you'd be a natural selection for the motor pool in Alaska."

The two wrapped up dinner fifteen minutes later. "You probably should get a good night's sleep, so you'll be fresh and alert for tomorrow morning's meeting with Bill."

"I am in need of a good night's sleep. Thank you again, for making this trip happen. Perhaps I'll see you again, in the coming week."

"I suspect not, as I have to be in Chicago on Monday and back up in New York by Friday. I'm hosting another one of those bond sales for the blue bloods of Manhattan."

"Will Hedy Lamarr again be giving out kisses to each bond purchaser?" teased Charles.

"Ha, I'm afraid not. Apparently, she's in the middle of making some movie, but Hollywood is instead sending me Veronica Lake to help with the auction."

"Only Veronica Lake. My, how you do suffer. Well, there is a war on and one must do with what one can get."

He gave Mr. Astor a firm handshake and bid him goodnight.

Once back up in his room, he returned to the task of putting down on paper the important facts of the case, so as to have ready a written report of events for Donovan in the morning. He then left a wake-up call time with the Front Desk and crawled into bed.

Charles took a taxi at 0815 hours to the OSS Headquarters Building in downtown Washington, after having breakfast in the Club dining room. He greatly enjoyed having an omelet made from real eggs and fresh milk, straight from a cow – nothing powdered. It was only a fifteen minute cab ride to his destination, but he wanted for sure to be there promptly at 0900 for his appointment with the General. The same all-business secretary who'd been there before he'd left for Moscow was still at her desk when he arrived. She obviously knew he was coming, whether he was "officially" on the calendar or not, and simply pointed him in the direction of a chair in the waiting area. He noted that the wall clock proclaimed it to be 0850 hours. He closed his eyes and reviewed his opening lines to explain to Donovan what had happened in Moscow.

Promptly at 1000 hours, she called out "Captain Worthington" and walked over to the General's door. She knocked twice, then opened it without waiting for a response. "Captain Worthington is here to see you, sir."

Charles approached the massive desk, stopped, saluted and then stood there in silence. Donovan neither rose, nor returned the salute.

"You cleverly arranged this meeting, Captain, so tell me what it's all about." He picked up his coffee mug and then leaned back in his chair and sat there in silence.

Charles stood at ease, and began. "Well, it all started two months back, sir, when a member of the NKVD contacted me and wanted to make a deal to trade his information for an eventual relocation to America as he wishes to start a new life here. Over these past weeks, he has alerted me to the fact that the NKVD has recruited someone within the U.S. Military Mission Moscow. He has given me some identifying clues, but not a specific name. Not knowing who their mole was is why I felt that I could not report this operation through the normal communication channels."

Donovan stirred a little in his chair, but remained silent.

"More importantly than this alleged mole in Moscow, he claims that the NKVD has at least three penetrations of a super-secret weapons development program here in America called the 'Manhattan Project.' The research is centered at Los Alamos, New Mexico and has something to do with 'splitting the atom.' This would somehow create a bomb that has never before existed and be of incredible power. He's provided me some small identifying facts about two of the three moles. He knows this because he was recently put in charge of the file section for these cases, and for the distribution of the reports to the appropriate Soviet research offices, which are trying to build such a bomb. Let me stop there for a moment, if you have any questions. I can go back to fill in minor details of the operation if you wish, but that's it in a nutshell and here is a summary of the major points." He stepped forward and placed on Donovan's desk his hand-written report he'd finished the night before in his room at the Cosmos Club.

Donovan read quickly through it, then rose from his chair and muttered, "son of a bitch." He then proceeded in silence over to the coffee pot in the corner of his office and refilled his cup. He was obviously thinking. He returned to his desk and began to read the report a second time. He'd still never told Charles to sit down or help himself to some coffee, so Charles remained right where he was.

Finally, he looked up. "I don't normally approve of circumventing official channels, but I can see under these peculiar circumstances of not knowing who might be the mole out there in Moscow that you couldn't just send in a telegram from the Military Mission. As for the other, I'm not sure what to think. I've never heard of any program called the 'Manhattan Project', so I don't know if this Sasha is just bullshitting you, or it's so secret that not even I've been made aware of it. That could be the case, as there is probably nothing the OSS could contribute to such a research effort.

"You've met this Sasha character several times now face-to-face, right?"

Charles nodded affirmatively.

"What's your gut feeling about the guy? You think he's playing straight with you, or is he taking you for a ride, maybe just to get his free ticket to America?"

"Well, it could be the latter, but I'm inclined to believe most of what he's told me. The reason he so desperately wants out of Russia before the war ends is because he had been working for the Gestapo up until June 1941 and the German invasion. He's afraid that once the Red Army captures Berlin, the NKVD will find his name in the Abwehr's files as having been an asset for them, and then it's goodnight Irene for him."

Donovan shook his head. "Jesus, you sure know how to pick'em. You violate Allied policy about recruiting a citizen of an Allied country and then he also just happens to be a former German collaborator as well!"

"There's one other possibility that's crossed my mind as well, sir. What if the NKVD has only vaguely heard about this secret project, but for the moment doesn't know much about it, other than that it will make an incredible bomb? What if Sasha's story about penetrations in New Mexico are just red herrings to disrupt and slow down the project, while Army G2 rips the place apart with investigations?"

Donovan nodded his head slowly in agreement with Charles' idea. "That would be pretty clever. You've been interacting with some of those NKVD fellows for several months now. Do you think they're capable of such a subtle ruse?"

"Absolutely, sir. I think being devious is in their blood. They are all quite accomplished chess players. This maneuver would be a classic sacrificing your pawn to lure your opponent in a direction you desire. The NKVD gives up a lowly agent within our Military Mission in Moscow so as to prove Sasha's bona fides and thus we believe his allegations about penetrations within this secret weapons program."

"Which possibility do you think it is?" asked the General, as he sipped more coffee.

"Well, my conclusion at the moment is about 70-30 in favor of Sasha's story being true about the Manhattan Project. Part of my positive conclusion is connected with my respect for how clever the Russians can be. I think a "deception story" of there being three penetrations within the project is overkill. If this were really an NKVD deception ploy, I'd think they would have pushed the story of there being one mole at Los Alamos, or maybe a hint at there being a second, but who would believe that they're running three assets at a super-secret program out in the middle of nowhere New Mexico? The NKVD would be risking making Sasha sound like he was simply a fabricator, with such wild claims of three assets within the program."

"I see what you mean and I think I agree with you – at least enough that we better investigate this further, beginning with confirming that there is such a secret atomic bomb making program going on somewhere in the government. I have a meeting this afternoon with someone who would have to be aware of such a research program, if there is one. Let me just directly ask him if he is aware of something called the Manhattan Project, and see what answer I get. You meet me back here at 2000 hours on Monday and we can discuss this further."

"And what about the allegation of there being a mole in Moscow?"

"Well, I'll speak personally with FBI Director Hoover on Monday. This an FBI matter and they will have to be brought in to investigate. I'll ask Hoover if they can immediately send a man to Moscow to discreetly look in to this allegation." They both then simultaneously laughed at what the FBI would consider discreet!

Donovan stood and came around and shook Charles' hand. "You've done a good job in a very difficult situation. Now let me do my part. Go out and enjoy your few days back in America, and I'll see you on Monday."

CHAPTER 13

Later the same Saturday that Donovan met with Captain Worthington, he attended a high-level policy meeting at the State Department. Normally, he'd beg off at the last minute and send one of his deputies to such tedious affairs, but he knew that Secretary of State Cordell Hull always chaired these meetings, so he decided to actually attend himself. Donovan managed to stay awake and even pretend that he cared what US foreign policy towards South American countries was going to be after the war. Hull was a decade or so older than Donovan, but both men's hair were pure white. Hull had been the secretary of state for almost eleven years and wore a permanent well-wearied look on his face. The 1930s had not been easy years, but the previous two years since America entered the world war had clearly taken a toll on him.

As the meeting was breaking up, Donovan approached the Secretary. "Cordell, have you got a moment?"

"Certainly, Bill, what's up?"

Donovan led Cordell by the elbow off towards a corner of the large, dark wood-paneled conference room, away from the others.

"I've had something very troubling come up. Have you ever heard of a classified weapons program called the Manhattan Project?"

Hull had been known back in his home state of Tennessee as quite a good card player, but even he couldn't keep a "poker face" upon hearing that code name – even the name of the project was classified Top Secret.

He was about to deny ever having heard of such a name, but then thought better of lying to the Director of the OSS, particularly since he already knew the program's code name. He leaned in towards Donovan and in a lowered voice replied, "Bill, I'm surprised you even know that code name. I didn't know you were on the cleared list for that project. Did the President brief you on it?"

Donovan smiled. "No, I've just heard about it from the goddamned Russians!"

"Look, I won't insult you by saying that there is no such program, but you had better go through channels on this one. Go see Alger Hiss. He works for Stanley Hornbeck and he's the State Department's representative to an inter-agency committee that controls access to this project. If you want to know anything about this subject, please first go see Hiss and get cleared to be added to the access list."

They shook hands and parted. As Hull walked away, Donovan recalled why he thought so poorly of diplomacy and diplomats. Hull clearly knew of the program, but wanted him to first go see some underling and get on a god-damned list! Hull had never impressed him as having a set of balls larger than two grapes – very small grapes!

Before he left the State Department that afternoon, he tried to track down Alger Hiss, but finally learned from a weekend duty-desk that Mr. Hiss was not in the building and that someone thought he'd gone out of the city for the weekend. Donovan shook his head as he walked along one of the main, ground floor corridors of the impressive building, his heels echoing down the totally deserted marble – never let a little thing like a world war interfere with the weekends of diplomatic cookie-pushers!

Donovan's secretary finally managed to get Mr. Hiss on the telephone on Monday morning, when he arrived at work at 0930 hours, and she immediately put him through to General Donovan.

"Hiss, this is General Donovan."

"Yes, General. Lovely morning isn't it."

Donovan hadn't called up to get a weather report and jumped straight to the point. "I've had something come up that you might be able to help me with. At least, Cordell thought you were the right man to contact. I'd like to see you this morning."

"Of course, General, I'd be glad to be of any assistance to you that I can; although this morning, I'm already booked for several meetings. Perhaps, we could…"

Donovan interrupted him in mid-sentence. I'll be at your office in thirty minutes. Either you can clear your calendar, or I'll call the Secretary of State, who will clear it for you. Please stay on the line and give your office room number to my secretary." Donovan hung up even before Hiss could start to say, "Yes, I'd be happy…"

Hiss, dressed in a beautiful gray suit and matching bow-tie, was waiting down at the main entrance of the State Department when General Donovan's car drove under the portico. An Army captain jumped out of the front passenger seat to open the General's door.

The armed guard on duty at that entrance was wise enough not to ask a brigadier general for his identity card. Hiss recognized General Donovan and immediately came over to him.

"Good morning, General. I'm Alger Hiss. I've arranged for us to use a small conference room just down the corridor here on the first floor, rather than you having to come up to my office." Hiss couldn't resist adding, "up on the seventh floor," just to let the General know that Hiss was up on the same floor as the Secretary and other leading officials of the Department.

Donovan followed him in silence a short ways down the hallway and into a small conference room. Hiss had arranged for coffee and hot tea to be placed in the room in advance.

"May I offer you something to drink, sir?"

"No, thank you. I'm a little pressed for time this morning, so I'll come straight to the point. Secretary Hull told me on Saturday that you're State's representative to an inter-agency committee for the Manhattan Project. Is that the case?"

Hiss was taken aback by the question, given the small circle of government leaders who even knew of this research effort. "Well, I am… I mean, I am a member of the committee that approves people to be added to the list of people who are allowed to know about this project. Are you wanting me to bring up your name at the next meeting of our committee for consideration to be cleared for you to be read-in on the project?"

"No, I'm asking right now as to whether there is in fact such a secret weapons development project? I asked this simple question of Secretary Hull on Saturday and he sent me to you."

"Well, I guess since you already know the Top-Secret code name for the project, there is no harm in my confirming to you that it does indeed exist. May I ask you, why do you want to know about it?"

"I don't need to know any intimate details about the research. I've just had an overseas visitor who told me of a volunteer he's had, who's claiming that there is a security leak in this program. I'm just trying to confirm if this volunteer is legitimate or not?"

"That's very interesting. Who is this volunteer and what is his nationality?" asked Hiss.

Donovan just ignored his question, as he had no intention of sharing such details with a State Department officer. "My man is leaving to go back overseas in the next 48 hours and I need to be able to tell him whether such a leak is very serious and how hard to bother pursuing the case."

"Any leak of any government research is of course serious, but I can tell you that this project is still very much at an early, theoretical research stage and may never turn in to an actual weapon. So, if your man can find out more, I'm sure someone will be interested, but I'd say he needn't consider this situation as all that critical. Does that help you?"

"Yes, it does, thank you."

"So, would you like for me to proceed in putting forth to the committee your name for possibly being given access to this project? It could be a few weeks before this happens, but I'll be happy to pursue this if you wish."

"No, thank you. If I want to know any further details, I'll just ask the President when I see him twice a week."

Donovan then turned and headed for the door. "Don't worry. I can find the exit on my own."

Donovan's next stop was at the FBI Headquarters, up on Pennsylvania Avenue in downtown Washington DC, where he had an appointment with Director Hoover at 1100 hours. Donovan and Hoover had known each other since 1942 when the OSS had been created and neither man even pretended to like the other. Hoover had fought vigorously to prevent the creation of the organization at all and then to limit its powers as much as possible, when it did come in to existence in June 1942. He had managed to get the OSS banned from operating in Central or South America, as well as within the United States itself. Donovan could forgive him those actions – just a man protecting his bureaucratic fiefdom. It was Hoover's self-promoting behavior in all matters that annoyed Donovan.

Despite their opinion of each other, after the door opened and General Donovan was ushered in to Hoover's palatial personal office, Hoover had a wide smile on his bull-dog face with fleshy jowls, as if his best friend had just arrived. Hoover knew that Donovan was known about Washington as a man who had the ear of President Roosevelt and thus needed to be shown some respect, at least to his face.

"Bill, come in and make yourself comfortable." He pointed at a set of leather chairs off to the side of his actual desk. "You're looking well. War news must be good this Monday!"

Donovan again passed on an offer of coffee and proceeded to the point of the visit. "J. Edgar, one of my overseas officers has just brought me very disturbing information about Soviet espionage against the United States. Counterespionage is of course a matter for the FBI and I wanted to brief you first, get your thoughts and then see what should be done next."

Hoover's entire body visibly relaxed. He decided that perhaps he'd misjudged Donovan up till now. He always liked anybody who recognized the Bureau's preeminence in fields that Hoover believed belonged exclusively to the FBI.

"I certainly appreciate this. Tell me what we're dealing with here and I'll be happy to give you my opinion on how to proceed." He lighted a cigarette and leaned back in his large leather arm chair.

"Actually, we have two cases of espionage you'll have to deal with, but I must emphasize that they must both be dealt with in a very delicate and sophisticated manner; otherwise, not only will my officer's life be in danger, but the Soviets will instantly kill our source – and you may never be able to figure out who the American traitors are and arrest them. Again, that's why I came directly to you, so that your view on how to carry out these investigations in a subtle manner will get passed down your chain of command. One case is in Moscow and the other one is here in America."

Hoover was practically smiling. He already was envisioning headlines in the major newspapers of the country when he personally announced the arrests of foreign spies. "Alright, let's get started. Tell me first about the one in Moscow."

OK, a volunteer recently approached my officer there in Moscow and claimed that the Russian NKVD has recruited within the last six months an American official in Moscow, probably at our Military Mission, but the State Department boys over at the Embassy can't be totally excluded either."

Donovan didn't mention that the "volunteer" was a Soviet citizen as that would have raised the question about the prohibition against recruiting citizens of Allied nations. Donovan knew that Hoover didn't give a damn about such silly prohibitions, but this way he didn't put Hoover in an awkward bureaucratic spot, by actually stating the obvious."

Hoover's smile disappeared. This sounds serious. Do we have any identifying details at all on who this traitor might be?"

"Not much, I'm afraid. I'd like to suggest that you send one of your men to Moscow to do some investigating, perhaps under some innocuous sounding cover so as not to alert this mole – if there is indeed one."

"Absolutely, I'm sure we can work out a cover story to justify my special agent's presence there for a week or two, while he discreetly checks on things. I can see that we need to go gently here, so as not to put your volunteer in danger by tipping our hand to this penetration in Moscow."

Donovan was glad to hear that Hoover appreciated the danger that could come to Charles' volunteer. He suspected that Hoover didn't give a damn about the welfare of the foreigner working for the OSS, but Hoover recognized the value of getting important intelligence out of such a source, not only now, but in the future – and that required that he stay alive and in place.

"Excellent. How soon do you think you can get a man out to Moscow?"

"I'll have to check on whether we might have a Russian-speaking officer we could send, but I'm sure we can get a man on his way by the end of this week, at the latest."

"Good," replied Donovan.

"Does this volunteer of yours have any sort of track record with you on reliability? I mean, has he given you to date any other leads or information that have been verified as accurate? Anything that would allow us to precisely assess how much validity to place on this accusation of there being a mole in Moscow."

"Not much, I'm afraid. He's a fairly new asset. He's also spoken of an even bigger security problem back here in America and I'm hoping that a confirmation of a mole in Moscow would allow us to place more credence on this other reporting, which frankly is much more serious."

"That's the one that is taking place here within the United States?"

"Yes. Let me begin by asking if you are aware of a secret weapons development program called the Manhattan Project?"

"It does sound vaguely familiar, where is it located?"

Donovan wasn't sure if Hoover was just being cautious, or in fact he'd never heard of it and just didn't want to admit it. "Truth be told I'm not even officially supposed to know about it, but I spoke briefly on Saturday about it with Secretary of State Hull, who at least admitted that it does exist, but didn't want to get into details. He asked how I'd heard about it and he about turned white when I told him I'd heard about it from the Russians."

Hoover laughed. "I suspect he did."

"About all I know is that it has something to do with splitting the atom, which will make one hell of a bomb, which is why the War Department has gathered up every top notch physicist and shipped them off to Los Alamos, New Mexico to work on the project. And most importantly, according to our source the Soviet NKVD has recruited at least three Americans working on this research. The information they're stealing from our project is being given to their scientists who are also trying to build such a bomb."

"Holy, Mother of God," mumbled Hoover. "I keep telling people not to trust those God-damned Commies, but all of the lefties Roosevelt has placed within his own Administration makes it impossible to do anything about this threat."

"Yes, well the politics of this matter is another reason it will have to be handled very quietly until you've identified all of the traitors out in New Mexico."

"Does your source have any specific clues as to who these three men are?"

"He's given us a few details with which your men can get started and he's been told that finding out more details is his highest priority. I'm hoping that within a few weeks, I'll be able to give you more, but here is what we know right now." He pulled out a sealed envelope from his inner coat pocket and slid it across the desk to Hoover.

Hoover grabbed up a letter opener that once supposedly had belonged to Chicago crime boss, Al Capone and carefully slit the envelope open. He took out the one-page letter and carefully read the few details that Charles had brought from Sasha.

"Not much here, but we've solved cases starting with less than this." He pointed at the last line about how the OSS source believes that all three men were working for the NKVD for ideological purposes. "Hard to believe we have that many God-damned traitors in this country!"

"I know, but at the moment you know our policy – anybody who's fighting against the Nazis is a friend of America. Maybe they've hidden well their true political feelings, or maybe they still obtained a security clearance despite their political leanings because the Soviets are supposedly our friends."

"The Bureau has been busy with this Manhattan Project from the start, doing the background checks on all these flaky academics they've brought in to work on building this atomic bomb. We'll start by reviewing the security files on everybody working out at Los Alamos and a few other places and put a red star on the folder of everyone who's a socialist or communist."

"You've got a big task ahead of you J. Edgar and given who is the threat, you'll have to be careful about the political views of anybody you're going to bring in to work in this case."

"I'll personally hand pick every man who will be part of this special task force. Did you go in to any details with Cordell about these penetrations?"

"Not really."

"Good. So he's not expecting any updates or anything from you?"

"No."

"Until we get well in to our investigation, I don't intend to tell anybody at the State Department anything. And the same goes for the White House. The President is the worst gossip in all of Washington. You'd be appalled at the secret information he shares with various journalists!"

"Keeping anything a secret in this town is a miracle," replied Donovan with a chuckle.

"Back to the Moscow problem for a moment. You do have a man out there in Moscow now, don't you Bill? Do you want him brought in to work with my agent while he's there?"

"I do have an officer in Moscow, but I think it'd be best to leave this investigative work solely to your man. In fact, it's probably best if the two of them had no direct contact at all, unless something comes up where your agent needs some backup assistance."

Hoover was loving what he was hearing, to the point that he was almost getting suspicious as to why Donovan was being so considerate of what was FBI jurisdiction. Still, he smiled and promised to keep him informed of how soon his agent would be headed for Moscow.

Donovan stood. "Well, I know you have lots of work to do, so I'll get out of here and leave you to it."

"Thanks for personally stopping by to bring this to my attention. Always glad to work with the OSS."

"Same here," replied Donovan with his own feigned sincerity.

Everybody lies.

Donovan told his driver to take him back to his office. He'd confirmed that there was indeed a sensitive program called the Manhattan Project and he'd set a few wheels in motion. There was little else for him to do until Tuesday morning, when he'd go brief Secretary of War Henry Stimson on this threat. The War Department would obviously be in charge of this secret program, so he might as well start at the top with Stimson. As he rode along, he thought about how ironic it was that when Stimson had become the Secretary of State in 1929, one of his first acts was to shut down the secret American code breaking operation called the "Black Room." Donovan recalled his famous phrase about how "gentlemen don't read other gentlemen's mail." He suspected that since becoming the Secretary of War in 1940, Stimson had regretted several times that 1929 act of naiveté!

Back at his office, Donovan learned that unfortunately, Secretary Stimson was out on the West Coast until the following week. His secretary then tried getting him an appointment with Admiral Leahy, head of the Chiefs of Staff, but he was also traveling until Thursday, so the best she could do was an appointment for the coming Friday morning.

Charles arrived promptly on time Monday evening and Donovan's secretary was ushering him directly into the General's office, when Duncan Lee came into the outer office to drop off a report Donovan had requested. He just briefly saw Worthington, but Lee remembered him from a meeting they'd had in Lisbon, and had seen him around the building a few times before Charles had departed for Moscow. He didn't think Worthington had seen him, as his focus was ahead on Donovan. He was curious as to why Charles was back from Moscow after only a few months, nor had he seen any mention on the General's daily calendar of him. He lingered around for a few seconds after putting the report in Donovan's in-box, until the secretary came back to her desk.

In a casual manner he said, "Say, wasn't that Captain Worthington? I didn't know he was back from Moscow."

"Yes, it was. I believe he's just making a brief courtesy call on the Director, while he's passing through town. Thank you for the report, Mr. Lee." She then sat down and turned her eyes to her desk, letting him know he was no longer needed. She'd worked for Donovan for many years and knew when some junior official was being nosey – a habit of Lee's that she'd noticed on many occasions around the front office.

Donovan was in a much friendlier mood towards Worthington than he'd been at their first meeting, two days earlier. He was smiling.

"Take a seat Charles, and I'll bring you up to date on what I've learned in the last forty-eight hours." He then summarized his encounters with Secretary of State Hull and subsequently with Alger Hiss.

"So, there is in fact a secret program called Manhattan Project, but we still don't know much about it," observed Charles.

"Correct, and from the way the two of them acted when I even mentioned that name, I can tell you this isn't just any old 'secret program', of which there are many around Washington. I'd hoped to see Secretary of War Stimson in the next day or two, but he's traveling until next week. I do have an appointment on Friday with Admiral Leahy, who heads the Chiefs of Staff. I'll put this question before him. Surely, he's on the approved list and will be more forthcoming with me than those two State Department characters!

"But at least we now know that Sasha didn't just make up some name out of his imagination. There is in fact some special weapons development program underway here in America."

"Correct, though we still can't positively conclude as to whether there really are three penetrations of it, or as we discussed on Saturday, is this a clever Soviet ploy to disrupt this program."

Charles simply shrugged his shoulders, to indicate he had nothing new to say about that question.

"I'm as ignorant as you are about what an esoteric physics topic concerning 'splitting the atom' could have to do with a potential new weapon, so I had my personal secretary call around the country today to several individuals who are supposedly our leading physicists. I thought I'd just ask one of them what happens if you split an atom.

Charles was intrigued, "And what did anyone have to say?"

Donovan picked up a sheet from his desk. "She phoned the home and office numbers for: Robert Oppenheimer – not at his home nor office.

Enrico Fermi – not at his home nor office

Leo Szilard – not at his home nor office

Hans Bethe – not at his home nor office.

Nor did anybody admit to having any idea where they might be reached or when they would be back home."

"Quite a coincidence, that all these top physicists are out of town at the same time," remarked Charles."

"Well, I don't believe in coincidences. So, I personally called over to the Central Switchboard at the Pentagon and asked for the Base Commander's number for whatever fort we have at Los Alamos, New Mexico and guess what? The head operator informed me that there is no US Government facility for any branch of the service or any civilian entity listed as being in Los Alamos!"

Charles let out a small laugh – "Must be a hell of a project, at which no one works and there isn't even a building!"

"Oh, you'll be happy to know that Albert Einstein's housekeeper admitted that at least he is there at Princeton, but he taught this afternoon and she said that he then likes to ride his bicycle around campus while he thinks, so she couldn't say when he'd be home and might possibly give me a return call."

"Well, at least we know in what town he is!" Changing subjects, Charles inquired about how the planned visit to FBI Director Hoover had gone, in regard to Sasha's allegation that there was an NKVD asset within the Military Mission in Moscow? "Did you get any joy out of Mr. Hoover?"

"Yes, that went quite well. He took the allegation seriously and is going to send a man out there by the end of this week, under some sort of cover, to 'discreetly' do some investigating. He'll make no direct contact with you, unless he has some sort of emergency need for assistance. I made it clear to him that this was clearly an FBI matter, so he was in a very cooperative mood. We'll see what his man turns up."

Charles was a little skeptical about anyone from the FBI doing anything discreetly, given his limited experience with them, but he kept that opinion to himself and returned to the subject of the penetrations of the Manhattan Project.

"I just want to mention again, sir, that according to Sasha, the Russian word that the NKVD uses in the files for these three, refers to them as people assisting the Soviet Union out of political beliefs, not doing it for money or because they're being blackmailed. They truly believe in socialism or communism. Though having seen 'communism' first hand in Moscow these past few months, I don't know how anybody can believe that crap."

"Yes, well this whole communism thing, not to mention the Americans who believe in it, is a problem that our nation is going to have to face up to and deal with once this war with Germany and Japan is over."

"So, what should I do next? How do you want me to handle Sasha, and what about his demands, particularly the one about moving to America before the war ends?"

"I imagine the legal guys will have to be brought in to tell us how to do this according to the book, but we'll make his entry into America happen one way or the other – even if it's just flying his ass into some remote airfield. That's assuming that what he's been telling us is reasonably accurate. So, go ahead and tell him we'll bring him to America. After several years of war, nobody knows who's legally in America anyway. And tell him we'll give him a generous one-time payment to get him started in his new life, especially if he helps us find any of these moles within this secret project. Has he given any indication of what kind of money he might be expecting?"

"I've been using the figure of $10,000 as a likely amount and he seemed happy with that – not that I think he has any clue as to how much that is or isn't."

"I take it he speaks English reasonably well?"

"Quite well, sir. He has an accent, but he understands well and can speak well enough to be understood, so language won't be an issue upon his arrival."

"Alright, between you and me, if any of this pans out, we'll give him what he's asking for, but that is totally dependent on any of his allegations turning out to be true. And for God's sake, tell him to never mention again that he once worked for the German Abwehr! You can imagine how some Congressional Committee would love to grill me someday about us working with a former Nazi spy, much less bringing him in to the United States!"

"I've already discussed that with him. Just one more outstanding issue, sir, how can I keep you updated on what's happening and send you information given me by Sasha, since I don't know if I can trust the Military Mission's comms?"

"I've been thinking about that this afternoon. Given the possibility of there being an NKVD mole within our Mission out there, I agree that we can't trust using the normal Army communication system there at the Mission." He handed over to Charles a leather bound book, about the size of a small, personal bible, but which was in fact a codebook. You will use this One-Time-Pad system to double-encrypt messages to me, or to read anything received from me. You remember from your training how to use one of these?"

"Yes, sir, I do. It will raise a few eyebrows in the Communications Section, but nobody knows exactly what I do out there anyway."

"Well, if anybody questions you about it, up to and including General Deane, you tell them to feel free to contact me directly if they have a problem."

"Anything else, sir?"

"Not that I can think of at the moment, except to state the obvious – press your agent as hard as you can to come up with more identifying data on these three traitors."

"I will."

"Will you be ready to take off as soon as Wednesday morning?"

"Yes, sir, what little personal and shopping business I had to do is completed."

"Good. I'll have my secretary get on to making you travel orders right away, hopefully, with a departure date of say Wednesday?"

"Wednesday will be fine."

"What are you planning on telling colleagues back in Moscow was the purpose of your trip? We obviously don't want them to think there is anything special going on in Moscow that involves the OSS."

"Before I left, I suggested that my trip home might have something to do with an operation I was involved with when I was in Lisbon. I think I'll stick with that explanation."

"Sounds good." Donovan stood up and came around to Charles. He gave him a firm handshake and said, "You're performing a hell of a service for your country, Charles." He smiled. "You may have to go to prison for some of the things you've been doing, but you'll always have my thanks."

"Will you come visit me in prison on Saturdays?" joked Charles.

"Every weekend, son. Have a safe journey back to Moscow and be extra careful once there. If this thing is as important as it sounds, the NKVD won't be obeying any niceties of diplomatic protocol!"

And then Charles was out the door

Donovan lighted another cigarette and sat there staring at the door for several minutes. He was very proud of young men like Charles. He thought to himself that it was easy for old men like himself to sit around in the comfort of nice offices in Washington and plan this or that clever operation. But it was the young men and women who went overseas, generally working alone, who were to be praised. Whether in a Burmese jungle, in Occupied France, or out in the snow of Moscow, they were the ones getting the job done, in secret. The American people would never even know their names, much less what they'd done for them, but they should be grateful!

Two days after Alger Hiss had met with General Donovan, Hiss was sitting on a park bench just before 11:00 pm, in a small park in upper Georgetown. A woman approached him and sat down at the other end of the bench. Without saying a word to her, Hiss simply rose and walked off into the night, leaving his folded newspaper on the bench. After a few minutes, the woman moved over to the paper and picked it up. She carefully placed it in her large purse, making sure that the envelope inside the paper remained in place.

Elizabeth took the first train the following morning up to New York City and in a similar maneuver in Central Park that afternoon, she passed it along to an NKVD officer, working undercover at the Soviet Consulate in that city as an administrative clerk. Within another twenty-hours, Hiss' report had been translated, encoded and transmitted by HF radio signal to Moscow. His report raised quite a stir when presented to the NKVD colonel in charge of the American Desk.

CHAPTER 14

Seven days after his last meeting with General Donovan, Worthington was back in the land of perpetual winter. He'd traveled back to Moscow on a priority basis, which again raised a few eyebrows at the US Military Mission Moscow as to why he was accorded such special treatment, but Charles was happy to have been spared a lengthy ship voyage to reach Archangel! When questioned by several colleagues about such VIP travel treatment, Charles smiled and hinted that having had "dinner" with the young lady in Donovan's outer office who arranged travel orders, she was just doing him a favor. He left the rest to their imagination.

The first day after his return, he spent mostly sleeping. He'd flown all the way, but he'd barely slept on the journey for more than two-three hours at a stretch. On the second day after his return, he phoned Captain Nosenko at the NKVD and arranged for a meeting with Colonel Suvarov for Friday morning at 1000 hours, so as to restart their weekly liaison meetings. He hated attending these pointless meetings, but he had to maintain the pretense that that was the only reason he was in Moscow. Shortly after speaking with Nosenko, he phoned the British Embassy and asked to speak with Miss Summerfield.

After several minutes wait, she came on the line. Charles always wondered in what far off corner of their Embassy she worked, as it always took a long time for the operator to find her.

"Jane Summerfield, here," said that lovely, British accent that Charles had been missing.

"I told you that they'd send me back."

"Oh, Charles, how nice to hear your voice! When did you get back to Moscow?" There was so much more that she wanted to say to him, but knowing that the NKVD was certainly monitoring the public phone line in to the British Embassy caused one to be rather reticent.

"I think it was yesterday, but my body clock is so screwed up, I'm not even sure what day this is, much less when I arrived. Have I missed anything special while I was away?"

"No, not much. Oh, it snowed once while you were gone," she teased.

"Snow, amazing! Say, I believe I was promised a home-cooked meal when I returned. Is that offer still good?"

"Absolutely. I've been practicing while you've been away and our doctor says that both of my recent dinner guests will likely survive."

Charles laughed. So, when do you want me to come over?"

"How about tomorrow night, say 1900 hours. You remember my address don't you?"

"Indeed, I do. I'll see you tomorrow night."

He'd had lots of time to think about her on the long journey back, not that he'd come to any real conclusion. He loved her company, but was there something more he'd like to see develop? Of course, there was the minor little detail of her still being married, if only on paper. What kind of a bum steals another soldier's wife while he's possibly sitting in some POW camp? Likely, he was dead, but "likely" and knowing he was dead were two different things. Well, he'd see how things went with her the following night. Aside from her lovely face and soft voice, he also enjoyed her sense of humor and the intelligent conversations they had on a variety of topics. She may never have gone to university, but she'd clearly read a great deal and had an inquisitive mind. God, he humorously thought to himself, did the fact he admired her mind as much as her body mean that he was actually becoming more mature!

Several of his colleagues drifted into his office throughout the morning, once word had spread that he'd returned. Most just said hello and welcomed him back, but several were naturally curious as to why he'd flown all that distance, for barely a week's stay. Among the more curious ones were Bobby Penkovsky and Barry Singell. Charles just tried joking them off by saying that President Roosevelt had wanted to consult personally with him on how things were going on the Russian Front. Penkovsky had remained the more persistent of the two.

"Hey, did you hear anything back home about the US sending troops up through the Black Sea to start an offensive down in the Balkans?"

"No, I didn't hear anything about a new offensive anywhere, to be honest. Where'd you hear about a Balkan campaign?"

Oh, just guys in the mess hall one day at lunch talking with a couple of the pilots that ferry between here and Archangel. That's kind of down in the area where I got distant relatives – that's why I was asking."

"No, I didn't get any decent rumors on much of anything. Calling me back was, as I'd suspected, connected to a couple of things I'd been involved with before I left Portugal."

"Oh, well, good to have you back. I'll probably see you at dinner tonight."

"Yeah, see you at dinner."

After Bobby left, Charles made a mental note to himself about how he'd been pretty curious as to the purpose of his trip to Washington. Maybe it was just natural curiosity on something that might affect his distant relatives, or maybe he was the mole and had been tasked with finding out why Charles had made such a speedy trip to Washington. And in that same regard, why had Singell been so curious about the same thing?

By lunch time, Charles was again barely able to stay awake, so he cleaned off his desk and decided that soon as he ate lunch, he was going back to bed. As he entered the grounds of Spasso House, he saw the back of Viktor just doing down the stairs to the basement warming room. Charles went up to his room and grabbed the two books he'd brought for the old man and headed down to see him, before going to lunch.

Viktor heard the door open and saw Charles entering the small room. A big smile came to his face. "So, they sent you back to us for some more chess lessons!"

"Yes, I was told I couldn't return PCS to America until I'd finally beaten you at a game." They both laughed and they shook hands. "And by the way, President Roosevelt asked me to pass along his warm regards to you."

Viktor noticed the books in Charles' left hand. "What do you have there?" he asked as he pointed at Charles' hand.

Charles laid the two books on the table in front of Viktor. "A little something for you, my friend."

Viktor looked at the two titles and read them aloud: "*The Great Gatsby* by F. Scott Fitzgerald and *The Adventures of Huckleberry Finn* by Mark Twain. I've never heard of these. Are they good?"

"Well, my American Literature professor at Harvard made us read them, so I guess they're considered good, or maybe he gets a percentage of the sales of these two books." Charles had kept a straight-face while saying that, but Viktor had become accustomed to his dry sense of humor and he smiled. "I think you'll enjoy them. They're both about the problems and challenges that face people."

A look of delight came to Viktor's face. "I shall begin one of them this very night. Thank you very much for your thoughtful gift. How was your visit back to Washington?"

"Typical Army nonsense – just some questions about activities that I'd been involved with at my last assignment in Portugal. Things we could have handled by telegrams, but I appreciated the trip home." Charles gave Viktor a wink of the eye, indicating that that was something he could pass along to his NKVD handler to keep him happy.

Viktor gave a knowing smile in return. "I hope you at least got to visit some old friends while you were home."

"I did. I had half a day's layover in New York City and had a lovely Italian meal with two old pals."

Charles saw that Viktor didn't know the word, "pals." "The word pals means friends or old buddies."

"Ah, I see. Well, when shall we have our next chess game?"

Charles laughed. "Give me a couple of days to get my brain back on Moscow time, so I'll have a fighting chance against you. Perhaps Monday at the end of the day."

"Excellent. I look forward to it."

On Friday morning, Charles arrived at NKVD Headquarters promptly on time and Captain Nosenko was waiting for him as usual at the main entrance. They saved discussion of his trip to America until they were with Colonel Suvarov, so Charles wouldn't have to repeat the same answers for him.

"Charles, how are you?" said Suvarov in English, as Charles entered his office. Nosenko had obviously taught his boss this one phrase to impress Charles. Suvarov gave him a big bear hug, before pointing his

American partner to a chair. The Russian seemed genuinely glad to see he had returned. This was a little puzzling as he'd previously shown little excitement when Charles showed up at any of their previous meetings.

Charles took out of his leather satchel a bottle of Jack Daniels Tennessee Whiskey and presented it to the Colonel. "A little gift from America. They've had to recently stop producing this product because of the war, but there are still a few bottles around if you have the right friends." Nosenko translated and Suvarov smiled and nodded in agreement – he understood well the concept of acquiring hard to find items if you had the right friends. Charles didn't bother telling him that the Cosmos Club had cases and cases of the stuff down in its cellar and that Astor had convinced the manager to share an unopened bottle with Charles, so as "to help the war effort."

Instead of trying to explain the difference between Scottish whiskey and American whiskey, Charles just told him to enjoy it on some special occasion. He suspected that the bottle would probably wind up on the desk of some general at the NKVD. With hindsight, Charles realized he probably should have brought two bottles. That way, Suvarov could have tasted one and given the other one as a gift up the chain of command.

They spent the next twenty minutes discussing Charles' trip and drinking tea. Having to work through a translator, doubled the time needed to exchange the same amount of sentences if both weren't speaking the same language, so it was really only a ten minute conversation. He repeated once again his "story" of how his Headquarters had only wanted to discuss with him some details about his activities back when he'd been in Portugal. He did claim, almost truthfully, that he'd also met with General Donovan while in Washington, who'd expressed his pleasure at how the liaison relationship was developing.

Charles smiled. Suvarov smiled. They both understood that that was just the usual, protocol bullshit that was demanded in such situations.

Everybody lies.

Purely by luck, a packet of exchange material had arrived from Washington while Charles was away that was actually of interest to the NKVD. OSS Headquarters had sent him the schematics for a very small, seven-shot revolver that could easily be hidden on the body, or in a package. The Smith and Wesson Company had developed it especially for the OSS and OSS officers going into war zones had been issued the revolver for the last six months. Charles could tell that the two Russians were excited about it as they spent several minutes talking in Russian and pointing at various parts of the drawing, before coming back to him.

"This is excellent," Nosenko translated for his boss. "I shall have a few very good reports for you early next week."

"Excellent. I look forward to meeting with you next week"

In just a few more minutes, Charles was out the door and being escorted back to his car by Nosenko. Charles felt he'd done the necessary to keep up the pretensc that his only purpose for being in Moscow was to maintain this liaison exchange.

Charles arrived at Jane's small apartment at 1900 hours with a bottle of French white wine in hand, which he'd bought off Sergeant Kowalski. Charles was smart enough never to ask where the clever Kowalski acquired such items! He also had in his pocket his gift from America for Jane. As she opened the door, a wonderful smell drifted to his nostrils, and his eyes were treated to the sight of Jane in a lovely green dress, a matching scarf around her neck and her hair all perfectly coiffed. She'd obviously left work early that day to not only cook, but to properly prepare herself for his arrival.

She gave him a big hug and greeted him warmly.

"There's some color in your cheeks. Don't tell me you actually have sunshine in America in April!" she teased.

"Well, it is rationed like most everything else, but I was entitled to an extra portion, since I'd clearly not had any in several months."

"So, tell me everything. Did you manage to meet up with any old friends?"

"Yes, as a matter of fact, I did. As I passed through New York City on the way to Washington, I had time to have an excellent lunch with two old pals down in the district called Little Italy."

"And I presume you had Italian food?"

"Yes, and down in Washington, I had a very nice dinner one night with my old boss, where I had a giant steak that actually came from a genuine cow." They both laughed.

He presented her with the bottle of French white wine.

"My goodness! Where did you come up with a bottle of French wine?"

"A sergeant I know procured it. I suspect the fewer questions asked about how, the better."

She laughed and gave that wonderful smile of hers. "Ah, we have a sergeant like that at our Embassy. I suspect all armies have such talented men in them, who can make all sorts of hard to find items appear like magic."

"I think you're right. And speaking of which, would you like your present from America now or later?"

"Hmmm, now I think, otherwise I'll just be thinking about it until it appears and I might burn our dinner."

"OK, close your eyes for a moment."

She did as instructed and Charles pulled from his pocket the pair of silk stockings he'd brought her. He'd consulted with Salvatore and Lou as to what a lady might want from America and their instant answer was silk stockings, given how they'd almost disappeared since the war had started. Salvatore naturally knew a guy who knew a guy who had some for sale – even in wartime!

He held them up in front of her. "You may now open your eyes."

She did and nearly shrieked when she saw what was before her and took hold of them and felt that they were genuine silk. "Where on earth did you find these?"

"I know a guy in New York named Salvatore and I'll match his skills with any Army sergeant in the world, for coming up with hard to find items. I hope they're the right size. I had to guess on that point, not having any... well, I just guessed." Charles actually blushed on this subject of no familiarity with her legs.

"I'll be right back." She dashed off to her bedroom and returned a few minutes later, modeling her new stockings. "They're perfect!" She lifted the hem of her skirt to a height to give him a good view, that no doubt her mother would have thought scandalous. She came over to him and gave him another hug and gave him a kiss squarely on the lips. There was then a moment of awkward silence. "Well, I better get back to my stove before I burn our dinner."

"We wouldn't want that to happen."

"Oh, I can't even remember the last time I had on a proper pair of stockings," she gushed as she stirred some onions in the hot skillet.

She'd prepared a dish with chicken, which had no special name other than "my mother's recipe chicken." The accompanying peas and carrots were out of cans, but to Charles, they tasted wonderful. Maybe it was the candlelight that improved the taste of canned vegetables. Amazing also how your dinner companion affected your taste buds.

"Tell me more about New York. I don't suppose you paid any attention to whether hem lines are going up or down this year?"

"No, as a matter of fact I didn't. Sorry."

"Never mind." As she stood to go get dessert, she again lifted her skirt quite high so as to show off her new stockings, and her entire legs. "And just how did you get the perfect size for my legs?" she teased.

"Well, that's a military secret."

Over the course of their dinner, he told her all about his trip, at least anything that he didn't mind if the NKVD heard or not. Both of them suspected that there might be a few microphones about her apartment. The topic of how the war seemed to be going led naturally to the question of what both of them might do after the war, once they'd returned to civilian life.

"I suppose that I'll have to finally face up to the fact that my husband is dead and get on with my life as a single woman." That was the first time she'd openly acknowledged that he was most likely dead. She really had no idea as to what she would do for a living as a civilian.

Then it was his turn. "I'll probably go back to work as a lawyer, though doing exactly what I can't say. I'll just see what happens when I get back home and I'm in civilian clothes again. And as for romance… since we're being very honest with ourselves tonight, I doubt there's any chance of me and the young lady I've mentioned in the past ever seeing each other again. So, I guess I'll have to get on with my life in that regard as well."

There was a long silence at that point as they stared at each other. Charles reached across the small table and squeezed her hand.

"Getting out of Moscow will be great," added Charles, "but I'll certainly miss our times together."

"Yes, that will be the only negative aspect of leaving here. Of course, eventually this horrible war will come to an end. But perhaps your renewed law work will bring you over to England one day on business, and I can show you around my home village. It really is lovely in spring and summertime."

Another awkward moment of silence. "Absolutely, I'll have to come over and have a proper look round. All I've seen so far are a couple of your English airports."

Neither of them was willing to say out loud what they were both clearly thinking about – was there to be any sort of "them" after Moscow?

They moved to her one small couch for coffee after dinner. She put on a few old records from before the war. She finally wound up snuggled against him, his arm around her shoulder. It was the first time in a long while that she'd felt so safe and protected. Charles was starting to feel rather sleepy and checked his watch and saw that it was almost midnight. It was the most pleasant five hours he'd enjoyed in a long time.

She turned enough so she could whisper in to his ear and thus not worry about any microphones in her flat. "The reason it always takes you so long to get me to the telephone at the Embassy is because I work in the code room and they have to come get me out of the vault."

He whispered back, "I see."

"I tell you that because I want you to know I do know how to keep a secret."

He nodded, not understanding quite where she was headed in her conversation.

"Charles, I don't believe that the OSS flew you 5,000 miles just to review old files with you. Is there some special operation going on here that involves you?"

Charles had lied to so many people throughout his life and especially since joining the OSS, that he easily and smoothly lied to her, "Of course not. Why do you ask?"

"It's just that I'm afraid. I've already lost one man I loved and I don't want to lose another person who's becoming very special to me. You're not involved in any operation that could cost you your life are you?"

"There's nothing going on. I swear to you." He pulled her close to him, her head upon his chest. She liked that. She felt safe and soon they were both asleep.

About a half hour later, he awoke and gently nudged her. "I suspect I better be getting back home. I wouldn't want the Russian Army guards at Spasso House to become worried about me, staying out so late."

They were standing, with their arms around each other. "It's been a grand evening," she said in almost a whisper.

"It has," was his response and then leaned forward and gave her a long, passionate kiss. As they finally broke apart, he asked, "So, are you going to wear your new stockings and show them off at your Embassy on Monday?"

"Are you joking? Never. These will be saved just for very special occasions – with you!" She gave him one of her million-dollar smiles, and lifted her skirt up one last time before he departed to show him again how good they looked on her legs. "How do I compare to your Betty Grable?" she teased. "I read that the American G.I.'s voted her as having the best legs in the world."

"That's just because all those guys haven't seen yours!" He kissed her once more and then he was out the door.

He was smiling during the initial part of the drive back to Spasso House, but then he started seriously analyzing his situation with Jane. First, Olga hadn't truly, totally disappeared from his mind and secondly, he didn't want to be hurt so badly again. He was very fond of Jane and she appeared to feel the same about him, but he knew that wartime stresses, especially in tough places like Moscow, sometimes made people desperate for someone to love – a feeling that maybe wouldn't be there once the setting was no longer the same. Also, his focus had to be at the moment totally on the Sasha operation, not on Jane. He had to keep Sasha safe to get his intelligence, but most importantly, this operation was to be his ticket back in to the good graces of General Donovan and a successful career. And related to his operation, he wondered why she had asked him whether he was working on something secret in Moscow. Her explanation that she was worried about losing him made sense, but her query made him feel uncomfortable. God, he thought to himself, he was getting paranoid if he was going to consider even Jane as working for the NKVD!

After Charles left, she poured herself the last of the wine and sat thinking on her couch about her predicament. She'd told Charles the same lie about her background as she'd told everyone in Moscow. Since he was clearly from a family with money and breeding, a Harvard graduate and a lawyer, she'd stuck with that lovely story of being from rural East Anglia. Had told him how her dad was a school teacher and about the lovely garden in the back of their house. It hadn't mattered at first, but now that she was falling in love with him, should she tell him the truth or just stick with her lie? He doubted he'd be too impressed that her father had been a dock hand at the small river port of Ipswich and had died one night while drunk and had fallen in to the water. Or that her mom had been a bar maid in a rundown seamen's pub for many years. Her claimed singing lessons had been when her mom had put her up on a table in the pub as a little girl and she'd sing sea shanties for the sailors and dock hands – and they'd throw her a few coins. Her mom's large victory garden behind their house was in fact one small window box of flowers outside the kitchen window to their one bedroom flat on the second floor of a cheap apartment building in a seedy part of town. She had been quite fond of the man she'd married, but she'd only known him for a month before the nuptials and she'd married him just in hopes of getting out of Ipswich. Then three weeks later he got shipped off to the Middle East and had never once written her. She did hope that he was in fact still alive, but she rather doubted it. Look in an encyclopedia for the term "foolish wartime wedding" and it would say, see entry for Jane and Nigel Summerfield. God, what a mess she'd gotten herself in to with Charles. She'd have to eventually tell him, but maybe later would be better.

Everybody lies.

Charles had decided he'd wait a full week after his return before phoning Sasha to suggest a chess evening. He didn't want to give the NKVD even the slightest impression that he was in any hurry to see Sasha after his visit back to Washington. The leadership of the NKVD, however, was in a hurry in regard to Charles and the possibility of there being a mole in their service. NKVD Chairman Lavrenti Beria himself chaired a meeting on Tuesday morning to discuss the possible compromise of their assets within the American Manhattan Project, based on the report that their asset within the US State Department had just sent them. The forty-four year old Beria had been the head of the NKVD since 1938 and was feared by everyone. He'd overseen the purges within the NKVD's own ranks in 1938-39 and had allegedly personally shot dead his predecessor, once his show trial had ended.

The nearly bald Beria, who looked more like a timid school teacher in his rimless eyeglasses than a ruthless leader of the NKVD, sat at the head of the table which had nine senior NKVD officials around it.

"This report from our agent in Washington is most disturbing." As he began to speak, his eyes shifted around the table to his various deputies and particularly to the head of the department in charge of the spy effort against the super-secret American atomic bomb program. "The fact that the head of the American military's spy organization, the OSS, was inquiring of this program is a cause for worry. But his vaguely worded statement about how he had to advise one of his officers before that man went back overseas at least gives us a clue to pursue. It's unfortunate that our agent that Donovan spoke to was not able to get from him any particulars about this foreign source who'd told the OSS about our penetrations of their Manhattan Project. We obviously must quickly find the traitor in our ranks. General Parshenko, please give us the results of your initial investigation in to this matter."

Despite his Ukrainian-sounding name, Parshenko was the most ethnic Russian-looking person in the room. He had large bushy eyebrows, a full head of hair and the traditional high Slavic cheek bones. He had a striking face, in part because while the hair on the top of his head was still dark brown, his prominent eyebrows were almost completely white. Parshenko never smiled, which perhaps came with the job of being the head of the Counterintelligence Department of the NKVD – the man whose task was to discover any foreign spies within its ranks, or anybody not seen as being totally loyal to Comrade Stalin. Not surprisingly, no one ever wanted to sit with Parshenko for lunch in the NKVD cafeteria. Everyone was afraid of accidently saying something that Parshenko might interpret as being "disloyal."

"Unfortunately, we have little to go on at this early date." Parshenko spoke slowly and methodically, as his eyes moved slowly from each man's face to the next one around the table. "The Director of the OSS has claimed to the US State Department that 'the Russians' have penetrated the Manhattan Project, although, he pretended that he personally didn't know anything about this program. I'll come back to this point in a minute, but let's for the moment proceed on the assumption that General Donovan told the truth about having an asset somewhere who has told an OSS officer serving overseas about our efforts against their program. Donovan refused to tell our agent within the State Department anything about this source of his, not even his location, but I think we can safely assume that this source of theirs is here in the Soviet Union."

"Couldn't we have a leak at our residency in America?" asked Colonel Bakunin. He was one of the very few men at the table who dared to interrupt Parshenko, for the simple reason that he had an uncle on the ruling Politiburo, plus another uncle and his father were both generals in the Red Army.

Parshenko didn't even bother to turn his head in the direction of Bakunin to reply. He simply stared straight ahead and said, "Mikhail Petrovich, the OSS does not operate within the United States. Donovan claimed that one his officers had just informed him of this information and that the man was about to leave Washington to go back overseas. Therefore, the information must have been acquired overseas by the OSS. As I don't believe any Soviet official serving in Asia, South America, Africa or in Occupied Europe is aware of our operation against the Manhattan Project, I think the conclusion that the leak is here within the Soviet Union is the correct one. It's possible that the leak is from one of our scientists out in Central Asia at our research facility, but most likely the leak is right here in Moscow."

Beria interjected himself back into the discussion to prevent any further exchange between Parkshenko and Bakunin. "Any other points, Nikolai Nikolaiovich?

"There is the question of what to make of OSS officer Charles Worthington's sudden trip from Moscow back to Washington just before General Donovan started his inquiries about the Manhattan Project. For those of you not aware of this, the OSS sent a man to Moscow in early January to open a liaison channel between us and this American organization. My understanding is that he generally meets once a week with Colonel Suvarov and while nothing of great value has been exchanged, Worthington has fulfilled his part of the agreement. Our occasional surveillance on him has reported no suspicious behavior by him and reporting from our various informants who have had contact with him also have not reported anything unusual about his behavior. Our penetration of the US Military Mission, a man who has regular interactions with him every week, also has reported nothing inconsistent with his official liaison duties. According to that source, Worthington has claimed that his trip back to Washington was in connection with some operation or operations that he had been involved with at his last posting, in Portugal. Our recruited source on Donovan's staff has reported that he saw Worthington going in to Donovan's office early on a Saturday morning, back on the seventeenth of the month. He has not been able to learn any explanation for the purpose of Worthington's trip back to Washington. That is the summary of the facts as we know them."

"Thank you for your excellent report, Comrade Parshenko. Now, gentlemen, allegedly you are among the best and brightest officers we have within the NKVD – so what are some ideas on how we should proceed?"

Bakunin was the first to speak. "Is this Worthington the only OSS man in Moscow?"

"He is the only one we officially know about, nor has our source within the Military Mission reported any indication of another such officer. That doesn't mean there isn't someone else, assigned here in a deep cover position, but we know of no other OSS officer here," replied Parshenko with a barely disguised distain for another pointless remark by Bakunin.

A timid voice from the far end of the table spoke. "I presume that we have now placed full-time coverage on this Worthington, to see what he does when not coming to our Headquarters building for meetings?"

"We have, but we have tried being very discreet in our coverage and thus on a few occasions we have lost him for short periods of time. We have to be careful. We don't want him to realize that anything has changed since his return to Moscow and that he is now being surveilled twenty-four hours a day."

"But why hasn't this American spy been covered twenty-hour hours a day all along?"

Parshenko looked agitated by the question. He replied, "Perhaps because we are at war and I only have so many men and so much gasoline, and many people to watch. And up until now, we had no reason to believe that this Captain Worthington who only knows twenty words of Russian, and seems rather lazy, posed any kind of threat. Now, that we know differently, we shall make adjustments."

Beria looked around the table and inquired if there were any more questions. That was generally understood to be his way of saying the discussion period was over. "What other steps will you be taking General?"

"Given that our work against the Manhattan Project is of the highest priority, I have compiled a list of everyone here at NKVD Headquarters who is aware of this operation. I have ordered the transfer of two hundred extra men down from Leningrad. Too many of our NKVD colleagues on this list know many of our Moscow surveillance squad members, so we must have 'new' faces to do this surveillance. As soon as the Leningrad people have arrived in the next few days, we will be instituting around the clock home telephone monitoring and physical surveillance of all thirty seven men on the access list, with the exception, of course, of you, trusted comrades. We will have to move slowly and carefully so as not to alert this traitor. We will also be conducting surreptitious entries into the apartments of all these men, looking for the usual espionage paraphernalia that they might have hidden there. For those with wives, children, etc. who are normally at home during the day, we will have to contrive reasons to get them out of their living quarters for several hours so we can do these searches."

Everyone at the table nodded in agreement to these actions and those who had been around for many years suspected that their phones also would be tapped and they would be surveilled as well, despite Parshenko's assurance to the contrary.

Beria brought the meeting to a close. "Alright, we have a plan of action and I'm sure that all of you understand that we must keep the knowledge of this investigation strictly to ourselves." They all nodded in agreement and rose to depart. Beria cynically thought to himself that with the nine men at that table, within twenty-four hours the number of "knowledgeable" people would probably have doubled – fools trying to impress someone else within the NKVD or the Red Army, or various mistresses!

Parshenko lingered behind to speak one-on-one with Beria, once all the others had left. "Do you have a minute more Lavrenti? There's something I didn't want to bring up in front of all the others."

"Of course. Is it your question of why doesn't General Donovan know about the Manhattan Project. I noticed that you never came back to that point."

Parshenko smiled. He could see why Beria had reached the high position he had; he never missed anything. "Yes, that is point one. I find it difficult to believe that the head of the US military special intelligence service, would not have been made aware of this secret weapons-development program. It's as if you had not been made aware of own secret program to develop an atomic bomb."

"That does seem a little strange."

"Second point – Donovan goes to the Secretary of State and then to our agent Hiss to ask about the program and told them that an OSS officer from abroad had just brought him this intelligence about how there were foreign agents within the Manhattan Project. He claimed that Secretary Hull had sent him to Hiss, but how do we know that for certain."

"And what would be the purpose of Donovan lying to Hiss?"

"What if the Americans are suspicious of Hiss? Donovan makes him aware of this supposedly terribly important bit of intelligence, with a strong hint that it was Worthington who'd acquired this intelligence and had just brought it to him. So, what if all of a sudden we start surveilling Worthington; a man we've rarely watched in the past? Would that not be a confirmation to the Americans that Hiss was an agent of ours? That is why our surveillance on Worthington has to be very subtle. He must not realize that suddenly we are constantly watching him."

Beria was smiling. "That would be very clever of the Americans, but how do we know which is the truth?"

"For the moment, we can't know. We'll have to proceed with our internal investigation, in case there really is a leak, but we should at least keep in mind that this is all a clever American deception simply to confirm that Hiss is our mole."

Beria had taken off his glasses and was slowly cleaning them with his handkerchief. "Do keep me closely updated on how your investigation is going."

CHAPTER 15

On the Monday of his second week back, Charles phoned Sasha at his office.

"Captain Turgenev, it's Captain Worthington. I'm back from America."

"Ah, Captain Worthington, how nice to hear from you. How was your journey?"

"It went very smoothly and I also managed to see a few old friends while back in Washington."

"Were any of those friends female, young and lovely?" teased Sasha.

"Perhaps one or two were, but now those are just pleasant memories and I've been hard at work the past week. However, now that I'm caught up, I thought we might have another evening of chess."

"That would be very nice. I would like to hear about your journey, but I myself am quite busy right now. Let me phone you back in a few days when I have a better idea of what my following week looks like."

"Certainly. Just give me a call when you have a free evening. And if you suddenly find yourself free towards the end of the work day, just give me a call and perhaps we can arrange something even on short notice.

"Very well, I'll be touch."

"Goodbye," said Charles and hung up. He didn't think he'd heard any stress in Sasha's voice, or anything peculiar in his words used, to indicate that anything was wrong. He hoped that Sasha just didn't want to appear too eager to see Charles, but again, he would just have to sit and wait.

Over the next several days, Charles thought he saw surveillance, but he didn't actually have many reasons to be out and about in his car, so it was hard to say. He never saw the same car or person twice – the usual yardstick to determining if one had surveillance, as taught at the OSS School – but he had a "feeling" several times that a vehicle was tailing him for a period. The car in question always seemed to stay the same distance back from him, regardless of whether his lane was speeding up or slowing down. And one evening when he was headed for the British Embassy to a party, a suspect car one lane over to the right, seemed to always remain in the "blind spot" of his rearview mirror – and thus Charles couldn't note its license plate number, or see who was in the car. Another "tell" he'd been taught at OSS School. He never did decide for certain if he really was getting exemplary surveillance, or his paranoia was just making him see "ghosts" that weren't really there. Given the high stakes that were on the table, he could be forgiven feeling a little paranoid. He also remembered the old joke by one of his OSS instructors, a fellow who'd previously been a New York City detective and had personal experience at following bad guys around for almost thirty years before coming to teach at the OSS: "It isn't paranoia, if there really are people following you!"

He got to see Jane for a brief period at a party at her Embassy early one evening. Unfortunately, that week was her turn for evening "administrative" duty, so there would be no chance to get together for another dinner until the following weekend.

When she came up to him at the party, she was wearing her typical, unflattering WREN uniform. Charles simply gave her a polite kiss on the cheek. They'd decided to keep their much more personal relationship a secret from their colleagues – and from the NKVD – unless there were indeed microphones in her flat, in which case the secret was already known to them. She thought it funny that she didn't mind so much the NKVD knowing about the state of her personal life regarding Charles; she just didn't want her embassy colleagues to know.

"Charles, how nice to see you. How have you been?"

"I've been very well, and you Jane?"

"Oh, keeping busy. Say, there's a rumor going around that your Ambassador has gotten hold of a copy of the movie *Casablanca* with Humphrey Bogart and Ingrid Bergman, and is having a showing at Spasso House this weekend. Is that true?"

"I believe it is. I'm pretty sure that it's to be at 1400 hours on Sunday. Would you like to come see it? I'll even buy you some popcorn."

"You take subtle hints quite well. I would love to see it. I've heard wonderful things about it ever since it came out, but I've never seen it. I'm not sure yet what my schedule is going to be on Sunday. Can I phone you Thursday morning and confirm that I'll be free on Sunday?"

"Sure, that will be fine."

"By the way, we're supposedly getting in next week a large food shipment from England. I might be able to offer you soon another home-cooked dinner, depending on what's on the plane."

"That would be delightful."

They continued chatting about mundane matters for another five minutes. Jane's desire to keep their new relationship confidential had one flaw. Anyone who happened to be watching them, could tell from their looks at one another that they were now more than just casual friends. Major Singell happened to be one person who indeed had been watching them that evening.

On Wednesday at lunch, Major Singell came to the mess table where Charles, Tom Parkington and Ted Collins were eating. After the usual greetings, Singell said, ostensibly to Ted, "Say, have you noticed that attractive WREN over at the British Embassy? I think her name is Summerfield." He gave Ted a wink. "I think Charles here knows her pretty well, don't you Charles? What's her first name?"

"Jane, I believe and yes, she is quite attractive," replied Charles.

Ted joined in on the fun. "So, you been seeing a lot of Miss Summerfield?"

Charles wasn't biting. "Only in my dreams," he responded with a smile.

"Oh, come on Charles," said Barry. "I saw you two together at the Brit party the other evening and you looked like a couple of teenagers out on your first date."

Charles looked a bit embarrassed, but then recovered and told Barry, "I think your lack of sex, being this long away from your wife, is starting to make you delusional."

"I doubt if it's a lack of sex that's making him imagine things," stated Ted.

It was then Singell's turn to look embarrassed and he quickly changed the subject. "How was General Donovan looking when you saw him back in Washington? There was an Army colonel through here while you were gone who said he'd been looking pretty tired in recent months."

Charles had hoped to avoid any discussion that he'd even seen Donovan while back in Washington, but he didn't want to get caught in a lie about even seeing him. "Oh, he'd heard I was in the building and had me stop by for a two-minute chat. My assignment here was his pet project and he just wanted to hear how it was going, so I only got a quick look at him, but he seemed the same as always to me."

"Any good rumors out of your Headquarters?" inquired Tom.

"None that I'd put any credence in," he replied and smiled.

The conversation then drifted off to when would be their next poker night.

On Thursday morning, Jane called Charles at his office and confirmed that she would be free on Sunday to come to the movie at Spasso House.

"I can come pick you up at your flat and give you a ride, if that would be convenient."

"Actually, I'll be working at the Embassy in the morning. You know, it's almost time for the monthly report. Anyway, I believe a couple of people here at the Embassy have gotten invitations as well and I'll just catch a ride over with them. But I might need a ride home afterwards."

"OK, great, I'll look for you on Sunday."

Charles went off for lunch at Spasso House with a smile on his face, having the pleasant thought in his brain of getting to see her in just three more days. He'd barely returned to his office when he received a call from Sasha.

"Hello, Captain Worthington. It's your chess instructor calling. How are you today?"

"Fine, thank you. By the way, is there a season called spring in this country?" Charles had woken up that morning to discover at least a foot of brand new snow on the ground and the temperature had fallen below zero Fahrenheit once again. He was really getting sick and tired of snow and cold!

Sasha played along. "This is spring!" They both laughed. "Listen, if you're still interested in having me 'kick your ass' on the chess board again, how about this coming Sunday afternoon at that same restaurant?"

Charles was in a panic. He'd just been heard on the Mission phone line, which was no doubt monitored, when he'd agreed to a movie date with an attractive British woman. How could he now agree instead to play chess with Sasha on Sunday afternoon? What NKVD listener would believe he was going to cancel his date with Jane and choose instead to play chess with some Russian guy?

"Unfortunately, I'm already booked for Sunday afternoon – and she's much prettier than you are!"

"Ah, I'm being thrown over for a pretty female face!" teased Sasha. He was actually upset, but hid it well. He was quite anxious to hear from Charles what had happened in Washington and hoped to find out details as to how he would be smuggled out of Russia.

"Don't suppose you'd be free on Saturday sometime?" asked Charles.

"Let me think a second. There is the monthly Communist Party meeting for my apartment block that morning at 1000 hours, but I'd be available after 1200, until 1700 hours, when I'm to meet with some friends."

"How about 1300 then, at that same restaurant as before?"

"That will be fine. I will see you on Saturday Captain Worthington."

Charles had made it 1300, so that he could have some decent food for lunch at Spasso House instead of eating any of the terrible stuff offered under the pretense of being called food at that restaurant! He also thought again about how Jane was interfering with his work life, but he had to admit he did enjoy her company.

Shortly after the phone call from Sasha, Charles decided to try his hand at using the code book Donovan had given him, to send his first "secret" message back to Donovan. He wanted to tell the General that he was going to meet Sasha that Saturday, but also wanted to tell him that he thought he'd been getting constant and very subtle surveillance since his return to Moscow. He locked his door and first wrote out in English what he wanted to say. As for the surveillance, he didn't want to get in to much speculation as to why that might be occurring, but suggested Donovan might want to review with whom he'd discussed their "special project." He figured Donovan was bright enough to draw his own, correct conclusion as to one reason that Charles had suddenly started getting surveillance – that there was an NKVD mole back there in Washington. He then began the laborious task of converting his English words in to a coded message, using his book. He made a mental note to self to keep his messages as short as possible in the future!

He wondered as he walked his strange message down to the Communications Room if anyone was going to give him shit about sending an already coded message, which no one there in the code room could read. Fortunately, the mystique of the OSS took care of everything and this unusual procedure was just written off as one of those weird things that the OSS did. Nobody seemed to care in the least that he'd already encoded his own message, which would then be encoded a second time by the Commo room. He hoped that there wouldn't be any talk around the Military Mission of his special procedure for a message. He was optimistic on that point, as generally, the guys in the Communications Room were a pretty tight-lipped bunch. Despite the pain of doing this encoding by hand, he decided to send other similar messages, once or twice a week to General Donovan, just so there'd be no correlation to his meeting with Sasha and his sending a message. In his actual text, he'd decided never to use Sasha's true name and that he'd always simply refer to him as his "special friend."

Having sent his message, arranged for an agent meeting on Saturday and a movie date with Jane on Sunday, Charles decided he'd accomplished enough for one day. He locked up and headed off to Spasso House for lunch, to be followed by a little afternoon reading and then a nap.

After a quick lunch on Saturday, Charles headed for his chess date with Sasha. He didn't make any stops along the way, or any other maneuvers to try to flush out surveillance, but still he thought he'd spotted at least one car that seemed to be following him at a distance to the restaurant. Sasha was already at the small table off in a corner and waved as Charles entered. Sasha looked tired and a bit anxious. Perhaps it was just his genuine work, or perhaps the stress of being a spy for Charles was taking its toll on him.

"It's good to see you Sasha, how have you been?"

"I'm fine. How was your journey back to Washington?"

"Uneventful, but rather long and tiring."

After they were seated, Charles pulled out of a cloth bag, two items he'd brought him as souvenirs from America. A small statue of Miss Liberty in the New York Harbor and a carton of American cigarettes. He knew that Sasha wasn't that much of a smoker, but he was certain that he could barter the packs of American cigarettes for a variety of desirable items, especially food products. They discussed Charles' trip to America in general terms, but let almost an hour go by before turning to issues related to their secret relationship. By then, they'd both spotted one gentleman who'd arrived shortly after Worthington and who never left the room. He was either the keenest chess observer in Moscow, or he was their surveillant that afternoon. The two finally decided that he was far enough away that he couldn't hear what they were actually saying. Thus, they turned to the issues of their clandestine relationship and what Worthington had learned in Washington, while outwardly continuing to focus on the chess game.

"I spoke directly with General Donovan and he asked me to pass along his personal appreciation to you for your efforts so far."

"That's nice, but when am I going to be moved to America?"

Clearly, Sasha didn't care about having his ego stroked; he just wanted to know the facts.

"It's all agreed, as I told you before I went on my trip. Nothing has changed. You said you wanted to be gone before the war ended and unless you know something I don't, that is probably still a year or two away."

"The end of the war might still be far away, but I'd hoped to travel to America while still alive."

Charles gave him an odd look, not understanding at what he was trying to say.

"I've been noticing over the past week what I'm sure is surveillance on me. But what is odd, in discussing this in a roundabout way with several of my closest friends at work, it seems that all three of us have noticed what we thought was surveillance. But not by anyone that we know from the Moscow surveillance squads."

"And what did your friends think was the cause for this surveillance?"

"No one is sure. It could be that the Counterintelligence Department is simply conducting a periodic check on a number of us and it's not necessarily tied to any particular reason."

"I hate to add your worries, but I've noticed almost from the first day back what appears to be very subtle surveillance on me. If it is surveillance, it's by a large team, as I'm never seeing a repeat of a person or a car."

Sasha kept staring down at the board as if worried greatly about his king. "Who all knows about me? I've told you about our mole in your Mission here in Moscow and our recruitments in this weapons project.

Who knows where else the NKVD has recruitments —maybe even at your Headquarters?"

The same thought had crossed Charles' mind, but he wanted to be reassuring to Sasha. "There are only two or three people besides General Donovan who know about you. And my messages from here to Donovan and back to me from him are double encrypted. That means only I hold the code book and encrypt my telegrams before I even give them to our Communications Section, who then encrypt them again, so even they can't read my messages. Same thing happens when I receive a return message from Washington, so I don't see how your service could have learned about you. Still, we should be extra cautious in the coming weeks."

"Agreed. Let's not play chess again for maybe three weeks. I went to Petrov after your call to me to see if he still wanted me in contact with you. He didn't answer right away, as he had before. He said he wanted to think about it, which meant he had to check with somebody higher up the hierarchy. He obviously got the approval, because he told me to have another meeting with you, but he told me in particular to try to find out why you really traveled to Washington."

"Hmmm, that is interesting. I'm sticking with my story that there was a particularly important operation that I'd been involved in back in Portugal and Headquarters wanted to talk to me face-to-face about it, not just exchange telegrams on the subject. But here's a little twist that you can claim you got from me today. Tell Petrov that it had something to do with how the US military will respond if the Germans send troops into Portugal to secure the wolframite mines, if the Portuguese Government suddenly decided to quit selling the stuff to the Nazis."

"What is this wolframite?"

"It's needed to make steel extra hard and Portugal is the only place in Europe where the Germans can get it. Tell them that if the Germans send in troops, the OSS has plans in place to dynamite the mines." Charles grinned. "That should make Petrov happy."

"Is there any actual truth to that story?"

"A little, but it sounds good doesn't it?"

It was Sasha's turn to smile, in part because he did like the story, but he'd also just captured Charles' queen.

"As for further contact, we'll wait three weeks for the next chess game, for which I will take the initiative to phone you with a proposal. In the meantime, I'll check to see if there will be any more social or musical events at Spasso House and try to get you put on the guest list."

"That would be good. Try to invite Petrov as well. It makes him feel important."

"Ok, now what more about the Manhattan Project have you learned? Have you gotten any more details on who are your moles at Los Alamos or how they pass the information to the NKVD in America?"

"Generally, what I see are simply reports from our moles, with technical information about their work, not messages dealing with operational matters of the cases. However, I did get one item that should help identify one mole. The fellow with the code name of "old man" that I told you about before. He did some sort of graduate study at a famous university in Germany in the 1920s. It wasn't clear if that was for his doctorate or just some sort of research there, but that ought to make it pretty easy for your people to figure out who he is."

"It should certainly help; although, I don't know how many American scientists might have studied in Germany."

"Charles, what will you Americans do when you finally figure out who the moles are? You do understand that if even one of them is suddenly arrested, there will be a severe investigation back here in Moscow to see if there has been a leak about the case. I won't be of much value to you if I'm dead!" Sasha moved his bishop. "Check," he said loudly.

"I discussed just that point with General Donovan and he told me not to worry. He would make sure that your information will be handled carefully and that there'd be no dramatic, public arrests of anyone." Charles hoped Sasha believed that story, at least more than Charles did when Donovan had said it to him. Given FBI Director Hoover's reputation for loving headlines, Charles wasn't sure how Donovan could keep Hoover in check, regardless of what it might mean for the OSS asset, or even Charles himself.

"Perhaps I should be flown to America before anyone is arrested," suggested Sasha.

We'll see. And now, any more thoughts on who might be the NKVD mole here at my Mission in Moscow?"

"Just one little hint. I was drinking again with my old colleague who'd first told me of his 'success' and he said something that made me think that the recruitment had something to do with a woman."

"What did he say?"

"Well, you wouldn't understand it, because when I had managed to ask about why any foreigner, especially an American, would agree to spy for Mother Russia, he simply replied with an old Russian proverb. It sort of says, 'the biggest danger for a man to trip over is his own dick.' I presume you understand the meaning?" Sasha smiled, then shouted out, "Checkmate!"

"I understand."

"Well, my dear friend Charles, thank you for my gifts, and by the way, your chess game is getting better. However, now I need to leave, as I need to get out yet today and do a little shopping. I don't have a nice place where they feed me three times a day like they do you at Spasso House."

Charles leaned forward and lowered his voice, "You know, before you leave here, I'm going to beat you at this game!"

Sasha smiled. "Mozhet beat, mozhet beat – maybe!"

They then shook hands and parted. On his drive back to Spasso House, Charles again spotted one suspicious car, possibly following him, but couldn't be sure. He drove in a straight route back home, so there was little chance to flush out surveillance, if it really was there. He did think that the further identifying detail on the NKVD asset in New Mexico, "Starik", ought to greatly help the FBI identify the man. He also thought again about the problem there would be of stopping the man from spying without putting Sasha in danger.

For the rest of the afternoon, he put Sasha behind him and spent it reading one of his new Dashiell Hammett books he'd brought back with him from Washington. After dinner, he found himself again thinking about Jane, and where, if anywhere, was their relationship headed.

On Sunday, Jane and three other British officers showed up at Spasso House for the showing of *Casablanca*. He was loitering around the front door and when she saw him, she immediately came over to him.

"Jane, what a pleasant surprise. I didn't know you were coming today," he teased.

"I hope my showing up isn't a problem for you. In case you already have some little Russian 'blondinka' lined up to sit with you."

"She cancelled at the last minute, so I am available to sit with you. Shall we get some popcorn and a coke on our way to our seats?"

"Absolutely, I'd love some popcorn."

The lights dimmed as the movie started, which allowed Charles to slip his hand in to hers in the dark. Charles had in fact already seen the movie a couple of times, but was happy to watch it again. He thought it an excellent movie.

When the movie ended and the lights came back up, he saw that Jane was crying. "I'm not sure you're supposed to cry at the end of this movie," commented Charles, as he offered her his handkerchief to dry her eyes.

"How could any woman not cry with that finish? Rick's just given up the woman he truly loves and will never see her again."

After the movie, the two sat on a comfortable sofa in one of the small rooms off from the main ballroom and discussed the movie.

"So, did you like it, other than the sad ending?"

"Oh, it was wonderful. It has romance, intrigue, bribery, corruption, alcohol, humor, great songs and murder – what more could you want in a movie!"

"Be serious, did you like it?" asked Charles a second time.

"Yes, I loved it, for all those things I just mentioned, but also because it poses a great philosophical question – what is most important in life? It is an individual's personal desires and happiness or are there bigger, more important issues like patriotism and the good of mankind that have to take precedence?"

"And which did Rick Blaine choose?"

She looked surprised at his question. "Well, the big picture obviously. He gives up the woman he loves and does the noble thing that is best for the war effort against the Nazis – he sends Ilsa off with Victor Laszlo."

"Maybe. Perhaps Rick really just decided that she'd dumped him once for Lazlo and maybe she'd do it again, so better to just send her off now with the guy."

She couldn't decide if Charles was kidding her or not. She knew he was rather cynical about life, but surely not that negative about women and life in general. A thought came to her. "I think you've been hurt very badly by a woman. Is it the woman you've mentioned who you said you probably wouldn't be seeing again?"

Charles hesitated for a moment and then decided to just tell her the truth, or at least most of the truth. "Yes, there was a Russian woman that I'd gotten to know in New York City before America entered the war and maybe we were falling in love at that time, but then she had to go away. She reappeared in my life in Portugal and just as we were getting our relationship going again… I mean we were in love, or at least I was, then she betrayed me and disappeared once again from my life. Why shouldn't I be cynical about life and especially about women, given what I've experienced? The world's a horrible place and I've had some other things happen to me as well that I can't go in to with you, but what I've learned is that you should look after yourself first, second and last. What Rick does in that movie is indeed terribly noble, but that's just a Hollywood movie. I don't think the real world operates that way."

She gave him a sad look. "I feel very sorry for you, that you were hurt so badly, and that you now view the world that way."

Charles didn't know what more to say. He could tell she was very upset at his view of the world, but there was no sense pretending he wasn't a realist about how the world worked. He just sat there in silence.

"I see my colleagues are getting ready to leave. I think I'll just catch a ride home with them. We'll talk in the future."

"OK. I'll be in touch." He didn't like how their conversation had ended, but he couldn't think of anything to say to her to change her mind about him. He walked her over to her three British friends, smiled and bid all of them good night. He hoped she might feel a little differently in a day or two.

On the following Monday, the FBI special agent, posing as a State Department file clerk/administrative specialist arrived in Moscow to determine whether the Embassy or Military Mission needed more safes, etc. He insisted that he had to visit Ambassador Harriman first and that he be alone with him, which was rather uncommon for a lowly administrative officer. Once they were, he told Harriman what he was really doing in Moscow. FBI Director Hoover had tried getting the travel approved by the Department of State with agreement that his man wouldn't have to even brief Ambassador Harriman in Moscow, but got told "no." The Assistant Secretary of State told Hoover he didn't care how "sensitive" the subject matter was, the TDYer would tell the Ambassador what he was really doing in Moscow or he wasn't going. So, on his first day in Moscow, undercover special agent Jimmy Commee had his meeting with Ambassador Harriman. Commee was thirty-two years old, stood six feet one inches tall and on his most recent firing range score with a .38 revolver, he'd shot a perfect score. His trip to Russia was the first time he'd been more than a hundred miles from his home town in southern Pennsylvania.

Harriman didn't understand why he'd been scheduled to meet with a visiting Administrative Officer, to be briefed on a survey of filing cabinets and safes at his embassy, but cordially welcomed the man into his office.

Once he'd shaken the Ambassador's hand, the visitor sat down and got straight to the point. "I'm actually with the FBI. The Bureau has reason to believe that one of your staff may have been recruited by the Soviets to spy for them. It may be a civilian State Department employee; it might be one of the military people over at the US Military Mission."

"And how is it that the Bureau knows this?"

"I'm not at liberty to discuss that, sir." The fact that Commee himself didn't have a clue as to where the allegation had come from didn't impact on the standard FBI response to most any question from outside the Bureau – "it's none of your business."

"Any idea on how long you will be here in Moscow?"

"I'm hoping to be done in a couple of weeks, but that depends on how well my investigation proceeds."

"I see and just how will your investigation proceed? I mean, how will you go about your task of finding this Soviet mole on my staff? I don't care to see the entire Embassy turned upside down. I understand you're here posing as an Administrative Officer doing a survey on whether we need more safes and looking at how we store classified documents. Is that correct?"

"Yes, sir, that is correct and I will be as discreet as possible as I do my work. Usually, if someone has been recruited by a foreign country, there are telltale signs of this that can be spotted just through casual conversation with the person and chatting with their colleagues."

"Interesting, and just what are a few of those telltale signs you just mentioned?"

"I'm not at liberty to discuss those, sir."

"But I take it that you've had a good bit of experience with these sorts of espionage cases?"

"I'm not at liberty to discuss my background, sir. If you have any particular questions about me or my work here, I suggest you put them in writing back to Washington and a person of the appropriate rank at the State Department can raise them with Director Hoover."

Harriman could see he was wasting his time trying to have an intelligent conversation with the young man and simply reminded him one more time that he didn't want everyone upset thinking some witch hunt was underway. "Everyone here is under enough stress from the work and the living conditions, without being made to feel we suspect them of disloyalty as well. So, do please go about your investigation with tact, Mr. Commee."

"Yes, sir, certainly."

After the FBI man had left his office, the Ambassador shook his head in amazement. Not that he'd dealt with that many FBI agents, but they all had that same arrogant, superior attitude, just like their boss.

The fact that Mr. Commee, a lowly Admin man from Washington, merited a private meeting with the Ambassador raised a few eyebrows and started a couple of rumors on his very first day. It being wartime and after being around Russians who saw conspiracies in everything, stories ranged across the spectrum. One was that "obviously the man had personally brought some news that was so sensitive that it couldn't even be put in a classified telegram, possibly about a Second Front about to launch." Worthington's favorite was that "the man was actually an MGM screen writer from Hollywood, in Moscow undercover, so as to get atmospherics in order to write a screenplay about life at an important embassy abroad." This story was tied in to Sam Spewack's background in the New York theater world.

On his second day in Moscow, Commee came to Worthington's office in order to ask him directly about Charles' colleagues and if he had any suspicions about any of them in particular. He was a tall, athletic-looking man, who immediately struck Charles as a man who would be useful if you needed a door broken down.

After closing the door behind him, he came over to Worthington to shake his hand and in a barely audible voice stated, "I understand you're the OSS man here and I believe you know why I'm really in Moscow Captain Worthington. Mr. Hoover wants you to know he really appreciates the fine work you're doing here in Russia. I was told that you'd be available to assist me if I needed anything while I'm here conducting my investigation."

"Yes, I was informed that you were coming." Charles found the phrasing interesting – that he was there to assist Commee.

Charles must have had an odd look on his face, for the next question to him was, "You are aware of the allegation that some American here is a traitor?"

"Yes, vaguely." Clearly, Commee hadn't been made aware of the background to the case – like the fact that the "allegation" had come from an asset of Charles'.

"I can't go in to the background of my investigation, but let me get straight to my work here. Any of your colleagues seem to have a gambling problem, maybe are out playing around with Russian prostitutes, or are out and out Communists?"

There was that phrase again, "my investigation." Given the poor impression the man had made on Worthington in the first two minutes, he decided to just keep his views about any of his colleagues to himself.

"No, nothing special about anybody comes to mind. Just a bunch of soldiers trying to do their jobs in a tough situation. We do have an in-house poker game every couple of weeks, in which I myself play, but nobody ever wins or loses more than twenty or twenty-five bucks."

Commee looked a little disappointed that Charles didn't have any suspects for him to zero right in on, but no matter, Commee knew he'd get to the bottom of the problem quick enough, just by conversing with the staff in the days ahead. He'd been a success at his previous job at the Philadelphia Field Office, ferreting out Commies among Union organizers, and he'd soon have a suspect in custody here in Moscow – or at least have managed to slander someone's reputation without any evidence.

"Well, thank you for your time Captain Worthington. I was told back in Washington that there was no need for us to be in regular contact while

I'm here, so I doubt if we'll have any further contact. But if you do think of anything that I ought to know, do feel free to contact me."

Charles just shook his head in amazement as the man left his office. In the coming days, the FBI man made little effort at living his cover story of being there to check on secure records storage needs and simply bluntly started "chatting up" everyone on the staff he encountered at meals or around the Mission as to who was drinking a lot, sleeping with Russian girls or saying negative things about America. By the end of his fifth day, everybody was talking about how the man must be some sort of CI spook checking on something. The only mystery was whether he was Army Security, FBI or just what. Worthington sadly concluded that the mole within the Embassy would have likely reported to the NKVD about this guy's clumsy attempts. Thus, the Soviets could logically suspect that they had a mole within the NKVD who had told the Americans about their recruitment of someone within the US Military Mission in Moscow. And perhaps, even worse, about the NKVD assets in the Manhattan Project.

Charles was livid. So much for the FBI concept of being subtle and discreet! He saw the man on the street outside the US Military Mission one day while Charles was in his car. He gave serious thought to running the idiot over and thus helping the American war effort, but at this point, the damage had already been done. Besides, he figured that Donovan might have been a little upset with such an unconventional solution to the problem! On the sixth day, Ambassador Harriman sent for the FBI man to come see him immediately. Their meeting was once again private. On the following morning, the man was on the plane back to Archangel, where he could wait to catch a ship for England. Harriman also fired off a private channel telegram, Eyes Only Secretary of State, telling Hull what an idiot Hoover had sent to Moscow and he would never let another FBI special agent set foot in Moscow as long as he remained Ambassador.

Given the almost comical, yet dangerous, performance of the FBI man, Worthington decided to send no further "routine" reports back to Donovan, special code or not, as he had no faith in what would be done with such reporting back in Washington, particularly if they might be shared with the FBI. If Sasha came up with any specific details on any of the American moles in the Manhattan Project, he would send those to Donovan, but otherwise, he'd report nothing! He did feel he needed to warn Sasha and managed to have him sent an invitation for a reception the American Ambassador was throwing one night at Spasso house for a visiting American admiral. Charles was mystified as to why an admiral needed to "consult" in Moscow on how the aid shipments were helping the Soviet Army, since it was entirely a land war on the Eastern Front, but he was glad for an excuse to see Sasha on short notice. He kept trying to think of a way of breaking this news to Sasha, without making it sound too horrible, but it was horrible and he wasn't looking forward to their next conversation. He also had Major Petrov sent an invitation to the reception, as Sasha had recommended.

CHAPTER 16

Three nights later at the Ambassador's reception for visiting American Admiral Walter Koon, Charles saw Sasha across the room and casually headed towards him. This took almost ten minutes to navigate as various people kept stopping him to chat. Charles finally managed to maneuver himself next to Sasha by the food table. After a few typical sentences of greeting, Charles turned the conversation to more serious matters, while smiling mindlessly and looking around the room.

"I have some possibly dangerous news for you. The American FBI sent one of their men to Moscow, supposedly to discreetly investigate who might be the NKVD mole here at the Military Mission or the Embassy. Unfortunately, the man was as subtle as a Cossack at the Tsarina's afternoon tea party."

Sasha was impressed that Charles knew that old Russian proverb, but he was uneasy as to where this story was going.

"By now, almost every American at the Military Mission and within the Embassy have talked about how some security official has been poking around, looking for somebody for something. The only good news is that some Americans think he was here looking in to embezzling of money or something like that. The Ambassador sent him packing two days ago, for being such a jerk."

Sasha was as upset as Charles had anticipated he would be. "Are you trying to get me killed!" he exclaimed. "Now the NKVD will know that they have a leak within the service and someone has told the Americans about our mole in your Mission."

"I'm very sorry, but there is nothing to do now, except be very cautious."

"Yes, there is something to do. I want to be out of the Soviet Union within thirty days. I have a few items to give you tonight, but I will give you nothing else until I arrive in America. I will gather all information that I can, but you get nothing more until I am out of Soviet Union. I think that is only way I can trust you to do what you have promised me you would do."

Charles knew Donovan wasn't going to like this, but he could see there was no point in debating the issue further with Sasha that very night. "There is a movie night coming up in a week. I'll see to it that you are invited."

Sasha had taken a pack of Russian cigarettes out of his pocket and pulled one out of the pack. In order to light it, he laid the pack down on the buffet table and then left it there for Charles. "I know you are starting to like Russian cigarettes."

"Indeed, I am. It's been very nice seeing you again." He reached out and shook Sasha's hand. "Good night."

Sasha said, "Good night," then turned and slowly walked away.

Charles waited a minute or so, then reached to pick up a small pastry from the table with his left hand, and with his right, casually picked up the pack of cigarettes and placed them in his pocket. He then saw Major Petrov on the other side of the room and made his way over to say hello to him for a few minutes. Petrov seemed very glad to talk with Charles. He presumed that was because Petrov could now boast to some superior as to how he had brilliantly arranged to have direct contact with Charles.

Once that obligation was over, Charles quietly slipped away from the reception and went up to his room. It hadn't been a great evening. Sasha had threatened to withhold any more information until he was out of Russia, which he wanted to happen within thirty days. Also, he'd sent an invitation to Jane for the reception that evening, but she hadn't shown up. He'd tried calling her a couple of times since their unpleasant discussion after watching the movie *Casablanca* together, but was told each time that she wasn't available to come to the phone at that time.

He hoped that there might be some great intelligence in the cigarette pack, but that was also rather disappointing. All Sasha had additionally learned about their mole in Los Alamos called "the old one" was that he had a Ph.D. in physics and had been with the program since its beginning. Charles mused that probably half of the personnel involved in the Manhattan Project had degrees in physics, but he'd pass it along to Donovan and hoped it would help.

There was one little bombshell in the note; Sasha announced that he now wanted to take his girlfriend, Anastasia, with him to America. He loved her, she was four months pregnant with his child and he was greatly worried by what would happen to her once he disappeared. Several of his colleagues knew enough about her that the NKVD would easily be able to track her down once he was gone. Therefore, he now wanted Charles to not only get an NKVD officer out of the Soviet Union, but to also smuggle to America a young pregnant Russian peasant girl who spoke no English. At the end of the note, he provided her full name, physical description and her date and place of birth. Charles was getting a terrible headache and decided to simply take two aspirins and go to bed. He'd think about his Sasha problems tomorrow.

Washington D.C.

The six men who constituted the War Department's vaguely named Interagency Committee on Policy Review Procedures were all in their chairs when Colonel Bishop called them to order promptly at 1000 hours three days after Charles' last, brief message had arrived from Moscow. The committee had to have some sort of name so as to book a conference room when needed and one titled "policy review" sounded boring enough that no one would care what it did. This was the fourth meeting to discuss the allegations that there were not one, nor two, but at least three Soviet spies within the Manhattan Project. It included one representative from the F.B.I., who on the first day let it be known that Mr. Hoover thought the committee should meet at the F.B.I. building and be chaired by one of his men. The other five just ignored that comment. There was a rep from Army Security, one from the Manhattan Project Security Office, one from the White House and one person representing the OSS. Colonel Bishop was a career Army officer, who'd started his military career in the cavalry. He couldn't spell atomic fission, but had a reputation for being able to keep secret things secret and to get things done.

"Gentlemen, we still don't have a whole lot to go on in trying to identify these three alleged moles, but I think we've made some real progress on the one the Russians are calling the "old one." We believe that he is a physicist, had studied in Germany, possibly was once at the Carnegie Institute in Pittsburgh, was in Chicago within the last few months, is possibly married and is probably doing this for political reasons, i.e. he believes in socialism or the Soviet Union. And of course, his code name possibly hints at his age, although it's possible that this is a bit of humor by the NKVD and he's actually quite young, but for the moment, we're looking particularly at men over the age of forty. Now Mike here from the Manhattan Project Security Office has been doing research through the personnel files of the employees at Los Alamos, and just informed me this morning that using these criterion he has created a short list of six possible suspects. Mike, why don't you take it from here."

"Thanks Colonel." He then passed out to the others a one-page document containing a brief bio on the six suspects. It was stamped Top Secret at the top and bottom of the sheet. "A person made the list if he matched at least four out of the six facts we believe are accurate about our target. I'll give you a minute to scan down the list." He then leaned back and lighted his pipe while the others read the material.

When all had finished and were again looking at him, he continued. "Each is simply referred to as Mr. A, Mr. B, etc. and by which we will refer to them in future discussion or correspondence, so as to keep the identities on this list held as tightly as possible. As you can see, I've listed them in alphabetical order, not in rank of suspicion, as frankly I don't think anyone particularly stands out above the others at the moment. Any questions or comments?"

The FBI representative spoke first. "I see that Mr. B actually studied in Vienna, Austria not in Germany."

"That's correct. I still put him on the list because I decided that the OSS source might have actually learned that the man was a German speaker and had studied in Europe and simply jumped to the conclusion that he'd been in Germany. Anyway, I thought it worthwhile to keep just this one extra suspect on the list for the present."

Most everyone around the table nodded in agreement with that step.

"Would you like for me to run these six names through the F.B.I. records and see what comes up?" asked Robert of the F.B.I.

"No, I don't think so," chimed in Colonel Bishop. "The names of all employees were checked with the Bureau before they were initially hired and I want no special attention drawn to these six for the present by doing another name check on them specifically."

Mike again took control of the meeting, as he passed out a blank sheet of paper to everyone. "This may seem like a children's game, but I would like each of you to now mark down you're top three suspects, as you see the situation, in the order of suspicion. We all know the same facts, but come from different backgrounds and I would like to see which of these six strike each of you as most likely as being one of our moles. Don't ponder this for a long time. I actually want your first, quick thoughts."

All turned their attention back to the biographical sheet. Within one minute everyone had given Mike their sheets with their rankings of the suspects and he did a quick tally.

He then laughed. "Well, this ought to be easy to find the mole. We have five votes and all of you have a different person as the number one suspect!"

All of the others, except the F.B.I. man also laughed. They then began a two hour discussion of the six suspects. At the finish, they did at least all agree that all six merited further investigation, beginning with a surreptious entry to be made into their residences and to try to keep a closer eye on them while at work and during their leisure time. This couldn't be typical surveillance for fear of being spotted and thus alerting the mole they were on to him.

"Rich, how would the OSS stay in touch with an agent working at the Los Alamos facility out in the middle of nowhere New Mexico?" asked Colonel Bishop. He slid a large map of New Mexico into the center of the table.

Rich had been a New York City detective for fifteen years before the war started and he joined the OSS. He thus had more experience than anyone else present on how to discreetly meet with police informants, or for the past two years with foreign spies working for the OSS.

"Well, I wouldn't go directly into Los Alamos. I understand it's hardly even a town with only a few burger joints and a couple of bars; there'd be no place to have a quiet meeting with an agent. Plus, there'd be too much of a chance of coincidentally bumping into someone from the base who knows the agent. No, if I was holding an occasional meeting with an agent, I'd have him come over to at least one of these little towns like Espanola or White Rock." He pointed at little dots on the map. "But I'd probably prefer Santa Fe, which is a real city. I understand that many of the scientists out there have their own cars at the base and there are several buses a day that run between Los Alamos and Santa Fe."

"I presume you've never been to Espanola or White Rock?" asked Chuck of Army Security, who'd grown up in the Southwest and had been posted at Los Alamos until two months ago.

"No."

"Well, they're hardly more than a few streets with one gas station and a diner. You'd probably have to go to Santa Fe if you wanted to be able to go unnoticed by the locals.

"Good point. So let's say our first choice to cover is Santa Fe. We still have the problem of following any of our six suspects when they leave the base and go to the city, without the risk of being spotted." He paused and looked around the table, in case anyone had a good idea. "Now, if I was still a cop and the place was Brooklyn, I'd use about twenty cops in plainclothes who could blend in and just have each man stake out one particular block. They don't move more than one block with the target. They'd mostly just sit and watch. It might take a few times as I moved my net around, but eventually I'd have a pretty good idea of where my suspect went and what he did."

Again, silence from the others, then Rich spoke again. "I've never been to Santa Fe, so I don't know what kind of guy could just sit around on street corners all day, but I'd get as many of those guys as possible and have them at the ready. When one of our six heads for Santa Fe, you alert the team and have them spread out around the city. Have them memorize the six photos and then they just sit and wait – and we hope we get lucky."

Chuck spoke up again. "I have an idea. I grew up as a young boy out in Dallas, Texas. And I'll tell you who can just sit around on park benches and at bus stops and no one notices – old men. And I'll tell you where you can get a bunch of trustworthy old men." He paused a moment for dramatic effect – "retired Texas Rangers."

He got no response from the table, so he continued. "There are many of those good ol' boys who spent twenty or thirty years as Rangers and are now just sitting around here or there in Texas. They know law enforcement work and I don't think we have to worry about any of them being closet communists." That remark got a laugh even from Robert.

Colonel Bishop spoke. "I like it. We find ourselves twenty or so retired, old Texas Rangers and have them staying in different motels or boarding houses in Santa Fe on call. Each will know in advance his stakeout location and when he's alerted, he goes to his spot for that day."

He looked around the table, waiting for comments. He saw only heads nodding in agreement. "All in favor raise your hands." It was unanimous.

"Alright, Chuck, get out your ten gallon hat and spurs and fly out to Texas to start hiring. Let's have this up and ready in ten days. Pay whatever is needed to get us twenty of these guys and say, another five in reserve. It's nice for once in my life to able to say that money is no object. And Rich, you head out to Santa Fe in a few days and you'll be in charge of whatever training is needed for these guys. Chuck will meet you in Santa Fe and you two can pick out the initial twenty street corners to have staked out. Also, get a list of names of motels and boarding houses in the city. Each man coming in will make his own reservations, but we'll at least give them suggestions to use to start their search"

"Should we coordinate this with anybody in Santa Fe?" asked Chuck. "Perhaps the Chief of Police, just in case any of our guys get arrested for vagrancy or anything. I don't mean tell him the true story, but give him something plausible to believe. Maybe a story that the Army is on to a group of criminals stealing weapons and we have some people in Santa Fe watching for them, etc."

"Not a bad idea," replied Bishop. "I'll fly out there and take care of that myself since I have the nice looking Army uniform to wear while I'm meeting with the Chief of Police."

Several of the members had started to push their chairs back from the table, thinking they were done for the day when Bishop again spoke. "One more item I wanted to bring up, just for you to give some thought to, not that we need to come to any conclusion on it today."

A very serious look had come to Bishop's face. "Gentlemen, what will we do if we are able to identify one or all of these moles?"

"What do you mean, what will we do? We'll prosecute the SOBs of course," responded the F.B.I. agent without hesitation. "It's treason. It's wartime. We can probably get the death penalty."

"But they're not spying for the enemy; it appears they're spying on behalf of an ally, so I'm not so sure you'd get a death penalty, regardless of the evidence. But that's not what I'm talking about. I see two other scenarios here. First, let's say that we can find evidence that we can take into a courtroom. Do we really want to have the public spectacle of an ally having been caught spying on America and stealing our military secrets? The second situation is perhaps even worse. What if we conclude that one or two people at Los Alamos are definitely spying for the Soviet Union, but have obtained no legally admissible evidence that we can take to trial? What if we only have the word of this Russian agent working for the OSS in Russia? How do we bring that guy into an American courtroom so that the defendant can confront his accuser? Isn't there something like that in our federal laws, Robert?"

"Something like that, yes, but there are of course exceptions," replied Robert, as his voice petered out.

"No need to decide anything today, but I'm saying we could find ourselves in an awkward situation wherein we know one of these scientists is working for the NKVD, but can't legally prove it. Are we just going to sit by and let that guy go on spying?"

Mike jumped into the discussion. "Surely, the government can fire anybody it wants from the Manhattan Project, no explanation needed?"

"Yes, it can, but after he's fired, how do you keep the fellow from still going off and giving everything already in his head to the Soviets? What if he goes down to the pier and is going to get on a Russian freighter headed for Archangel?"

The others could see where Bishop's logic was leading and nobody, including Bishop, liked it. They all stared down at their notepads.

"These are extraordinary times and eventually we may have to consider extraordinary solutions." He then went silent.

SANTA FE

Elizabeth was already seated in a booth towards the back of the low-priced diner in a working-class section of Santa Fe when the young man she'd met before at the bus stop walked in and headed her way. The décor was plain, but the floor was clean and ceiling fans slowly turned, so as to at least keep the warm air moving. They offered a blue plate special every day of the week. The only other customers in the place at 2:30 on Saturday afternoon were two middle-aged ladies having coffee at a table near the front window. They clearly lived in the neighborhood and were old friends, judging from the way they were talking and interacting. They always sat at the same table so that they could look out the window and see if anything was happening out on the street – not that much ever did.

The youngish-looking man came straight to her booth and sat down. He once again had what looked like several books wrapped in brown paper and tied with string. He laid it beside him on the seat. He didn't shake her hand, but simply nodded and gave her a smile and inquired if she was well.

"I'm feeling quite well. It's a journey of several days to reach here by train, but it's lovely country. I actually quite enjoyed the trip."

"Where do you come from," he innocently asked.

"Back on the east coast," she vaguely responded.

"I thought Harry might be back for this session. Is he OK?"

"Oh, yes, he's fine. It's just that he's busy with some other work that only he can do, so I came."

The waiter/soda jerk/cashier/manager came over and took their orders. They both ordered the blue plate special of the day and a Coca-Cola.

Her NKVD handler back in New York had instructed her to chat a bit with the young man this time, in order to get a feel for how he was handling the pressure of his clandestine work. Ivan had explained to her that when an agent was all alone and far from home, he might start getting the jitters. She should bring back this time an evaluation of his state of mind, if she could do so.

She figured she couldn't just directly ask him how his state of mind was. Was he losing his nerve? So, she decided to start with a question about his motivation for helping the Soviet Union.

"How did you get started helping the cause?"

"Well, even to a young person, it was clear to me that capitalism didn't work. The Great Depression cost my father his small business and millions of Americans were starving. My older brother had already started college and would go to meetings of socialists. He would bring home some of the brochures and I started reading the material. I found the proposals quite interesting with solid scientific reasoning as explained by Marx. However, it was the fact that the Russian workers had seized control of their own destiny and that Mr. Stalin was building this new workers' paradise that really excited me. I knew I wanted to be a part of that grand experiment, but then the war started and there was little I could do, except finish my studies."

"Such logical thinking by such a young man as yourself is very impressive. I've been told that Mr. Stalin himself has seen some of your reporting and has been very impressed." Stalin of course had never even heard of the fellow, but she knew that this statement would stroke his ego.

"As I was finishing my academic work, I suddenly was asked to join this secret military research program and I immediately saw my chance to be useful to the Soviet Union. If we are successful in building this new, special sort of bomb, the Soviet Union must have one as well to keep the capitalists of America from ruling the world."

She noticed that he always referred to the "Soviet Union", never Russia.

"You're absolutely correct. The workers of the Soviet Union must have one of these as well, so as to survive and prosper." He again had a smile all the way across his face."

She looked at her watch. "Well, I need to be headed for the train station. I'm glad we had a chance to chat this time. I'm not sure if it will be me or Harry next time, but thank you again Comrade, for your help for the workers of the world."

"I know the date, time and place for the next meeting, so all is set. Thank you for coming out to New Mexico to meet with me." He took the small parcel and slid it across the table to her. "Goodbye, Comrade."

She rose and left first. He stayed and paid the check. Elizabeth began her three day journey back to New York City. She felt very proud to be working for a cause that so motivated such a young and talented person as he was – working to build a new world.

MOSCOW

The Special Committee of the NKVD, formed to determine if there was a leak within the service and chaired by Director Beria himself, had just come to order for their Tuesday afternoon meeting.

"Gentlemen, our penetrations appear to still be reporting excellent information about the American's Manhattan Project, but we have made little progress in confirming whether we have a mole within our service, and if so, who he is." He then turned to General Parshenko. "Would that be an accurate summary of the situation, General?"

"Yes, we're still getting reports from our three sources within the atomic bomb project – that is the good news. However, we have made no progress at identifying a mole within our service, and I am fairly well convinced that there is indeed a leak of some kind. Perhaps, we just need to be patient in our search. Unfortunately, I am not a patient man! Our special coverage on everyone within the NKVD here in Moscow who has knowledge of our three sources has not produced any leads, neither from the searches of their homes nor from discrete surveillance on them."

"What about coverage of this fellow Worthington?"

"We are conducting round the clock surveillance of him, but in a very delicate manner on most days. Once or twice a week, we continue to show him obvious coverage, so as to make him think that he is still only getting the typical surveillance that he's received in the past. We don't want to alert him that we are paying any more attention to him now than in the past. And all of our informants who have any dealings with him at all are being pressed to provide us something about his activities and interests. He has been spending some time recently with a woman from the British Embassy, but in general he leads a very boring life. He expresses no great passion about politics or life in general." Parshenko then simply shrugged his shoulders, as if to say, "What more is there to do?"

Beria spoke again. "If we don't make some progress soon in other areas, we might consider at least removing this Worthington from the equation. I think we're all of the opinion that as the only OSS man in Moscow, he must be playing some role in this spying operation. If he suddenly had an accident, it would at least be harder for this mole to be able to communicate with Washington."

Everyone around the table silently nodded in agreement.

"Well, we can think about that idea for a while. There could be unfortunate repercussions if an American intelligence officer mysteriously died in Moscow. Let's hope that Parshenko's efforts will bring us a better solution."

CHAPTER 17

Charles had risen early, had breakfast and returned to his room, while most of his colleagues in Spasso House were still showering and preparing for the day. He then cracked his window, sat down in his one comfortable chair and lighted a cigar as he turned his mind to the issue of smuggling two people out of Russia. Now that he had a firm deadline by which to get Sasha, and his girlfriend, on their way to America, Charles had to get moving on coming up with a workable plan. He'd previously toyed with a few ideas, but that was when he thought such an exfiltration might be six months or more in to the future. Now, he only had a few weeks within which to actually do it.

He considered simply sending Donovan a telegram, seeking Headquarters' assistance, but he knew that wouldn't really bring a solution. First off, Sasha still hadn't provided convincing proof of such traitors or their identities, upon which Donovan could justify undertaking such an extraordinary exfiltration. An action, which if it failed, would raise a hell of protest from Stalin and probably result in Donovan himself being fired, not just that of Charles. Second, on a more practical level, he'd spent enough time at Headquarters to know that such a request would bring in the lawyers and then it would take HQS longer than thirty days to even get a committee formed to address the issue, never mind shipping fake passports or anything else useful out to him. And the wider the circle of people in the know, the more likely questions would arise as to why was the OSS sneaking citizens of an allied country out of their country? Worse, there was also the question of whether there were any other moles in the OSS, besides Duncan Lee, who might report to Moscow about such a plan and thus the NKVD could thwart it. No, he concluded, to give Donovan some "deniability" and as a practical matter, Charles was on his own for this tricky little task.

First, he considered whether to "openly" take them out, posing as Americans or Russians traveling on official business, or to try to hide them in a box or something? By lunchtime he'd concluded that given the length of the journey, hiding them in a box stamped "diplomatic cargo" was impractical. Sasha could pass for an American soldier, if he had the correct uniform and documents. Sergeant Kowalski worked in the office that created identity and travel documents for the Mission, so he constituted a good possibility for acquiring the needed papers. Sasha could read and understand English well enough; if he just didn't have to speak English and thus reveal his heavy Slavic accent. At that point, Charles looked at his watch and realized he'd been at it for almost four hours. He decided to go down to lunch and hope for inspiration from a canned vegetable.

The peas didn't speak to him, but the bandages on a colleague's right hand did give him an idea. The poor guy was obviously right-handed and was having a hell of a time trying to eat with his left hand. He pondered, what if a guy had bandages across his lip and around parts of his mouth? Other people wouldn't expect him to speak much, and if he did, it would come out sounding kinda funny anyway, given the tape and gauze. So, having a "wounded soldier" possibly solved the problem of Sasha, but how to deal with a woman who presumably looked Russian and couldn't speak nor understand English?

After lunch, Charles retreated to his room with a cup of coffee to continue thinking about the challenge of getting Anastasia on an American military plane. He was down to the last sip when it came to him. He wasn't sure where the inspiration came from – it just popped into his mind. Don't try to disguise her being a Russian, let her be a Russian, but make her a prisoner. Maybe get her some fake Russian identity papers, surely Sasha would know how to accomplish that trick, but make her under arrest. She'd be a Russian who'd been caught cooperating with a German spy and who was being sent to America for further interrogation as she claimed to know of a German spy operating in New York City. It was just so simplistically stupid sounding that it might actually work. She could be handcuffed and Sasha could be an American M.P. who was escorting her to America. He'd have a Slavic family name, claim to be second-generation Russian and thus he knew enough Russian language to communicate with his prisoner. The story could even be that it was she who'd hurt his mouth while trying to escape earlier in the day. Therefore, the M.P. wanted to keep her isolated as much as possible for the safety of others. Brilliant! Now, all he needed was an American M.P.'s uniform and various documents. He went in search of Sergeant Kowalski.

The day got even better a few hours later at his office when Jane phoned him with an invitation to a small dinner party at her Embassy on the coming Friday evening. Perhaps, she'd forgiven him for his cynical view of the human race. He didn't really care. He was happy that he'd be with her again in just a few days. Charles admitted to himself that he'd really missed her.

Charles left messages for Kowalski at various offices around the Mission that afternoon and just before 1700 hours he knocked on the door of his office.

"Ah, Sergeant Kowalski, how are you?"

"Fine, sir. I heard you were looking for me."

"Yes, come in and close the door. Have a seat."

Kowalski was getting worried. When an officer sought him out and even invited him to sit down, he knew the officer had a big favor in mind.

"What can I do for you, sir?"

Worthington saw that there was no point in beating around the bush on this topic and he might as well simply bill it as a "request" for a volunteer. He walked over and turned the radio up quite loud. Charles never felt one hundred percent sure that there weren't NKVD microphones about the building, regardless of what the State Department Security Officer said.

"Kowalski, this has to remain strictly between you and me. I need your voluntary assistance on something a bit unusual, but it does have the approval of General Donovan himself. That's why I was recently in Washington. If you don't want to hear anymore, you can leave now and we'll simply forget this brief conversation ever happened."

"Will this really piss off the Russians?"

"Oh, yeah, whether we succeed or fail, it will definitely piss off Uncle Joe and the NKVD." Charles grinned.

"Well then, count me in."

"Great. I'll give you more details when we get a bit closer to the date. I suspect this will take place in maybe two-three weeks. The timing will depend on the turning of a few other wheels, but the game clock has already started ticking."

"Lucky for you then I happen to be free every night for the rest of the month."

"What I need for you to do in the coming days is to come up with an M.P.'s uniform, winter coat and boots – the whole outfit, for a guy two inches shorter than me and a little thinner."

Charles could see Kowalski's brain whirling through its card file on where he could beg, borrow or steal such items. "The boots might be little tricky – those go at a premium around here. Any idea what size this guy wears?"

"Not right now, but by early next week, I should be able to find out."

"OK, anything else you want to tell me right now?"

"I can tell you that you're going to go out one evening and pick up a man and a woman. He'll be wearing this uniform you're going to get and does speak English. You're going to drive them to the American section of the airport and see to it that the two of them make it onto the flight that leaves the next morning at 0600 hours for Archangel. They are to then be on the flight that departs from Archangel at 1600 hours that same day for England."

"We sneaking them on the plane or will they have travel orders?"

"They'll have all the official paper they need, especially since you do work down in the section that creates such orders." Charles gave him a broad grin and handed him a small piece of paper with the name of the imaginary M.P. "I'll get for you in a few days the name and particulars on the female Russian prisoner he will be escorting."

Kowalski smiled. "Ah, I see now why I got chosen to 'volunteer' for this assignment."

"In part, yes; I presume that on occasions when the captain is busy down there, you have been known to put his signature on certain documents!"

"True, he is a busy man and I hate to bother him for his signature on every single document." He then paused before asking, "How many years you think I'm going to spend in the stockade if this operation goes belly up?"

"If this goes belly up, you're probably going to get shot, so I wouldn't worry about any jail time."

It was Kowalski's turn to grin. "Great, this just sounds better and better, the more I learn! Just tell me one thing. After farting around out here for more than a year, am I going to do something that actually makes a difference?"

"Oh, this will really make a difference, my friend. And if I don't get shot, I might even put you in for a medal."

"What sort of orders should this woman be traveling under? Just so I know what correct form to have on hand when the day comes."

"She's going to be a Russian POW, being escorted by this M.P. back to New York City for further interrogation."

"OK. If that's about it for now, I'm going to take off. I'm hungry and I'm going to head on over to the mess hall for dinner."

Charles reached over and shook Kowalski's hand and gave him a nod. "And besides you being able to come up with needed documents, you're also my first choice because I know you're a guy I can depend on when all the chips are on the table."

Kowalski just nodded and walked out. He didn't say anything, but he did think to himself that that was one of the nicest compliments he'd ever received.

Plan "POW" was underway.

Charles arrived at the British Embassy promptly at 1900 hours on Friday. Jane met him at the door with her usual lovely smile and acted as though their unpleasant conversation after the movie *Casablanca* had never occurred.

"Charles, how are you?"

"I'm fine, thanks for inviting me."

"My pleasure. I'm so glad that you could come tonight. This is the semi-annual 'nobody's dinner.' A gathering for people from embassies who have absolutely no rank at all and are rarely, if ever, invited to any diplomatic event."

"Sounds like a wonderful idea," replied Charles with a grin as he continued to hold her hand that she'd extended to shake his upon meeting.

She leaned towards him and whispered. "I had to get special dispensation to invite you as captains would normally be considered a bit too important in the world, but I assured our head administrative officer that you really were a 'nobody' at your Mission."

"Indeed I am nobody of any consequence," he replied with feigned seriousness.

They went in to a main dining area where there was a long table set for twenty people. He vaguely recognized one or two people there, but after introductions were made, he confirmed that the guests really were the lowly administrative staff people who rarely got invited to diplomatic functions, but who, of course, were crucial to making any embassy function.

He kept wondering whether he should even bring up in conversation with Jane the movie night, or just pretend it never happened and hope they'd returned to their previous, happy relationship. She solved the problem for him towards the end of the dinner, when she leaned close to him and said, "After the dinner, please stay a bit longer. I've arranged for us to use our 'secure conference room' where we can freely talk about a few issues."

"Sure."

He then understood. The unpleasant movie night topics hadn't been forgotten. She'd simply been putting on a good show until they could again discuss them, in private.

About a half hour later, most of the guests were exiting and she led Charles off to a small room, built within a room on the second floor of the chancery. The inner room was raised slightly off the floor of the outer room on thin stilts, so that one could see if any microphone wire was leading to the inner room. The "secure" portion had no electricity connected to it for lighting. There were only battery-powered lights within it. Charles was quite impressed with the structure. He'd never seen any such room at the U.S. Embassy, but then the British had been at spying much longer than the Americans and understood much better the technical threats.

Once they were inside the room and the door latched, she finally spoke. "I thought it would be better if we were in a room where we could talk quite freely and maybe finish the conversation we'd started that day at Spasso House after the movie."

Charles figured it was her "show" and simply nodded in agreement and remained silent, so she could raise whatever topic she wanted.

"Charles, I feel there's something really bothering you. It's not just your cynicism about your fellow man, it's, well, I don't know what it is, but my feminine intuition tells me that there is something that's affecting your whole outlook on life. I've come to care very much for you, and I think you for me, and I'm wondering if there's anything I could do to help you?"

"I have several work things going on right now, which I can't really go into, but which are certainly causing me stress." He shrugged his shoulders to indicate that was all he could think of for his behavior.

She decided to go at it from a different angle, since she still felt that there was something else he wasn't sharing with her. "Charles, what is it you want out of life?"

"I suppose the same things most people want – to be loved, to be happy, maybe someday have children and have a decent income and home."

"And do you think you're headed in that direction? If you don't, maybe that explains the unhappiness I sense in you."

Without having given it any forethought, he suddenly decided to share with her his family secret that he'd shared with no one, except a couple of people years ago back in Chicago. "There may be something that affects me and is what you're sensing." He took a deep breath. "I'm not Charles Worthington. That's a totally fictitious name and background that was created for me by a Chicago gangster long ago. My father had been an accountant for the Capone organization; he simply kept the books. Unfortunately, both my parents one day happened to be in the wrong place at the wrong time and were gunned down by a rival mob. I was fifteen years old at the time. One of Capone's lieutenants felt sorry for me and he took on the job of looking after me. I didn't live with him or anything, but he arranged for me to start attending this private boarding school. He gave me this alias name, so nobody could associate me with my father and the mob. When I was about to graduate from high school, he paid the headmaster of that school to create impressive phony school records for me going back to first grade, letters of recommendation, etc. I suspect he might have even paid a person or two at Harvard to make sure I was admitted, and thus began the prestigious life of Charles Worthington."

"Oh my god, Charles, I'm so sorry." She didn't really know what else to say.

"So, you see, other than the kindness of that one man, I've seen pretty much how horrible life can be, and my experiences at the OSS have also taught me that you need first and foremost to look out for yourself. While I was working in New York City before America entered the war, I met and fell in love with this Russian woman, but she had to suddenly leave America. When I was posted to Lisbon, she briefly came back into my life. She said she was still in love with me, but then she had to make a choice between me and her beliefs and she chose the latter. She left me, but not before she stole a few million dollars' worth of gold, which didn't exactly do anything for my career."

Jane was almost speechless. She leaned over from her chair and just hugged him. After a full minute of silence, she spoke again. "I still think you're going to be a very unhappy and lonely man if you let the past control how you see everyone around you for the rest of your life. There's nothing I can say to magically make you see the world differently overnight, but I think you need to start trying to change. And you need to know that I'm here to try to help you do that. I'm touched that you decided to share these details with me. Let's just leave it there for now and maybe in a few days we can talk again."

Charles was moved by her words, but didn't know what else to say to her at that moment. He settled on, "Yes, let's just leave it there for now and we can meet again in a few days." He left a minute later and drove straight back to Spasso House. He lay awake for several hours thinking about her and of her advice. "Changing" was easier said than done.

Across town, Jane lay in her bed wondering if the meeting with Charles and his revealing his true past to her would have been the right moment to have told him the truth about herself. She'd thought about doing so, but just hadn't been able to muster the courage to take such a big step.

The following morning he put his mind back to the task of getting Sasha and Anastasia out of Russia. The more he'd considered the M.P. and a Russian prisoner ploy, the more he liked it. Charles didn't doubt that Kowalski could come up with the required Army uniform pieces and was fairly certain that he could also generate the proper travel documents that would get the two of them on the plane from Moscow to Archangel. The

American authorities in England might ask a few more questions than there would be in Archangel, so Charles decided to send along with Sasha a formal letter from himself, stamped Confidential. It would explain as to how the M.P. was escorting a Russian prisoner back to Washington D.C. in connection with an OSS investigation into a Nazi spy ring. He added in the last paragraph a sentence as to how General Donovan would greatly appreciate any assistance provided to the escorting sergeant in getting this dangerous prisoner back to America as quickly as possible. Charles thought that that added a nice touch, and would probably carry more weight than the signature of a mere captain at the bottom of the document.

Having finished the letter, he sat in his office smoking a cigar and thinking about Sasha. He contemplated whether Sasha was truly ideologically motivated against Stalin, or was he simply an opportunist?

When the Bolsheviks took over, Sasha abandoned his own upper class origins and joined the revolution. When the Purges were getting underway in the 1930s, he laid low in the records section of the NKVD. On the verge of Hitler's invasion of Russia in June 1941, he made a deal with the German Abwehr, but when the war turned in favor of Stalin, he returned to being a good, loyal communist. Then when he realized that the Red Army might find in Berlin one day the records of him having been an agent of the Abwehr, he came to Charles looking for a ticket to America by once again selling out Stalin and the communists. So, was Sasha an ideologue, an opportunist or simply a survivor in an ever changing world?

Charles didn't like being blackmailed over Anastasia, but he grudgingly admired Sasha for doing what it took to have her come with him to America and not just abandon her. He hoped the girl truly loved Sasha, as he certainly appeared to be in love with her. If she did, he was a lucky man.

He realized that he needed to meet and talk with Sasha one more time, so as to explain to him the escape plan – and to measure his feet for the American boots. He checked the schedule for entertainment nights at Spasso House and found that there was another movie night of Laurel and Hardy comedy shorts on the following Monday. He immediately prepared invitations for Sasha and for Petrov.

He also contemplated how he would get the American soldier's uniform to Sasha. Charles was certain that he was now getting surveillance every time he went out. It was still very subtle, but definitely closer and heavier, as if they didn't wish to lose him again. He concluded he'd have to press Kowalski into service for one more task. He hoped that a mere sergeant from the Military Mission didn't merit surveillance, particularly after the many months he'd already been in Moscow. A horrible thought did cross Charles' mind – what if Kowalski himself had been recruited by the NKVD while in Moscow? He dismissed the thought. In part because Kowalski's Polish hatred for Russians had seemed quite genuine that day when Charles first arrived in Moscow and ever since. And second, because the thought and the consequences would be so disastrous, he just couldn't let himself believe that prospect might be true.

In the intervening days before the Monday movie night, he also gave further thought to who might be the mole within his own Mission. He went through the same short list of possible suspects he'd contemplated for weeks of Captain Tom Parkington (the friend of traitor Duncan Lee), Captain Ted Collins (former member of the American Communist Party), Bobby Penkovsky (with family members living in the Soviet Union) and finally, Major Barry Singell (with the odd sighting of him going into a local apartment building with a young, attractive Russian girl). And then, of course, there were dozens of other military personnel in the Mission that he hardly knew. One of them could be the mole, and he just didn't know enough about them to realize they were the traitor.

Fortunately for Charles, the week rolled by quickly and suddenly it was Monday evening. In case he didn't get a chance to speak privately with Sasha at movie night, he wrote out in a note as much detail as possible all that the soon-to-be traveler needed to know. Surely, he would at least have a chance to slip him a note. He also needed to get Sasha alone for thirty seconds so as to measure his footwear! He didn't know how to plan for that and figured he'd just have to take advantage of whatever opportunity presented itself.

Unfortunately, Petrov arrived first of the two on movie night and clearly was quite keen on chatting with Charles. He seemed quite intent on learning as much as possible about Charles' background; it was as if Petrov had orders to quit being subtle and "learn" something useful about Charles. He didn't like that development in connection with the heavier surveillance he'd been getting. He sensed he'd definitely become the focus of NKVD attention. He saw Sasha arrive, but it was another fifteen minutes before he could get away from Petrov and get into conversation with Sasha. He only had about ten minutes before the first movie started.

They finally "accidently" crossed paths at the buffet table.

"Good evening, Sasha. How are you?"

"I'm good, thank you, though I am still seeing very subtle surveillance on me every few days. How are you, Charles?"

"I'm also good, but very busy these days. I'm arranging for two people to travel to New York City in about a week or so."

"That will be very nice for them. I hear New York City is a lovely place to visit, or even to live."

This time, it was Charles who laid a packet of local cigarettes on the table, next to a plate of cheese slices. "This will give you specifics, but the basic idea is that you will pose as an American soldier, a Military Police officer. You've perhaps seen them around our Mission building sometimes?"

"Yes, I've seen them, with those arm bands that have the letters, M and P."

"Correct. You will have some bandages near your mouth, which will explain why you don't care to speak much and also explain why you sound a little funny if you get asked any questions before you board the airplane."

"And why will they allow me and Anastasia on the plane?"

"You will have all the travel documents you need. You will be an M.P. escorting a Russian prisoner, Anastasia, back to America for questioning, as she is suspected of working for the Nazis and knows about some Nazi spies in America."

Sasha grinned broadly. "I like your story. Where do I get my American soldier's uniform?"

"You remember the pond where we first met at the polar bear swim?"

"Yes."

"Did you notice the very tall tree, with the three main branches? It was halfway between the pond and the street and it had thick bushes around it."

"Yes, I know it well."

"This coming Saturday morning, very early, you will find a cloth sack laying by its base. In the sack will be your uniform. When my colleague picks you two up on the evening of the following Saturday for the flight, he will have for you your identity and travel authorization documents. Will that day work for you?"

"I will make sure that it does, but if for whatever reason your man or I'm not there that Saturday, do we have an alternate date?"

"The alternate will be the following Saturday, if we can, but I'd suggest you try real hard to be there the first time, as there may not actually be a second chance. If you can, schedule a meeting with someone at work for Monday. And remember, bring nothing with you, no photos or mementos. Your apartment, and hers, should look as if you both planned on returning, but something unexpected happened to you. Maybe you were robbed and killed. The NKVD may suspect you defected, but we want to leave your fate and whereabouts a mystery."

"I understand."

"Your female prisoner speaks only Russian and in general refuses to speak at all. You will fly to Archangel and then to England. From there, on to an airfield near New York City and that is when the two official travelers will simply vanish. You'll have a phone number to call two very good friends of mine who will take care of everything from that moment onward."

Sasha kept nodding in agreement with what he was hearing. "And they will have my $10,000 and new identity documents?"

"They will have everything for you."

"And will we meet again in America?"

"Of course and we can play some more chess."

Sasha listened to Charles' statement, but something in the American's facial expression told him that they'd probably never meet again.

"It won't be right away, because it would look strange if I suddenly left Moscow within a few days of your disappearance. I'll stay here another three or four weeks, but my friends will take good care of you. Anything that you have learned since today, you can just pass in writing to them and they will get it to General Donovan. I don't suppose you have anything important for me today?"

A slight smile came to the Russian's lips. "I have found for you something very important, but as I told you before, you get nothing more until I am in America – that way I will know that you will work very hard to keep me safe."

"I will try my very best for you regardless, but I'm not going to argue further with you tonight." They both stared at each other in silence for several seconds. "Don't suppose you at least want to give me a small hint at what you've found for me?"

"Nothing much really, it's just one little name." Sasha grinned like the proverbial Cheshire cat. He knew it was cruel to tease Charles like that, a man who he'd come to admire and even like, but he trusted no one and felt that his silence now was the only true guarantee he would reach America alive.

"Is it the name of an old man" asked Charles."

"Perhaps, perhaps," replied Sasha as he picked up the pack of cigarettes from the table. He did take a little pity on him and decided he could give Charles just a little something right then, as it might be important in helping Charles arrange for his exfiltration from Russia. "By the way, your local mole has two children."

"Excellent, that should help me identify who he is."

"Just don't go arresting him until I am out of the country, please!"

"One last thing. You will need to be wearing American Army boots that night, to go with the uniform. I doubt if you know your foot size in American measurements, do you?"

"No."

"Not a big problem. In about five minutes, go into the Men's Room, down at the end of that hallway. I will come in and put a piece of paper on the floor and trace the outline of the boot you are wearing."

"Five minutes, OK." He reached out his hand to shake Charles', as any two men saying "good night" would do, but Sasha held onto Charles' for a few seconds longer than usual. He looked the American in the eyes and said, "Thank you for everything, my friend." He then turned and strolled back into the crowd of guests while putting one more piece of bread covered in caviar in to his mouth.

CHAPTER 18

Charles awoke early the next morning, but continued to just lay in his bed while he thought about how he could insure on the upcoming "special" Saturday evening that Sasha would not have the periodic surveillance he'd told Charles about the previous day. It had been the subject on his mind as he finally fell asleep the previous night without having come up with a solution. The exfiltration plan simply could not work if Sasha and Anastasia were being watched that particular evening. Either Sasha would have to execute some clever escape from coverage, or Charles would have to…what? Kowalski might be able to pick up the two Russians even if they were being watched and get them to the airport, but the Soviets would never let an American flight take off from the airfield until they had the two under their control. He finally decided to come back to that problem later, but in the meantime, he would go find Kowalski and give him the tracing of Sasha's boot.

Kowalski came by Charles' office at 1000 hours to report that he'd already procured the needed American uniform and took the tracing of the needed boot size.

"Do you think the Soviets ever bother following you around the city?"

"I doubt it, but then I've never been trained in how to properly try to detect if I'm being followed or not. I'd noticed a car following me now and then in the first few months I was here, but it was so blatant, anybody would have noticed the car." A bad thought came to Kowalski's mind. "Why are you asking?"

"I'm going to have to get this uniform and those boots you're looking for in to the hands of my Russian friend this coming Saturday morning. He knows to go to a spot under a particular tree in a city park that morning to find his needed stuff. I'm seeing surveillance on me just about every day recently and I just can't risk putting down this package of clothing. That leaves only you as an option and that's why I asked if you ever had surveillance."

"Well, I usually do my shopping for alcohol and other hard to find goods that you officers have put in a request for on Saturday mornings and I've never seen anybody following me on those days."

As Kowalski hadn't actually said "no", Charles proceeded as if he would do it. "Do you know Patriarch's Pond Park, where there's a large pond in which crazy Russians go swimming during winter on Sundays?"

"I do. A few of us went there once to see a lot guys swimming in the freezing water. You're right, they're crazy!"

"You happen to recall a very tall and weirdly shaped tree near the pond? It has bushes around it at the base. It's the only real tree near the pond."

"Yeah, vaguely. It's oddly shaped?"

"Correct. That's the tree under which the clothes and the boots are to be placed this coming Saturday by 0900 hours."

"Could I put them down there at say 0300 hours? This might be easier to do at the end of a Friday night out and about, rather than doing it on Saturday morning."

"You're call. If late Friday nights is your regular pattern and nobody seems to follow you, then just go there in the wee, small hours of the morning."

"Consider it done."

"Great. Now, a second question for you. You've gotten to know most of the officers and men here at the Mission this past year. Who has precisely two children?"

"Hmmm. I presume you want an absolutely accurate account?"

"Afraid so."

"Well, in that case, I better just go steal a look through the personnel files. I know a few of the guys well enough to be able to answer that question, but not everybody. I can let you know by late this afternoon."

"That will do fine. I'll see you this afternoon."

After Kowalski's departure, Charles leaned back in his chair and lighted a cigar. He didn't know why, but he thought better while smoking a cigar. He returned to the challenge of how to insure that Sasha wouldn't have surveillance on the evening of X Day, as Charles had begun to call the exfiltration day. How could he make sure that most all of the surveillants in Moscow working on a Saturday would be too busy to cover Sasha? He was about to the end of the cigar forty minutes later and still nothing had occurred to him. He'd spent several minutes considering the idea of setting off an explosion somewhere in the city, which would draw NKVD surveillance teams to it. However, aside from the challenge of setting off an explosion, he then realized it would draw fireman, policemen and soldiers to the sight, but he couldn't think of any reason that surveillance teams would go there. At this point, he realized he needed a break as his brain was scraping the bottom of the creative barrel for ideas. He'd just put his feet back on the floor, when there was a knock on his door.

"Come in," he said loudly.

"How you doing, Charles?" A cheerful looking Major Singell entered. "Not interrupting anything important am I?"

"No, I was just sitting in here and thinking."

"About anything special, or just about the meaning of life in general?"

"Oh, just something I'm trying to figure out."

Singell's face turned serious and he lowered his voice slightly. "By the way, you know, if you ever need a little unofficial help with something, you can come to me."

"Thanks, Barry. That's good to know, but this is more of a 'I just need to make up my mind about something,' rather than actually doing something."

Barry laughed. "Well, if it doesn't require actually doing anything, I'm definitely your man. Listen, I came by to see if you're up for a little poker one night later in the week?"

"I suspect so. Just let me know when and where."

"Any particular nights good or bad for you?"

"No, I'm free any night."

"Great, see you later." He closed the door behind him as he left.

Charles looked at his watch and decided he'd head on over and be there for lunch soon as the mess hall opened at 1200 hours. He thought that some instant potatoes from a box might stimulate his brain to coming up with a clever idea. At least walking over to lunch would get some blood back into his butt. He'd been sitting just about the entire morning.

After lunch, he brought one of his novels back to his office, which would give him something to do while waiting for Kowalski to return with the data about who had two children. The Sergeant knocked on Worthington's door a bit after 1400 hours. He handed Charles a sheet of paper with nine names.

Charles was glad to get the list sooner than expected, but a bit disheartened at seeing so many names on it.

"I gotta run. Let me know if you need anything else."

"Thanks. I'll mention your name to FDR the next time I see him."

"I'd rather you mentioned my name to Heddy Lamarr," he replied as he shut the door behind him.

Charles thought of the newspaper picture of Mr. Astor with Heddy Lamarr at the war bond sales night in New York City. He laughed and thought to himself that he'd have a better chance of getting in to see Miss Lamarr through Astor than seeing President Roosevelt.

Charles started going down through the list. He knew three of the nine – Bobby Penkovsky, Barry Singell and Nick Haberly. He vaguely recognized two more – Lt. Jack Malmedahl and Lt. Bill Watts, but the other four, he'd never even heard their names before, much less met them. He already had something "suspicious" on the first two. Penkovsky, because he possibly still had relatives down in the Caucuses through whom the NKVD could possibly blackmail him. As for Singell, there was the incident of Charles probably seeing Singell with a young Russian woman that day going in to a local apartment building. Haberly had always struck Charles as a total straight-arrow and a very loyal American. Other than matching the criterion of having two children, he saw nothing suspicious about him. Charles would have to try to find out a little more about the others, or at least meet them.

He wound up his mental review of the nine colleagues with two children still focusing primarily on Barry Singell. There was the incident of the Russian girl at an apartment building, but more intriguing to Charles was Barry's coming by that morning and offering to "unofficially" assist Charles, if he ever needed a hand. If Singell was indeed the mole, Charles pondered whether there was some way he could take advantage of that offer to assist Charles. Singell had been particularly friendly to him ever since he'd first arrived in Moscow. Granted, he'd never been overly inquisitive as to what Charles did in Moscow, but their conversations had on several occasions touched upon the work of the OSS in general. Maybe the guy was just naturally friendly, but he concluded that if he had to rank his suspects that very afternoon, Major Singell was at the top of the list for being the mole.

Charles bumped into Kowalski late in the afternoon in the corridor and asked him to come back to his office for a quick moment. After closing his door, Charles simply asked him if he knew or strongly suspected whether any of the nine people on the list he'd given Charles earlier were having flings with local girls.

Kowalski clearly looked uncomfortable answering such a question, but finally did say, "I feel fairly certain about Singell, based on having seen him once in an odd part of Moscow with a blonde gal on his arm. There was also some talk one night among some of the enlisted guys in a bar about Lieutenant Haberly, but that may have just been the beer talking."

"OK, thanks. It may be nothing, but I was just curious. I'll see you tomorrow."

Charles cleaned off his desk and headed for Spasso House. For the first day in a long time, it hadn't snowed the entire day! Maybe there was a springtime in Moscow after all. He still had time before dinner was served, so he decided to just continue walking around the neighborhood, instead of going to his room to wait for the dining hall to open. There wasn't exactly sunshine, but at least it might be called light cloud cover. He thought back to his days at Harvard in wintertime, where it also got pretty cold, but he remembered a lot more, clear sunny days and bright blue skies up in Massachusetts. He wondered if maybe his memory was just playing tricks on him. No, he definitely remembered there being many days of cold, clear skies around Boston.

As if by magic, he suddenly had an idea as to how to draw lots of surveillance to one part of Moscow, while Kowalski picked up his two passengers in another part of the city one evening soon. The idea involved using Singell to mislead the NKVD. The plan was so simple, he couldn't understand why he hadn't come up with it sooner. He wanted to keep an open mind for a few more days as to who was the mole, but his gut told him it was Barry. Charles just kept walking in circles in the blocks near

Spasso House. His surveillance team was beginning to wonder if he'd lost his mind and somehow forgotten where he lived.

The plan was quite simple. He'd request Singell's assistance in an upcoming tricky operation. He'd tell him that he was going out X-night to meet an important Russian agent and that it would be in a certain area of the city. How exactly he told Barry that information he'd work out later. Barry tells the Soviets and they pull in all the surveillants they have in Moscow to provide "static coverage" of many, many blocks, in order to catch whomever Charles would meet that night. Yes, it just might work, if he could convincingly make Barry aware that something "big" was happening that specific night. Charles began to smile. He then became cognizant of the time and that he was a good ten blocks away from Spasso House. Much to the relief of his surveillance team, whose members all wanted to go off duty and go home, he immediately turned around and headed back home.

Charles was positively cheerful during dinner, chatting away with his tablemates as if he enjoyed being posted to Moscow. Later that evening up in his room, he returned to thinking about his plan. It suddenly dawned on him that after the NKVD had noticed that Sasha vanished from Moscow the same evening that Charles had led them on a wild goose chase, they'd be none too happy with him. He had diplomatic immunity, so what could they actually do to him? Slit the tires on his car maybe? It wasn't his personal vehicle, so what did he care? Maybe they'd rough him up some night out on the streets of Moscow and make it look like a robbery. Of course, this was a country where Stalin had caused the deaths of hundreds of thousands, maybe even millions of his own citizens. There were worse things than a faked mugging that could befall him late one night on the streets of the city. His thoughts drifted to "value judgments" as an old ethics professor of his at Harvard had called them. His situation was beginning to look a bit like Rick's dilemma in *Casablanca*. What had more "value?" Charles' safety or the delivery of Sasha safely to America, so he'd reveal the name of the Soviet mole within the Manhattan Project. Charles had a half bottle of Jack Daniels in the bottom drawer of his dresser. He pulled it out and poured himself three-full fingers worth of the tawny gold liquid. He and his old buddy Jack would have to think about the question together.

Over the next hour or so, he debated the pros and cons of his plan. Granted, he'd been screwed a number of times in recent years and he talked a good game of looking out for nobody but himself, but when it came right down to it, he knew he didn't really believe that. His parents hadn't taught him that as a young boy. Several influential professors at Harvard hadn't taught him that either and Vincent Astor would be appalled at his selfish thinking. He finished the bottle of Jack at about the same time he admitted to himself that he knew what he had to do, regardless of what might be the personal consequences to him afterwards. He also knew he was going to have a terrible hangover in the morning.

He went the following morning at 1000 hours for his weekly meeting at the NKVD, which as usual, was polite, but didn't accomplish much of anything. He felt as if Colonel Suvarov was staring at him with a hard, suspicious look, but he decided afterwards that it was only his imagination playing tricks on him. He wrote up a short report to send back to OSS Headquarters about the meeting as soon as he returned to the Military Mission. He wanted everything to appear routine and normal back at his Headquarters as well as in Moscow. Duncan Lee might not be the only NKVD mole within the OSS. There should be no hints in either capital that anything special was about to happen.

Charles then headed back to Spasso House for lunch. He joined Captain Collins at a table and a new lieutenant who'd only arrived a few days earlier. Charles thought it funny that after only four months, he was considered an "old timer" with knowledge worthy of passing on to a new guy. After answering a few questions from the newbie and jokingly asking Collins how the working proletariat were doing in America, he excused himself. He headed down to see if Viktor was in the worker's room. He was, just finishing his lunch he'd brought with him. One other Russian was in the room, but he was busy reading a newspaper at the other end of the table.

"Viktor, it hasn't snowed for two days now, you might soon be out of a job!"

The Russian laughed. "I wouldn't put away your winter coat quite yet Charles. In fact, I think it will snow tonight, but in any case, when there is no more snow for the year, I will begin gardening."

"It's good to be essential twelve months of the year. By the way, are you anywhere near retirement age in the Soviet Union?"

Viktor again laughed. "Retirements have been suspended for the duration of the war. And in any case, it's good to keep working, as one can't really live on just a monthly pension check."

The other Russian had finished reading and stood up. He nodded to Charles and put on his coat, hat and gloves and departed.

Charles poured himself a glass of tea and sat back down with the old man. He wasn't sure exactly what Viktor's age was, but he presumed that twenty years in a Siberian labor camp hadn't done anything good on the fellow's health, so his actual physical condition might be "much older" than his chronological age.

"Viktor, you've read much more of what people call 'classical literature' and you've experienced a much harsher life than I have, so perhaps you can address a question I have about life better than I can."

He shrugged his shoulders. "Maybe. If by classical you mean Tolstoy, Dostoevsky, Chekov and writers like them, yes I have read quite a bit. As for life, well I survived Siberia, though I'm not sure that taught me anything important, but I can try to answer your question."

"I think surviving twenty years in Siberia teaches a person many things, so, here is my question. When a person has to choose between what is good for him personally and what might be called a higher good, say over a matter of principle, or the good of a nation, which path do you think most people choose?"

"Ah, that is a hard question. As I told you once, I saw the worst and the best of men out in the labor camps. I think most of us would like to think that if ever faced with such a hard decision, we would choose the better option – by which I mean what is best for society, for mankind. However, I don't think anyone really knows how he'll act until actually forced to make such a decision. It's like the question of bravery. We all want to think we will be brave in battle, but until the bullets start to fly, no man really knows. Does that help?"

"So you think that choosing a path that leads to the good of the many over the good of the one is the correct choice?"

"Absolutely, it's what separates us from the lower animals and even some animals are higher on the ethical ladder than most other animals.

I've read that a mother elephant will fight to the death and give her own life to protect her calf, and that all of the females of the herd will do the same, even if the calf isn't hers. They have a sense of the welfare of their community. Surely man must choose the same path. You don't have to read 19th century Russian authors to know that."

"I suppose not, but I did want a second opinion. Do you think a man's pride plays a role in such a decision? In other words, will he do the 'right' thing because of his concern of what others will think of him, of his reputation, even if after his death?"

"Perhaps that is a small factor, but I still think a person knows what he should do, regardless of whether anybody else will even ever know." Viktor sipped from his tea glass.

"I suppose."

"Do you have a calf that needs protecting?" asked Viktor with a smile.

Charles laughed. "No, nothing in particular. I'm just in a philosophical mood. Well, thanks for your thoughts. We should have another chess game soon."

"Yes, I think you are understanding the game better and better, and after you achieve that, you will play better."

"Good evening, Viktor."

"Good evening, Charles."

The rest of the week dragged slowly by. Charles hated waiting, but at this stage there was nothing left to do. He'd gone over the exfiltration plan in his mind time and time again, considering each step that needed to occur and trying to even calculate how to get back on track, should something go awry at any stage. He'd checked several times with Kowalski to confirm that he'd correctly procured every official Army document that Sasha, AKA the M.P., and his female Russian prisoner, would need to board the planes in Moscow, Archangel and in England. The U.S. Army had a form for every situation. Kowalski actually found a "transfer of prisoner" form and had it properly filled in, complete with the forged signature of his supervisor down in the Administrative Section, and countersigned by Captain Charles Worthington. There were nine documents in total, each one just waiting for a date to be put on them. Kowalski had suggested that they only be added at the last moment, in case there was an unexpected delay in the initial departure from Moscow. As a final nice touch, Kowalski had even thrown in a pair of GI-issue socks and pair of his own American boxer shorts, though he admitted that if someone was down to examining the Russian's underwear, he probably had a real problem!

The end of the work day on Friday finally arrived and Kowalski left with the cloth bag to be hidden at the base of the large tree in the park that Sasha would pick up on Saturday morning. It also included a short note with instructions of where and at what time Sasha and Anastasia were to be waiting on the following Saturday evening. It also told Sasha that the friend who was going to pick them up "to take them to the party" would have the bandages that Sasha needed. Charles had forgotten at the last personal meeting with Sasha to explain who would actually put the bandages around his mouth, so that issue needed to be addressed in the note. Kowalski printed the note in semi-accurate Russian. Charles figured that it was better to have the note in bad Russian rather than English, just in case it was found by someone else. Charles wished Kowalski luck as he departed, then Charles went to Spasso House for dinner. He ate a quick meal and went straight to his room. He wasn't in the mood to chat with anyone. He spent the evening alternating between reading one of his mystery books and looking over at the clock. He finally started feeling sleepy and at 2300 hours he crawled into bed. He'd find out from Kowalski at breakfast in the morning if the "drop" had successfully been accomplished. His staying awake wasn't going to make the mission any more successful than if he was asleep.

Charles was in the mess hall Saturday morning promptly at 0830 hours when it opened. He'd finished eating powdered eggs and biscuits by 0900 and then continued to drink coffee until Kowalski strolled in for breakfast twenty minutes later. He came over and sat down at a table where Charles and another officer were discussing whether Major League Baseball should continue while the country was at war. Charles was in favor. Kowalski didn't need to say anything to Charles. The grin on his face told him that all had gone well the night before – actually at 0200 hours on Saturday to be precise.

Charles spent most of the rest of the day in his room. He wrote a few letters to friends back in the U.S. and started a new Dashiell Hammett detective novel. He phoned and left a message at the British Embassy for Jane in the afternoon, but the British duty officer didn't think she was working at all that weekend, so he doubted if she'd receive Captain Worthington's message until Monday. Unfortunately, she had no phone at her apartment. On Sunday, the temperature almost reached the freezing mark – surely spring was coming soon. It was the end of April!

Jane returned his phone call on Monday morning. "Sorry I didn't get back to you on Saturday. I had the whole weekend off for a change and just found your message this morning. How was your weekend?"

"I didn't do much of anything. I read mostly and wrote a few letters. How about you?"

"On Saturday morning a few of us girls went to the main farmer's market and in the afternoon to one of those commission stores, where you can buy old jewelry and clothes. That was fun."

"Did you buy anything?"

"No, there wasn't much that I actually needed, and the things I did like, I couldn't afford. Then Sunday was laundry day."

"Pretty exciting lives we lead!" Charles teased. "Listen, would you be free for dinner, say Tuesday or Wednesday evening?"

"I think either day is good for me. I've just seen my schedule for the week. You want to go out, or come over to my place for whatever happens to be in my cupboard?"

"If you don't mind, let's just eat at your place. You fix the side dishes and a dessert and I'll see what I can find for the meat dish, and I'll bring some wine as well."

"Fair enough. How about you show up at 1900 hours? That will give me a chance to get home and put on something suitable for entertaining a gentleman caller, as my mother refers to people like you."

"Ha, well I'll just be showing up in my uniform and I didn't do laundry on Sunday, so I may or may not have on clean socks, but I promise I'll shave before coming over."

"Sounds like we have a plan. I'll see you tomorrow evening."

"Till tomorrow."

He heard the line go dead as she hung up, but he sat at his desk with the receiver in his hand and a smile on his face for another twenty seconds. He loved the sound of her voice.

A minute later, his phone started ringing again and he thought that perhaps Jane had forgotten to tell him something, so he happily picked up the receiver and in a very pleasant voice, said "Hello."

He was rudely brought back to the present real world when he heard the male American voice down at the reception desk informing him that he had a phone call from some Russian named Turgenev on the line.

He heard the transfer click and Charles said, "Captain Worthington here."

"Good morning, Captain. Sasha Turgenev here. How are you today?"

"I'm fine, as well. I had a very relaxing weekend."

"Listen, I only have a minute, so let me quickly ask you about having an evening of chess again in the near future?"

"That sounds good, but I'm rather busy this week. How about I phone you next week and we can see what day might work later in that week?"

"I understand," replied Sasha. "I will await your call next week."

"Excellent. I wish you a good week."

"And to you, goodbye."

"Goodbye."

Charles hung up the receiver, as a satisfied smile came to his face. The instruction sheet left with the sack of clothes under the tree had instructed Sasha to phone on Monday morning to suggest a game of chess if he had safely received the clothes. Step one had been achieved. His smile disappeared and a serious, almost sad, look came to Charles' face as he realized that might have been the last time he would ever hear Sasha's voice. Some days, Charles thought of Sasha as quite the unethical opportunist, but today, Charles decided to think of him as a man who was doing very valuable work for the good of America under dangerous conditions. He made a mental note to himself to call Sasha's office number several times in the coming week as he'd just said he would. He would have no ostensible reason to know that Sasha had vanished on Saturday.

He was about to seek out Sergeant Kowalski to put in an emergency scavenging order for some meat for the Tuesday dinner and a suitable bottle of wine to go with whatever he could find when he had a clever idea. It was only 1000 hours, but he headed back to Spasso House and sought out the chief cook in the mess hall.

"Hey, Sarge, you got a minute to chat?"

"Sure, what you need?" Sarge had liked Worthington ever since his first meal there when he'd inquired if seconds were allowed.

"I got a dinner date over at my British gal's apartment tomorrow evening at 1900 hours. She's offered to cook for me, but I thought I might surprise her by showing up with an already prepared meal. I know you guys don't sell food to every peasant in Moscow, but would a suitable contribution to the 'kitchen coffee fund' perhaps get me two dinners to go tomorrow evening?"

"You're absolutely correct Captain that we can't sell Army food out the back door, but if you had a pressing military need, say to work late in your office till past the end of the serving time in the mess hall – and wanted a little take-out food to sustain you while conducting Army business, well, that's a totally different matter. We're serving baked chicken with some vegetables on the side for dinner tomorrow evening. Would that assist in your Army-related business that evening?" Sarge didn't even crack a smile while saying that.

"I believe that would do quite nicely."

"And you look like a pretty big eater, Captain, I better send two dinners with you, so as to truly fill you up tomorow evening."

Charles leaned over to the floor, as if picking up a US$20 off the floor. He'd had the Jackson in his palm since he'd entered the kitchen. He held the bill out to the Sergeant. "Sarge, you must have dropped this earlier while working in here. Your kitchen, your floor. Whatever's laying on it must belong to you."

The cook smiled. "So that's where it got to. I been looking for that twenty that I won in cards last night. Thanks for finding it for me." He took the bill and smoothly slid it in to his right side pants pocket. "You know, I'm thinking of trying my hand at baking a cherry pie in this oven. Would you be willing to taste test my first try tomorrow? I could just send you off with a pie, along with your dinner, and you could let me know on Wednesday if you thought the men might enjoy my pie some Sunday in the near future."

"You know me, Sarge, anything to help out the US Army. I'll come by here about twenty minutes before you up open for business tomorrow evening."

They shook hands. "See you tomorrow, Captain Worthington."

251

When Charles got back to his office that afternoon, he phoned Jane and gave her the good news. "You don't have to cook at all tomorrow. I've made arrangements to use a kitchen and I'll be preparing dinner for us."

She laughed, not believing a word he said. "Excellent. Well, that will leave me even more time to make myself look extra nice tomorrow."

"I'll see you on Tuesday."

"Till tomorrow."

Just as he put the receiver down, Captain Parkington came through his doorway. "Did you just get informed that you're going home this week?"

Charles' mind returned to the present time and place, and he responded to Tom's question with a, "Huh, what are you talking about?"

"Well, from the way you're grinning, I figured you must have gotten some pretty exciting news, like they're about to promote you straight to full colonel and immediately send you back to Washington!"

"No, I'd heard that you'd suddenly come in to some money and were finally going to pay me that $20 you still owed me from our last poker evening. That's why I was smiling."

"Me owe you, you sure about that?" teased Parkington.

Charles pulled out his desk drawer and took out the scrap of paper upon which was written Tom's I.O.U., with his signature and the number twenty written on it. He held up the paper, "Yep, I'm sure."

"O.K. Just as soon as we get paid again, I'll settle my account with you."

"Good, I could use some cash."

"Say, I just got a letter from our mutual friend, Duncan Lee. He said he thought he'd seen you a few weeks back at OSS Headquarters and asked how you were doing here in Moscow?"

"I don't remember seeing him back in Washington. Must have been my good-looking twin back there," joked Charles. "Anything in particular bring you to my office, or are you just lost?"

"Nothing special, I just got tired of filling out requisition forms for everything the Red Army wants and needed a break. Apparently, they don't make anything in this fucking country. It's unbelievable the variety of things they ask for, down to kitchen sinks!"

"Oh well, I'm sure they're going to pay us back someday for all this stuff we're giving them now, right?"

"You been drinking some of that cheap wine Kowalski comes up with, or are you trying for a Section 8 discharge on the grounds of mental incapacitation? The day the Soviets ever pay us back one single ruble for all the millions of tons of stuff we've shipped over here, I'll go down and do a back flip in Red Square, while singing a chorus of *Swanee*!"

Charles laughed. "Hey, I'd pay a ruble to see that. In fact, I'd pay two rubles!"

"Alright, I'll keep that offer in mind, if I'm ever short of rubles. See you later, and I'll get you that $20 I owe you at the end of the month when we get paid." He stopped in the doorway and turned back to Charles. "You will still be here at the end of the month, 'Colonel' Worthington?"

"Yeah, I'll still be here."

Tom pulled the door shut on his way out. Charles put his feet up on his desk and crossed his arms on his chest, as a worried look came across his face. He thought to himself, that that was the weirdest coincidence, if it was true. Soviet mole Duncan Lee had written to Parkington and "happened" to ask about him, just as Charles was about to launch a very sensitive operation. First of all, Tom had never just dropped by Charles' office in four months, and now he does – simply to kill time? Charles had convinced himself that Major Singell had to be the NKVD mole in the Military Mission, but suddenly Parkington's unusual behavior brought him back in to the running as a serious possibility. He spent another twenty minutes pondering Tom's visit, then decided to call it a day and go home to Spasso House. He had just a few chapters left to read in his current detective novel and thought he'd finish it before dinner. He wished he could find case-solving clues as easily as Sam Spade and Charlie Chan did in all those novels! He grabbed his coat and left.

CHAPTER 19

A little before 1700 hours on Tuesday, Charles stopped by the mess hall and picked up his two baked chicken dinners and a cherry pie. It was still warm and smelled wonderful. He doubted if it would stay warm for long and was tempted to scoop out a few fingers worth, but decided that would be a bit gauche – perhaps if they ate it as soon as he arrived, it might still be warm.

He drove as fast as he could on the way to Jane's; he didn't care whether surveillance might think he was trying to lose them or not! Upon arrival, he practically ran up the stairs to her flat. As both hands were full, he just tapped on the door with his foot instead of trying to ring the buzzer and risk dropping the food. When she opened the door, he still almost dropped the food. Instead of wearing a dress, or blouse and skirt, she was only wearing a very sheer, pink negligée. Sheer enough to see that she was wearing no bra, only matching pink panties, garters and her prized silk stockings. He was speechless for several seconds before he could manage to whisper, "Wow!" All of his preconceived ideas of how prim and conservative English women were, vanished.

Jane herself felt a little embarrassed, but did like the reaction she'd gotten out of Charles. "Is that our dinner?"

"Yes," he barely managed to utter as his eyes continued to work their way up and down her body.

"Then I suppose you'd better come inside," she said softly as she offered him a welcoming smile. She closed the door behind him and took the pie out of his right hand. She brought it up to her nose to smell. "Where on earth did you get a warm cherry pie?"

"I know people in low places," he replied with his own broad smile. He placed the box with the dinners on a table, quickly removed his coat and hat and took her in his arms to kiss her. He'd forgotten all about the cherry pie.

After a long and passionate kiss, Jane pulled back and said, "Shall will get on with dinner?"

"Absolutely, but how about we start with dessert? We can enjoy the pie while it's still warm," suggested Charles.

"Splendid idea. Anything needs to be done with the dinners?"

"Just put them in your oven I suppose, to keep them warm."

She brought out two plates and quickly cut two slices of the enticing pie. They both put a fork full of the gooey, delicious concoction in their mouths at the same moment, and both immediately uttered a soft "yum."

After a few minutes of idle chitchat about how their days had been, Jane brought up the topic of her "provocative attire," which Charles continued to stare at while enjoying his cherry pie.

"I take it you like my clothing choice for this evening?"

Charles puckered up his lips and replied, "Oh, it's OK, if you like those sort of things." He managed to keep a straight face for about three seconds, before he broke up laughing. "What's not to like!"

"Want to know why I'm wearing this outfit?"

"Yes."

"Well, I've decided that it's time for me to move on with my life, especially with a nice guy like you. I've felt that you might be interested in being, well, more intimate shall we say, and that tonight might be the night. I thought I'd just save us both a lot of awkward conversation along those lines, if I wore this outfit for dinner. It does say 'yes', doesn't it?"

Charles laughed, "Yes, I think even an Army captain could correctly interpret the message your negligée is sending."

"Good." She wiped the last bit of cherry pie filling from her plate with her first finger and sensuously licked it off with her tongue.

Charles was rapidly losing interest in dinner, but figured to maintain some slight appearance of being a gentleman, they should enjoy the baked chicken, before he suggested they move to her bedroom. However, he didn't plan on lingering at the dining table afterwards, drinking coffee! The same thoughts were going through Jane's mind as well.

She quickly served up the baked chicken, green beans and yellow corn. After a few bites, Charles commented, "Our cook's chicken has never tasted this good before."

"Maybe your special waitress tonight is the difference," teased Jane.

Charles gave a lecherous grin and replied, "Maybe."

Half way through dinner Charles brought up his recent conversation with Viktor. "I had an interesting chat with Viktor, our snow shoveler at Spasso House, about life and responsibilities."

"My, how philosophical. And did you learn anything?"

"Well, he was very well educated as a young man prior to the Revolution, plus I think surviving twenty years at a Siberian prison camp probably gives him a few observations on his fellow man that most of us don't have."

"Oh my, you'd never told me before about that part of his past. I would think that has made him pretty cynical about his fellow man."

"Surprisingly, quite the contrary. He speaks rather highly of people. And as for 'responsibilities', he and Rick Blaine of *Casablanca* see the world quite similarly. Viktor said the good of society takes precedence over the individual's happiness. Of course, that's pretty close to what Comrade Stalin has been saying as he's gone about creating his nice little dictatorship, so who gets to make that decision as to what is best for society is an important question."

"Well, Stalin aside, I think Viktor is a pretty smart guy. And if you're talking about the individual getting to make the call on what is best, not some dictator, then I think you're on ethically sound ground. But why all this discussion on such a weighty philosophical issue? You about to make a life changing decision on something?"

Charles laughed. "No, no, I've just been thinking more about the movie and how Rick gave up the girl just to fight the bad guy Nazis. They don't touch on this in the movie, but after Rick's sacrifice, I think it did place a certain moral burden upon Lazlo and Ilse to be the best people they could be afterwards."

She reached over and squeezed Charles' hand. "Well, I don't even know a guy named Lazlo, so you don't have to worry about giving me up." She offered him that wonderful smile of hers.

"Well, we've had a good dinner and deep, meaningful discussion, I think it's time that we go get better acquainted in your bedroom. Otherwise, your lovely attire will have been wasted."

"Why Captain Worthington, what an excellent suggestion". She stood and blew out the one candle that had been burning on the dining table, then took his hand and led him to her bed.

As the wee hours of the morning passed, the eight members of the NKVD surveillance squad who'd been on Charles that evening had a mixture of envious thoughts of what Charles was doing with the lovely English girl all night long up in her apartment – and hateful ones for their having to spend the night sitting in cold, uncomfortable cars!

Charles didn't get back to Spasso House until 0800 hours. He grabbed a quick shower, changed clothes and headed down to the mess hall. He wanted to tell Sarge how good the food had been the previous evening and he finally showed up at the Military Mission at 0930 hours. Being known in the building as the OSS "spook" was occasionally quite convenient, as no one questioned him when he arrived late or left his office early. He gave some final thoughts to Step Two of his plan for the next hour and then went to seek out Sergeant Kowalski, but he was out on some errand for somebody and no one in his section knew exactly when he'd be back. He left a message for him to come by Worthington's office when he did return and then went back upstairs to sit and wait. His favorite activity – waiting!

He closed his office door as he wasn't in the mood to talk to anyone. He had nothing left to plan or review. He'd gone over the scenario for Saturday evening a dozen times. There was nothing left to calculate or improve. He'd brought one of his mystery books with him, but wasn't in the mood to read either. He spun around, put his feet up on a table and looked out the window. He thought about the previous magical evening with Jane and what might lie ahead for them. He believed now that there might be a "future" for them. He had to get through the coming week or so and there certainly was risk to his plan, but he told himself that he was probably being overly concerned about how the NKVD would react, and possibly retaliate in some way. However, they weren't stupid and once they realized that Sasha had vanished the same night that Charles had been out playing games with their mole on the south side of Moscow, they'd be angry. They'd figure out he'd tricked them. It was just a question of how angry they'd be. He recalled his childhood days in Chicago of the Prohibition Era and the various ways that the different mobs had for letting people know if they were annoyed! He'd definitely be extra cautious in the coming weeks and not go out alone anywhere.

Yes, he concluded, he did have a good shot at there being a future with Jane, but just in case, he was pleased he'd gotten certain things said to her last night. He was particularly glad, he'd brought himself to tell her he loved her. Having finished thinking about Jane, he turned his thoughts to his own possible future. Assuming, and it was a big assumption, that all went well this coming Saturday and that Sasha really had learned the true name of one of the Soviet moles at the Manhattan Project, Charles delightfully thought about recall to Washington, promotion, maybe even a medal.

Charles was about to head off to Spasso House for lunch when there was a knock on the door and Kowalski entered. "I found your note that you'd been looking for me this morning. What's up?"

"Nothing urgent. I just wanted to go through with you one last time the steps that you'll execute Saturday night." He could tell by the look on the Sergeant's face he thought they'd already walked through the steps enough! "This is the last time, I promise."

Kowalski sat down in the straight chair in front of Charles' desk and started reciting the plan.

"One: I leave the Mission at 1710 hours and drive to the store down on south Leninsky Prospekt that sells wine and buy a couple of bottles."

"Two: I head off to that Commission Store we went to together last month, and take a quick look in there."

"Three: If I've not seen any signs of cars following me, I then start driving in the general direction of north, as if heading for Spasso House, but use some side streets so as to flush out surveillance if its there.

"Four: If clear, I then head for Point X and try to arrive there at 1805. I pull over to the curb and hopefully, your two 'friends' come out and get in the back seat of my car. We then head straight for the airport."

"Five: At the airport, I show my pass to the guards and presumably they let us through the gate. Once within the American Section, we just park in the dark and wait till 0300 hours when I put the bandages on the guy and then escort them inside. Presumably, they know their roles as M.P. and prisoner. Everybody in there knows me, so I really don't think there will be any trouble if we've gotten that far. I walk with them as far as the plane and hopefully it takes off as scheduled, and then I return directly to my quarters."

"Six: I come to Spasso House Sunday morning at 0900 hours for breakfast and if I see you there, I'll know nobody shot you Saturday night. If you see me smiling, you'll know they at least got on the plane and left here safely."

Charles smiled. "I know my part. You know your part. Hopefully, the two Russians know their roles and if the NKVD doesn't fuck it up, we'll all live happily ever after."

"Sounds good. Say, if this works, could you smuggle me out of here the following week? I'm tired of Moscow myself." Kowalski grinned as he stood up to leave.

"Maybe we should smuggle both of us out of here. The Soviets are going to be very unhappy people, soon as they realize these two people are gone and they figure out I probably had something to do with it."

He stood, reached out and shook Kowalski's hand. "I'll see you on Sunday morning for breakfast."

"Yep, till Sunday."

Late morning Thursday, Charles left his office in the Mission and went down the hall to find Major Singell. He was at his desk filling out some form or another. "Barry, you got a minute?"

"Sure, what's up?"

"Let's go down to my office."

"OK." He rose, picked up his coffee mug and followed Worthington down the hallway, curious as to what was afoot.

After Charles had closed the door and turned up his radio, he got straight to the point. "You remember telling me recently that if I ever needed a little 'unofficial' help, I could call on you?"

"Yes, and I meant it."

"Well, I need some assistance this Saturday."

"OK, what's up?"

"First, the ground rule here. You can say 'yes' or 'no', but the contents of our conversation stays strictly between you and me. Agreeable?"

"My word, this is strictly off the record between you and me."

"OK, I have to meet a guy this Saturday evening. It's still early in the game with him and I'm not sure yet I trust him one hundred percent."

Singell nodded. "Understood."

"I'd like you to be standing by in your car – maybe four-five blocks away, holding a sack of money and some papers for me. I'll go to meet him and check out the situation. If all looks good, I'll come back to you and retrieve those items. You then get the hell out of the area and I'll go back to meet my guy."

"You don't want me to stick around and watch your back?"

"No, I appreciate the offer, but I want to keep you out of this as much as possible. Just hold my stuff at a safe distance and then get out of there. That way, no matter what happens, you're not involved. If this meeting turns to shit, General Deane isn't going to be a happy man and I don't want to screw up your career."

"OK, so first, you go off to meet this fellow. What if you don't come back to the car in twenty-thirty minutes? What should I do?"

"If I'm not back in twenty, I'm probably not coming back, so just go back home and forget you were even out that night."

"And what do I do with this money?"

Charles smiled. "Well, if I'm not back by the next day, if I were you, I'd just put it under your mattress and forget we ever had this conversation."

Singell smiled. "So, it's that unofficial is it?"

"General Donovan knows what's happening, but nobody else here in Moscow does."

"Ah, so this is why you went back to Washington a few weeks ago?"

"Yes. Any other questions?"

"Just one if I may, since I'm going to be out there with you on a dark night. I don't want to know any details, but will you be meeting with a Russian?"

Charles hesitated for several long seconds, pretending as if he was deeply debating whether to answer or not, just to build the suspense.

"Fair enough. It is a Russian, but he claims to know of a Nazi spy within the Soviet NKVD – that's why it's considered worth the risk of my meeting with him."

Singell let out a low whistle. "For that kind of information, I'd agree with you and Donovan that it's worth the risk. You're going to ride with me to the area of your meeting?"

"Yes."

"And where is the meeting?"

Again, Charles hesitated a long moment for effect. "I'll give you specific directions Saturday evening after we leave Spasso House, but in general, we'll be headed for Komsomolskaya Metro Station – an area near there actually, but I'll have you wait just a few blocks from the metro stop."

"And what time will we depart?"

"I'll get back to you about that Saturday morning, but it will be early evening – say 1730 hours. I want you to have some dinner before we head off."

Again, Singell smiled. "You're a very considerate master spy of your underlings!"

"Thanks very much for your assistance. You're one of the few people around here I know I can trust." He stood and reached over to shake Barry's hand."

"Think nothing of it. I'm just glad I can really do something to help win this war. Pushing paper day-after-day does get pretty boring!"

"Well, if all goes well, this should definitely help the war effort. I'll see you Saturday morning at breakfast time in Spasso House, say 0900 hours."

"See you then." Singell headed back to his own office. Charles sat back down at his own desk, quite satisfied with how his gambit had gone with Singell. He still couldn't know for certain, but simply the fact that he'd agreed to participate in an activity clearly out of his assigned Army duties, made it pretty clear that Singell was the mole. Maybe he was just ignoring Army regs and being very patriotic, but Charles doubted if that was the explanation. He felt fairly confident that Barry would pass the word to the NKVD about a "special meeting" on for Saturday evening and he hoped that the Soviets would then react as anticipated!

Every fifteen minutes or so Charles would step out in to the hallway and confirm that Singell's office door was still open. At 1215, he saw that it was closed, so Charles hurried over to Spasso House to see if Barry was there having lunch. He was not. Charles had a quick bite to eat himself, then returned to the Mission building and again discreetly looked around for Singell. It was nearly 1500 hours before Charles saw that his office door was again open. He wondered where his suspect mole had gone for nearly three hours.

Major Singell came in to the mess hall just shortly before Charles finished his dinner and sat down with him. They both avoided any reference to their "secret" discussion of the morning and just discussed the usual mundane topics of life in Moscow – whose tour was about up, what's the new guy like, whether a new issue of Stars and Stripes had arrived, etc. After about five minutes of such chit-chat, Charles slipped in one innocuous sounding question, but very important to Charles.

"Did you get much done today, Barry?"

"I pushed a lot of paper, if that counts as getting something done."

Charles laughed, "Kept your butt glued to your office chair all day, huh?"

"I got up twice today to pee; otherwise I hardly left my desk all day. I've got to find a little pillow to put on my chair, or by the end of this assignment I'm going to be permanently injured!"

Just as he was finishing his statement, two other officers came over and joined them and the conversation turned to the news received that day by one of them that his wife was four months pregnant. "She's been waiting to tell me till she was positive and that all seemed to be going well."

Charles finished the last of his dinner and slipped away as the conversation continued on the question of whether the young lieutenant wanted a boy or a girl. Charles went directly up to his room and lighted himself a "victory" cigar. As far as he was concerned, the fact that Singell lied about having gone out somewhere for almost three hours in the middle of the day confirmed Charles' suspicion that Barry was the mole. There was a one percent chance that the Major had gone out for some legitimate reason, but a ninety-nine percent chance he'd slipped off to report to his NKVD handler that Charles had something big going down on Saturday evening. Charles opened the Charlie Chan mystery he was in the middle of, to enjoy reading while he finished his cigar.

CHAPTER 20

At 1300 hours on Friday, Comrade Beria called the special investigative committee to order. They were meeting in emergency session to discuss the latest news that had come to their attention Thursday evening. All of them had been given a numbered copy of the agent report to read that morning, and which all had brought to the meeting.

Beria began in a very calm and steady voice. "It would appear that our suspicion about this Captain Worthington being connected with a traitor within our own organization is correct. Perhaps he's running two different agents, but from the extraordinary steps he's taking for this agent meeting on Saturday evening, the logical conclusion is that he is to meet with a source within our organization. The traitor who has leaked word of our having penetrated the Manhattan Project." He looked around the table to see if there were any dissenters with that conclusion. There were not.

He turned toward his colleague from the Counterintelligence Section. "Comrade Parshenko, what are your plans for coverage for Saturday evening?"

His bushy, white eyebrows went up high as he began to speak. "Well, we don't want to scare this Worthington off from going to the meeting, so we'll have no coverage on him and his colleague when they leave Spasso House on Saturday. There is really no need, as we already know where in general he is headed – the area around the Komsomolskaya Metro Station. We will simply flood that area with stationary surveillance for ten city blocks in all directions, so we'll have an eye on him wherever he goes He will see people about, but no one will follow him. Every man will have an excuse for why he's standing or sitting in each spot and will be appropriately dressed. I will also arrange that there will be no uniformed Moscow Militia officers around who could inadvertently screw anything up."

"Do you have enough men to cover that much area?" asked Beria.

"We will pull coverage off of all the targets we have been concentrating on for the past several weeks with the special squads we brought down from Leningrad. That should give us a sufficient number of men."

When a few others mumbled about whether that was a good idea, Parshenko explained his reasoning. "First of all, I will need all the men I can get for that night. I must have every street covered. Second, and more importantly, if one of our current targets is the mole, I don't want him to see surveillance earlier in the day and thus possibly scare him off from coming to the meeting with Worthington. We want to catch the two of them together, red-handed." He slapped his hand down on the table for emphasis.

Colonel Protkin of Security asked, "And what exactly will you do with this Worthington? He has diplomatic status, doesn't he? Do we have the legal right to detain him?"

Beria fielded that question. "We will detain him, gently but firmly, and take him to an office at the Foreign Ministry, on the justification that we had to confirm that the person claiming to be Captain Worthington really was that person. On Sunday afternoon, Deputy Foreign Minister Suslov, who normally deals with the American Embassy, will demand that General Deane personally come to the Ministry. He will be confronted with the blatant evidence that OSS officer Worthington has been engaging in espionage against the Soviet Union, in gross violation of the agreement by the Allies not to spy on one another."

Everyone at the table nodded in agreement that this was an excellent plan.

"We will of course respect his 'diplomatic immunity' and then release him in to the personal custody of General Deane. We will demand that he be gone from the USSR within twenty-four hours. We will also demand a personal apology, in writing, from Ambassador Harriman." Beria then just sat there smiling.

About that same time on Friday afternoon, Worthington called over to the NKVD Headquarters to speak with Captain Nosenko to make an appointment for Tuesday or Wednesday in the coming week with Colonel Suvarov. Charles wanted to maintain the impression that all was as usual. He got an appointment for 1000 hours on Tuesday. He thought about calling up Jane and arranging a dinner with her for the next week as well, but was afraid that she might announce that she was free over the weekend and suggest he come over. He didn't want to be heard on the city telephone system claiming to her that he was too busy Saturday or Sunday to see her.

Suddenly his phone rang. It was General Deane's scheduling adjutant.

"The General would like you to accompany him to a ceremony on Monday afternoon at a Red Army cemetery. They are commemorating all the Soviet soldiers who died last year fighting in the Battle of Kursk."

The last thing Charles wanted to be doing on Monday was going to some ridiculous Red Army ceremony, but he would have to have a pretty good explanation to give to General Deane as to why he would be too busy to attend. And again, he wanted to maintain the picture as to how everything in his life was just the usual, boring activities. He did make one mild attempt to get out of it.

"Any reason that General Deane wants me in particular to attend this ceremony with him?"

"He doesn't. It's just that we try to spread this sort of thing around to all officers below the rank of major and from my chart, I see that you haven't participated in one since your arrival in Moscow."

"I see. Of course, I would be happy to attend the ceremony with the General."

"Excellent. Please be here at the General's office and ready to go at 1400 hours on Monday. I'll go ahead and advise the Red Army's Protocol Office that it will be General Deane, you and First Lieutenant Peter Murau attending the ceremony."

"Thank you. I'll be there at 1350 hours on Monday."

"Perfect. You have a good weekend, Captain Worthington."

Charles immediately cleaned off his desk and left the building. God knows who might call next and invite him to a Red Cross tea, or some other absurd event that would screw up his life in the coming days. If he wasn't reachable, he couldn't be invited to anything!

As he entered the grounds of Spasso House, he saw Viktor shoveling the couple of inches of snow that had fallen that morning. He waved at the kindly old gentleman, but did not go over to him. He just wasn't in the mood to talk to anyone. He went straight to his room and locked the door. He would simply pretend not to be in to whomever might come knocking.

He went down to dinner promptly at 1700 hours, grabbed a quick bite to eat and returned immediately to his room. Solitude was what he wanted that evening before the big day on Saturday.

He tried reading to pass the time, but his mind kept drifting back to Sasha, the exfiltration plan and how the NKVD might react when they figured out that he had hoodwinked them. Old Chicago came to his mind. He'd heard that on occasion when somebody had really annoyed Al Capone, he'd put out the word that the guy had twenty-four hours to get out of town and never return – a pretty civilized approach. But then there was also the St. Valentine's Day massacre of 1929. Capone had had enough of a rival north side gang headed by "Bugs" Moran and ordered the machine gun killing of seven of Moran's underlings lined up at a brick wall. There was no point in reviewing the risk versus gain again. Sasha had invaluable intelligence related to the Manhattan Project and it was worth whatever risk to give him the best possible odds of getting safely to America. He just hoped it worked.

At 2200 hours he decided to go to bed, even if he couldn't go to sleep. It was several hours before he did finally drift off, but at least while horizontal in bed, his thoughts turned to Jane and her negligee, which was much more pleasant than thinking of Al Capone.

He awoke at 0700 hours and other than showering and shaving, he had nothing to do until the mess opened on weekends at 0830 hours. He was the first guy in line when the door finally opened, although there were four other officers right behind him. Presumably, guys who also had nothing else to do on a Saturday morning. Charles went for the scrambled eggs, two pancakes and a cup of the Ambassador's good Brazilian coffee. The pancakes weren't exactly soft and fluffy, but the Aunt Jemima Maple Syrup made them quite tasty.

He grabbed a copy of Stars and Stripes that was only two weeks old and went over to a small table by a window and read what was happening back in America as he ate. As he looked around the room, he started getting a little nostalgic about Spasso House. Regardless how the operation went down this weekend, Charles figured he'd be back in the States within three or four weeks – either as a hero, or in a pine box. Despite the horrible winter weather, he'd enjoyed a number of things about being in Moscow, mostly the people. Jane was at the top of that list, but several of the fellows he'd played poker with were good guys and Kowalski was in a class all by himself for his willingness to "unofficially" help out Charles. Even Moscow itself, when covered in sparkling white snow, was attractive. His formal liaison duties had been a farce, but it had justified his being in Moscow and thus available to be contacted by Sasha, who'd already provided important intelligence. If he showed up in America with the actual name of one of the Soviet moles within the Manhattan Project, he'd be considered quite a star, as would Charles himself. His mind turned back to people he'd met and liked, and among them was Viktor. Even if he was an informant, he was still quite a unique and charming Russian. Charles admired the fact that while he'd certainly been dealt a tough hand in life, being sent to live for years in a Siberian labor camp, he still held an optimistic view of life and his fellow man. He was really a very likeable fellow. A smile came to his face as he wondered just what Viktor had come up with week after week to report to the NKVD about him, so he could keep his relatively cushy job as handyman at Spasso House.

He took a second cup of coffee back up to his room and spent the next half hour writing a letter to Jane. It wasn't a sad, farewell letter or anything like that, but he liked to have all his bets covered. Just in case things didn't go well that night, he wanted to tell her again what a special night it had been when he'd stayed till dawn with her – and how he hoped there would be thousands more of such nights in the years ahead for them. He sealed it in an envelope and would leave it in the Military Mission for Kowalski to deliver to the British Embassy on Monday. He passed the rest of the morning reading. He wanted to finish his current Charlie Chan novel before he headed out that night.

Finally, evening arrived and it was time for him and Singell to start their "drive" around the city. He wore his uniform and his regulation Army outer coat. He didn't want to give the Russians any pretext that whoever might "mug" him that night didn't know they were attacking an American military officer.

Singell was waiting down in the mess hall when Charles came in. He'd finished a light dinner and was just drinking coffee. He nodded when he saw Charles at the door, picked up his tray and began his exit.

"All set?" asked Barry.

"We're good to go." He held up a small Russian-style shopping bag, in which he'd placed US$2,000 from his OSS contingency fund. Money he kept in his locked filing cabinet in his office that no one else knew about. He'd also drawn up a list of fake questions about Soviet intentions toward Finland and Poland once fighting with the Nazis ended. He presumed that Singell would sneak a peek at the contents while he was out of the car. Charles wasn't exactly sure what good it would do to fool the Soviets about his mythical agent, but saw no reason to help point a true finger at Sasha. He placed such a large amount of money in the sack as a tease to any Russians who might hear from Singell as to what was in there. Maybe if other NKVD officers saw what kind of big money there was to be made from working for the OSS, it might give somebody else ideas.

Singell drove. "Where to?" he asked.

"Just head as if we're going down to the Metropole Hotel for dinner, but stay out on the main streets."

"I thought we were headed to Komsomolskaya Metro area?" asked Singell anxiously.

"We are. I just want it to look initially as if we're headed somewhere they'd expect."

Singell looked much relieved. "Ah, very clever."

For the next twenty-five minutes, the only talking was Charles giving Barry driving directions. Finally, he said, "OK, pull over here to the curb." He put the bag down on the floor of the car. "You're in charge of this until I return. I should be back in 25-30 minutes, but give me one hour. If I'm not back by then, go home and keep the sack safe until you've heard from me, or about me."

Barry reached out his hand shook Charles'. "Good luck and stay safe."

Charles exited the car and headed off in to the night. There were very few street lights in Moscow. Fortunately, it was early enough that residents had lights on in their apartments and some light shined out on to the sidewalks. No one seemed to be following him, but he did note that a number of people seemed to be standing in doorways smoking or waiting at bus stops. He wondered if all of them could be surveillants. He hoped they were, for if that was true, there couldn't be anybody left to be watching Kowalski or Sasha that night. Not even the NKVD had that many surveillants!

Charles finally came to a stop at an intersection and stood in the doorway of a closed bread store. Every few minutes, he stepped out on to the sidewalk as if looking up and down the street for someone. Each time he did this, he tried to look ever more anxious. After twenty minutes, he had one last look around and then started walking rapidly back towards the car.

Singell was still sitting in the car. Charles tapped on the passenger side window and he unlocked the passenger door. The bag was still on the floor. Charles entered and closed the door.

"Change of plans. Let's head straight back to Spasso House."

Singell looked a little frantic. Obviously, sitting alone in a car at night on a very dark street was not his idea of fun, even when he knew he was safe.

"What happened?" he asked as he started up the car.

"The guy never showed. I waited at the designated spot for twenty minutes and then left." Charles tried to show that he was a bit upset and mystified. "Could be a dozen innocent reasons as to why he didn't make the meeting, but of course it could be he got cold feet. Or worse, he's been arrested. Let's get out of this area as quickly as possible."

"So, what happens now?"

"The plan is that we try again at this same spot in two weeks, when hopefully I'll learn that he simply had to work a weekend shift or fell and broke his ankle, but all I can do now is sit and wait."

"You don't have any way to contact him?"

"No, it's just a pre-arranged street corner on certain dates and times."

"But you do know where he works?"

"I know the name of the department, but I don't even know physically where it's located." Charles simply shrugged his shoulders.

Singell wanted to ask what department that was, but couldn't think of any explanation of why he would ask such a question, so he just drove on in silence until they reached Spasso House. He pulled up near the outer gate.

"I'll let you off here. I was invited to play a little poker over at Fred's apartment. Since it's still pretty early, I think I'll head on over there. Sorry things didn't work out for you tonight."

"Well, few things ever work out exactly according to plan in my business." Charles shrugged his shoulders and exited the car. "Thanks for your help in any case. We can try again in two weeks, if you're still willing."

"Absolutely, you can count on me any time. Good night."

"Good night, Barry."

Charles took his bag and headed in to Spasso House. Ambassador Harriman was having some sort of dinner party, so Charles used the side entrance and went up the back staircase to get to his room. He managed to maintain a somber look until he had closed and locked the door, then he let a wide smile spread across his face. He'd successfully carried out his part of the plan in drawing lots of NKVD surveillants off to watch him for the evening. He presumed that Singell had run off to meet with his NKVD handler to explain what had happened, not to play poker.

Hopefully, Kowalski had been equally successful in getting Sasha and Anastasia in to the airport, and in just another seven hours or so, their plane would be on its way to Archangel. There was nothing more for him to do that night. He wouldn't see Kowalski until Sunday morning breakfast and learn how things had gone the night before. He got out of his closet his last bottle of Jack Daniels with the last two inches of bourbon in it. He would optimistically go ahead and have a celebratory drink to having outwitted the NKVD. He lighted a cigar to go with his drink. Yes, all-in-all, a pretty good evening he silently thought to himself. Too bad Jane didn't have a phone. He would have liked to call her up, just to hear her lovely voice. He had to settle for his memory of it and the wonderful feel of her body. He then undressed, turned off the lights and laid down in his bed. He fell asleep fairly quickly. He'd been on an adrenalin rush earlier, but now he was unbelievably tired.

Morning came quickly and it was barely light when he awoke a little before 0700 hours. He would have ninety minutes to kill before the mess hall opened and perhaps even longer before Kowalski showed up. The sergeant wasn't by nature a morning person, but perhaps he'd make an exception since he knew Charles would be going crazy, waiting to hear the results of the previous night.

Sometimes, the cook would do something special for Sunday morning breakfast. As Charles went down to the serving line ten minutes after it opened, he was delighted to see crisp bacon and fried hash brown potatoes to go with the scrambled eggs. He must have gotten in a special shipment of a couple of slabs of bacon and a big sack of real potatoes! There probably wasn't enough to feed everyone who would eventually show up that morning, but that would be a lesson to the late-comers not to come so late! Charles took the excellent breakfast as an omen that Kowalski would arrive with good news. Promptly at 0900, his partner in crime strolled slowly through the door. Soon as their eyes locked, his fellow Chicagoan's mouth widened in to a large smile. It was good news.

Soon as he'd filled his tray, he came over and sat down with Charles and one other officer. They both greeted Kowalski. Moscow was just too small and too miserable a place not to let non-coms eat with the officers.

"How you doing?" politely inquired Charles of Kowalski.

"Pretty good. How about yourself?"

"I didn't sleep too well last night, but I'm doing better today. You do anything fun last night?"

"No, pretty quiet night for me."

The young lieutenant who was sitting with them inquired, "What the hell is there to do that's fun in this place?"

Charles smiled and replied, "Wait till you've been here longer. Your definition of 'fun' sinks ever lower and soon you'll think playing cards or finding a newspaper only three weeks old qualifies as fun!"

"I've already been here six months and still nothing seems like fun." He stood up and picked up his tray. "I'll see you guys later. Taking a crap after breakfast is probably going to be the highlight of my Sunday!"

Worthington and Kowalski both laughed.

Soon as they were alone, Charles asked, "So, how did it go?"

"Smooth as silk. They were both at the rendezvous point promptly on time and there wasn't another soul in sight on that small street. The Russian guards on duty last night at the airport couldn't care who drove in and the three Americans who had Saturday night duty didn't care who flew out. The plane left on time this morning and I was back in bed by 0600 hours."

"Excellent. Any way of discreetly finding out this afternoon if the plane has left Archangel on time without problems?"

"I stopped by the duty desk at the Military Mission on my way over here this morning to get a book out of my office. If there'd been any flap up at Archangel since the plane landed there, the duty officer would have known about it and said something." He looked at his watch. "The plane is scheduled to leave in about six hours. I'll swing by the Mission again in seven hours and can find out if the flight left on time without incident for England. If there was a problem, I'll come back here to find you. Otherwise, you'll know everything went smoothly."

"Well, so far so good. You might as well just leisurely enjoy your breakfast. It isn't every day that we get bacon and real potatoes!" Charles stood to leave.

Kowalski put on a big grin. "No, sir, it isn't," he said loudly and then softly added, "Or to fuck over the Russians!"

Charles replied, "No, not every day." He then slowly strolled out of the mess hall, hands in his pockets like a man without a care in the world.

The NKVD special investigative committee met at 1400 hours on Sunday as scheduled. This session had been planned as a celebratory one and to discuss just who had been found to be the traitor. Before Chairman Beria arrived, everyone around the table had been briefed on what had happened, or rather what had not happened on Saturday evening. His face was even gloomier than those of his colleagues. He already had a meeting scheduled for 2000 hours that evening with Comrade Stalin, in anticipation of giving him good news. Now, he would have to show up with bad news, never a good thing to present to Stalin!

"We all know what appeared to transpire last night. Any thoughts on what really happened yesterday? Did Worthington's alleged agent not show because something unavoidable came up and the agent simply couldn't get to the meeting, as does happen sometimes in agent work? Or have we been cleverly deceived and we just don't know yet to what purpose? Personally, I suspect that it's the latter." He looked around the table at all his colleagues who were studiously staring down at blank notepads in front of them. Apparently, they thought if they didn't make direct eye contact with Beria, he wouldn't call on them to speak.

After several long seconds of silence, General Parshenko raised his head and began to speak. "I don't know what actually happened last night, but as of 1000 hours this morning I sent orders to the special surveillance squads brought down from Leningrad to go to the homes of every NKVD officer on our suspects list and question them on what they were doing from noon Saturday until the moment they were asked that question. Most had easily confirmable answers, such as dinners with friends and two are out of the city on business. Three initially claimed to have simply been out drinking with a friend or two, but once they were out of sight of their wives, two admitted they had been with prostitutes. We're checking the stories of all three of these men. That leaves only three men who have yet to have been found. Two are single and one married. I have men waiting at the apartments of these three until each one returns. We are also contacting their work colleagues to see if any of these three had mentioned what they might be doing over the weekend. All of this is taking some time to do, but I hope that by 1700 hours we will have talked to all the men on our suspects list." He looked over at Beria and added, "Thus, you might have something positive to tell Comrade Stalin tonight."

"Well, that's at least something," replied the Chairman of the NKVD. "I have to go to another important meeting now. When I return in an hour, I want you to have suggestions for me on what other actions to take this very day. Also, your thoughts on what, if anything, we should do about OSS officer Worthington?

Charles never ventured out of Spasso House on Sunday and was back in the mess hall for dinner at 1730 hours. By 1800, he'd still seen no sign of Kowalski. He took his no-show as positive news. Sasha by that time should be well out of Soviet airspace and on his way to America. Charles wished he'd saved just a little of his Jack Daniels for another toast, but his glass of powdered milk would have to do.

Just minutes before Beria was to meet with Stalin, General Parshenko reached him via phone at the Kremlin.

"Comrade Chairman, we have accounted for all of the suspects, except for one. He is Captain Alexandr Turgenev. Everything seems in place in his apartment, but there is no sign of him and none of his neighbors remember seeing him since Friday evening. One of his colleagues has told us he has a girlfriend named Anastasia, but he doesn't know her last name or have any idea of where she works or lives. So, perhaps he's simply spending the weekend with her."

"You may wish to be optimistic Parshenko. I can't afford to be so. What is his position within the service?"

"He is the archivist and records keeper for all Manhattan Project reporting we receive from America."

There was total silence from the other end of the line.

"Did you hear me, Comrade?"

A feeble voice replied, "Yes, I heard you. Good god!"

"Do you still wish to proceed with the other measures we discussed this afternoon?" asked Parshenko.

"Let me confirm these with Comrade Stalin and I'll get back to you within the hour." There was a long pause and then he added, "I hope."

CHAPTER 21

On Monday morning, Charles waited until four or five of his colleagues had finished breakfast and were leaving Spasso House for work at the Military Mission, so as to walk with them. He figured no action could be taken against him during the ten minute stroll if surrounded by a number of other American military officers. He went to his office and locked the door behind him. He took out his one-time pad code book and began the slow task of encrypting by hand a message to General Donovan giving him the good news of the safe departure of Sasha for America via England. He estimated that he would arrive in New York City within two-three days and advised that Sasha had instructions on how to get in touch with Donovan via a mutual friend. He then asked that General Donovan send word once there was confirmation of the Russian's safe arrival in America. He figured Donovan could learn about Sasha's girlfriend from Sasha. He preferred only sending "good" news at the moment. Charles decided to send a separate message later that morning identifying Major Barry Singell as the mole within the Military Mission, as that information would be shared with different offices. He took his hand-coded message to the Communications Section where he was informed that there would be no incoming or outgoing classified communications for at least twenty-four hours as the section conducted a full maintenance and update on the equipment.

Charles was dumbfounded. "Who ordered this maintenance check for this morning?"

"Major Singell was here bright and early this morning and personally ordered it. He is in charge of this section you know."

"Any explanation by him for this action today?"

"Not really, he just said that orders had come down from on high."

"OK, well here's my message to send once you're back in business. He figured it was as safe leaving it with the Commo officers as it would be in his personal filing cabinet with lock. He didn't like this attempt by Singell to cut him off from communicating with Washington for the next 24 hours or more, which he was sure is what this "maintenance check" was really all about. There was however, one other channel available to him that not even Singell could shut down – the unclassified US Postal Service bag, which would be going out from the Embassy that very day at noon. He'd never expect Charles to use it to communicate classified information back to Washington.

Charles locked his office door and began a very chatty letter to his former boss, Mr. Astor. No matter what else happened in the coming days, he would insure that Donovan would eventually get word about Singell being the traitor in the Mission. He wrote about signs that spring might soon reach Moscow, of improving his chess game and even a little bit about the English girl, Jane Summerfield. He didn't want to get the censors too excited, so he left out about her negligee attire at their last dinner! Buried towards the end of the second page of the handwritten letter, he inserted the key sentence. "When you see Bill, please tell him I recall how at our last meeting, he'd asked me to recommend someone for a position in his office. After careful thought, the obvious choice is Barry Singell, a very special fellow." Donovan would clearly understand the meaning of those two sentences. Charles then added two more paragraphs about books he'd recently read, quite enjoyed and highly recommended to Astor.

He sealed the envelope, addressed it to Astor's home in New York City and stamped it. He put it in the inside pocket of his tunic and headed down to the mail room, with thirty minutes to spare. When no one else was in the hallway to observe him, he slipped his envelope into the mail slot. On the way back to his office, he passed Singell's. The lights were on, but his door was closed. Maybe he figured he'd get fewer questions about shutting down communications for a day if nobody actually saw him. Back in his office, he mentally composed what he would write about Singell in an official telegram, once he knew that communications were back up and running.

As it got closer to time for heading over to General Deane's office, he tracked down Lt. Murau to suggest they go over together. He even requested a duty car and driver, just to surround himself with one more person while out on the streets of Moscow that day. He was probably being overly cautious, but better safe than sorry. Murau was quite amenable to the idea of going together. He was actually looking forward to having a little "face time" with General Deane and admitted he'd actually volunteered to go to this ceremony. They arrived promptly on time and were sitting in Deane's outer office when he came out to depart for the Soviet memorial ceremony. The sun had even appeared in the afternoon, which would make the affair a little less gloomy.

The General was carrying with him a recent Time magazine to read in the car. Murau's face turned down. He might be seen by Deane, but the lieutenant presumed he would be expected to sit quietly and not speak while the General read to and from the cemetery! Worthington smiled and thought to himself, "Ah, the best laid plans of young lieutenants." Charles looked at his watch and calculated that they should be back in time for dinner. He'd heard a rumor that the mess hall cook, Sarge, was going to be offering Italian spaghetti and meatballs that night, Charles did not want to miss that.

Phone calls started flying between General Deane's office, the Embassy and the Military Mission about 1530 hours. Initially, the story was that General Deane had been shot and killed by a sniper at the Soviet cemetery, along with five or six other officers present on the podium. However, at 1545 General Deane himself rushed through the doorway of his outer office, dispelling that rumor. He was wearing no coat.

He shouted to his adjutant, "Get me Ambassador Harriman on the phone, right now. I don't care if he's meeting with Stalin himself or taking a bubble bath. I want him on the phone now! We've got a dead American soldier." He headed straight for his 18th century desk and sat there waiting for the connection to be made over to the American Embassy.

A few seconds after Deane, a stunned looking Lt. Murau came through the doorway. There was blood over the upper portion of his outer coat and dried blood on his face. As all the office staff stared at him, he said softly, "His head just exploded and he dropped to the ground. Then two Russians went down as people started diving in all directions." He didn't look at anybody in the room. He just stared vacantly straight ahead.

"Whose head exploded?" shouted one staffer.

"Worthington," mumbled Murau. "He's down in the car, covered with the General's coat."

Several people who'd had combat experience realized Murau was in shock and led him over to a chair and sat him down.

The General appeared in his doorway. "Go down and get that boy's body out of the car. Bring him up here."

The adjutant at the desk turned to Deane. "I have Ambassador Harriman on the line. I'll transfer it now to your desk."

General Deane closed his door and returned to his desk.

By dinner time, the Soviets had posted dozens of extra soldiers around the American Embassy, the Military Mission, Spasso House and any apartment buildings where Americans resided. The Americans as well posted extra soldiers at all the official buildings and all civilian and military staff were ordered to stay off the streets until further notice.

All conversation in the Spasso House mess hall that evening was about the shooting. The most recent version of events circulating was that some Nazi sniper had tried taking out General Deane, but after the first shot hit a Russian, Worthington stepped in front of Deane and took the next bullet. Another Russian or two were also killed, but nobody knew a final body count.

Kowalski spoke up. "How do we know it was a Nazi sniper?"

There was silence around the room. Finally, one man replied, "Well, who else would be shooting at American and Russian soldiers?" Most of the others nodded in agreement. Kowalski said nothing more, but remained skeptical, given what he knew had transpired over the weekend. He figured that by now, the NKVD had realized they were missing somebody from work, and that Captain Worthington had somehow had something to do with it. They might not yet have put two and two together and started wondering about who the man and woman were who flew out on Saturday night, but he decided that he'd just sleep on some couch right there in Spasso House that night.

At about the same time, a Soviet NKVD captain came in to General Parhsenko's office with the latest news from the hospital where the two Soviet Army lieutenants who'd been shot had been taken that afternoon.

"Unfortunately, both men have died, General. Our sniper sends his apologies, but in all the chaos and people running around, it was simply too difficult for him to make shots to non-vital parts of the men he was aiming for on the podium."

Parshenko shrugged his shoulders and lighted a cigarette. "Send him my congratulations for a job well done. It's understandable what happened to our two men."

The captain looked ill at ease.

"Is there something else?"

"I was just thinking that it's tragic that we had to shoot two of our own men."

"If some mystery sniper had only shot the American OSS officer, it would have raised suspicions, but this way the Americans will believe it truly was a an accidental tragedy and that the prime target had probably been General Deane. So, these two men had to die for the good of the Soviet Union. I will personally see that they are both awarded Red Stars for their sacrifices. And if it makes you feel any better, I had asked for the names of two of the most incompetent officers within the Moscow Military District. They may have done more for their country by dying, than had they lived." A thin smile came across Parshenko's lips. Anything else, Captain?"

"Still no sign of this Captain Alexandr Turgenev, sir. No one in his office had any inkling of him going away for the weekend, nor did any of his neighbors. And we're still trying to find out the last name of his girlfriend, this Anastasia."

"Have any of his colleagues or friends noticed any changed behavior by him in recent weeks or months? Spending more money, or anything like that?"

"Not that anyone is reporting so far. It seems the fellow led a very quiet life. He wasn't much a party goer and he'd even voluntarily chosen to work in the records section several years back. Only after the war started did he come back in to operational work. Wife and son are both dead. According to his record, he speaks English fairly well. We have several men at his apartment now, thoroughly going through every inch of his two-room apartment."

A deep frown came across Parshenko's face. "It's those quiet ones that you always have to watch carefully," he mumbled to himself. There was no definitive proof yet of a link between Worthington's strange behavior Saturday night and Turgenev's disappearance, but Parshenko knew in his gut they would eventually learn of some connection between the two men. He suspected that Turgenev was long gone from Moscow, but to where? It was a long way to the Finnish border and what idiot would go towards the front lines with the Germans? He'd personally been assured that morning by the Soviet Air Force colonel in charge at the airport that there were very tight controls on who could enter the American Section of the airport. It would be three more days before Parshenko would learn that that statement wasn't exactly accurate and in fact, there'd been a man and a woman in the back seat of one American vehicle that came to the airport on Saturday night.

On Tuesday morning, as Jane entered the British Embassy for work, the receptionist on duty at the front desk, asked her, "Have you heard the news, Miss Summerfield, about the shooting?

"No, what shooting?"

"Some Nazi-sympathizer tried killing American General Deane yesterday at an outdoor ceremony, in a cemetery no less."

"Was he hurt?"

"No, one of the yanks who was there with him stepped in front of the bullet and saved him, but he died. And so did two Russian officers who were there."

Jane felt a cold chill go up her spine. "Do we know the name of the American who was killed?"

"William Worth, or Worthington, something like that. Let me look. I've got it written down here." He looked down and started fumbling around with the papers on his desk. "Here we are, a Captain Worthington, poor bugger."

He looked back up at the WREN, who looked as if she'd just seen a ghost. "You alright, Miss?"

Jane didn't answer. She just turned and walked slowly down the corridor. She managed to get to their small canteen and took the first chair she came to, put her head down and started to softly cry. The two other people in the room looked over at her and finally the woman came over to her and put her arm around Jane's shoulder.

"What's wrong, dear? Is there anything I can do for you?"

She raised her head. "I just received some bad news about a friend. I'll be OK in a few minutes."

"Would a little water help, or a nice cup of tea?" The woman nodded over to Harry still sitting at his table. "Get her some tea." Russians thought that vodka was the medicinal cure for any problem; the English thought it was tea.

Soon Jane was sipping at a cup of fresh, hot tea. She'd stopped crying.

"Would it help to talk about it?" tentatively asked her female colleague.

Jane shook her head in the negative. "I need to go to my office. Thanks for your help." She stood and walked on down the hallway, almost in a state of shock. When she finally got within the small code room, she sat down and at least knew she'd be alone in there. She started thinking back to some of Charles' comments the last time they'd been together. A few of the things he'd said at the time had struck her as a little odd, but now made more sense. His talk about living life to the fullest and his statement about having to do the right thing for society, not just look out for yourself. It was like he knew he was about to die, but how could that be?

She got on the phone and dialed the American Military Mission. "May I speak to Master Sergeant Kowalski, please? It's the British Embassy calling."

"Let me check to see if he's around this morning. Hang on." She heard the receiver being laid down on a hard surface and several shouts in the background. After a long minute, another voice came on the line.

"Sergeant Kowalski here. May I help you?"

"It's Jane Summerfield calling from the British Embassy. Charles had mentioned your name several times. I believe you were friends."

"Yes, ma'am, I'd say we were friends." He wasn't sure what else to say.

"We just got word here that Captain Worthington has been killed. Could you confirm that that is true?"

Kowalski knew they were not supposed to be talking about the shooting, but he decided to ignore such orders, as he knew that Charles had been seeing this woman. "Yes, I'm sorry to say that the Captain is indeed dead. He died yesterday afternoon. I don't really know any of the specifics."

"Sergeant, could I ask a favor of you? Could you stop by the British Embassy some time today so that we might speak in person?"

Kowalski didn't look forward to dealing with a situation of a crying woman, which he suspected is what the meeting would turn in to upon his arrival, but it was impossible to say no. He also still had the letter left by Charles on Monday in his in-box that he was supposed to deliver to Miss Summerfield. He'd forgotten all about it in the chaos of the previous day. He looked at his watch. "Yes, ma'am. I could arrive there at 1500 hours, if that would work for you."

"Yes, that would be fine. I'll be waiting for you down at the main entrance. Thank you. Goodbye."

"Goodbye."

Kowalski suspected that this woman didn't believe any more than he did that the shooting had been an "accident." Charles smuggled two Russians out of Moscow on Saturday night and on Monday afternoon, a Nazi sniper just happens to shoot and kill Charles out of dozens of people on a podium! Mrs. Kowalski hadn't raised an idiot for a son and he was convinced that Charles had been set up. He also figured he'd better not go walking down any dark streets himself in the coming days.

Just after lunchtime that Tuesday, General Deane's adjutant came in to his boss. "Sir, I think you should be aware that Lt. Murau has been telling everybody in the Mission that Captain Worthington stepped in front of you and took a bullet headed for you. He's saying that one of the Russians near you was hit first and that Charles then stepped in front of you to protect you. I was over at Spasso House for lunch and all the men are talking about what a hero Worthington was."

"Yes, what about it?"

The adjutant hesitated a moment. "Well, sir, I recall you saying yesterday, right after you came in from the ceremony, that Worthington was hit first. Unless he could see the shot being fired and could move faster than a speeding bullet, I don't see how he could have intentionally stepped in front of you, sir."

"You say all the men are talking about what a hero Worthington was?'

"Yes, sir."

Deane leaned back in his chair, thinking for several long moments. "Well then, what Lt. Murau is saying is the correct version. I'll draft up a recommendation for the Bronze Star this afternoon for Worthington. Let the poor man's family and friends have the satisfaction that he died valiantly, and not that he just happened to be standing in the wrong place at the wrong time."

"Yes, sir. I understand, sir, but I drafted up a report of the incident yesterday afternoon and it, well, it reads a little differently..."

Deane looked at his adjutant. "No you didn't. There is no written account of the shooting yesterday yet. I'm about to put down on paper what happened yesterday at the cemetery. Are we clear?"

"Yes, sir, there is no draft report."

"Do we have any information in his file about next of kin for Captain Worthington? I'll personally do up a letter of condolence to his family."

"I've already checked his personnel file, sir. He has no living relatives listed, not even a distant cousin."

"That's quite unusual, but doesn't he have to have someone listed to be notified in case of his death?"

"Yes, sir, he does."

"Well?"

"He listed Vincent Astor, 5th Avenue, New York City, New York."

"Are you shitting me? The Vincent Astor?"

"I doubt if there is more than one Vincent Astor on 5th Avenue in New York City, sir."

"OK, let's get a message off priority to the Secretary of the Army, asking him to personally phone Mr. Astor and break the news to him. I'll write the condolence letter this afternoon to Astor. Do we have anyone traveling back to America in the next day or so, somebody who could hand-carry the letter to mail stateside?"

"I'll check immediately on that."

"And bring me in the form for the Silver Star. I'll be putting Worthington in for that award."

"Yes, sir, the Silver Star."

"Oh, and one last thing. Find some way to get Lt. Murau transferred back stateside, permanently – preferably to some supply depot in Texas or some place where he can cause no harm. I've never seen any soldier fall apart at the sight of one dead body as he did yesterday. I'd hate to think of him ever actually being in a combat zone!"

"Yes, sir. I'll look in to that as well." The adjutant was grinning as he walked out of the General's office.

Everybody lies, sometimes for a good reason.

Sergeant Kowalski pulled up to the entrance of the British Embassy promptly at 1500 hours. He'd brought two recently arrived corporals with him, on the justification that it would do them good to know where the British Embassy was located. He figured if he just happened to die that day, he wanted witnesses. The Brits did in fact have a spectacular location, right across the Moscow River from the Kremlin, with a splendid view of the massive structure. He left his colleagues in the vehicle as he went in and asked for WREN Summerfield.

She was waiting by the reception desk.

"Sergeant Kowalski, thank you for coming so quickly."

"My pleasure ma'am."

"How about a cup of coffee down in our canteen?"

"That would be great."

Once they had their coffee, she got straight to the point. "Sergeant, Charles and I had dinner at my place last week and he was sounding very philosophical about life that evening – and now he's dead less than a week later. I know this sounds crazy, but with hindsight, it's almost as if he knew was going to die. Is your Mission sure this was some purely coincidental sniper incident?"

Kowalkski had had a bad feeling on the drive over that she might raise such a question. "Do you want our Embassy's official position, or mine?"

She smiled. "I think yours would be more enlightening and I promise you, it stays with me."

"Well, the Captain and I were up to something on Saturday pretty important, which the Russians probably didn't like. I can't go in to detail, but let's just say it was pretty crafty what Charles had worked out. That guy had balls bigger than… sorry, ma'am I didn't mean to be so graphic."

Jane smiled. "That's quite alright, Sergeant. I'm surrounded by British soldiers all day long here. Go on."

"First of all, he didn't know that he was going to die. He wasn't that much of a pessimist; although he knew that there was danger involved with this operation on Saturday and maybe he wanted to say some things to you that night, just in case. But he was too self-confident and competent not to think he had at least a fifty-fifty chance.

"Thank you for telling me that. And the shooting on Monday?"

"Yes, well, I personally find it quite a coincidence that he pulls a fast one on the Commies on Saturday and then he just happens to be shot at a Soviet ceremony on Monday by some mysterious Nazi sniper! Like I said, that's just my personal opinion. I'm sure General Deane's official account is much more accurate." They both grinned.

"Thank you very much for sharing that with me. I'm just glad that Charles' death was linked to something important. I'm going to miss him terribly."

"If you're wondering, Charles wouldn't have felt a thing. One second he was standing there just fine and the next second, he wasn't. He wouldn't have even heard the bullet."

Jane just nodded and was fighting back the tears.

"If I may speak freely, ma'am. I know Captain Worthington was crazy about you. His whole face just lit up when he spoke about you and about a week back he was asking me if I had any idea what an apartment for two people might cost back in the New York area? I don't want to go putting words in his mouth, but I took such a question to indicate that he was thinking about marriage when he got back to America."

In truth, Charles had never said a word about Jane directly to him, but he could tell by the smile that suddenly came to her face that he'd made the right decision. What was one little exaggeration for a good cause, in a city where everybody lied?

He then pulled out the letter from Charles addressed to her. "He'd left this envelope in my in-box yesterday. I just found it this morning and was going to bring it over some time today and then you phoned me. "Here.""

She took the envelope and looked and saw that it was unopened. Kowalski saw her look at the seal.

"No ma'am, nobody's opened it. It's addressed to you and only you."

"Thank you, Sergeant, I'll open it a little later, when I'm..."

He saw a tear come from her left eye and run down her cheek. She couldn't speak.

"Well, Miss Summerfield, I'd better be getting back to my Mission. If there's ever anything I can do you for you, you just phone."

She held out her hand. He shook it and then left without saying another word. She continued sitting there for a while longer, thinking about Charles and his advice to her a couple of times that last evening together for her to get out and live. Don't live in the past of her long missing husband he'd said to her that night. She made a silent promise to Charles to do just that in the future. She'd read the letter that evening, when she was alone at her apartment.

Major Singell had been in a fretful state ever since Saturday night. He didn't know exactly what had gone down that night, but he thought it a very strange evening. He imagined that Charles had at least a strong suspicion that he was working with the NKVD and that night had been some sort of test. And then when Worthington was shot and killed on Monday afternoon, he like Kowalski, didn't believe Charles had just randomly been shot that day! He'd shut down outgoing communications from the Military Mission on Monday morning as the NKVD had instructed him to do. He'd explained to his Russian handler that it could only be for twenty-four hours, but he hadn't seemed to care that it would only be for one day. Of course, with Charles dead, he couldn't be writing any more messages to Washington. Unbeknownst to Singell however, Charles had left his hand-encrypted message with the Communications Room guys on Monday morning and indeed, it went out about 1000 hours on Tuesday. There would be quite a surprise waiting for General Donovan when he came in to work that day and decoded the message from Charles. It would be like getting a message from the grave.

Donovan had learned on Monday afternoon about Captain Worthington's death. The Secretary of the Army had phoned Mr. Astor as General Deane had requested and Astor had then immediately phoned Donovan. Everybody knew that in wartime men died, but it was still a rude shock when it happened to someone you knew personally and liked.

The hand-coded telegram he received on Tuesday morning explained to General Donovan about the exfiltration and he anxiously awaited word from somebody that this "Sasha" had made it to the United States. He also received a telegram from General Deane on Tuesday as a courtesy, explaining how his man had died at the ceremony in Moscow. The fact that two Russian officers were also killed in the shooting incident did make it look like Worthington's shooting had been coincidental. Still, Donovan was a little suspicious. Given his profession, he didn't believe in coincidences and the fact that less than forty-eight hours after smuggling someone out of Moscow, Charles "just happened" to be shot and killed – well, that was one hell of a coincidence!

He put the message in his personal safe for the present. He thought about scheduling a meeting of the special committee dealing with the Manhattan Project mole for later in the week, but decided he'd best wait until he'd heard that the Russian was safely in America. And more importantly, actually handed over the name of the mole. He hated to second guess Charles, especially since he was dead, but he hoped his officer in Moscow hadn't simply been duped by Sasha, so as to get out of the Soviet Union. As excited as he was, he'd just have to patiently wait a few days to take any action.

NEW YORK CITY

On Friday morning, someone with heavily accented English phoned Salvatore. "You are Mr. Salvatore, friend of Charles Worthington? This is Sasha."

"Yeah, what's can I dooze for ya?" It actually took Salvatore's brain a few seconds to remember the instructions that Charles had left weeks earlier with him and Lou.

"My friend and I have arrived in your amazing New York City and I am supposed to phone you, yes?"

"Yeah, glad's to hear from youse. Welcome to America! Where's youse calling from?"

"What you say?"

Salvatore guessed that his new friend didn't speak such good English, being a foreigner and all, so he spoke slowly and simply as he could, as if to a child. "Where you standing at now?"

"We are in place called Grand Central Station."

"Great. You see big hall and information booth in the center?"

"Yes, we were just in there. I saw booth."

"Great. You two go stands by there and I comes in twenty minutes to meet you. Whats you wearing?"

"I am wearing clothes of American soldier, of Military Policeman, with bandages on face. Girl is beautiful girl." Sasha gave Anastasia a big smile and told her in Russian what he'd just said about her on the phone. She smiled back.

Salvatore figured that it should be easy to find the two, even in Grand Central. "I be there in twenty minutes. Goodbye."

"Goodbye."

Salvatore shook his head and turned to Lou. "Geez, I's exhausted from having's to talk likes Mr. Astor. You'd think diz foreigners would learns better English befores they come to America. Let's go."

Sasha turned to his girlfriend and said to her in Russian, "I would have thought that a friend of Charles would speak better English." He shrugged his shoulders. "Let's go stand by information booth in the big hall."

Hundreds of people passed by them in the ensuing twenty minutes. Finally, an Italian-looking man, in an expensive pin-striped gray suit and wearing a gray fedora hat came up to them. "Youse looking for Mr. Salvatore?"

"Yes, are you that man?"

"Dat's me, Salvatore. Youse got any luggage?"

Sasha showed a big smile, having finally made contact with Charles' New York friend. "No, no suitcase. This is Anastasia. She no speak English."

Salvatore tipped his hat at the woman, who smiled back at him and held tightly to Sasha's arm.

"OK, let's goes. Follows me."

They headed out one of the large doorways and found parked just up the street a big, beautiful Packard. Salvatore pointed at it. "Get in." He took a look around to see if anybody seemed to be watching them.

Sasha let Anastasia enter first, as he also took a look around them to see if anybody was paying any particular attention to them.

Sally pointed at the bandages. "Youse OK?"

"Oh, yes." Sasha started pulling off his various bandages and showed that he had no damage. Sally realized that they had just been part of a disguise.

"We're goings to a nice Italian restaurant." He gestured with his hand as if bringing a fork up to his mouth. Anastasia smiled at him and nodded. "We can talk there." All three of them nodded in agreement.

In fifteen minutes the Packard pulled up to Mama's. Sally had warned Mama earlier that he'd be by with two special friends for lunch, so she was waiting to greet him soon as he came through the door.

Sally went over to her to kiss her cheek and quietly said to her, "Da girl don't speak no English and da guy's ain'ts so good, but he seems to understand if you speak real slow and clear for him."

Mama nodded and went over to the two guests. "Welcome," she said and gestured for them to come to a small, semi-private dining area near the back of the restaurant. Mama gave the two a big, warm smile. The two Russians smiled at her and followed her to the back. The table was all set with plates for four, bread and wine.

Mama poured all of them a glass of good, red Italian wine, and also filled a glass she'd set there in advance for herself. She raised her glass in a toast and said, "Welcome to America!" They all drank. Sasha could tell already he was going to like this New York City!

A few minutes into the conversation over the first course, Salvatore figured he'd better bring up the bad news about Charles and get that unpleasant task out of the way.

"Abouts our friend, Charles." He hesitated.

Sasha smiled. "Yes, how is my friend? Has he already arrived back in America?"

He looked over at Lou for any suggestion on how to proceed. Lou just stared down at his plate. Mr. Astor had called them on Monday after he'd gotten the news about Charles' death. Salvatore didn't know if that would affect what the two Russians were to do for Charles in coming days, but he figured they would want to know as soon as possible about their mutual friend.

"Charles won'ts be coming back to America, ever." He lowered his face.

"I do not understand. He told me it might be a few weeks, but that he would see me here in America."

"I don'ts knows all da details, but apparently der was a Nazi sniper at dis ceremony for dead Russian soldiers at some cemetery on Monday. He was trying to kill dis American general, but Charles stepped in fronts of him and took da bullet. Two Russian officers also was killed."

Sasha's smile disappeared from his face. "He was a good man. He gave his life for me." He quickly translated for Anastasia what he'd just learned and her smile also disappeared.

"Who is telling this silly story about a Nazi sniper?" asked Sasha.

"Da American Embassy. Da Secretary of the US Army himself called Mr. Astor with da news on Monday. Mr. Astor called me yesterday."

"Govno" mumbled Sasha. "I don't know this word in English, but that story is nonsense. Two days after he takes big risk to help me and Anastasia escape, a Nazi just happens to shoot Charles!"

"Does seems quites a coincidence doesn'ts it," offered Lou.

Sasha shrugged his shoulders. "Well, if that is silly story that your government wants to tell its people, is OK by me. I guess everybody lies when it serves their purpose."

Sasha crossed himself and then raised his wine glass, as did the others. "To a good man, Captain Charles Worthington. May my future days be worthy of this man."

Towards the end of the lunch, Sasha took Salvatore out to the main restaurant for a private chat. He took a folded piece of paper out of his pocket. "I promised Charles that when I safely arrived in America I would give him name of an American traitor working for Soviet Intelligence Service. Name is on this paper. Charles died for this name. Do you know how to get it to General Donovan?" He held it out.

Salvatore very solemnly took it and put it in his pocket. "I will's personally takes care of dis. I knows who to call. General Donovan will haves dis by tomorrow."

"Thank you."

After dessert, Salvatore brought up about the new identification papers. "It will takes two-threes days to get you and da Mrs. some high quality American identity documents. Any's name in particular youse wants?"

"Not really, no wait, make my new first name, Charles."

Salvatore smiled, "Yeah, Charlie boy would like that. And I'll finds out by tomorrows about when youse can get your money." He pulled a thick money clip from his pants pocket and peeled off three hundred dollars in twenties. "Here, dis will give you somes eating money till we cans get youse your money Charlie tolds us about. Plus, youse will need to gets some clothes and things for youse and the little lady."

Sasha was astounded. He'd never seen so much money in his life. "Thank you very much."

"One mores thing? Anybody maybes looking for you? American police? Russian police?"

"I'm sure the Soviet Government is looking very hard for me, though hopefully, they don't know I am in New York City."

"Well, we gots a little apartment overs in Brooklyn wheres you can lay low for the coming days. I got's a cousin who lives on da first floor. He'll keeps an eye out in case anybody comes around snooping, but just in case." Salvatore took a .45 out of a side pocket and handed it discreetly under the table to Sasha. "Dis will keep youse safer than my cousin."

Sasha grinned and took the gun.

"Ok, let's gets youse two over to Brooklyn."

CHAPTER 22

WASHINGTON DC

Not that he liked them much, but Salvatore took a late afternoon train down to Washington DC that Friday. He'd phoned ahead to Mr. Astor and simply said over the long distance phone line that he was coming to town and had the name of a horse that Charles wanted him to have. Astor quite enjoyed meeting and speaking with Salvatore and Lou and by the end of a conversation, the multi-millionaire was throwing out "youse" and "deese guys" like one of the boys from Brooklyn. They agreed on the phone to meet in an Irish pub near Union Station at 11:00 pm. Astor thought that might be a little less conspicuous than having Salvatore come to the Cosmos Club.

Astor was "dressed down" to only a cashmere sport coat and he'd removed his tie before entering Danny Boys Pub. The chauffeur dropped him off a block from the bar. He was enjoying some Irish whiskey at a corner table when Salvatore came in and headed over to him. "Goods evening, Mr. As…" Astor cut him off with a hand gesture.

"My name is Jones. I believe you are Mr. Smith from New York, here about a race horse."

Salvatore grinned and reached out to shake hands. "Yeah, I'm Smith and youse is Jones. How's youse doing tonight?"

"I'm doing well. I guess you've had a visitor from the other side of the ocean?"

"Yeah, twos of them in fact. Da guy Charles told me about and he brought this skirt with him, from da same place."

"Ah, I didn't know there was to be a woman brought along? His wife?"

"Naw, dey don'ts act married, but clearly he's sweet on her. I've gots both of dem stashed in Brooklyn for safe keeping and I'm setting dem up with some new names."

"Anything youse needs from General Donovan or me?"

"Just da ten grand Charles promised this guy and then I thinks he plans on taking a powder soons as possible. When I tolds him about Charles getting wacked, he started looking pretty worried. He said it weren't no coincidence."

"No, I'm pretty suspicious about that story as well. I'll see General Donovan tomorrow and probably gets back to youse by Monday with the cash. If it will be any longer than that, I'll just use my own money and then Donovan can repay me. Anything else?"

"Yeah, I gots something hot for da General." He took an envelope out of his inner breast pocket and slid it across the table to Astor. Der's a sheet of paper in dis envelope with a name on it. Our new friend said it's da name of the traitor here in America that Charlie has beens waiting for."

"Is it any name youse recognized?"

"I never looked. I figured dat name is secret and none of my business, so I justs put it in da envelope withouts looking at it."

Astor put the envelope in his coat pocket. "Excellent. I'm sure General Donovan will be very happy."

"One lasts thing. Tells da General, if he wants dis traitor to just quietly disappear some night, well, just have him calls me and Lou. No charge, we'd considers it ours patriotic duty."

Astor resisted smiling as he was certain that Sally and Lou were quite sincere in their offer. "I'll pass that offer along to General Donovan and let you know. And I'll travel up to Manhattan on Monday to pass youse da ten grand."

"Perfect."

"When are youse going back to New York City?"

"First train in da morning."

"You have a place to stay tonight? I know it's tough to find a vacant hotel room in this town. I might be able to help you get a room."

"No needs. I gots a little friend here in Washington, if you knows what I mean." Sally started smiling. "I suspects she'd be willings to share her bed tonight in dis emergency situation."

"Yes, I knows what youse means," replied Astor.

Astor ordered two last glasses of good whiskey and proposed a toast. "To our departed and dearly admired young friend – Charles."

"Yeah, to Charles."

They emptied their glasses, then Salvatore departed while Astor took care of the check.

Mr. Astor met briefly with General Donovan at the latter's office on Saturday afternoon. "It's very sad losing a fine young man like Charles," stated Donovan.

"Yes, he had such a bright future ahead of him. I trust whatever is in this envelope was worth his life." Astor slid the still unopened envelope with the name of the traitor across the desk. "And despite what the Secretary of the Army told me, I presume you don't believe that BS that this was an accidental, random shooting in Moscow?"

"That's the story that our Embassy in Moscow is sticking with, but that would be a hell of a coincidence. Charles cleverly arranged the exfiltration of two Soviet citizens out of Moscow and within forty-eight hours, he's accidently shot."

Donovan got $10,000 out of his personal safe for Astor to pass to Sasha through the two Italians in New York City. After Astor passed along what Salvatore had said about Sasha's plans to just disappear, Donovan wasn't entirely comfortable with the idea, but figured he could live with that. Although, he knew FBI Director Hoover wouldn't be happy at all. They chatted a few more minutes about Charles, then Astor departed with the money and made plans to travel to New York City on Monday morning. Afterwards, Donovan set the wheels in motion for the Interagency Committee on Policy Review to meet at the War Department on Tuesday afternoon. He decided to attend the meeting himself on Tuesday, to deliver the mole's name and to be directly involved in a decision as what to do next.

On Tuesday afternoon, the six members of the Committee, headed by Army Colonel Bishop, were already around the large oak table when Donovan arrived. He took the envelope from his coat and took out the slip of paper upon which Sasha had written the true name of the NKVD agent with the code name of the "old one" and handed it to Bishop.

"I hope that this will be useful to your committee's work, as my man in Moscow gave his life so that that scrap of paper and name would reach me."

Bishop passed it around the table.

"Is it known to you?" asked Donovan.

As chairman of the committee, Bishop answered. "Yes, he was one of our top suspects, based on details that your source had previously provided. I take it you have absolute confidence in this name from your source?"

"The source was asked for the true name of the NKVD penetration of our Manhattan Project known as 'the old one' and that is his answer. As you recall, according to him, there are two others, but that is the one true name he was able to get. He worked in the NKVD's records/archives section for their spying on our project and thus all the reporting that came in from their three moles passed through his hands. He did not see operational traffic on the cases, but he managed to elicit from colleagues the details he has provided to date. In sum, I have absolute confidence in that name."

"Very well. Your source certainly sounds like a man who should know what he's talking about. Do you think he will eventually be able to get us the names of the other two penetrations, or at least more identifying details?"

Donovan hesitated. He didn't really care to admit that the man was in America, but had chosen to just disappear, so he carefully phrased his answer like a good lawyer that he was would do. "At this time, I don't believe we will be able to have further contact with this source and in fact, we're not sure where he is."

The group then went round and round for thirty minutes as to what to do next, given the legal and political perplexities of the situation.

Robert of the FBI pointed out the weakness of taking legal action against an American citizen based on the word of a single foreign source, who couldn't even be brought into the court room to personally testify in a prosecution against the accused. "Even in wartime, it would be tough to get a judge to even admit this evidence to the jury."

The representative from the White House then stated the obvious, "Having a trial against this man and accusing him of spying on behalf of a key ally, the Soviet Union, would certainly not make it easy to convince

Congress to continue sending the Soviets millions of dollars of aid as part of the Lend-Lease package for the USSR."

"And a public trial of this nature would no doubt eventually reach the ears of the Japanese and the Germans, and make them aware of a special weapons program here in America," added Colonel Bishop.

At this point, everyone pretty much lapsed in to silence, as there was little left to say. Bishop officially brought the meeting to an end. "Let's wrap this up for today. Everybody go home and think about it and we'll meet again next Monday."

Everyone nodded in agreement and started filing out. Donovan remained seated and Bishop asked Rich and Chuck to stay for a minute, "on another matter" as he stated it.

Once it was just the four of them left, Bishop spoke. "I raised this possibility several weeks ago and told you that you should be thinking about what we do in just such an awkward situation that we now find ourselves in – guilty but unprovable in a court of law."

Rich nodded and replied, "We'd occasionally run in to this situation on the Homicide Squad in Manhattan."

Chuck chimed in, "Yeah, in talking with a number of those retired Texas Rangers we've hired in recent weeks, a few of them got to telling me stories of situations where everybody in the state knew who'd committed several murders, but they couldn't bring the guy to trial."

Bishop turned to Donovan. "Now, you see why I asked you earlier, how confident are you in this name. I ask you that again, off the record."

"My man who died believed in the accuracy of this agent and if he did, I do."

"Thank you, General. Well, I'm sure that you have many things needing your attention for the war effort and I won't ask you to stay any longer, while we three chat among ourselves. And if ever asked, remember, you left this meeting before any further actions were discussed." Bishop gave Donovan a hard stare as he stood to shake the General's hand.

"I understand. Thank you all for your efforts." He softly closed the door behind him as the other three proceeded with working out the details of what all of them understood needed to be done.

General Donovan had two other important tasks to do that day. He sent a message to the Chief of Personnel of the U.S. Army, requesting the immediate transfer of Master Sergeant Jan Kowalski, currently serving at the US Military Mission in Moscow, to the OSS Headquarters in Washington. He then sent a priority message to General Deane in Moscow, asking as a personal favor to Captain Worthington's family that Sergeant Kowalski, personally and immediately, bring Worthington's effects back to Washington. He'd read in Charles' last telegram of Kowalski's role in the exfiltration of Sasha. He intended to make sure there weren't any more "accidental" shootings of Army personnel in Moscow.

MOSCOW

General Deane had been told that Captain Worthington had no family, but agreed to the personal request of a fellow general and ordered Sergeant Kowalski to immediately depart for America with Charles' personal possessions. Kowalski took all of Charles' books and gave them to a very sad Viktor. Kowalski, after fourteen months in Moscow, gladly got on the plane, after expressing in Polish one last time to the Russian sergeant on duty at the airport what he really thought of Russians, the Red Army and Moscow. He suspected that he wouldn't be returning to Moscow and left an envelope in his room with instructions as to how to dispose of his personal possessions, in case he didn't come back to Uncle Joe's capital.

Captain Charles Worthington was buried with full military honors in a Red Army cemetery, although with some thought to the feelings of General Deane, not the same cemetery in which Worthington had been killed. Charles' liaison contacts, Suvarov and Nosenko, attended, as did Major Petrov and even General Parshenko. Parshenko attended as a sign of respect for one of the few people who'd ever outwitted him. Viktor stood a ways back from the official mourners, but had wanted to be present for the burial of a young man he'd come to quite like, even if he did have to inform on him. Jane could not bring herself to attend. She wanted to remember Charles alive – so charming and funny. She burned the silk stockings he'd given her. She knew she could never wear them again without having sad thoughts of the man who was now gone from her forever.

Even the weather cooperated and a gentle spring rain fell, giving just the right setting for the funeral service. General Deane gave a brief, but very moving speech and mentioned how Charles' brave action had saved his own life from the actions of a Nazi sniper that day. General Beria himself was present and said a few words about how the death of Captain Worthington was a symbol of the close cooperation between the United States and the Soviet Union, which would guarantee the eventual defeat of Nazi Germany. Nobody was certain what religion Charles practiced, but the Patriarch of the entire Russian Orthodox Church was on hand to offer a prayer.

Everybody lies.

The NKVD eventually did figure out how Captain Sasha Turgenev and his girlfriend had gotten out of the country, but there was no way to prove it, so no formal complaint was ever made to the American Embassy. Captain Worthington was dead and the America sergeant who'd driven a man and woman into the airport that Saturday evening had already been transferred back to America. Sasha's NKVD colleagues and neighbors were told that he'd been killed in a car accident near a village south of Moscow that fateful weekend and had been buried there. As for Anastasia's work colleagues, no explanation was ever given to them. People had been disappearing in the Soviet Union with no explanations for over twenty years. She was just one more.

As the subsequent weeks passed, Major Singell was starting to feel more at ease. Perhaps, he'd been wrong that Charles had had any suspicions about him, or if he'd had, his "untimely" death must have prevented him from reporting those suspicions about him. If any formal actions were going to be taken against him, surely the Army would have acted by then. He returned to visiting several times a week his blonde, nineteen year old Russian girlfriend he was in love with and engaged in sex with her even more passionately than before.

EPILOGUE

Several weeks after he threw it in the Moscow Military Mission mail slot, Charles' personal letter fingering Major Singell as the mole finally reached Mr. Astor via the US Postal Service. He took the train down to Washington the next day and again made a quiet visit to see General Donovan to deliver it. The General said he understood what it meant. Donovan had little time for Astor that day, as he was very busy. Apparently, something big was about to happen in early June, though he couldn't go in to details, even with Vincent Astor.

General Donovan went the following morning to make a personal visit to Admiral Leahy, head of the Joint Chiefs of Staff. There were several delicate issues to be considered and discussed. The reputation of the US Army for one. The feelings of Singell's wife and family. The bad feelings that the arrest of an American Army officer, charged with spying for the Soviet Union, would create within Congress and the American public at large towards the Soviets. That same afternoon in late May, a priority message was sent to the US Military Mission in Moscow, ordering Major Barry Singell to report immediately to the 1st Infantry Division, currently training somewhere in England. He arrived there on June 1, 1944. Donovan managed to place a secure phone call to General Huebner, head of the 1st, a few days before Singell's arrival and explained, off-the-record, a few things about the Major.

As a result of that unofficial call, Singell was in one of the very first landing crafts to hit Omaha Beach on D-Day, the 6th of June, 1944. The men in his craft were very proud that a senior officer had been assigned to lead their platoon. The official notification letter to his wife back in

Oregon, received by her in late June, said that he had fought very bravely that day. At least he did for the thirty seconds he survived after hitting the beach.

In late June, the Chicago Tribune carried a small article stating that a native of Chicago, Captain Charles Worthington, US Army, had been posthumously awarded the Silver Star for gallant action in Europe. There were few details, other than that he had sacrificed his own life to save a superior officer.

Tommy brought the paper, turned to that page, over to Murray Humphreys who was enjoying his breakfast in his luxurious apartment that overlooked downtown Chicago. Life as one of Capone's lieutenants and subsequently as a major mob figure had provided very well for Humphreys' quality of life. He'd carefully tucked the white linen napkin up around his neck, so as to protect his white silk shirt and black tie. The pin-striped jacket of his expensive suit was over the back of a nearby chair.

"Hey boss, check out this article about young Charlie."

Humpheys quickly read the article and looked up. "Is that our Charles, you think?"

Tommy shrugged his shoulders and raised his hands. "How many Charles Worthington's can there be from Chicago, particularly since you made that name up back in the early thirties?"

"Yeah, that must be our little Charlie. The Silver Star! Huh, his ol' man would be proud of him. So am I."

"That was a good thing you did back then for that kid." He noticed that a small tear had started rolling down the check of his boss, so he turned and walked over to look out the window and said no more. The boss wouldn't want anybody to see him crying.

Another small notification appeared in the obituary section of the Tribune a few days later.

Famous Physicist Livingston Dies in Auto Accident

World famous physicist, Thomas Livingstone, age fifty-six, has died. He had lived in Chicago for many years before the war, while working at the Fermi Laboratory. New Mexico State Police reported yesterday that his car had gone off a steep cliff while driving alone near the town of Los Alamos. He had been vacationing in the area over the 4th of July holiday weekend. He is survived by his wife and two grown children.

Everybody lies in wartime.

Printed in the United States
By Bookmasters